MARAUDER

Also by Gary Gibson

Angel Stations
Against Gravity

The Shoal Trilogy

Stealing Light
Nova War
Empire of Light

Final Days
The Thousand Emperors
Marauder

Gary Gibson

MARAUDER

TOR

First published 2013 by Tor
an imprint of Pan Macmillan, a division of Macmillan Publishers Limited
Pan Macmillan, 20 New Wharf Road, London N1 9RR
Basingstoke and Oxford
Associated companies throughout the world
www.panmacmillan.com

ISBN 978-0-230-74890-3

1 3 5 7 9 8 6 4 2

A CIP catalogue record for this book is available from the British Library.

Typeset by Ellipsis Digital Limited, Glasgow
Printed and bound by CPI Group (UK) Ltd, Croydon, CR0 4YY

MARAUDER

Marauder is set a few centuries after the events described in *Stealing Light*, *Nova War* and *Empire of Light*, and is a standalone work.

HISTORICAL ARCHIVES SUBSECTION C/5
category ALPHA

[From the offices of the Corso Institute of Non-Human Languages & Ciphers, in collaboration with the Accord Stellar Archaeology and Weapons Research Division. Presented by the Department of Alien Affairs during a plenary session of the Accord Central Chambers of Government at Ymir in 2745.

Please note this document contains restricted information and is rated PRIORITY RESTRICTED ACCESS.]

SUMMARY

The first Nova War of record is known to have taken place a hundred and sixty thousand years ago in the Large Magellanic Cloud, a dwarf galaxy orbiting the Milky Way. This conflict, which is believed to have lasted millennia, was made possible by the same 'nova drive' technology that enables our own starships to travel at faster-than-light speeds. The Magi, a multi-species collective that then dominated the LMC, had discovered that the nova drive was also a weapon of enormous destructive power – one capable of obliterating entire star systems, and billions of lives, at a single stroke.

Fragmentary Shoal records show that the nova-drive technology originated not with the Magi, but with a far older alien civilization known as the Makers, who appear to have been responsible for seeding caches of this and other advanced technologies throughout both the LMC and our own Milky Way. No other species is known to have independently discovered a means to travel faster than light, and attempts by Accord researchers to reverse-engineer existing drives have so far met only with failure.

Our extensive analysis of recovered historical records, several hundreds of thousands of years old, lends credence to the idea that these caches were intended as a kind of trap, albeit of a highly sophisticated nature. Any species sufficiently advanced to develop interstellar civilizations without the benefit of faster-than-light travel, so the thinking goes, would naturally exploit the contents of any Maker cache they might stumble across in their process of expansion. Given sufficient time to discover the drive's inherently destructive properties, they would ultimately destroy themselves either through internal unrest or during conflict with other species.

Following the cessation of this earliest known Nova War, the surviving Magi built fleets of autonomous starships and directed them to seek out Maker caches and destroy them. The majority of these 'Magi ships' were later destroyed by the Shoal Hegemony who, forewarned by events in the LMC, created a stable empire controlling interstellar traffic throughout much of our own Milky Way – until they, too, were destroyed by internal factionalism and an aggressive territorial war conducted with a neighbouring species two centuries ago.

The Shoal Hegemony's departure from the greater galactic stage has since allowed for humanity's rapid expansion, by making use of nova drives recovered either from derelict Shoal craft or from the Maker cache in the Tierra system. Such rapid growth, however, makes it difficult to keep track of the devices – and, given their hugely destructive potential, we recommend prioritizing the acquisition *by any means necessary* of all extant nova drives, including those recently recovered by independent human colonies such as the Three Star Alliance.

Taking control of this technology is therefore an essential step towards preventing the occurrence of another Nova War.

We do, however, anticipate strong resistance from the Three Star Alliance in particular, and a draft proposal has been prepared regarding the possibility of military action should current negotiations fail to reach a satisfying conclusion.

ONE

Megan

June 2763, 82 Eridani System (the present)

Megan Jacinth watched as the ship that had carried her down to Avilon's surface lifted up once more, its drive-fields flickering as it passed through the former asteroid's atmospheric containment field. She had been the only passenger.

The stars overhead were still in visible motion, unsurprising given that Avilon had only jumped into this system within the last few hours. Avilon was a boosted world, after all – a landscaped rock barely a few hundred kilometres in diameter, with a gravity engine at its heart and a containment field to keep its atmosphere from dissipating. Light and heat came from fusion globes, orbiting outside the containment field like tiny suns.

She looked around at the wide, dusty plain on which she now stood. The horizon appeared so close that it made her feel as if a single step might send her toppling over its edge.

She reached into the satchel slung across her shoulders and pulled out a band, using it to tie back her shoulder-length dark hair, flecked here and there with silver. Then she started to walk.

Megan hadn't been walking for much more than an hour before some instinct caused her to glance up. She glimpsed a black outline occluding the stars and growing larger by the second as it descended towards her. It appeared that her arrival had not, after all, gone unnoticed.

She stumbled backwards as a machine came thudding down onto the cracked dirt before her. Starlight glittered from its glassy black skin and armour-plated struts. Judging by the markings on its carapace, it was one of Avilon's security mechs, set to guard against unauthorized intrusions.

Megan stared at it in shock. Even though she'd been prepared for something like this, actually coming face to face with such a deadly machine was another matter. Her body instinctively wanted to turn and run, but she was all too aware of just how much firepower the mech was carrying. She'd be dead before she could take a single step.

Moving with exaggerated care, she reached inside her satchel and removed a stubby tube made of copper-coloured metal and dark plastic. She held it out towards the mech, at the same time pressing a small switch on the side of the device.

She waited for something to happen – but nothing did. She stared at the mech, dry-mouthed and unsure of what to do next.

The mech began to probe the machine part of her consciousness with informational feelers, looking for possible points of entry. It had already detected the cerebral implants she used to interface with starships. A brilliant white light flared out from the mech's torso, dazzling her. Then a sudden gust of air from its turbo jets sent her coat flailing around her legs.

She kept the override unit held out before her in one trembling hand. But suddenly the idea that this little box – this cheap, prefabbed gizmo of hacked-together circuitry and stolen override codes – could possibly protect her seemed utterly futile. She was outclassed, and she knew it.

Kazim had assured her endlessly of the device's efficacy, but at that moment she found herself wondering whether she might have made a terrible mistake by relying on him. It had since occurred to her that if anything were to happen to her, all those contacts she had so carefully built up over the years would have no choice but to deal with him directly – and then Kazim's profits from the illegal exportation of *sans de sezi*, out of Corkscrew, would surely increase by a not inconsequential margin.

The machine's servos whined faintly, its carapace splitting apart to reveal intricate glittering machinery underneath. It was, she realized to her further dismay, focusing its attack systems directly on her.

At the same time, a low rumble built up somewhere deep within the machine's core, building towards a crescendo.

The paralysis that had gripped Megan until that moment suddenly slackened. She stumbled backwards, preparing to take her chances and run . . .

The noise cut off abruptly, the machine's attack systems folding themselves away and the carapace closing back over them once more.

She felt suddenly numb with relief. Maybe Kazim hadn't been lying after all—

A flickering beam of energy shot out at her from another section of the mech, propelling a flood of fire through her nerve endings. She fell backwards, slamming the rear of her skull on the ground, her jaw clamped in a rictus grin as her body twitched and shuddered.

She caught sight of the mech leaping back into the sky, like some oversized mechanical locust, before rapidly vanishing out of sight amidst the stars.

With an extreme effort, she was just about able to turn her head to where she could see Kazim's override unit lying near one outstretched hand.

I'll kill you, thought Megan, in those last moments before consciousness slipped away. *I should never have listened to you, Kazim, you lying piece of shit.*

Megan finally came to again some hours later, the grass feeling cool and damp beneath her cheek. Beside her knelt a heavily muscled man with intricate tattoos on his neck and a look of deep concentration as he searched through the contents of her satchel. She instantly noticed he had a rifle slung over one shoulder.

She tried to say something, but her tongue felt sluggish and unresponsive. Even trying to form a few words made the muscles in her throat ache, and she could barely feel her arms and legs as she tried to move them. Nevertheless, a faint tingling in her extremities suggested the return of sensation, though she could no more command them to obey her than she could sprout wings and fly away.

She glanced beyond the man and saw a spider-truck parked nearby, with two headless and bare-chested figures standing next to it. These were bead-zombies, she realized, their bodies controlled by microscopic devices implanted in the nub of spinal column that protruded from the healed-over stumps of their necks. Each carried a long, curved sword in one hand and a pistol in the other.

Bead-zombies were, she knew from experience, incapable of feeling pain. Taking them on in a fight was a good way of getting yourself sliced into chunks, regardless of how much damage you might inflict on them in the meantime.

But the zombies didn't worry her nearly so much as the neck-tattoos on the man still searching through her satchel. They signified that he was a Freeholder and a native of Redstone, and the tattoos represented the number of people he had killed in one-to-one combat. He wore a traditional Freehold blade on his hip, its haft wrought in a fine filigree the colour of jade and ivory, depicting stylized human figures in close combat.

He stood up suddenly, slinging her satchel over the shoulder not burdened by his rifle, and looked down at her. 'Can you get up?'

'What the hell do you think?' she tried to say, but the words emerged half-slurred. Her tongue felt like something that had crawled into her mouth for shelter and died there.

'Fair enough.'

He leaned down, took hold of her under her armpits, then began dragging her towards the spider-truck and the waiting bead-zombies. Her boots left dark grooves in the dusty yellow soil.

He slammed her upright against the side of the truck, between two of its legs, propping her there with one hand against her shoulder. The bead-zombies had turned towards him, from which she deduced they must both be slaved to his control.

'It's wearing off now, right?' asked the Freeholder. 'The stuff the mech shot you with?'

'Fuck you,' she mumbled, then coughed, though it was getting easier to talk. 'What the hell do you want with me?' she managed to ask. 'And who the fuck are you, anyway?'

'Sifra warned me you'd be a pain in the ass,' he replied, taking his hand away from her shoulder. 'He wasn't kidding.'

Megan just about managed to stand upright without his support. 'Sifra?' She swallowed hard. '*Anil* Sifra?'

One corner of his mouth curled upwards. 'So you *do* know him.'

'No.' Megan shook her head. 'No, I'm not going anywhere if he's—'

The Freeholder sighed loudly, then hauled her over to an open hatch at the rear of the truck. She yelled in protest as he pushed her inside a cramped and windowless compartment with a metal floor and walls before slamming the door shut.

I'm sorry, Bash, she thought, feeling all her carefully wrought plans slipping through her fingers like so much water. *Looks like I've failed you again.*

A few minutes later, she felt the vehicle stagger into motion. The ceiling was low enough to force her to sit bent over. Her head banged against the hard surface above her when the truck lurched suddenly as it picked up speed, but before long it had achieved a smooth, steady rhythm, bouncing only slightly as it leaped around the tiny planetoid's circumference.

Before long the numbness in her limbs had nearly worn off, but it was soon replaced by intense cramps. She flexed and stretched her arms and legs to try and ease the pain, but that was far from easy in such a confined space. When she felt sufficiently recovered, she banged and kicked at the door of the cramped compartment, throwing all her rage and frustration at it, until she finally ran out of physical energy.

She then made up for it by screaming abuse at her Freeholder captor at the top of her lungs, even though she knew he almost certainly couldn't hear her from where he sat in the truck's cabin. Which was a shame, because she thought some of the insults she'd just come up with were particularly inventive.

She finally slumped down again, her rage and fury replaced by a kind of numb emptiness.

Sifra.

How could he possibly have known she was coming here? Her plan had seemed so simple when she had first worked it out, back on Corkscrew, which lay a hundred and fifty light years distant:

1: Make her way to 82 Eridani, where the world of Redstone was located.
2: Avoid, by any means necessary, actually setting foot on Redstone itself.
3: Wait in one of the outer-system refinery settlements for Avilon to make its scheduled stop in-system.
4: Land on Avilon, bypassing its security protocols with the aid of the override device provided for her by Kazim.
5: Find Bash and rescue him from whatever hole Sifra had squirrelled him away in all these years.
6: Fly to the Wanderer and save the human race from all-too-certain extinction.

An agenda clean and uncomplicated – in principle at least. But, as ever, real life in all its complexity had got in the way. Just finding a way to land undetected on Avilon had required the negotiation of numerous deals and also the payment of bribes that had drained her remaining finances. Numerous favours had been called in. And, if not for Kazim, part-owner and investor in several ships used for smuggling *sans de sezi* as well as being the nearest thing she'd had to a friend these past several years, she would never have got even this far.

But, for all her preparations, there had remained the unanswered question of just how the hell she was going to get Bash out of the high-security medical facility he was supposedly being held in. And that, added to her discovery that Sifra's reach extended deep inside Avilon's global security network, made her job close to impossible.

It then occurred to her that her only remaining option was to admit defeat and turn herself in to Avilon's civilian authorities. She might not be able to save Bash, but it was still a hell of a lot better than letting Sifra get his hands on her.

She managed to access the local data-net via her implants and quickly found a responsive AI representing Avilon's civilian council. She explained to it that she had been kidnapped and gave a brief description of her abductor and the spider-truck.

A few seconds later, the truck came to a sudden, lurching halt. She heard the hollow thump of a door opening somewhere overhead, then the sound of boots hitting the ground.

The door cracked open once more, and the Freeholder peered in at her, haloed by bright artificial daylight that hurt her eyes.

'Don't do that again,' he said, holding up one fist and then flinging its fingers open. An Avilon Security ID materialized in the air, before fading after a few moments. 'Otherwise I'll have to knock you out for the rest of the journey.'

'You're . . . ?'

'The police,' said the Freeholder. 'Welcome to Avilon. Now shut the hell up.'

He closed the door hard, and she heard him climb back up into the truck's cabin. They were soon under way once more.

Well, that's that, then. She'd clearly walked into a trap, and a carefully prepared one at that.

She let her head fall forward on to her knees, giving herself up to hopeless exhaustion. As a result, she barely noticed when the truck finally came to a halt, a few hours later.

She squinted painfully as the compartment door opened again, letting daylight flood back in. The Freeholder reached in and grabbed the collar of her jacket, dragging her out and depositing her in a heap on the yellow soil.

She looked around, seeing they had come to a halt in front of a vast sprawling building that looked as if it had been modelled on a fairytale castle. It sat at the centre of a few dozen acres of carefully tended lawns and coppiced trees. It was, even by the excessive standards of Avilon's population of the ultra-wealthy, stunningly tasteless.

'Get up,' said the Freeholder, as the two bead-zombies came over to stand behind him.

'How long have you been working for Sifra?' she asked as calmly as she could, staring up at him. She was damned if she was going to let him see how frightened she really was.

'He told me to bring you here,' the Freeholder grunted. 'He didn't say whether you had to still be in one piece.' He gestured towards a nearby gate. 'So how about you shut the fuck up, and start—'

She jumped up and ran. One thing she knew about bead-zombies was that they weren't very good at moving fast.

For the first few moments, she thought her legs might actually give way beneath her. She was still afflicted by numerous aches and cramps, and one ankle felt strangely numb. But she ignored all that, letting her frank terror of ever again setting eyes on Anil Sifra empower her muscles to carry her away as far and fast as humanly possible.

She sped back along the same narrow road on which the spider-truck crouched. Just a few kilometres away she could see the glistening towers of Cockaigne – Avilon's primary settlement – rising up to pierce through the containment field more than a kilometre overhead.

The aching in her legs grew, her lungs burning in her chest like twin embers. She listened for the steady thump-thump of the spider-truck pursuing her, but heard nothing yet. Just when she began to think she might actually make it to freedom, she heard a yipping sound from somewhere to her right, and the noise of something running up behind her.

She risked a quick glance over her shoulder, and nearly stumbled in fright. Two mogs were closing in on her from either side: half-human, half-canine hybrids, bipedal like a human being but dumb, vicious and short-lived.

Not to mention wildly, incredibly illegal. Megan had once seen a mog rip a man's throat out within seconds.

They were closing in on her fast, and she knew she could never outrun them. But the thought of those long snouts equipped with their rows of gleaming teeth spurred her to even greater effort.

Damn Sifra. Damn him to hell. And damn Bash for losing his mind.

She suddenly stumbled, falling to the ground with a yell, and stuck out both her arms in a desperate bid to protect herself. The sleek grey bodies of her pursuers darted all around her, jaws snapping at the bare flesh of her throat but never quite coming close enough. She saw, at close quarters, humanoid hands tapering into long, black claws. She screamed in panic again, convinced she was about to die in a particularly horrible and unpleasant fashion.

Just then, a sharp, high-pitched sound cut through the air. Suddenly, the creatures pulled away, crouching on the soil nearby and continuing to watch her with hungry intent. The worst thing about them, she decided, were the eyes – because they were the most human-looking part of all.

'Do you know how easy it would be for me,' said the Freeholder, as he stood over her once more, 'to just let them rip you apart?'

'Call them off,' Megan managed to croak. 'Please.'

He whistled twice, pointing at each mog in turn. The creatures stood up in response, their long, pointed ears twitching as they rose from their skulls. They both turned and ran back towards the luxurious estate.

'Maybe this time,' said the Freeholder, unslinging his rifle and aiming it at her, 'you'll be prepared to go where I tell you.'

He led her back, past the parked spider-truck, and through the nearby gate, before guiding her inside an arched doorway. Megan found herself in a cool, dark interior with whitewashed walls and low-standing couches. Soft rugs and cushions lay scattered all around and, even though the building seemed otherwise deserted, a hidden projector filled the space with low-resolution holograms of intertwining naked forms. The air smelled of sweat, mingled with the burned-honey aroma of *sans de sezi*. They continued on down some steps into a starkly lit basement.

'After you,' he said, opening a heavy steel door and motioning her inside.

At first, Megan thought the room was empty.

The Freeholder had locked her in a basement room measuring maybe five metres by three, which was lit only by a single, faintly glowing panel in the ceiling. The walls were bare and undecorated, the illumination insufficient to reach even the corners fully. She saw a single narrow cot pushed into a narrow recess, the dark sheets balled up and rumpled, while a spigot, with a bucket placed beneath it, protruded from the wall facing the door.

Megan slumped against the nearby wall, letting her back slide down against bare concrete, till her head was resting on her knees. She risked accessing the local data-services again, but this time got nowhere. This room, she realized with a sinking feeling, was almost certainly shielded against her implants.

She closed her eyes, and saw again those two mogs yearning to rip her throat out. She reopened them quickly, clenching her fists tight until the fingernails dug into the soft flesh of her palms.

I have fucked this up so very, very badly.

Something moved on the other side of the room.

She froze, realizing with a start that what she had taken for a bundle of discarded sheets on the single cot was, in fact, a living body. Whoever it was, they seemed still asleep.

She got up and edged over to the cot, discerning the outline of knees pulled up close to the chest beneath the blankets. Reaching down with trepidation, she pulled the blankets gently to one side, before gazing down at the smooth, untroubled face of the man lying there.

She gaped in astonishment, hardly believing her own eyes. It was Bash – Imtiaz Bashir – the very man with whom she had once shared her deepest secrets and whom she had once abandoned to certain death.

He looked emaciated, half starved, and she lifted up one corner of his blanket to see that he was still fully dressed beneath it, although his clothes were filthy. He was in a terrible state, but she had never been so glad to see another living being in her whole life.

He showed absolutely no awareness of her, as his eyes stared past her into some unknowable place. His expression was calm and his lips slightly parted, as if just on the verge of saying something.

A terrible sadness came over her. Had he been suffering like this all these years, since Megan had last seen him? Was there still some part of him locked inside his head that knew where he was or what had happened to him?

From the look of him, that possibility seemed remote.

'I told you I'd come back for you,' she said softly, kneeling by the cot and stroking one hand across his forehead. He smelled terrible, and she guessed he hadn't been bathed in quite some time. *I'll bet they keep those mogs in better condition.*

Bash's eyes were large and brown and quite as beautiful as she remembered them. When she had first met him, she had been struck by his size – two metres of muscular mass accompanied by the sweetest personality imaginable. Now, much of that muscle was gone, leaving him so emaciated that Megan found herself wondering when he had last been fed.

His breathing faltered, and caught. His eyes seemed to focus on her for one brief moment.

Megan felt her own breath catch in her throat. *He knows I'm here. He must do. He . . .*

But then his eyes lost focus again, and once more he stared off into some unknowable vista.

She shakily exhaled, realizing it was foolish of her to have expected anything else. The Bash she knew was gone, and now all that was left was this sad, sorry shell of a man.

She stroked his scalp again, feeling for the ridges and crenellations beneath the skin that identified him as a fellow machine-head. Without him she could not reawaken the link that Tarrant had once forged between Bash and the alien entity known to some species as the Wanderer – but to others as the Marauder.

Megan rocked back on her heels, pressing her hands against her eyes. A long time ago, when she was much younger, she had convinced herself she was in love with Bash. When she told him so, he had laughed and informed her, not unkindly, that she wasn't his type. When she asked what his type was, he had glanced across the bar they were sitting in, towards a cluster of male Alliance officers gathered around a nearby table.

At first she had been crushed, but she soon understood that what she had mistaken for romantic love was instead something deeper and more lasting. It was a bond like that between brother and sister, or father and daughter: a bond that had first formed on the day of her sudden and unexpected rescue.

In a very real sense, she owed him her life.

It was easy for her to imagine what he might say now, were he capable of saying anything at all. She could picture his easy sardonic smile, hear the warm full tones of his voice.

'Remember the first time we met?' she whispered.

His unspoken reply echoed in her ears. *Sure I do, Megan. It was on Redstone. I remember it as if it were yesterday.*

'I was so scared that night.' She remembered how she had fled through crowded city streets, desperate to escape a terrible fate.

The first time I saw you, she remembered him once saying, *you looked so cold I wanted to wrap you up like a baby.*

'You were the only one I could trust. The only one I could tell the truth to.'

Your secret was always safe with me, honey. You know that.

His eyes still stared past her, betraying no hint of awareness. Megan smiled to herself, then felt her own eyes grow moist.

'You took me under your wing and I hid there for years,' she murmured.

And then she had stayed with him, following him all the way back to Kjæregrønnested and the Three Star Alliance; and then she had met Gregor Tarrant, and been forced to watch as he sentenced Bash to a fate worse than death – before tearing Megan's life apart forever.

TWO

Gabrielle

On the first morning of the Grand Pilgrimage, Speaker-Elect Gabrielle woke up with stomach cramps that made her wince. She waited for the worst of the pain to pass, then opened her eyes to see a look of concern on the face of the old woman standing by the foot of her bed.

'Madame Gabrielle?' enquired Mater Cassanas. 'Are you all right?'

Gabrielle stared across an ocean of linen at Cassanas's inquisitive expression, then looked away, bunching her fists tightly beneath the heavy restricting sheets as the pain returned, then faded just as quickly once more. She stared past the gold and silver statuary adorning the bedchamber, past its high ceiling decorated with scenes from the Book of Uchida, and out through the tall windows reaching from floor to ceiling. There, she could see the canals winding through the heart of Port Gabriel, whose pale blue waters were dotted here and there with the white sails of yachts and with automated sea transports.

Most of her attention, however, was taken by the barges crowding the riverside docks. They were huge flat-bodied vessels sprouting innumerable pennants and flags, all decorated with the red and gold seal of the Sacerdotal Demarchy of Uchida.

She had tried, as she had done every morning now for more than two years, to access the public parts of the Tabernacle information service. And, as ever, she failed.

'I'm quite all right, Mater Cassanas,' said Gabrielle finally, before sitting up carefully. Her machine-head implants were feeding her a constant drip of background data about her surroundings: the composition of the sheets between which she lay, or the trace elements in the air she breathed, even the current locations of orbital factories and Accord peacekeeper platforms above the surface of Redstone. She could track them, if and when she chose to, even follow them as they passed from one horizon to the next, and beyond.

But there was so much more information closer to hand to which her access was heavily restricted. It was for her own safety, they claimed, because too many public-data links could be subverted by the Demarchy's enemies and used to launch covert viral attacks against her. Even so, it was enormously frustrating to be gifted with so very powerful a tool and yet be prevented from making use of more than a tiny fraction of its capabilities.

What made it worse was the knowledge that machine-heads had, for a very long time, been regularly employed as the pilots of interstellar craft throughout the Accord and beyond. Their implants allowed them to interface directly with such craft, and the idea of being a starship pilot had never failed to fill Gabrielle with wonder. Yet it had always been an impossible yearning.

Cassanas looked doubtful despite Gabrielle's reassurances, pursing the lips of her long horse-like face. But Gabrielle glared at the old woman until she finally bowed in acquiescence, a flush of red colouring her withered cheeks.

'Of course, Madame Gabrielle,' Cassanas muttered, peering back at her with unmistakable hostility from below the yellow-and-black cap that identified her as an attendant.

The old woman's eyes dipped briefly towards Gabrielle's belly, swaddled beneath constricting sheets. In that moment Gabrielle felt suddenly, overwhelmingly certain that the old woman knew precisely what she was trying to hide.

But she also knew that Cassanas would say and do nothing, out of fear for her own son's life.

Even so, Gabrielle felt her heartbeat grow faster, her hands again forming into fists beneath the heavy linen, where Mater Cassanas could not see them.

She then thought of Karl – proud, strong Karl Petrova. Despite all their talk, she had never really believed a day might finally come when all their dreams of escaping could be realized.

'You're scheduled to have breakfast with your advisers, before departing for Dios,' declared Cassanas, clearly struggling to maintain her professional composure. She motioned with her eyes towards the door leading into an antechamber. 'Therefore I think perhaps we should get started immediately.'

'Of course,' said Gabrielle, aware of the slight quaver in her voice as she replied.

She waited, as taught from childhood, until Cassanas had peeled off the sheets, before swinging her bare feet out and onto the cold marble floor. She then followed the old woman into the antechamber, where her robes of office had been laid out on a chaise-longue, ready for the morning ahead.

Cassanas picked up several items, draping them over one arm in preparation for dressing her charge. As Gabrielle watched her, she thought back on the endless mundanity of all the days of her life up until now, each day barely distinguishable from the last. She could almost taste the sights and sounds and smells that lay in all their rich and infinite variety beyond the choking confines of the palace.

'I want to dress myself this morning,' Gabrielle said on a sudden impulse.

The old woman looked at her, perplexed. 'It's against protocol to—'

'Nonetheless,' said Gabrielle, her jaw tight, 'I insist.'

The old woman's face flushed with anger. 'You won't be able to hide it forever, you know,' she spat, her eyes dropping again towards Gabrielle's belly. 'Thijs and the rest will find out about your *little secret* soon enough. You'll ruin the whole Pilgrimage, and the Ascension too—'

'I think,' said Gabrielle, 'you should be careful what you say. Or should I inform Karl of how you've just spoken to me?'

Cassanas's nostrils flared, and she looked ready to make a retort, but instead swallowed deeply before replacing the robes on the chaise-longue with exaggerated carefulness. Gabrielle had the sense the old woman was barely resisting the urge to throw the clothes in her face.

'All I want,' continued Gabrielle, 'is to have a few minutes alone.' She forced a smile. 'It's a big day, after all, and you know it's hard enough, as things are, for me to get a little time to myself.'

Cassanas's mouth fluttered like an angry moth. 'Thijs and the rest will be arriving soon. If they discover I've left you on your own for as much as a moment . . .'

'Edith –' Gabrielle used the old woman's first name as she stepped closer to her – 'just a few minutes, no more. You know you'll hear them coming long before they reach my chambers.'

Cassanas nodded and left the room without another word, her face still taut with anger.

Gabrielle felt her shoulders sag with relief as, closing her eyes, she subsided onto the chaise-longue. She could hear Cassanas busying herself on the other side of the door, straightening the bedclothes or perhaps putting things away.

Gabrielle then stood up and stripped off her nightdress, taking the opportunity to study herself naked in one of the floor-to-ceiling mirrors that surrounded her. Placing her hands on her belly, she began gently probing her soft flesh.

Was it obvious yet? she wondered. Perhaps just the tiniest curve to her belly was evident – a sign of the scandalous new life growing within her.

Oh, Karl. She wondered how he'd react once he knew . . . but when would be the right time to tell him? Would it change their plans, or even give him a reason to abandon her?

No, she told herself adamantly. *Stop being ridiculous.* It was foolish to think any such thing.

She then dressed herself in the robes that identified her as the Speaker-Elect for the Sacerdotal Demarchy. She checked herself again in the mirror, turning this way and that, knowing she had to play the part for as long as necessary. And yet nothing could have made her happier than the idea of tearing these ridiculous robes off and burning them.

I'm only a girl, she reflected, for her twenty-first birthday was less than three days away. And too young to be a murderer, however much those she would soon help to kill deserved their fate.

She reached up to touch her scalp, feeling the faint crenellations and bumps of the machine-head hardware beneath her skin. Her long and lustrous hair hid most of the visible traces of the technology, except where faint lines could still be seen on her exposed temples. Unless people looked very closely, they might never guess, Karl had reassured her.

Gabrielle heard distant voices echoing beyond her chambers, coming closer.

Stepping back out of the antechamber, she let Mater Cassanas adjust the fastenings on her robes. Gabrielle did not resist when the old woman then took her by the elbow and guided her out of the bedchamber and into the reception room beyond the double doors, where Thijs and his entourage were already waiting.

Smalling turned as she entered, as did Lampard, Abramovic and Thijs himself, each of them dressed in his own distinctive robe of office. They stood in an untidy group by a long table that had already been prepared for the morning meal.

These men present were the true rulers of the Demarchy of Uchida, as Karl had once explained to her; she, by contrast, was little more than a means to an end, regardless of endless public pronouncements to the contrary. Accompanying these high officials of the Demarchy were a number of yellow-and-black-capped attendants, most of them acting as security personnel under Karl's direct command.

Gabrielle forced herself to unclench her shoulders, taking a deep breath and then exhaling slowly until the rapid thundering of her heart had slowed to a gentler rhythm. She avoided gazing directly at Thijs, whose eyes roved with obvious interest over the few curves of her body actually visible beneath her voluminous robes.

From the direction of the riverside docks came the sound of music – a recording of a choir singing a hymnal. The melody came and went with the wind blowing in from the river and the sea beyond.

'Mer Gabrielle,' said Thijs, his eyes finally finding their way back to her face. 'I can't tell you how happy it makes me to see you looking so well, and on the eve of such a special occasion.'

The Demarchy's chief of security, Thijs kept his hands locked in front of him like two sea anemones grappling over a fragment of food. Lampard regarded her with a cold and distant gaze, as if already engaged in the act of dissecting her alive. Abramovic remained as aloof and unreadable as ever; Gabrielle could recall no more than a very few occasions throughout her life when the master of sciences had actually spoken to her directly.

'Is everything all right?' asked Thijs, a flicker of concern crossing his face. 'You look a little pale, Mer Gabrielle.' He glanced to one side of her. 'Mater Cassanas . . . ?'

Gabrielle saw the old woman turn towards her, her gaze dipping briefly once more towards her mistress's belly before rising to meet her eyes.

I dare you, thought Gabrielle, staring back. Not for the first time in recent months, she had the sensation of her whole life hanging in the balance by the most delicate of threads. *Tell them how Karl's been blackmailing you. Bring the whole damn Pilgrimage crashing down around their ears, and see just how grateful to you they are.*

But when Cassanas turned to address Thijs a moment later, she was transformed into the very picture of smiling obsequiousness. 'Mer Gabrielle is just very tired,' replied the old woman. 'I think that's understandable, given the circumstances, as there's so much to do before we sail for Dios.'

Gabrielle forced another smile. 'Mater Cassanas – Edith here – she's been fussing over me all morning, haven't you?' She glanced at her, then turned back to Thijs. 'She's so *worried* about me.'

Cassanas nodded robotically, then flashed a sideways glance at Gabrielle that was just a few degrees north of absolute zero.

'Enough of this,' said Lampard, his eyes studying them both from out of that broad face. His voice had a permanently weary edge, yet carried a lifetime's experience of exerting authority. It was to Lampard here that Karl was expected – he had once told her – to report on a daily basis concerning her every movement and word. 'Mer Gabrielle,' he continued, 'if you have any concerns or queries about the Grand Pilgrimage before it begins, it would be best if you voiced them now rather than later. Let us know if there's anything you need, or anything you think might ensure things run as smoothly as they should. This is *your* moment, after all.'

You miserable, lying piece of scum, thought Gabrielle.

'Of course,' she replied instead, once again summoning up her every element of deceit within her as she met his eyes. 'I have no special requirements or requests. Perhaps we should waste no more time and just get started.'

Lampard smiled tightly and nodded, with a look in his eye that might have meant nothing to Gabrielle if Karl hadn't already described in detail the fate intended for her.

If Thijs should to be the first to die, she decided, then it was only right that Lampard should be second.

THREE

Gabrielle

The day was bright and chill, small airships and null-g platforms floating above Port Gabriel's skyline, as Gabrielle and her entourage exited the People's Palace. They were protected from the freezing weather and the unbreathable native atmosphere by a containment field that moved along with them, making breather masks or any other kind of respiratory aid unnecessary.

The voices of the choir were amplified across the plaza surrounding the palace as Gabrielle, Thijs, Lampard, Abramovic and an accompanying entourage of nearly a hundred made their way towards a bulk transport waiting just outside the palace gates. Parts of the transport's transparent hull had been painted over with broad gold and black stripes. Further away, close to the shores of the Ka River, Gabrielle could see the monument to the Port Gabriel massacre of two centuries before, towering over the surrounding buildings.

The details of the journey lying ahead of her had been drilled into Gabrielle from such a young age that she could visualize almost every step of the way. A barge would carry her a few hundred kilometres downriver, to the mouth of the Ka River and the city of Dios, not far from the Demarchy of Uchida's disputed border with the River Concord States. And, once there, she would be transported to her ultimate destination: the ancient Magi starship known to the Demarchy's citizens as the Ship of the Covenant. The alien vessel still lay half buried where it had fallen from orbit, centuries before, on the slopes of Ascension Peak, a stub of volcanic granite standing guard over the city below.

But there were other things she knew about the Ship of the Covenant that were not public knowledge, and were in fact known only to very few of the high officials accompanying her. The Demarchy's own long-term and highly secretive research project had demonstrated almost conclusively that, by the time the next Speaker-Elect was due to depart for Dios in another twenty-one years' time, the Ship of the Covenant would have nearly finished the centuries-long process of repairing itself – and, when that day came, there was nothing Thijs's or Lampard's successors could do that might prevent the alien craft's inevitable departure.

On that same day, the Demarchy of Uchida would, in one swift stroke, lose the technological and military advantage it had held over the River Concord States for so very long. There would no longer be any reason for the Accord to maintain its military orbital presence, and war between the Demarchy and its neighbours was only one possible outcome.

Given all that, there was a very real chance Gabrielle might be the last of the Speakers-Elect. It was therefore imperative for the Demarchy that they grab whatever data they could from the alien craft, which could then be traded to the Accord in return for continued protection, not only from rival states but from the renegade Freehold camps hidden deep in the Montos de Frenezo.

Even though she, like all the other Speakers-Elect who had come before her, was outwardly exalted by the Demarchy, Karl had taught her that it was solely because of the advanced scientific data they could each bring back from the Ship of the Covenant that they were in any way valued. And if that ship had only flown off long before now, Gabrielle might never have been forced to undergo this whole insane charade.

But then again, she reminded herself, if it hadn't been for the Ship of the Covenant, there would never have been a reason for her to be born in the first place.

They walked at a steady, unhurried pace for the benefit of the state propaganda and news agencies recording today's events. Joining the recorded choir now could be heard the massed voices of the pilgrims gathered beyond the palace walls, filling the air with their chattering and shouting and occasional singing.

They're here because of me, she realized in a daze. She wondered what it would be like to walk, unknown and unrecognized, through those same streets beyond the palace, to be able to engage fully with the Tabernacle, or experience life far from Redstone. She wondered how the pilgrims would react if they knew the truth of Gabrielle's purpose in life – a truth she had learned from Karl in her bedchamber after he had chased Mater Cassanas away with threats to her son's life.

She thought of those long evenings of lovemaking, when she had given herself all too willingly to him. She would lie in his arms as he described how her physical appearance, and that of every Speaker-Elect who had ever lived, had been carefully tweaked at a young age to hide the fact they were all clones of the same woman – the first human being ever to communicate with and then pilot a Magi ship.

At that moment she saw a figure wearing the armour of the Demarchy's security services step out from under the broad wing of the transport. His feet were clad in heavy black boots, a decoratively filigreed breather mask strapped over his nose and mouth. This was Karl Petrova: bodyguard to the Speaker-Elect, confidant, lover and, before very long, partner in crime.

Gabrielle struggled to hide her joy at the sight of him. His eyes, however, met hers only briefly before moving on to regard Thijs and the other members of the Demarchy's ruling junta with apparent equanimity. And yet she knew that Karl's rapid rise through the security services, despite his not being a citizen of the Demarchy – despite *not even having a faith chip* – had earned him the security chief's unending enmity.

Along with the rest of her entourage, she was swept through the palace gates and on board the transport. Steps had emerged from within its hull as they approached, the doors sliding apart like steel jaws. Almost as soon as she had taken a seat within the transport's opulent interior, it lifted off the ground on a cushion of shaped fields.

The journey to the docks and the Grand Barge took barely more than a minute or two, the transport seeming to drop towards its destination almost as soon as it had risen. She had a brief glimpse of the massed pilgrims filling the streets beyond the palace, before they dropped to make a landing on the dockside. The Grand Barge was riding low in the Ka's lapping waters, while an Accord dropship stood a short distance away, with defensive fields flickering around its outer skin.

They disembarked to find a thin sleet outlining the shape of the containment field around them. The Grand Barge, dwarfing everything in its vicinity, had recently been repainted and refitted, and its upper hull was now festooned with pennants.

Gabrielle tried to look appreciative. Indeed, under any other circumstances, the sights and sounds of this day would have struck her as extraordinary. Her younger self would have revelled in the commotion, in the smell of the water able to find its way through the containment field. Yes, that previous Gabrielle would have been thrilled, but she now had to force herself to pay attention – to conceal the tension and fear that gripped her.

Other barges, equally opulent if not quite so enormous, waited at alternative moorings. These would be transporting Abramovic's research staff, whose purpose was to analyse and measure all the data recovered from the Ship of the Covenant.

And then, unless she acted, she herself would be killed and her body secretly disposed of, as had happened to every Speaker-Elect before her.

Members of the security services expeditionary forces, under Karl's command, stood at attention on either side of the ramp leading up into the barge, their body armour glittering in the morning light. They had, she knew, arrived fresh from wiping out a Freehold stronghold in the Montos de Frenezo. Most Freeholders had long since fled Redstone, but a few fanatics stayed behind to strike against the Demarchy.

The hull sealed itself behind them as soon as they entered the Grand Barge, a deep bass rumble then running up through her feet and into her bones as the fusion-driven turbines began to power up.

They were under way.

FOUR

Gabrielle

There were endless civic duties to be performed en route, as the barges slowly made their way one by one downriver and away from Port Gabriel. She duly performed her part, having been trained for this day throughout her life. The final ceremony did not come to a close until the sun was long sunk beneath the horizon, and then it was time for Mater Cassanas to accompany her to her temporary quarters aboard.

Barely a minute had passed before a knock came at the door. Karl entered as soon as Mater Cassanas opened it.

'I'll speak with the Elect alone,' he told the older woman. 'I'll let you know when you can return.'

'I don't know what you're planning to do when we reach Dios, Pater Petrova, but—'

'Take care, Mater Cassanas,' said Karl, 'not to say anything you might regret. Your boy lives or dies by my word.'

'For all I know he's dead already,' she spat, rounding on him and visibly shaking with anger. 'How would I know?'

Karl studied her with clear contempt, and Gabrielle waited, heart in mouth, to see what he might do next.

He first made sure that the door was properly closed behind him, then made a gesture in the air to activate his Tabernacle link. In response, a bubble of light appeared before him, and within it Gabrielle saw a ragged-looking man aged probably in his late twenties, who was crouching on a dusty floor somewhere with his back pressed against a wooden post. His dark eyes were full of defeat, while a patch of hair on one side of his head was still growing out again where the faith chip had been extracted from his skull. His face was barely illuminated by a single lamp hanging from a piece of twisted wire, but the torn remnants of his Demarchy insignia were visible on one dust-specked shoulder.

Cassanas's son was, as Gabrielle knew, a member of the same elite guard that Karl commanded. He had been officially missing in action for some months now.

'Believe me,' Karl said to the old woman, 'he's in just about the safest place he could be right now.'

Gabrielle wondered what in the world he meant by that, but it didn't seem like the right moment to ask questions.

'I don't believe you,' said Cassanas, but her voice sounded full of defeat. 'How do I know this isn't just a fake recording?'

'If you prefer –' Karl took a step closer to her – 'you can watch his execution in real time, right now – if you don't get the hell out of here and *leave us alone.*'

The last shreds of defiance fled Cassanas's expression, her fingers busily working at the buttons of her robe as if she wanted to tear it off.

'Please,' she said, her eyes full of despair, 'at least let me speak to him just the once.'

Despite herself – and despite the long hatred she had built up towards Cassanas over the years – Gabrielle nonetheless felt an unexpected stab of pity for the old woman in her anguish. There were times when Karl could appear immensely cruel and heartless, as if in reality he was someone quite different from the gentle and passionate lover she had come to know.

'Here,' said Karl, extending the bunched knuckles of one hand towards Cassanas before flinging the fingers wide, thus sending a small, glowing icon from his hand to hers. The icon hovered in front of Cassanas, then vanished when she reached out to it.

'That's everything you need in order to talk to your son via a secure link,' said Karl. 'You'll have two minutes to speak with him. But tell no one about this, and make certain your conversation is private – or I will make absolutely sure that he takes a very long time to die.'

Gabrielle watched the old woman bow her head obediently, with what seemed like supreme effort, before stepping out of the bed-chamber and closing the door behind her with a loud thud.

Gabrielle flung herself towards Karl, and he took her in his arms. As he returned her kiss, his hands began roaming across her back, tugging at the fastenings of her robes until they slipped from her shoulders.

She let her garments tumble to the floor before locating the seams of Karl's own uniform with practised efficiency. Before long, they both stood naked, Karl sliding his hands through her hair as he bent to kiss her breasts, then lifting her up and carrying her over to the bed.

He laid her down on the soft sheets, taking hold of her wrists and pinning them against the pillows above her head. She responded by wrapping her ankles around his thighs as he slid on top of her. Within moments he was deep inside her, and thrusting hard.

She delicately nipped the soft tissue of Karl's neck with her teeth, hearing him groan in response. She was conscious that his hair had streaks of grey in it. Uchidans in general, and Demarchists in particular, did not approve of overt body modifications, seeing them as a slight offered to God, including even such changes as made one look younger.

Something about the confrontation with Cassanas had charged the atmosphere, so that Gabrielle felt her orgasm building more quickly than usual. She could see it was the same for Karl: barely a minute or two had passed before she felt the muscles of his body go tense. He let out a restrained grunt before collapsing on top of her, finally releasing her wrists and leaning his head down to kiss her.

Her orgasm, when it came, washed through her like a warm tide. She tipped her head back, her breath emerging in sharp gasps. She had carefully taught herself not to cry out; though Cassanas might be easily blackmailed, the same could not be said for others who might overhear them, should they be passing anywhere near the door to her chambers.

Karl finally slid over to one side. 'I can't stay long,' he declared.

'You never can,' she replied with a groan. 'I just want all this to be over.'

'Hey.' He squeezed her shoulder with one hand. 'It's going to be all right.' He was still breathing heavily from his exertions.

She laughed shakily. 'You say that, but . . .'

'But what?'

'We never talk about what comes after. After we've gone – after we've escaped. Where do we go? Where can we possibly live?'

'A long way from here,' he replied. 'I've made arrangements to get us off Redstone and out of this system as soon as possible.'

'But where, exactly, are we going to go?' she insisted. 'Aren't they bound to come looking for me?'

'And risk exposing the Demarchy of Uchida to the kind of scrutiny people like Thijs would rather die than allow?' He chuckled. 'I've been preparing for this day for a long time, Gaby. We'll soon have new identities and new lives.' He squeezed her shoulder again, then raised his fingers to tousle her hair gently. 'Picture us some place warm where it never gets as cold as it does everywhere on this damn world, and living under some other sun. There are a thousand places I could get work as a security consultant, and you'll be able to decide for yourself what you want to do with the rest of your life. Just another day or two, and all this will be behind you, I promise.' He tucked a loose strand of hair behind her ear and flashed her a reassuring smile. 'Why do you ask? Having second thoughts?'

She frowned. 'No, of course not.'

'There's no turning back after this, Gaby.'

'Haven't I told you often enough how much I hate every last one of them?' she hissed through clenched teeth. She remembered times before she had met Karl, when it had taken all her willpower not to scream and to suppress the raw red anger she kept so tightly bundled deep inside herself. 'I despise them all, more than you can—'

He reached down and pressed a finger against her lips. 'I know,' he said, 'but I still needed to ask.'

She pushed his hand away and laughed. 'I'm not sure you could ever really understand, Karl. Not without being a woman.'

Karl had not been her first. That had been Thijs, who had come into her quarters one night years before, when she had been little more than a child, chasing Mater Cassanas out of Gabrielle's bedchamber before raping her. It had given her an insight into her true value in the eyes not only of Thijs but also of Lampard, Abramovic and even Mater Cassanas herself.

'Gabrielle—'

She silenced him with a kiss. 'But it's true what you say. It'll all be over soon, and then the both of us will be gone from here forever.'

'Then there's something you need to do,' he said, sliding his legs over the side of the bed and standing up. She pushed herself up on one elbow as he started to dress.

'What is it?'

He pulled on his trousers, then removed something from his jacket pocket, holding it up where she could see it. 'Do you know what this is?'

Gabrielle saw a thumb-sized vial filled with a dark red liquid the colour of blood. 'What is it?'

'This,' said Karl, 'is our ticket to freedom. Nanocytes, carrying a neurotoxin cargo. They're entirely harmless unless activated by a remote signal. When that happens, they release the neurotoxin into the bloodstream. Death then follows quite quickly.'

'It looks so small,' she whispered, through suddenly dry lips. She felt a creeping dread at the sight of the vial. It was small, yes, but full of deadly promise.

Karl nodded, replacing the vial in his jacket. 'There's been a slight change of plans, since Thijs has decided he doesn't want me present at the banquet. I'm to wait outside with the rest of the guards.'

'Why? I thought—'

'He doesn't need to hide his dislike for me any longer,' he replied. 'In fact, he's probably planning to have me thrown out of the Demarchy as soon as you're dead.'

He buttoned up his shirt and pulled on the jacket, then tossed a slim device onto the sheets, landing close to her hand. Gabrielle stared at the object as if it were a poisonous snake.

'My original plan,' he continued, 'was to introduce the contents of the vial to the ceremonial wine, prior to the banquet. That much, at least, hasn't changed. Then I would use that device beside you to trigger the poison, once Thijs and the rest had taken a first sip. All those present but ourselves, of course.' He shrugged. 'But it appears that last opportunity is now to be denied me.'

'So what do we do?'

'I can't activate the poison if I'm not actually in the banquet hall along with the rest of them.' He picked the device up again, this time folding the fingers of her hand around it. 'Its range is much too short, and anyway the whole of the banquet hall is shielded. Which means, Gabrielle, that you'll have to be the one to do it.'

She felt a surge of dizziness wash through her. 'Me?'

'If not you,' asked Karl, 'who else?'

'But I thought—'

'That I would take care of everything?' Karl chuckled. 'This actually works out to our advantage. Once they're all dead, I can come rushing in and perform a daring rescue of the Speaker-Elect. The crew'll be cheering me on, even as I sweep you off the Grand Barge – never to be seen again.'

'What if I make a mistake?' she asked, her insides suddenly feeling hollow. 'What if it doesn't work? What if . . . ?'

He snorted with exasperation, sitting down once more on the edge of the bed and reaching over to grab hold of her hand. 'Belle's tits, Gabrielle,' he said, his expression fierce, 'don't you *want* to get out of here before they flush your mind away? This is your chance to be free, damn it!'

She stared into his eyes, her lungs frozen in panic. Everything he said was true, and yet . . .

'How can you be sure I have it in me to go through with all this?' she asked.

He smiled at her. 'Because I can *see* you have it in you. I *know* you can do this – and you will. It's for both of us, remember. My life was ashes before I met you, Gaby, and I can't imagine a future without you being part of it.'

'Both of us,' she echoed, her voice suddenly sounding hoarse. He was right, so very right: without him she would be dead within a few days. 'You can rely on me.'

She remembered the first time she ever set eyes on Karl Petrova, almost six years before. For a long time he had been nothing more than another adult amongst the many who surrounded her. Even in the years that followed, she had been only peripherally aware of his reputation, of those stories regarding his spectacular victories against isolated pockets of militant Freeholders.

Even then, however, she had known Karl was different from everyone else: an outsider born on some other world within the Accord. She had also seen the way Thijs and Abramovic's faces hardened whenever his name was mentioned, as if each fresh victory he brought to the Demarchy somehow carried him further and further away from their favour.

Ordinarily, his refusal to have a faith chip implanted would have excluded him from any position of power within the Demarchy. But his tactical skill – and his astonishing ability to predict what the Freehold's next move would be – allowed him to rise through the Demarchy's ranks with astonishing speed regardless.

Finally, after many years of service to the Demarchy, he had been appointed her bodyguard.

For an outsider to be given such an exalted position was extraordinary, but Karl had explained to her the reasoning. There had been, he told her, an attempt by unknown forces to kidnap the previous Speaker-Elect immediately prior to her Ascension, twenty-one years before. Drastic measures had been introduced to prevent any such attempt ever happening again, and Karl's military and strategic skill counted for far more than whether or not he happened to have a chip lodged under his scalp. As her bodyguard, he had gradually won her trust, albeit slowly. She had come to look forward to seeing that dry smile, those world-weary eyes.

After they had finally become lovers, just a year ago, he had told her that he originated from a place called the Three Star Alliance, which had acquiesced to the Accord's political demands rather than face a brutal war it could not possibly win. Deeply embittered, he had fled across the stars to Redstone, having learned there was a need for experienced mercenaries within the Sacerdotal Demarchy of Uchida.

When his rapid promotion attracted Thijs's enmity, he had sought to learn as much about the chief of security as possible. And, in the course of his investigations, he discovered what the Demarchy had in store for their Speaker-Elect. Moreover, he discovered that the Magi ship at Dios – known as the Ship of the Covenant – had crash-landed only after being very nearly destroyed by the woman of whom Gabrielle was a clone.

The mind of that woman, whose name had been Dakota Merrick, had somehow come to be encoded within the memory banks of the Magi ship. Following its crash-landing, the ship itself had by some means recreated Merrick in body as well as mind, apparently in the hope that she would be willing to negotiate with the Demarchy in order to ensure the ship's survival until that time, centuries hence, when it could complete its repairs and depart from Redstone.

Gabrielle had listened to all this while his hand caressed her hair as they lay together in her bedchamber, and her skin grew increasingly chill as awful detail followed upon awful detail.

At first, the Demarchy had been intent on dismantling the alien craft with the aim of penetrating its secrets. Extraordinarily powerful though it was, it had suffered incredible damage, for its drive-spines and much of its outer shell had been burned away during re-entry. But then this woman – this Dakota Merrick – had suddenly emerged, disoriented but physically intact, from the Magi ship. The Demarchy's investigators had interrogated her for days, running tests that confirmed her physiology to be entirely human.

And yet there was evidence that she was not the *original* Dakota Merrick. She was clearly a clone of some kind, one whose last memory, prior to emerging from the ship, was of dying halfway across the galaxy, some centuries before.

This clone proved to be entirely unwilling to fulfil the task for which the Magi ship had apparently brought it back to life; nor was it willing to cooperate with the Demarchy's interrogators. They had resorted to torture in the hopes of gleaning from Merrick any information relating to the Magi ship that might be turned to the Demarchy's military or political advantage.

Their attempt proved wildly successful, for Merrick's clone proved to be in some way able to tap into the wealth of knowledge contained within the Magi ship's memory banks, and it imparted some of this knowledge under duress. But then the clone died while fleeing its guards, and before they had a chance to extract any more.

That might have been that, but the scientific and technological data the Demarchy of Uchida had thereby gained was valuable enough to barter in return for financial and military aid from the Accord. With such support, the neighbouring River Concord States were beaten into submission, while the Freehold – once the dominant military force on Redstone – was eventually reduced to a few violent extremists living in mountain caves.

But even that wasn't enough for the Demarchy's rulers, Karl had told her, for they saw a way in which they could secure the Demarchy's future for as long as the Magi ship remained there by the shores of the Ka.

They took tissue samples from the clone's corpse, and from them fashioned a new clone of their own – one that they themselves could control. That first Speaker-Elect had grown to adulthood with its own personality and memories – and none of Merrick's – and had undergone surgery to install the machine-head implants that would allow it eventually to communicate directly with the Magi ship.

Once such a clone reached the age of twenty-one, the cerebral circuitry had matured sufficiently that the clone could be transported to Dios, and to the Ship of the Covenant. Each Speaker was forced then to enter the alien starship, after which she would emerge once more carrying within her mind a cornucopia of data offered up by the ship in return for it not being torn apart by the Demarchy's engineers and scientists.

The only problem, Karl continued, was that each time a Speaker returned from her encounter with the ship, her own personality and memories had been wiped and replaced with those of the long-dead Dakota Merrick. And, each and every time, she proved just as wildly recalcitrant and unwilling to cooperate as before. The Demarchy's interrogators found it necessary, on every such occasion, to torture the clone until she gave them the information they wanted.

At first, Karl explained, the Demarchy considered trying to keep each of the clones alive, or even to produce multiple clones, but the ship refused to divulge data to more than one such clone at a time, perhaps realizing the speed with which it might otherwise be drained of knowledge; it also set a limit on how much data each clone could siphon from its memory banks. In this way the ship ensured its indefinite survival, by giving the Demarchy of Uchida sufficient leverage to rapidly dominate the whole of Redstone. And since it would take a little over two decades for a clone's implants to reach maturity, that set a definite limit on the frequency with which the ship could be interrogated.

And what about the clone? Gabrielle had asked, as she lay curled up on top of the bedsheets, her hands clasped around her knees and shivering. Put to death, Karl had informed her, once a clone had outlived her usefulness. The physical remains were disposed of in secret, even as the next Speaker-Elect was being born to a secret birth-mother.

This process had been finessed over the intervening centuries, and embellished with ceremonies as a public demonstration of the Demarchy's growing power. The city of Dios – meaning literally, the city of God – had grown up around that grounded starship, becoming a place of devout pilgrimage for the Demarchy's citizens. Few outside a secretive inner circle, however, knew the underlying truth.

In this way, Karl explained in a voice full of regret and anger, he had learned the true reason he had been hired to protect her: for the sake of the riches she would unlock once she was of age.

He had cupped her face in his hands then, assuring her he could never allow her to suffer the awful fate that had befallen her predecessors. She would not, as she had been taught to believe, ascend bodily to Heaven after entering the Ship of the Covenant. Instead, she would become someone else entirely, and then die a miserable, painful death.

She had clung to him, hot tears burning a path down her cheeks, as he promised to take them both somewhere far away from Redstone, where no one could ever find them.

But to do so, he had warned, might require drastic measures – possibly very drastic indeed.

Karl gave out a sigh of relief as Gabrielle reconfirmed her willingness to aid him in his plan. She would help him murder the whole of the Demarchy's inner circle, rather than allow them to take her life, and then the two of them would finally make their escape.

'I'm glad to hear you say that,' he said, with a strange half-smile that left her feeling unsettled, without really knowing why.

'But what happens afterwards?' Gabrielle demanded. 'You haven't told me how we're even going to get ourselves off-world. What if Thijs sends your own soldiers out looking for us . . . ?'

He pressed a finger to her lips. 'I've made arrangements, Gabrielle. Believe me, there's no possible way anyone's going to stop us.' He grinned, and she again felt that same curious unease as she returned his gaze, as if someone else were hiding behind his eyes. 'I promise you this, though,' he added, 'they'll never know what hit them. Literally.'

*

Karl slipped out of her bedchamber not long after. She let herself fall back against the pillows and closed her eyes, thinking of Karl's seed now deep within her body.

She wondered why she had yet again failed to tell him about the new life growing inside her. *It's one less thing for him to worry about, before we escape*, she assured herself. But another part of her knew that she was just afraid to tell him she was pregnant – strangely fearful of how he might react.

Mater Cassanas stepped back into the room, her mouth pinched tight and her eyes refusing to meet her mistress's. She moved around the bedchamber, picking things up and then putting them down again, making a show of tidying up but without really achieving anything.

'I don't know what you're planning,' Cassanas said finally, her voice tight with emotion, 'but I'll tell you this: you're making a mistake in trusting Petrova. He's an evil man, with evil intentions . . . you have *no idea*—'

'Then you could have at least tried to protect me,' replied Gabrielle, unable to keep the venom out of her voice. 'But instead you left me alone with him.'

'With Petrova?' Cassanas stared at her. 'But you—'

'I meant with Thijs,' hissed Gabrielle. 'You could have told him no, that he had to leave . . . but instead you did nothing.'

Gabrielle watched the old woman's face as comprehension finally dawned there. 'How was I to know that he would—?'

'How could you *not* know?' Gabrielle cried. 'I remember the look on your face then! You *knew* . . . you knew why he was there. And yet you still let him in. You never once tried to protect me from him, *not once*.'

Cassanas swallowed a great gulp of air, in the manner of someone drowning, before she replied. 'I took care of you as if you were my own daughter,' she gasped, her voice growing husky. 'I fed you from my own breast when you were a baby. I—'

'Get out.'

'I taught you how to read and—'

'I said *get out!*'

Gabrielle screamed these last words at the top of her lungs. She kept shrieking them until Cassanas backed away – running out through the door, with the same two words still pouring out of Gabrielle's throat like the shriek of a wounded animal.

FIVE

Megan

2751 (twelve years before)

The first time Megan had ever heard of the Wanderer was on the command deck of the *Beauregard* – a Kjæregrønnested-registered exploration vessel in orbit above that same world – where she sat ensconced within the folded-up steel petals of the ship's astrogation chair.

<Valentin. There's a cargo pod requesting rendezvous with us,> she observed. <Who the hell's responsible for sending it up here?>

Although Valentin – the merchant officer in charge of supervising the final maintenance checks before the *Beauregard* was handed over to the Accord – was hidden from her actual view, she could see and hear him perfectly well via her ship-linked senses.

Thus she saw Valentin reach out to a console, information rippling under his touch. One or two other members of the skeleton crew assigned to this final check-over were moving here and there around the command deck, in order to supervise last-minute drive and systems diagnostics.

Looks like a standard supply shipment, he replied, his voice sounding flat and echoless as it was fed directly into her auditory nerves. *Seems a little weird that they'd be sending it up now, though.*

<There's nothing standard about it. That's one of the supply pods we use when we're gearing up for a deep-space expedition.>

I'll check the authorization. He paused, the data before him flickering into a new configuration. *Well, whatever it is, it's highest priority. Orders direct from Ladested: don't look, don't touch.*

Megan tried to puzzle it out. Why would they be *loading* supplies? The *Beauregard* had only just arrived back in-system, and it wasn't going anywhere for a good long while – at least not until the special delegation of technical staff on its way from the Accord had finished taking it apart and putting it together again according to their own stringent specifications.

<We should flag up a query. Ask what it is.>

Already did, Valentin replied. *But I'm pretty damn sure nobody's going to tell us anything. It's got a security rating like you wouldn't believe.*

Screw it, she thought; it wasn't her concern any more. <When are you heading back down?> she asked Valentin.

Maybe in another hour or so, he replied. *There's a bar in the port district of Ladested, place called the Mog & Bone. We're thinking of holding a wake. Fancy joining us?*

Megan grinned. <Why the hell not?>

Hey, wait a minute. She saw Valentin step towards another console, frowning at what he saw. *There's a message for you.*

<What is it?>

Take a look.

The message materialized before her. <It says there's a dropship on its way here. Except it doesn't say who's on board.>

It can't be the Accord delegation already, said Valentin. *We're not scheduled to hand the ship over to them for at least another forty-eight hours.*

<Well, whoever it is, the Kjæregrønnested Orbital Authority want me to stay on board until they get here.>

You don't have to do shit, Megan. Our contracts are null and void the moment we step on to the disembarkation shuttle. After that, this ship belongs to the Accord, not to the Three Star Alliance. Come on down with the rest of us and we'll hold a wake in its honour.

<Stop sounding so morose,> she replied. <You'll find yourself a new commission within a couple of months. It's us machine-heads who have to worry about our future.>

She reread the orders a second time, her sense of disappointment growing. More than anything, right now, she wanted to be around the people she knew and trusted. She wanted to be there with them when they all drank to the end of an era.

<I wish I could get out of this, Val, but I don't think I can. I swear I'll see you and the others just as soon as I can make it down.>

Sorry, Megan. That's really shitty luck.

<Seriously. Drink one for me, will you?>

Will do, Valentin replied, and Megan got busy monitoring the docking process, as the cargo pod slid inside the hull.

A few hours later, Megan found herself all alone aboard the *Beauregard*, as she waited for the unnamed delegation to arrive from Ladested, which was Kjæregrønnested's capital. It was like wandering through a deserted mausoleum – or maybe a museum dedicated to failed hope.

Like most starships designed for long-range reconnaissance, the *Beauregard* was not somewhere most people would be happy to call home. Comfort was at a minimum except for those few luxuries deemed necessary to maintain the mental and social health of its crew. Beyond the lounge, and the recreation and meditation pods, the ship was a tangle of narrow access tubes, utilitarian corridors, claustrophobically tiny personal quarters and cramped working spaces.

Megan Jacinth was not most people. She had fond memories associated with the *Beauregard*, but the handing-over of all the Alliance's nova-class starships to the Accord and the stringent terms of the new treaty virtually guaranteed the end of her career in piloting starships. It felt to her like a betrayal.

Even so, she had to admit to herself that there was a certain novelty to being entirely alone on board the ship, even if that was only for a little while. She took the opportunity to wander its deserted corridors and silent access tubes, staying remotely linked all the while to the control and navigation systems, fantasizing that she was marooned alone somewhere in the depths of interstellar space.

Give it up, she chided herself. *The life you built here is over.*

Maybe there would be other opportunities for her, other routes to the stars, but for the moment she found it impossible to envision them.

She soon retreated to the bridge and the astrogation chair, the petals once more folding up around her. She felt herself immediately relax as her machine-senses merged again with those of the surrounding ship.

When most people complained of the hardships of space travel, they tended to forget it was a natural environment for a machinehead. The physical body became a distant concern once locked in full interface. All the stresses of living in cramped conditions amongst a few dozen other human beings, of sharing their recycled water and air, tended to vanish when your senses conspired to convince you that you were floating naked in infinite space rather than sealed up within a set of steel petals.

It wasn't long before a dropship rendezvoused with the *Beauregard*. Megan fired an ident-request over to it, and confirmed it was carrying the unidentified passengers she had been ordered to wait for.

What she didn't expect, however, was to find that Bash was also on board the dropship. She could sense his proximity through her machine-senses as the smaller craft made to dock.

<What's up, baby?> he responded, when she fired an immediate query at him.

<What the hell, Bash? First I get told I have to wait up here alone, and without explanation, and now I find *you've* got something to do with this. What exactly are you up to?>

He paused just long enough before replying for her to know he was choosing his words carefully. <Something came up,> he sent back after a few moments. <There are some people here with me from Ladested who want to talk to you.>

<Talk to *me*? Who? Are they from the Accord?>

<No, Meg, they're our own people.>

<So, why come here just to talk to me?> she replied, unable to hide her exasperation. <Why not wait until I'm back on the ground?>

<Just hang on until we get there, and then they'll explain everything. Shouldn't be more than another few minutes before we're with you.>

He broke the connection, and she stared beyond the coloured nodes of information arrayed in deep stacks all around her, projected against the interior of the petals. Bash was the *Beauregard*'s co-pilot as well as her closest friend, and two days earlier he had departed the *Beauregard* for what she'd believed was the last time. There had been no hint of any furtive plans for him to come sneaking back on board.

Let's have one last drink before I abandon ship, he'd said to her as he stood in the door to her quarters, gripping a bottle of some brown liquid in one hand. *Before I take the dropship down and try to figure out just what in hell I'm going to do with the rest of my life.*

She now severed her connection to the *Beauregard*'s AI, and sat there in the silent darkness for a few moments before ordering the petals to unfold.

As she gazed around the command deck, it finally hit her that she would never pilot the *Beauregard* again.

She tried not to feel bitter about it. Just days before, Otto Schelling and other senior members of the Three Star Alliance's ruling First Families had signed a treaty handing over full control of the nova-class fleets of all three worlds of the Alliance – Kjæregrønnested, Al-Jahar and Alyeska – to the Accord. And, as an accord of civilized species, they had much more power to bring to bear than the weaker Alliance. This agreement had followed years of intense bargaining, a trade and communications embargo, and the arrival of a number of heavy Accord cruisers filled with troops ready to occupy the Alliance's major cities, should they fail to accept the proposed terms. The whole business had struck Megan as immense overkill.

She fired a message off to Bash, to let him know she'd be waiting in the ship's lounge. Then she exited the command deck without allowing herself a backward glance.

*

She had just got settled in, after grabbing a second squeeze-bulb of Irish coffee from the lounge bar, when Bash entered, accompanied by two other men. The first she didn't recognize but the second was immediately familiar, even if she couldn't quite place him straight away. He was broad-chested and not a little handsome, and he carried himself with a confidence just shy of arrogance. His companion, by contrast, was as thin as a rail, his hair a dense tangle of blond-brown hair above a goatee beard. Whenever he moved, it was in a slightly jerky, bird-like fashion.

'Megan Jacinth?' asked the moderately familiar one in a loud voice.

She raised her squeeze-bulb in an ironic salute. 'That's me.'

She watched as the three of them made their way towards the circle of couches where she was sprawled. From the ease with which the two strangers navigated in the zero gravity, she could tell that they had both spent a lot of time off-world.

'Thanks for agreeing to wait for us here,' said Mr Vaguely Familiar, pulling himself into a seat across from her and sliding an arm through a nearby loop to keep himself from floating away. His skinny companion pulled himself down next to him, while Bash took his seat right opposite Megan. 'My name,' said the more attractive one, 'is Gregor Tarrant.'

Gregor Tarrant. Megan sat up straight, suddenly embarrassed at her casual slouching. 'I *thought* I recognized you from somewhere. You're famous.'

Tarrant smiled self-deprecatingly, with a dismissive gesture. 'Not really.'

'No,' she said, 'you *are*. Bash – I mean, Pilot Bashir – told me all about what happened. What you did was incredible.'

Tarrant and his goateed companion both chuckled and grinned. 'I was just doing my job,' said Tarrant.

Tarrant had been a junior officer on the *Beauregard*'s sister ship, the *Chesapeake*, on an exploratory expedition to a white-dwarf system sixteen light years from Al-Jahar. There the *Chesapeake* had come under assault from automated attack systems left dormant since the Shoal–Emissary war of a few centuries earlier.

That attack had taken the expedition completely by surprise. As a result, the *Chesapeake* had suffered a devastating breach that vented its atmosphere and killed a full quarter of its complement, including its captain, most of its senior staff and one of its two machine-head pilots. Bash was the fortunate one who had survived.

Tarrant, despite his relative inexperience, had somehow rallied the survivors and, regardless of repeated attacks, he had managed to keep them alive inside a hastily pressurized cavern located on an airless moon, until rescue arrived nearly two months later. It was an extraordinary story, made all the more remarkable by the fact that Tarrant had been only twenty-four standard years old at the time.

'I think you're being coy,' Megan replied. 'But I'll say no more about it if you'd rather I didn't.'

'Just as long as you don't have any unrealistic expectations of me,' he said, and then gestured to his companion. 'This is Anil Sifra, and he's here in an advisory capacity, as a representative of the First Families.'

Sifra. Of course. He was from the same bracket as the Schellings and the Beauvoirs who – along with the Sifra Clan – were the most powerful of the Alliance's founding families.

Sifra nodded to her politely. 'I know you must be wondering what the hell we're doing here.'

'You took the words right out of my mouth,' Megan replied, then regretted sounding so flippant.

'We're here to make you a proposal,' Tarrant explained. 'One we've already made to Mr Bashir here. It was his idea to bring you in on this, by the way. I hardly need tell you that things haven't been going well for the Three Star Alliance lately.'

'If by not going well,' said Megan, 'you mean the Accord bent us over and ass-fucked us with the terms of their new treaty, then I'd be inclined to agree with you.'

'Now it's my turn to embarrass *you*,' said Tarrant. 'I heard all about what you did at Kappa 659. You're halfway to being a legend yourself, after the way you bypassed that blockade.'

Kjæregrønnested's First Families had made their fortune financing long-range expeditions after the Shoal–Emissary war inadvertently opened the galaxy up to humankind. One of those expeditions had discovered Kjæregrønnested as well as Alyeska and Al-Jahar, all three of them habitable worlds orbiting stars that were separated from each other by no more than a few light years.

Some amongst those same families had dreamed of creating a society based on their own values, one that reflected the pioneer spirit they believed necessary to the survival of the species out there in the wider galaxy. These three colonies soon signed a treaty, forming the Three Star Alliance, just a few short years after the Accord – an interstellar polity comprising not only humanity but a number of neighbouring species – had also come into existence.

The discovery of Meridian ruins beneath the kilometres-deep layer of ice covering much of Alyeska's surface had been rapidly followed by the further discovery of a derelict Shoal coreship out in the depths of interstellar space, no more than three light years from Al-Jahar. That abandoned, world-sized starship proved to contain an even more fabulous prize, one whose value could not be measured: a cache of dozens of undamaged nova drives, enough to allow the Alliance to build its own independent fleet of starships. In one stroke, the Alliance had thus gained the potential to challenge the growing economic and political power of the Accord.

But as the Accord grew in strength, it introduced more and more stringent regulations regarding the use of nova drives – including those recovered from the said coreship.

Megan was far from unsympathetic to the Accord's fear that these nova drives might be used as weapons if they fell into the wrong hands. Indeed, the conflict between the Emissaries and the Shoal had shown just how destructive the devices could be, for in just a few short years the two rival empires had laid waste to vast swathes of the Perseus Arm.

But where she and many others chose to differ was regarding the assumption that the nova drives would be automatically safer under the Accord's control.

The Accord had then demanded that the Alliance hand over control of their entire superluminal fleet, with the claimed intention of leasing those same ships back to them – but carrying a permanent contingent of Accord military and technical personnel aboard each of them.

That had been a demand too far for the First Families. When tensions reached a peak, Accord cruisers had set up a blockade of the derelict coreship, cutting off any escape route for the salvage team at work on removing the last remaining drives.

Megan herself had been the pilot for the expedition sent to try and rescue the blockaded salvage workers.

'The way some of the other machine-heads talk about you,' said Tarrant, 'it seems that what you did there bordered on the supernatural.'

Megan grinned. 'Now you really *are* embarrassing me.'

'Apparently you jumped your ship across fifteen AUs, and directly *inside* the coreship itself.' Tarrant shook his head. 'Something like that shouldn't even be possible.'

'I swear it wasn't such a big deal,' she replied. 'A large part of the coreship's outer hull had already been torn away, so that left a pretty big gap to aim for.'

'Maybe so,' said Tarrant, 'but crossing from a distance of even *one* AU would scare anyone else to death. Look, what would you say if I told you there was a way to change everything, and put the TSA back on top? In a way that the Accord wouldn't be able to do anything about?'

Megan glanced at Bash, then turned back to Tarrant. 'What is it you want from me, exactly?'

'We're here,' said Tarrant, 'because you're one of the best machine-head pilots in the Alliance . . . and because we also need the *Beauregard*.'

'You "need" the *Beauregard*?' She could hardly mask her incredulity.

'Please, Megan,' said Bash, 'hear him out.'

'We're here,' said Sifra, 'on the direct orders of Otto Schelling. What we're now asking you for will be entirely voluntary.'

'We need you to pilot the *Beauregard*, but leaving immediately,' explained Tarrant. 'As soon as you give us the word, Otto Schelling will authorize the payment of half a million shares in high-value First Family commercial patents, with guaranteed per annum returns, into a private account under your own name.'

She glanced at Bash. 'This is bullshit, right?' she asked him. 'They're having me on.'

'No bullshit, Megan – and I already accepted.' A grin spread across his face. 'Checked my account this morning and saw the sweetest line of zeros.'

'The transfer will be handled by the Schellings' own legal firm under the strictest secrecy,' continued Sifra, 'and the deal is cast iron, whatever happens. The Accord won't be able to trace it or touch it, either. If you decide you want to be part of this, we'll authorize that transfer immediately. Think about the opportunities that it could buy for a machine-head pilot.'

'It's enough to buy part-ownership in a ship,' said Bash. 'Hell, Megan, think what we could do if we pooled our money. Finance our *own* damn expedition.'

'Just what in hell is it you're planning to do?' she asked Tarrant.

'We first need to know if you're in or not,' said Sifra.

Megan rolled her eyes. 'In for *what*, exactly?'

'A new expedition,' said Tarrant, 'deep into the galaxy – to find something called the Wanderer.'

'What is it, precisely?'

'You might regret asking me that question, Miss Jacinth, as it's going to take me a while to explain.'

She looked down at her hand, and noticed the bulb of Irish coffee it was still clutching. She had entirely forgotten it was there.

She took a sip, then sat back, gazing off towards an image of Kjæregrønnested that was turning slowly on a screen at the far end of the lounge.

'I'm all ears,' she said.

SIX

Megan

The story of the Wanderer had started, Tarrant went on to explain, with a discovery made on Alyeska.

Until the discovery of the ruins beneath Alyeska's ice, the Meridians had remained almost entirely unknown to mankind. Like the Shoal, they had once spread far and wide across the galaxy, leaving colonies on hundreds of worlds. But, unlike other starfaring species, the Meridians had never stumbled across a Maker cache, and so never acquired the means of faster-than-light travel. It would therefore have taken any one of their ships tens of thousands of years to travel from one end of their empire to the other.

It rapidly became clear to the archaeologists studying their ruins that, despite this, the Meridians had nonetheless undergone a dramatic spike in technological and scientific development within a very short time frame. That meant either that the Meridians had indeed found a Maker cache – but somehow failed to take advantage of the faster-than-light technology contained therein – or that their newfound technological sophistication had arrived by some other route.

What that route might be, Tarrant explained, had remained a mystery until the Schellings came into possession of data attributing this sudden spike to a machine-entity with whom a Meridian expedition had made contact. They had named this entity – which had apparently been roaming the galaxy for millions of years at sub-light velocities – the 'Wanderer'.

The Meridians had found the Wanderer willing to communicate, and even to trade information. It was, it seemed, looking for something. But as to what that might be, the Meridians either hadn't asked or had failed to record the answer. Analysts working under strictest secrecy had cross-referenced the newly discovered data with the historical records of other known spacefaring species, quickly finding a correlation with the Atn, and even with the Shoal. They, too, it seemed, had had their own encounters with the Wanderer, albeit at a much later date.

The more they dug, the stranger the story became. The Meridians recorded that the Wanderer had been on the losing side of some kind of war, but there were no records to indicate who that war had been fought against, or why.

All of this was incidental, however, to the fact that the Wanderer had apparently been blessed with a cornucopia of knowledge far in advance of that possessed by the Meridians. For a species like the Meridians, however, knowledge was the only commodity of true value.

The Schellings reasoned that if the Wanderer still existed, and if it could be persuaded to impart some of the same knowledge that had triggered a technological and scientific renaissance amongst the Meridians, then the entire balance of power would shift heavily in the Three Star Alliance's favour – and then the Accord would finally be forced to come crawling.

Megan finished her coffee and let the bulb float away from her. 'But if this . . . thing, this Wanderer, is so advanced,' she asked, 'what could we possibly have to offer it in return, assuming it does even want to trade? It's not just going to give us whatever we ask for without expecting something in return, is it?'

She looked between the two men, noting that their expressions were suddenly neutral.

'You already have something in mind,' she said slowly, 'but you're not going to tell me what it is – is that it?'

'That has to stay a secret between me and Anil,' said Tarrant, 'and, of course, a few members of the Schelling family.' He shrugged amiably. 'Sorry.'

Megan made a face. She never liked being kept in the dark. 'You really think that if we can find this thing, it'll really make that much of a difference to the Alliance?'

'Just a few scraps of scientific knowledge gleaned from the Alyeska digs were enough to make the First Families enormously rich and powerful,' said Tarrant. 'Imagine, then, what the Wanderer could do for us.'

Megan leaned back, her fingers tapping a staccato rhythm on her couch's arm. Tarrant's enthusiasm was infectious. 'It still doesn't give us back control over our fleets,' she pointed out.

Tarrant leaned towards her. 'If this works out as well as we think it will, we'll be returning home with enough advanced scientific data to revolutionize our society completely. We'll be able to license that data to the Accord in return for full control of our fleet again. They'll bend over backwards to give us what we want.'

'At the very least,' added Bash, 'it has to be worth a shot. Otherwise, you and I are going to be stuck running automated mining traffic, or having to retrain for the Accord. And even if they do decide to let us pilot nova-class ships, it's not going to be like it was before.' He shook his head, slow and sombre. 'Jumpy bureaucrats breathing down our necks all day, wanting everything we do filed in advance, and in triplicate – that's not what I became a pilot for.'

She turned to Tarrant. 'Look, all of this sounds great, but there's already a delegation from the Accord on its way here to oversee the handover.'

'All the more reason not to waste any time,' said Tarrant, his hands clenching into fists. 'Let me be very clear about what we are proposing. We want to take the *Beauregard* – *immediately* – on a deep-space expedition to seek out the Wanderer, and then see if we can replicate what the Meridians managed on behalf of their own civilization.'

'So, since we're doing some straight-talking,' said Megan, 'I want to be absolutely sure of what you're saying. You want to *hijack* the *Beauregard*, with my help, and you really have Otto Schelling's backing for this?'

'I can put you in touch with him right this second, if you're still unconvinced.'

'No.' She shook her head, feeling a curious sensation of both terror and exhilaration at the scale of their plan. 'I believe you. But how do we know the Wanderer is even still out there, or where exactly it is? It must have travelled a hell of a long way since it ran into the Meridians, even moving at less than light speed.'

Tarrant made a practised gesture, and a map of the local stellar arm materialized overhead. 'We narrowed down the Wanderer's likely location to a number of possible target systems, extrapolating from its last recorded positions,' he explained, as he indicated a star cluster that was clearly a very, very long way away. 'Fortunately, the Atn and the Shoal recorded the coordinates of their own encounters with it, and that information let us extrapolate its probable direction and speed of movement.'

'After this amount of time?' She found herself unable to hide her scepticism. 'So it could be anywhere.'

Tarrant grinned. 'Ordinarily it'd be an impossibly long shot, yes. But the Meridians left some probes behind to track the Wanderer, and they're still functioning.'

'So you're not just *hoping* it's still out there.'

'Oh no,' said Tarrant. 'We *know* it's out there. We even sent out a pair of our own probes equipped with nova drives to perform a fly-by. Take a look.'

The image of the spiral arm expanded, fading at the edges as the view rushed in towards a tight knot of several thousand stars that were identified by supplementary information as the Calafat-Holt Cluster.

The view zoomed in again, slowing as it approached a nebula that made Megan think of what sunset in hell might look like. Supplementary data told her she was looking at a Wolf-Rayet star, a bloated ball of gas dozens of times larger than a standard Earth-type, and approaching the end of its life. It had been given the designation C-H45k.

C-H45k was losing mass at an enormous rate, throwing off great sheets of burning plasma that obscured the star itself from sight. Any kind of approach to such a system was going to entail some fairly unique challenges.

'It doesn't seem to want to make it easy for anyone to drop by and visit, does it?' she muttered.

Sifra chuckled. 'Just the same thing we were thinking.'

'This isn't a mere hop or a skip you're talking about,' said Megan. 'You're talking about a trip of more than *fifteen thousand* light years. I can think of maybe only a handful of expeditions that have travelled that far. In fact, you're talking at least half a year just to get there.'

'Then we need to set out straight away, Miss Jacinth,' said Tarrant. 'And the *Beauregard* is already stocked with every resource it needs for a long-range mission.'

Megan nodded. At least that explained the final, mysterious cargo shipment. 'All right, then. Let me see it.'

'Pardon me?'

'The Wanderer,' she said. 'You said there was a fly-by. I want to see what it looks like.'

Tarrant glanced at Sifra, who shrugged. 'All right,' said Tarrant.

More images appeared. At first, all Megan could see was a black outline against a field of stars. But then she pulled the projected data into her personal datascape, the lounge around her briefly fading from her sight.

She could make out a massive central body, dark grey and black, with what appeared to be numerous arms extending outwards from its central mass. It made her think of nothing less than the knotted roots of a tree that had just been ripped from the soil and exposed to the daylight. She might have assumed the branch-like structures were drive-spines, if she hadn't just been informed that the Wanderer travelled at sub-light speeds.

The images sent a trickle of ice running down her spine. There was something about those branching structures that made it look as if the Wanderer were reaching out for her, like some ragged and hungry beast amidst a forest of stars.

She exited her datascape, and was aware of Tarrant looking at her expectantly. 'Well?' he asked.

'All right,' she said, 'I'm impressed. But what makes you so sure I won't turn your offer down?'

'Psychological profiling says you won't,' said Tarrant. 'And, besides, Mr Bashir assured us that you wouldn't.'

'Having two machine-head pilots is standard operating procedure for any long-range expedition,' said Sifra, 'and this one is no different. And, as we've already pointed out, the rewards are *extremely* generous.'

'No,' said Tarrant, studying her, 'she's not really interested in the money. It's just like Mr Bashir said: life for a machine-head in the Accord means being tightly controlled and entirely dependent on the mercies of a distant bureaucracy. But the Alliance was never about that.' He leaned towards her, his gaze intent. 'This is your chance to get back the life you wanted – before it's lost forever.'

Something made it hard for her to pull her eyes away from his. It was uncomfortably as if he could see right inside her, to all the insecurities she worked so hard to keep hidden.

'But . . . just the four of us?' she asked, looking around at the other two.

'It's not as if we don't know that just one machine-head could keep a ship like this running indefinitely,' said Tarrant, sitting back again. 'I'd obviously prefer to take along a full team of specialists, but there isn't the time for that, and there's too much risk that it would lead to us being discovered before we set out. Not only that, but it's absolutely imperative that none of this is in any way attributable to the Schellings – or any of the First Families, for that matter. We need to make this look as if we just cut and run.'

Cut and run. Just take the Beauregard *and pilot her fifteen thousand light years, in search of some ancient ship travelling on an unknown quest.*

The whole idea was impossibly romantic, and – she was forced to admit – more than a little appealing.

But it was impossible, of course. Surely he knew that?

'You do know that all the Alliance's ships are equipped with failsafes, don't you?' she said. 'They're there to prevent machine-heads like me from doing *precisely* what you're suggesting. As soon as someone down in Ladested realizes I'm taking the *Beauregard* out of orbit without authorization, they'll shut me down remotely.'

'And Otto Schelling, as the primary financier behind the *Beauregard* and its sister ships,' said Tarrant, 'has the ultimate responsibility for that override. We won't be stopped.'

'I need more than just your word on that,' she said.

Tarrant nodded. 'I'd check the current authorization flags, if I were you.'

Megan dived back into her datascape just long enough to ascertain that numerous fail-safes had indeed been disabled. She blinked, feeling numb. It meant she could literally take the *Beauregard* anywhere she wanted.

'Why ask me to do this *now*?' she exclaimed. 'Why not yesterday, or a week ago?'

'We didn't have everything we needed, a week ago,' said Tarrant. 'And that didn't leave us much time.'

There's no turning back, she told herself, feeling a sense of standing on the edge of a precipice.

'Whatever data you have about the Wanderer,' she said, 'I'll need to see all of it.'

Tarrant nodded, as if he'd been expecting her to say just that. 'We'll upload everything we've got to the *Beauregard*'s data banks, the moment you give your answer.'

She glanced at Bash, noting his hopeful expression.

'Okay,' she said, 'let's do it.'

SEVEN

Megan

2763 (the present)

The morning after Megan found herself locked into a basement room on Avilon alongside Bash, Sifra appeared in their cell in the company of the Freeholder, who had Megan's satchel slung over his shoulder.

She had been asleep, curled up on the cold hard concrete next to Bash's cot, when they entered. Sifra held an antique Consortium-era assault pistol in one hand, and she saw he still affected a straggly blond goatee, although there were now a few silver streaks. His hair still stuck up in places, giving him the appearance of someone perpetually in the process of just waking up.

He gazed down at her, then nodded with satisfaction. 'Good work, Luiz,' he said to the Freeholder, then grabbed Megan by the arm, hauling her to her feet.

He pressed the barrel of the pistol against her neck and guided her towards the corner of the room farthest away from Bash.

'Hello, Megan,' said Sifra. 'Long time no see. Were you surprised to discover I was still alive?'

She found it hard to swallow with the gun pushed against her throat. 'How did you do it, Anil? I left you and Gregor for dead. Didn't the Wanderer try and finish you off?'

'It lost interest in us,' said Sifra, 'because we no longer had what it wanted. We were stuck out there on the wreck of the *Beauregard* for very nearly two years, and all thanks to you. Two whole years before General Schelling was able to send out a rescue drone. Plenty of time for me to think about what I'd do if I ever met you again.'

'*General* Schelling?' She laughed because, the last she'd heard, the former president of the Three Star Alliance had been reduced to the status of a wanted fugitive. 'That's rich. And how is the evil old fucker these days?'

Sifra responded by driving his free hand into her belly. She felt her legs give way beneath her, and she slumped back onto the floor.

Sifra stood over her, breathing hard. *Shut your smart mouth, Megan*, she told herself.

'Luiz,' said Sifra over his shoulder. 'Let's see what's in that bag of hers.'

Luiz emptied the contents on to the floor, then bent down to pick up Kazim's security override device, handing it to Sifra.

Sifra held the device up before her face. 'I know you got this from a friend of yours,' he said. 'Arturo Kazim, shipping agent and part-time *sans de sezi* dealer.'

Megan looked away. 'It doesn't matter where I got it from,' she replied in a voice now a monotone. 'It doesn't work.'

Sifra nodded, and let the device fall back on to the floor with a clatter. 'On the contrary,' he said, 'it works just fine.'

Megan looked up at him, confused. 'What the hell are you talking about?'

'Arturo was working for me,' he said, clearly relishing her look of shock. 'He got well paid for it, too.'

Megan stared at him, refusing to accept this betrayal. 'That's impossible.'

'Money talks, Megan. Kazim gave you that device on my orders. He told you it would allow you to pass safely through Avilon's security cordon, but in reality it was programmed to hack the security systems in such a way that I myself, rather than Avilon's civil authorities, would be informed of your arrival.'

She stared up at him, feeling sick.

'I know all about how you built up a nice little business acting as a go-between for men like Kazim and their counterparts on

Morgan's World and Al-Jahar,' Sifra continued. 'I know just how long you've been planning to come and rescue Bash here – ever since Kazim told you, on my orders, that he was still alive.'

The sick feeling intensified, and she swallowed sour phlegm. She recalled the time Arturo had – perhaps, in retrospect, a little too casually – mentioned Sifra's name in connection with the *sans de sezi* trade on Avilon. She had badgered him for more information, and found out that Sifra had established himself as a major drugs importer for that tiny world's rich and jaded inhabitants.

What hurt most, however, was that although Arturo Kazim had not precisely been a friend, she had at least allowed herself to trust him, even so far as to rely on his aid in finding a means of landing undetected on Avilon.

'All this,' she said, 'just to lure me here? But why? For revenge?'

'Frankly, that would be the preferred option,' said Sifra. 'But no.'

'Then . . . what possible purpose is there to all this?'

'That, Megan, is something you will find out before too long,' he replied. 'Instead, I'm going to give you a chance to repay your debts to the Three Star Alliance, to General Schelling and to Gregor Tarrant.'

Gregor Tarrant. Even the mention of the name made her skin crawl. 'Where is he?' she demanded. 'Is he here?'

'Never you mind where he is,' he said. 'First, I want you to answer some questions. Kazim informed me that you've been raising funds to acquire your own ship, and that you've been making enquiries about buying goods and equipment for a very long journey. Where were you planning to fly to, Megan? And what does Bash have to do with it?'

She stiffened. 'Bash deserves to be cared for by anyone but the likes of you. And my own ship means I can be independent. There are plenty of colonies that desperately need machine-head pilots.'

'I don't believe you,' he said.

'Why?'

'To take the first point, I know you're not so stupid as to think there's anything you can possibly do for Bash. He's been effectively brain-dead ever since our encounter with the Wanderer. He'll never again be able to look after himself or feed himself. He can't even walk without being guided. Even if you rescued him, there's not enough left of his mind for him ever to be able to thank you.'

'He's my *friend*,' she said. 'I know this is a hard concept for you to understand, but that means he's important to me. I couldn't live with myself if I thought there was any chance he might know where he was, or who was in charge of him. And I still have enough money left to pay for his personal care – maybe even find a cure for him.'

'And I might have believed you,' said Sifra, 'if it weren't for the scale of what Kazim tells me you've been planning – which is far more than you could possibly need just to become a glorified cargo pilot in some backwater system. I think,' he said, 'that you're intending to go back out to the Wanderer. That's the real reason you're here – because without Bash you can't communicate with it.'

It was all true, of course, but she couldn't possibly let him know that.

'That doesn't make any sense,' she said. 'What could I have to offer the Wanderer that would make it willing to talk to me, when the last time around it did its level best to kill us all?'

'I couldn't have put it better myself,' said Sifra. 'So why don't you just tell me?'

'In all sincerity,' she said, 'I think you're fucking crazy. Going back out there would be suicide. I'd just get myself and Bash killed.'

Sifra shook his head. 'There are so many things about you that don't add up. You came to the Three Star Alliance along with Bash, but your records from before that were clearly faked. You supposedly come from Redstone, but you've never received a faith chip. And you're as sure as hell not a Freeholder, because they all tattoo their children at birth.'

'Maybe I had it removed,' she suggested.

'Don't mock me,' he said, his fingers tightening around the hand grip of his pistol. 'The real mystery is why were *you* the only one who could ever communicate with the Wanderer, without the experience killing you?'

'Just a minute. What do you mean "the *only* one"?'

'We experimented with other machine-heads to see if they could communicate with the Wanderer, using Bash as a bridge.'

'You mean you've *already* been back out to visit the Wanderer?'

He shook his head. 'You don't understand. We discovered Bash is still remotely linked to the Wanderer, regardless of distance – even across light years. He doesn't have to be anywhere near the Wanderer to get in touch with it.'

Her mouth flopped open. 'You're fucking kidding me.'

'Unfortunately,' Sifra continued, 'the experience ultimately proved fatal for all of our test subjects. All, that is, except you. So why is that?'

She stared at him mutely.

He kneeled until they were face to face, his pistol resting on one knee. 'All you have to do is tell me the truth, Megan. Or else I'll burn Bash.'

'What?'

Sifra glanced over his shoulder at Luiz. 'Are you ready?'

The Freeholder's expression was uncertain. 'But don't we need him to—?'

'For pity's sake,' Sifra shouted. 'We talked about this already. Just do what you're told!'

Luiz glared at him sullenly, then withdrew a torch gun from the pocket of his jacket – a handheld plasma-arc cutter of a kind typically used for slicing through pipes and bulkheads in emergency situations.

Megan heard a click, and a steady blue flame emerged from the tip of the cutter, hissing loudly. She watched in mounting horror as Luiz lowered it towards Bash's face.

She started to push herself up and forward, but Sifra shoved her roughly back down.

'Stay right there,' he said harshly, standing up again and aiming the pistol at her head.

Luiz paused with the hissing flame just centimetres from Bash's face.

'What the hell are you *doing*?' Megan demanded. 'I thought you needed him!'

'We do,' said Sifra. 'But how badly, really, does he need a face?'

She stared at him, her bowels turning to liquid. 'Anil, please, don't do this . . .'

'Simple choice,' he said. 'Luiz is an artist when it comes to this kind of thing. He'll carve off the nose, ears, maybe the lips. And, let's face it, Megan, given Bashir's current lack of a functioning intellect, does he really *need* his eyes?'

'Anil,' she begged, 'for the love of God . . .'

'Five seconds,' said Sifra. 'Either Luiz burns his face off, or you tell me the truth.'

Megan hesitated just a moment too long. Sifra nodded to Luiz, and the Freeholder dipped the flame marginally closer to Bash's cheek.

'I'll tell you!' Megan yelled in panic. She could feel tears starting, but didn't care. 'Please . . . whatever you want, but just don't . . .'

Just don't hurt him.

Sifra snapped his fingers at Luiz, who switched the torch gun off and stepped away from the cot. His sullen glare had not faded, and it was clear there had been a serious argument between the two men.

'So now you'll tell me?' declared Sifra.

'Do you know,' began Megan, 'what a Maker Swarm is?'

He thought for a moment. 'Something to do with the Maker caches? Like the one found in the Tierra system?'

She nodded. 'The Swarms were created by the Makers, in order to construct the caches on their behalf.'

He frowned. 'Go on.'

'The point is, the Swarms are still out there, or at least one of them is – and it's heading straight towards the Accord. Towards *us*.'

'What is it, exactly? A swarm of what?'

'Machines,' she said. 'Millions of them, interlinked and autonomous, comprising a single hive mind. And every last one of them is equipped with a nova drive. Try and imagine the damage an entity like that could do to us – to all of humanity. They're on their way here, and we've got no more than a year or two at the most before they turn up in force.'

Sifra rubbed at his chin. 'What does this have to do with the Wanderer?'

'Back when I communicated with the Wanderer, I got a hint from it of something that could halt the Swarm before it reaches us.'

Sifra scowled at her. 'How in hell could you know of such a thing? Surely if something like that was really coming our way, it'd be headline news everywhere?'

She struggled to think of an explanation that might convince him. The worst thing she could do, she decided, was to tell him the truth.

'Look, sometimes I come into contact with other species – in particular the Atn,' she said, improvising wildly. 'And it's general knowledge that the Atn have records going back longer than any other species in the Milky Way, including the Shoal.'

'So you're saying the Atn told you this Swarm was on its way here?'

'There's an Atn clade in the same system as Morgan's World,' she said, her mind racing. 'It's a long story, but I found out that one of their other clades had reported a Swarm passing through their region of space, and . . .'

She heard Luiz give a snicker from the far corner of the room, and felt her face grow hot.

'Oh, man,' said Luiz, 'I was wrong. This is worth it just for the entertainment value alone.'

'I think,' Sifra said to her, his expression turned sour, 'that if you wanted to make me even angrier than I already was, you couldn't do better than all this bullshit about swarms and caches.'

'For God's sake,' she snapped, 'what do you *want* from me?'

'You're right about one thing, Megan,' said Sifra. 'Going out to the Wanderer on your own, with nothing to offer it, would be suicide. And you don't strike me as the suicidal type. Nevertheless, I feel sure that's just what you were intending to do.'

'There are things you don't know about me.' She chose her words carefully. 'You asked why I wanted to talk to the Wanderer – well, now you know.'

'God *damn it*!' he shouted, then turned to Luiz. 'Go ahead. Carve him up. And, while you're at it, let me think about whether he even needs his hands. Or his dick, for that matter.' He glanced back at Megan and snapped his fingers. 'Now I really should have thought of *that* first.'

'No,' said Megan, her voice calm despite her inner turmoil. 'You're not going to singe so much as one damn hair on Bash's head.'

'And why the hell not?' Sifra demanded.

Luiz, meanwhile, regarded her with apparent interest.

'Because I've had time to think,' she said, catching the other man's eye and speaking quickly. 'Luiz, listen to me. If you burn Bash, you run a risk of permanently damaging his implants. And if what you're telling me is true,' she said, turning back to Sifra, 'and he really can link to the Wanderer as you say he can, then you're taking a chance of losing that link forever if you do any lasting damage. And if that happened, I'm guessing Schelling would personally burn *your* dick off.'

He stared at her. 'And that story you just told me?'

'Take it or leave it,' she said. 'I don't care if you don't believe any of it or not.'

'She's right,' said Luiz. 'It's too much risk. You have her and Bashir both, and that's all that matters.'

'No,' said Sifra, 'I—'

Luiz sighed and shook his head, then pushed his torch gun back inside his jacket. 'No, Anil,' he said firmly, 'let's just concentrate for now on our departure for Redstone. That's the reason I'm here, not because you've got some personal vendetta against this woman.'

Megan watched as Sifra visibly struggled to control his temper. Then he exhaled noisily and stepped back over to the door. 'There's something you're not telling me,' he said, glaring back at her as Luiz swung the door open. 'And even if I don't find out what it is today, I will eventually.'

He nodded towards Bash. 'In the meantime, you'd better get used to each other's company, because you're going to be spending a lot of time around each other.'

As he left, he slammed the door shut and locked it, his and Luiz's footsteps rapidly receding down the passageway beyond.

Megan let her head tip back against the wall with a groan. *Redstone? Of all the places.*

She glanced over at Bash, lying unseeing and uncaring on his cot. In a life full of bad memories, the ones associated with that particular world were the worst for her.

The following morning, Luiz returned, accompanied by the two bead-zombies. One remained standing by the door, a sword clutched in one hand, while the other kept a cheaply fabricated plasma rifle trained on Megan's head. Luiz meanwhile busied himself with cuffing her wrists behind her back. He then started to drag Bash out of his cot by the arm.

'For pity's sake,' said Megan, 'take it easy. You only need to coax him a little.'

Luiz gave her a brief, sour glance and kicked Bash hard as he lay on the floor, half tangled up in his sheets. Luiz then knelt down to twist Bash's arms behind his back, before securing them with another pair of cuffs.

Megan eyed the two bead-zombies. She might not have access to the local data-net but, with those two headless abominations physically present in the room with her, she could see their electronic control systems as a shimmering matrix of data. Was it possible . . . ?

She let her breath out slowly, forcing herself to ignore the way Luiz was roughly pushing and shoving Bash towards the door. There wasn't anything she could do about that right now, anyway.

The two of them exited the room, leaving her alone with the zombies. They were almost certainly controlled by an AI somewhere else on Sifra's estate. But remote analysis with her implants rapidly made it clear that the encryption on their control beads was of a highly sophisticated nature. Were she to make a brute-force attempt at subverting them, Luiz and Sifra would soon know about it.

Then she felt a growing sense of excitement when her implants identified what appeared to be flaws – or possible points of entry – in the encryption. *Could* there be some way to subvert, or even take over, one or both of them?

Except, she realized belatedly, doing so would require her to be in the direct physical presence of these zombies for quite some period of time – more time than Sifra or Luiz were ever likely to allow her. Instead they would stick her on board some ship bound for Redstone, dump her in some other makeshift cell, and that would be that.

She felt her earlier sense of hopelessness return, grey and deadening, and she could hardly be bothered to fight it.

Luiz soon returned for her, leading her back upstairs and into brilliant simulated sunlight. The two zombies, she noted with interest, accompanied them.

A small flyer, with bulbous shaped-field generators on its lower fuselage and a translucent upper hull, sat waiting for them on a grassy lawn. Like the spider-truck, it was decorated with Avilon Security decals. Luiz guided her on board, where she found that Bash had already been strapped in.

She watched with deep interest as the two zombies followed them aboard, Luiz carefully strapping them one after the other into their own seats behind her and Bash. The thought of them sitting so close, yet out of sight, made her skin crawl. But it was still an unexpected opportunity to investigate the limits of their secured encryption more thoroughly. She wondered what would be used to run and control the zombies, once they were out of range of the estate's AI systems.

Sifra himself was the last to board. He threw a single, uninterested glance at her before stepping on through into the cockpit, closely followed by Luiz. The craft rose immediately, so Megan had only a last brief glimpse of Cockaigne.

Just fifteen minutes later, they dropped to a landing at Avilon's primary spaceport, where Luiz herded her and Bash towards a nearby dropship. A tannoy boomed indecipherably some way off in the distance, with the electronic chime of an automated cargo truck dopplering somewhere to her right.

There was, she realized, no one around to wonder why two of the people now boarding the dropship had their hands cuffed behind their backs – and even if they had noticed, Luiz's high-level security clearance would probably have given them the perfect cover.

They were led up the dropship's broad ramp and inside its cockpit, where Luiz again strapped first Megan and then Bash and the two zombies into acceleration couches.

As the craft lifted up, the force of acceleration pushed her deep into the couch. Within minutes they were weightless, and well on their way to whatever destiny Sifra and Otto Schelling had planned for them. And, despite the circumstances of her departure from Avilon, there was a part of her that nonetheless felt safer in being far from the constant tug of gravity.

EIGHT

Megan

Half a day later, the dropship rendezvoused with the *Liberia*, an inter-system transport ferry. This consisted of little more than a framework of girders, modular docking ports and habitats arranged around powerful anti-matter engines. It followed a perpetually looping orbit that threaded together 82 Eridani's scattered collection of planets. Avilon soon dwindled to aft as the *Liberia* boosted sunwards, carrying them and numerous other small craft towards Redstone and the inner system.

She watched as Luiz and Sifra unbuckled themselves, casually discussing as they did so the various entertainments and distractions to be found within the communal malls and restaurants of the *Liberia*'s bow as they made for the hatch.

'Hey!' she yelled from where she was still strapped tightly into her couch. 'What about me and Bash?'

'What about you?' said Luiz, looking back at her with a smirk.

'How long are you going to be?' she demanded. 'You can't just leave us strapped into these couches! What if I need to pee? What about Bash?'

'She's got a point,' Luiz said to Sifra.

'Come back later and take care of all that,' Sifra replied to him.

'But what if I need to pee *now*?' demanded Megan, hating the plaintive tone creeping into her voice.

'Then I guess you'll have to just hold it in for a while,' said Sifra, and the two men laughed.

'At least take the damn cuffs off!' she screamed after them as they departed, still chuckling.

She could already feel a mild pressure growing in her bladder. If she had to pee on their damn couch, it would serve them right. But then again, she was the one who'd have to sit in it all the way to Redstone.

She found a part of her hoping Bash took a dump right there on his own couch. It would just serve the two of them the hell right if they had to clean up his shit. Literally.

On the other hand, it was clear she was going to be left here alone with the zombies for quite some time. She almost couldn't believe either of the two men could be so dumb . . .

'Oh, but they are,' she said quietly to herself, through gritted teeth.

She twisted her head around until she could just about see the two bead-zombies in their own couches. Didn't *they* need to pee? Somehow she had never thought to wonder about that.

She rolled her shoulders to relax the muscles, then slowed her breathing until she could focus more clearly.

Then she went to work.

Focusing was always the hardest part of this kind of work. A single break in concentration could ruin everything. Through her implants, she studied the flow of data between the pair of zombies and the dropship control systems to which they had now been slaved for the duration of the journey.

There was, she knew, no way a dropship's auto-control was up to that kind of job. But hacking the two zombies was still going to take a great deal of effort, and not a little time. It looked, however, as if time were something she would have in abundance.

She painstakingly tested each potential point of entry, one after another. Buckled into the couch and with her arms cuffed behind her back, it was far from easy to get a line of sight on the two zombies, to see if either of them reacted in any way to her remote prodding. Soon her neck was starting to throb like a bitch.

She took a break after a couple of hours that were rewarded with little success, and tried not to let self-doubt and despair swallow her up. Then she got back to work, studying and exploring each potential backdoor into either the dropship or the zombies themselves.

It wasn't long before she felt a band of tightness across her forehead that heralded an oncoming migraine. *Respond, damn you.* She kicked her feet against the couch in frustration, but it made no difference. No matter what she tried, it just wasn't working.

She glanced around at the zombies, and . . .

Had she imagined it when she saw the hand of one of them twitch?

Of course she had.

She squeezed her eyes shut and tried to ignore the throbbing of her muscles and the dryness of her throat.

Maybe she hadn't imagined it.

She restructured various custom routines she had created in order to probe the potential points of entry she had identified, keeping her gaze focused on that zombie in particular.

This time, she saw it. Definitely a twitch.

Megan rocked her head from side to side to try and alleviate the painful kinks that had developed in her neck and shoulders. Her wrists were sore and chafed from the cuffs they had left on her.

She modified another routine and set it loose. The zombie twitched again, then shifted suddenly in its seat, the fingers of both its hands spasming in a kind of rippling motion.

Megan let herself fall back with a laugh of triumph, all her pain and despair suddenly forgotten. She still wasn't home free yet, not by a long shot; and it wasn't long before elation gave way to fatigue. She had slept barely at all on that cold basement floor.

She closed her eyes, intending to rest them for just a minute or two, and fell immediately asleep.

She began to dream of the events following her return from the disastrous *Beauregard* expedition twelve years earlier. She had used the money she got from Sifra and Tarrant to rent an apartment in an upmarket district of one of Corkscrew's principal cities, and soon discovered there were easy ways of attaining the mental oblivion she now craved.

She slowly immersed herself in the city's street culture; the highly narcotic drug known as *sans de sezi* was everywhere on Corkscrew, which was hardly surprising since the medusa trees from which it was derived grew wild there. At certain times of the year, if the weather was just right, these trees released their orange spores in clouds ready to be gathered and processed before being smuggled off-world.

The streets were littered with the casualties of the drug, but this made no difference to her. She soon became something of a connoisseur of the orange spore, and before long a considerable portion of her fortune had thus evaporated.

But, in the end, even those hazy visions produced by the drug hadn't been quite enough to wipe out the memory of what had happened on her trip out to the Wanderer, and consequently Megan had slowly, albeit reluctantly, found her way back to the real world. She had even managed to re-establish some kind of career for herself as a machine-head pilot, but this time taking advantage of her growing inside knowledge of the routes by which *sans de sezi* found its way off Corkscrew. Before long she had found a way to gain employment through men like Kazim who had an intimate knowledge of the underworld and its workings.

In this way, she eventually found herself a new life. It was one that led her to believe she might finally lead a normal and happy existence, but her discovery regarding the approaching Swarm had put an end to all that.

Now on the *Liberia*, she dreamed that Bash was talking to her as they walked along one of Ladested's broad avenues, back on Kjæregrønnested.

Megan Jacinth, as I live and breathe, he began in surprise, gazing at her sideways.

She stared back at him in wonder, wondering how he could be here, and able to speak to her. Then she remembered that it was a dream, and not actually real.

I came back for you, Bash, she said. *Maybe not for all the right reasons, but I did, as soon as I knew you were still alive.* A breeze whipped at her hair. *But you don't know how much it broke my heart when I saw you lying there in that basement. You didn't even realize I was there.*

Didn't I? He chuckled. *Well, I've been away from the old place for a while.* He shook his head as they walked on. *But I figured it was time to come and pay you a visit, in view of the way things are shaping up for the future.* He glanced at her with a grin. *The things I've seen, baby, you just wouldn't believe.*

She began to have the uncanny sense that this was not, in fact, a dream after all.

I've missed you so badly, she said, a lump forming in her throat. *I've been so alone all these years since I returned – so alone you can't even imagine.*

I'm always with you, baby, he said, coming to a sudden halt. She did too, and he reached out with one hand to brush the hair away from her face. *I'm here right now, aren't I?*

I know you are, she said, looking up at him. She realized she was crying. *Just not the way I need you to be.*

His expression grew troubled, and he touched the side of his head with trembling fingers. *It's like having to share a house with an unwanted guest. Do you understand? I used to hide away where it couldn't find me, deep inside. But nowadays I can't even come and visit that house too often, except for when I get to sneak in and say hello, like now.*

Are you talking about the Wanderer? she asked, with a horrible chill. Her dream muscles were rigid with despair. *I'll find someone who can fix you, I swear I will.*

He brought his hand back down and folded it around one of hers. *You don't understand*, he said, shaking his head. *There's nobody that can fix me. I know that.*

His smile faded, his gaze becoming blank and vacant even as the intelligence faded from his eyes. She thought of candles guttering out in an abandoned house.

Wait! she cried, grabbing hold of him. *Stay with me. Please.*

I'll be there when you really need me, baby, she heard him say, as if from the far side of the universe. *You just take care of yourself until then.*

She woke with a start, to find Luiz unbuckling her restraints.

'Time for you to take your pee,' he said. 'We brought you something to eat as well.' He waved a hand at some food on a cardboard tray set next to her couch. The two bead-zombies had been given their guns back, and had them pointing at her.

'Dumb and Dumber here are going to keep an eye on you,' he said. 'And, while you're at it, take your buddy to the head as well, before he shits himself or something. I am right in thinking he'd do that, if we just left him there long enough?'

'You tell me,' she said. 'I'm not the one who's kept him locked up in a fucking dungeon.'

'You keep talking as smart as you do; see where it gets you,' said Luiz, finishing with the restraints. 'Turn over on your side so I can get your cuffs.'

Megan did as she was told and felt her wrists suddenly coming free. She tried to rub at them, but hissed between her teeth from the pain. It felt as if the skin had been scraped raw.

'Now go get yourself to the head,' said Luiz. 'And don't take too long in case I have to come looking.'

She got up out of the couch, feeling her muscles stretching painfully, and then waited while Luiz also released Bash. Once he was out of his couch, she took hold of Bash and led him, not without difficulty, out through the cockpit hatch.

'Down the far end,' Luiz shouted after her. 'Second cubby on the left.'

Fuck you too, she thought, and wondered if it had been Luiz's job to clean up Bash before her arrival on Avilon. If so, he'd been doing a very poor job of it.

She pushed Bash up against a bulkhead next to the head and stared into his empty, unseeing eyes. 'Were you inside my head just a minute ago, Bash? Or did I really just dream all of that?'

It hadn't felt like a dream. It had felt *real*.

But if it *had* been real, that meant there was at least some part of Bash that was still aware of everything happening around him.

The implications chilled her. If that really was the case, then Bash had remained locked in the prison of his own body, unable to communicate with the outside world . . . for more than a decade.

NINE

Gabrielle

Gabrielle had hardly slept during the night, and when she woke the next morning, on the Eve of Ascension, Cassanas was still avoiding her gaze. When Gabrielle asked to dress herself, the old woman's only response was a mumbled nod.

An hour later, Gabrielle made her way up through the tiered decks, trailed by several of Karl's guards, until she came to an observation deck on the very uppermost level of the great barge. More guards under Karl's command waited in an anteroom as she leaned against a railing, looking out towards the distant horizon, a view coloured slightly by the containment field keeping a breathable atmosphere around the deck itself.

In all of her life, Gabrielle had only rarely set foot outside Port Gabriel. Most of her existence had been spent within the strict confines of the People's Palace, and she now felt almost dizzy from the sight of so much sky. She gazed at canopy trees rising out of the frozen soil of the nearby eastern shore, the tiny black dots of one-wings circling beneath huge frond-like branches that overshadowed the ground beneath.

The Ka River was wide enough here for the western shore to have become little more than a dark line on the far horizon. The nearer shore was lined with the primitive-looking sealed domes and glittering biomes of small towns that looked like they had hardly changed since the days of the pioneers.

She glanced aft to see the rest of the barges strung out along the river behind them. Dios lay a hundred kilometres further downriver, yet she found it easy to imagine that, if she squinted hard enough, she could see the steep cliffs against which the Ship of the Covenant rested.

She remembered the excitement in her youth when she had once looked forward to this day – and the slowly building dread that had come to replace it. These two emotions merged and clashed in her thoughts. She had always wanted to visit Dios, as so many pilgrims did, but to do so under the present circumstances would be at the cost of her life.

She fanned her fingers, then stirred them through the air to activate the Tabernacle. A patch of air before her darkened, becoming opaque to her view.

She conjured up a real-time image of the Ship of the Covenant. Bridges were constructed all around the hull of the ancient craft, interconnecting with ramps and platforms built up the cliff face on either side. A number of buildings, part research establishment and part religious retreat, had been constructed around that portion of the ship that rested on the ground, and all of these in turn were surrounded by constantly patrolled walls and guarded gates. The Demarchy was extremely keen to protect its investment.

She heard a noise behind her, and guessed she had company. The image before her rippled and faded, and she turned to see Karl Petrova standing just inside the entrance to the observation deck.

He closed the glass doors behind him and came towards her. 'Are you ready?' he asked, his voice kept low. 'It's very nearly time.'

She swallowed hard. 'Surely the banquet is still hours away?'

'This is the last chance we'll have to speak to each other until afterwards,' he explained, reaching out to tidy a lock of her hair that had come loose. 'Everything's in place.'

She thought of that vial of poison, and felt a thrill of terror mixed with excitement lancing through her. 'I won't fail you,' she said, so quietly that she could barely be heard above the crashing of the waves on the nearby shore. He reached out and caressed her waist. 'You know that I love you, don't you?'

Gabrielle took a step back from Karl, eyes widening as she

glanced instinctively towards the doors behind him. They were both hidden by curtains from the direct view of his guards, but still . . .

'Karl,' she warned, 'if anyone heard what you just said—'

'But they didn't,' said Karl, his tone cool and confident, 'and they won't. You remember everything you have to do?'

She nodded. 'I remember,' she said, her voice sounding stronger this time.

'Say it again,' he coaxed.

She stared up at him. 'I remember,' she repeated, her tone almost defiant. Then: 'I love you too, Karl – more than you can imagine.'

He smiled at that, but again there was something unreadable in his eyes.

TEN

Gabrielle

'To our Speaker-Elect,' said Thijs, raising his glass high in a toast. Its contents sparkled, reflecting the flames of the fireplace that took up most of one wall of the Grand Barge's banqueting hall.

He then turned his gaze from the assembled dignitaries of the Demarchy towards Gabrielle herself. Their eyes met briefly before she looked quickly away.

'To Gabrielle,' confirmed Thijs, 'on the eve of her Ascension.'

More glasses were raised, their contents as dark and red as arterial blood. There were perhaps thirty men and women here altogether, arranged on either side of the long dining table carved from out of a canopy tree's taproot. Gabrielle sat at the head of the table, able to feel, through her feet, the distant vibration of the powerful turbines as the barge carried them onwards.

Semi-transparent glow-globes floated just beneath the ceiling, filling the room with a warm and pearly light. Tiny insect-like shapes occasionally flitted through the air – autonomous recording devices, nominally under Thijs's control, but secretly slaved, she knew, to Karl's command. Tonight, he would make sure they recorded nothing.

Gabrielle nodded to Thijs in acknowledgement. 'Hear, hear,' said someone further down the table, their voice slurring.

Thijs sat down again. This banquet for the Demarchy's leading bureaucrats and politicians had been going on for nearly three hours now, yet the after-dinner speeches had still not come to an end.

The first bout of speechmaking had come from a number of

minor adjutants, each of them in turn summarizing the various technological benefits that the Demarchy of Uchida had acquired thanks to previous Ascensions. After them had come the lower-level bureaucrats, detailing the Demarchy's continued happy relations with the Accord, while their equivalents from the security department had reported further on the Demarchy's continued successes against both the River Concord States and the pockets of Freehold resistance still scattered amongst the higher peaks of the Montos de Frenezo range. After these had come the senior researchers from Dios, with a summary of the financial and military aid received from the Accord, and finally the senior security and bureaucracy, whose speeches consisted mostly of congratulations to everyone else for their part in keeping the Demarchy safe from its neighbours and its enemies for another twenty-one years.

At last, just when it seemed that these interminable eulogies might go on for the rest of eternity, the remains of the dinner were cleared away by waiting staff, and the ceremonial wine was finally brought in. Gabrielle watched with sick fascination as the glasses around her were refreshed. She reached carefully into the folds of her gown, letting her fingers touch the device that would activate the neurotoxin, as if to remind herself she had not imagined last night's conversation.

When a glass of the poisoned wine was set before her, she stroked its stem with her thumb and forefinger, and forced herself to control her breathing. *I will not panic.* She reminded herself that Karl was just metres away, at the far end of a corridor leading to the banqueting hall. He was accompanied by twenty Demarchy troopers, whom he insisted were absolutely loyal to him.

Just another few minutes, and they would finally be free.

Thijs stood again, waiting for the conversation to die down.

'Tomorrow,' he said, 'Mer Gabrielle will be granted the privilege of communing directly with the Ship of the Covenant, as so many of her predecessors have done for nearly two centuries now. In return for this act of selflessness, the Demarchy and its benefactors in the Accord will benefit from a priceless cornucopia of scientific and technological wisdom.'

He looked around at the attentive faces. 'But this sacrifice is also a blessing for her,' he continued. 'After passing on to us this sacred information, Mer Gabrielle will, as all before her have been witnessed to do, ascend bodily into the highest realms of the informational matrix, there to reside next to God the Master Programmer. She will thereby be invested with a glory that even the most devout amongst us could never hope to attain. For this, Mer Gabrielle,' he declared, turning to face her, 'we here all salute you.'

Someone started clapping, and it spread. She watched entranced as the assembled leaders of the Demarchy, every last one of them, raised their glasses to their lips and swallowed the tainted wine.

She lifted her own glass, barely pressing the rim to her lips before placing it back down with the wine untouched. How many of those here knew the truth about her existence? she wondered. Was it no more than a few – Thijs, Lampard and Abramovic perhaps, and one or two others – or was it indeed the case, as Karl had assured her, that all of them were privy to this age-old conspiracy? Could there possibly be anyone here innocent of the crime against her?

There was no way of knowing, and if she did not act – if she allowed her doubts to get the better of her – she would surely die.

Gabrielle stood up suddenly, feeling as if her bones had turned to jelly. For a moment she feared that everyone present was entirely aware of her part in Karl's conspiracy, and they were simply waiting for the right moment to deliver their denunciation.

She glanced towards Thijs; surely he could detect the guilt radiating from her every pore? But instead he gave her an inquisitive smile that seemed in stark contrast to the iciness of his gaze.

'You have something to say, Mer Gabrielle?' he enquired.

It was not yet her turn to speak, therefore she was breaking strict protocol. But this would be her only opportunity to say things she had for so long ached to say.

'I do have something to say, Pater Thijs,' she replied, doing her best not to let his reptilian gaze put her off. She could feel her skin flushing red, and there was a deep thrumming in her veins that pounded in her ears like drums. 'In return for this honour, I wish also to thank you.'

A smattering of mild, uncertain applause, for Thijs had not finished his speech when Gabrielle had stood up and interrupted him. He sat down nonetheless, folding his robes neatly around him, and waited for her to continue.

She found the strength and will to go on by reminding herself of just how long she had dreamed of this moment. All she needed to do was picture his pale, sweaty face looming above hers, and remember the pain she had then felt.

'I do not think, Pater Thijs,' her voice grew marginally more steady, 'that I truly understood my role within the Demarchy until you came into my bedchamber when I was only thirteen years old and raped me.'

Thijs's eyes looked as if they had turned to glass, his entire face frozen, but he recovered quickly.

'Mer Gabrielle,' he stood up once more, 'perhaps asking you to take part in this banquet has put too much of a strain on you. May I suggest that you now retire for the night . . . ?'

A door banged open, and one of Karl's guards came running in. He stepped over to Abramovic and whispered urgently in the man's ear.

Abramovic turned in his chair to look up at the man, his expression incredulous.

Thijs looked genuinely relieved by the interruption. 'What is it, Pater Abramovic?' he asked.

Abramovic gestured in the air to summon his Tabernacle link. He kept it private, however, so only he could see what information lay there. He then shot upright in his seat, and looked at those sitting around the table with terrified eyes.

'We need to abandon the barge,' he said, in a voice suddenly husky. 'We need to get the hell out of here right *now*!'

The guard hurried back out of the room and, as the door opened, Gabrielle could hear a murmur of voices from beyond, and what might have been shouting from up on the main deck.

'What in hell is going on?' demanded Thijs.

Now, thought Gabrielle in a panic, suddenly sure that she and Karl had been uncovered.

She took hold of his activation device and pressed the button set into it, with a satisfying *click*.

At first, nothing happened. No one was even paying any attention to her now, because they were all busy staring at Abramovic.

'There has been an attack on the Demarchy,' announced Abramovic. 'From off-world.'

The banqueters broke into a hubbub of questions and demands. 'From the Accord?' asked one voice.

'I don't know,' Abramovic replied. 'There's only limited data coming through at the moment, but it appears there has been a . . . an impact of some kind in the ocean several hundred kilometres south of Dios. All I know is that *something* just landed there – something big. It might be a comet or a meteor . . .'

Someone at the far end of the table coughed violently.

'That's impossible!' cried Thijs. 'We have planetary defences for such things – not to mention the Accord forces in orbit. How could this possibly . . . ?'

'*How* isn't important,' Abramovic yelled, and then himself coughed violently. 'The point is that there's a tidal wave coming towards us. We have fast-launch flyers on the aft upper deck, enough for all of us. We must evacuate the ship immediately if the Demarchy is to . . . is to . . .'

He stopped then, a perplexed look on his face. His chest heaved, and he again coughed explosively into one hand.

Gabrielle watched in horrified fascination as he peered down at the specks of blood on his palm. 'I don't understand,' he said, looking over at Thijs before slumping forward.

One of the other banqueters half-stood before vomiting violently into his neighbour's lap. Then his face twisted in a grimace, and he collapsed right across the table. Over the next few seconds, the rest followed, their bodies contorting as they stumbled up from their chairs or tumbled to the floor.

Thijs stared at Gabrielle with a horrified expression, as if he realized what she had done. He tried to push his chair back, but instead fell to his knees, continuing to stare up at her with hatred.

'I used to dream of a moment like this,' said Gabrielle, gazing down at him. 'Ever since that night.'

'You . . .' Thijs managed to gasp.

'Not just me.' A strange calm came over her. 'This was all Karl Petrova's plan . . . and he's a far better lover than you could ever be, Pater Thijs.'

Thijs's eyes finally lost their focus and he slumped to the floor. Gabrielle stared around the suddenly silent banquet hall, at all the bodies surrounding her, their eyes bulging and faces contorted.

The door at the far end burst open, and Karl himself strode in, dressed in cold-weather gear. A pair of breather masks dangled by their straps from one hand, and a spare jacket was slung over his shoulder. She had never been so relieved to see someone in all of her life.

'Where are the rest of the guards?' asked Gabrielle, puzzled to see him alone.

'Up on the main decks, preparing for the evacuation,' he said, kneeling by the body of a banqueter sprawled on the floor. 'As far as they know, I'm here to round you and everyone else up.'

'What are you doing?' asked Gabrielle, as Karl touched two fingers of his free hand to the dead man's throat. He then glanced around the rest of the room, before nodding to himself in satisfaction.

'Checking they're all dead,' Karl replied, then threw her a look that sent a shiver through her. 'I thought perhaps you wouldn't be able to manage it, but you've proven yourself a regular little angel of death, haven't you?'

'Don't call me that,' she snapped, horrified that he could say something so vile.

'Here,' he said, stepping forward and handing her one of the masks. 'We don't have much time.'

She pulled the mask over her mouth and nose, strapping it on as Karl affixed his own. He then handed her the jacket, which she pulled on over her robes, before tugging her towards the door with unexpected roughness.

'Why is the barge being evacuated?' asked Gabrielle, as Karl dragged her after him by one arm. They were almost running along a passageway. 'What's going on? Abramovic said a tidal wave was on its way here . . . that there had been some kind of impact in the ocean. How could that be?'

'I guess it's just coincidence,' he replied, as if not greatly concerned. 'At least we won't be here when it arrives.'

Something horrible then occurred to her. It simply wasn't possible such a thing could be just coincidence . . . could it?

'Karl,' she asked, her voice trembling, 'do you have anything to do with it? With that wave or whatever just landed in the ocean?

They had now arrived at an airlock, beyond which lay the main deck. He pulled her inside, then grabbed her by the shoulder, twisting her around until she was facing away from him. She gasped with shock as something was stabbed into the soft flesh at the top of her neck, just below her skull.

She tore herself from his grasp, automatically bringing her fingers up to probe the punctured skin. The flesh was puckered, and she could feel something hard beneath. Despite the shock, it had hurt very little, and now the entire back of her neck felt numb, as if anaesthetized.

'What the hell was that?' she demanded, seeing him pocket a silver device with a needle-like nozzle at one end.

'You're a machine-head,' he said. 'That makes you easy to track. But the inhibitor I just put in you should take care of that.'

'Damn you, Karl, What have you done to me? And why won't you answer my question? What makes you think you have the right to—'

'I'm trying to keep you alive,' he rasped, hitting the release on the airlock door, his voice muffled by his breather mask.

There was a brief, powerful gust as the air pressure equalized with that of Redstone's natural atmosphere. Even with the jacket over her robes, the shock of the freezing air directly against her skin made Gabrielle's lungs cramp.

They were outside now, on the main deck, beads of rain sprinkling her neck and face where they weren't covered by the breather mask. A wind from the sea flurried the tops of the waves, and it was so cold that she offered Karl no more resistance as he hauled her along.

Within moments she stood at the bow of the Grand Barge, looking over the railing at a much smaller vessel directly below them, which rose and fell with the motion of the waves.

Shouting filled the air, coming from behind. Something thundered overhead, and Gabrielle glanced up, catching sight of a security services flyer lifting from one of the barge's upper decks and quickly vanishing into the night.

She had a sudden intuition regarding what Karl had in mind for them. She had pictured the pair of them roaring off into space on board some luxuriously appointed dropship, but that clearly wasn't what he had planned.

Karl glanced back along the main deck and, from his expression, Gabrielle could tell he was listening to someone over a Tabernacle link.

'What is it?' she asked.

'Someone's found the bodies,' he replied tersely. 'And now they're looking for us. Get ready to jump.'

Gabrielle tried to frame a response, but by now her teeth were chattering so uncontrollably under her breather mask that it made it extraordinarily difficult to get any words out. 'No,' she said at last. 'Not until you tell me what's going on. How can there possibly be a tidal wa—'

'*Now*,' Karl shouted, putting his arms around her waist, lifting her up and heaving her over the railing before she had a chance to resist.

She shrieked as she fell, hardly getting a chance to draw breath before she hit the water. The shock of the icy cold drove all other thoughts from her head.

She drew in a ragged breath, hands clawing desperately at the surrounding water. She had never been taught to swim because what need, after all, would a Speaker-Elect have for such skills?

Just when she was absolutely sure she was about to die, she felt a hand take hold of her wrist. Then more hands seized hold, lifting her up and pulling her on board the boat she had seen from the railing. By some miracle, her breather mask had remained in place.

Strong arms carried her through a hatchway and into a cabin smelling of mould and paint. Once the man carrying her set her back down, she felt the deck beneath her feet begin to throb. After a moment there was a slight lurch, and the boat began to move, picking up speed and rocking from side to side hard enough that Gabrielle was forced to shift her feet in order to keep her balance.

She looked around to see she was sharing this cabin with four men, all wearing worn-looking combat suits and breather masks, including the one who had fetched her inside. She realized with a shock that they were all Freeholders – and therefore enemies of the Demarchy of Uchida.

Karl was the last to enter through the hatch, water pouring from his soaking garments. He must have jumped into the water right after her. The cabin was not particularly small, but with all six of them it felt crowded.

One of the four Freeholders stepped over behind Karl, snapped the hatch shut and then touched a panel set into a bulkhead. The air throbbed with the sound of pumps, as Redstone's inhospitable atmosphere was swiftly replaced with breathable air. Another of the men threw a heavy towel towards Gabrielle and gestured brusquely to a door leading further inside the boat.

'There's dry clothes in there,' he said, pulling off his breather mask. His accent sounded barbaric to her ears.

She nodded numbly and stepped towards the door, too frightened to do anything but obey.

The door slid open on hidden rollers, revealing a toilet and sink beneath a ceiling so low that she had to duck down. She pulled off her freezing wet clothes and dried herself as best she could, but the cold had already penetrated deep inside her body.

Finding the dry clothes, she quickly pulled them on. The overalls were clearly a man's, and therefore much too big, but at least they were dry and, she discovered with relish, had heating elements woven into the fabric.

She touched an orange patch on one shoulder, and after a few seconds blessed heat caressed her skin. Even so, she knew it would take some time for the heat to truly permeate. She next dragged on a pair of heavy boots that were at least a couple of sizes too large, but she compensated for this by tying them tightly around her ankles.

When she stepped back through into the main cabin, Karl was still there, with one of the Freeholders. The others had all disappeared from sight, although she could hear their muffled voices echoing along a narrow passageway that appeared to run the full length of the boat.

When Karl glanced towards her, it once again felt uncomfortably like looking into the eyes of a stranger.

ELEVEN

Megan

2751 (twelve years before)

It takes time to move a starship measuring three hundred metres in length, and massing several thousand tonnes, out of orbit. Drive-fields used for manoeuvring and short-distance propulsion need to be activated, and even then it can take hours or even days before such a ship can put sufficient distance between itself and objects possessing large mass – such as planets – that can prevent a superluminal jump taking place.

Thirteen hours after agreeing to help Tarrant and Sifra hijack the *Beauregard*, Megan finally climbed down from the astrogation chair, feeling weary and exhausted. Kjæregrønnested still loomed large in the command deck's monitors, but they were accelerating now, headed for the outer system. The *Beauregard*'s drive-spines were scraping raw energy out of the quantum vacuum and storing it in preparation for a jump that would carry them across light years

Bash took over in the chair and Megan made her way to her own quarters. She collapsed, exhausted, in the cubbyhole where she slept. But it was nearly impossible to rest, with so many conflicting thoughts and feelings churning through her mind.

They were committing an act of piracy, after all; the punishment, if they failed, would be severe. She wondered if she had too easily let Bash's enthusiasm push her onto a path of recklessness. For a moment, she wondered if she should tell him to halt the flight, to return to orbit above Kjæregrønnested and then suffer the consequences of their foolishness.

And yet she remained where she was, stretched out fully clothed on her bunk, with one booted foot dangling over the edge. Whatever doubts she might retain, the fact remained that Tarrant was offering them both a chance at a real future.

She had no trouble in picturing the chaos that must already be erupting back in Ladested. A squall of increasingly frantic queries was already chasing them, and undoubtedly the engineers, drive-specialists and military advisers who had been waiting to assume effective command of the ship on behalf of the Accord would by now be aware of what was happening.

Finally, sleep stole her away, and she woke some hours later to find that the ship's steadily building acceleration had returned gravity to the ship.

She accessed the navigation systems and saw that Kjæregrønnested had slipped away into the stellar darkness. The initial squall of transmissions had blown into a storm, and she now accessed some of them, along with some of the major news feeds.

The strongest threats, it seemed, were being delivered by the Accord forces already in station above Kjæregrønnested. She was not surprised to learn that two of the Accord's own nova-class ships were setting out in pursuit of them. But this was nothing more than a gesture; without a clear idea of just where it was they were going, it would be impossible for anyone to track the *Beauregard* after its first significant jump into deep space.

It's out of your hands, she told herself, and she let out a shuddering breath. They were entirely committed now.

She suddenly felt all the tension ease out of her body, like the first flush after sex, and a grin spread across her face.

She deliberately brushed against Bash's mind and saw, through their shared data-senses, that he was still locked into the astrogation chair after more than half a standard day. She pushed some of her good feeling towards him.

She felt, more than heard, his chuckle emanate through the connection. <If I didn't know better, I'd think you were flirting with me, girl.>

She laughed. <As if. I thought I'd be terrified once we were past the point of no return, but instead it's as if all the tension and worry just slipped away.>

<I knew this guy back in my military days – another pilot – and he told me one time he'd been guiding a transport down from orbit some place when all the systems quit on him at once. He dropped like a rock and he knew he was going to die. Absolutely knew.>

<But he didn't?>

<Nope. Just like that, all the systems came back online, right before he was about to pancake into the dust, and that's how he managed to pull out of it. He suffered some serious injuries, of course, but nothing they couldn't fix. And he told me that, right before those systems came back online, he felt utterly at peace. He said that was because he knew there wasn't a damn thing he could do.>

<Oh, great, so we're doomed. Is that what you're saying?>

He laughed. <No way. I didn't mean it like that. But once you know there ain't no turning back, just as you said yourself, there's no point in worrying any more. So you don't.>

<Thanks,> she sent back, with a tinge of sarcasm. <I'll remember that next time I'm on the verge of some fatal accident.>

This time he really did laugh. <Not even a few lingering doubts in that head of yours?>

<A million and one,> Megan replied. <But I haven't changed my mind. I know now this is the right thing to do.>

<Same here,> he sent back.

<There's a long and lonely journey ahead of us, Bash. If ever you're harbouring any doubts about your sexual orientation, feel free to come to my cabin and let's discuss them in private.>

<Girl, you are just incorrigible. What about our man Tarrant? I saw the way he looked at you, first time he set eyes on you.>

<Tarrant?> She was surprised at how flustered the suggestion made her. <I hadn't noticed.>

<Bullshit. He's a good-looking devil – we can both agree on that, can't we?>

<I guess so. But I'm sure he's not really interested.> The words sounded lame even to her own ears.

<Like you said, it's going to be a long journey there and back.>

<Any more scintillating insights you'd like to share with me?> sent Megan.

<Well, there is one thing. Tarrant uploaded a bunch of data about the Wanderer to the ship. Did you check any of it out yet?>

<No, not really. I had a quick glance at some of it before I fell asleep, but that's all.>

<Well, go take a look now, before you take over from me in the chair. It ain't light reading, but it's a hell of a story.>

Over the following days, the constellations visible aft of the *Beauregard* shifted and morphed with each successive jump until they had become very nearly unrecognizable. They were travelling spinwards, following the direction of rotation of the Milky Way. Megan spent the first weeks of their voyage poring over all of the data related to the Wanderer; there was, she quickly discovered, enough material there for a lifetime of study, much of it highly academic in nature. She downloaded a variety of specialist-knowledge sets to her implants, so she could at least have some kind of idea just what it was she was looking at whenever it came to any of the more esoteric information.

Most other machine-heads Megan had met dreamed of buying into an expedition that made a big find, much as the Schellings had achieved with Alyeska. The Wanderer seemed to represent precisely such an opportunity, and yet the more she dug into the data, the more she had the sense that some of the information was missing. As if, she surmised, it had been deliberately omitted.

She left it alone for a while and tried to concentrate on her shipboard duties. There were replacement drive-spines to be manufactured and manoeuvred into place on the *Beauregard*'s hull, along with a thousand other tasks involving general maintenance and life-support that would normally be taken care of by a full crew. But with just the four of them on board, they were having to do triple, even quadruple, duty in order to keep things running.

All this work had the added advantage of distracting her from the strangeness of being on board this familiar ship without its usual complement of crew. In her imagination, the passageways and drop shafts seemed to echo with the voices of those who had accompanied her on previous trips. She regularly found her thoughts drawn back to those faces, and wondered when she might see them again, if ever.

Given that unaccustomed solitude, it was perhaps inevitable that she and Tarrant would become lovers, just as Bash had predicted.

Barely more than a month into their voyage, Megan made her way to the command deck to start her usual shift in the astrogation chair. Bash stood next to it, in an otherwise deserted deck, one corner of his mouth twisted up in a wry and knowing grin.

'What did I tell you?' he said, as she approached. 'I knew Tarrant would find a way into your pants.'

Despite herself, Megan's face coloured, and Bash almost choked from laughing.

'How the *fuck* did you know?' she asked.

He reached up and tapped the side of his head. 'You were broadcasting loud and clear,' he told her.

'Belle's tits,' Megan exclaimed. 'You were *listening in*?'

'Not intentionally, no.' Bash shrugged, still grinning. 'You've really got to learn how to hide it better when you're having sex. So?'

'So, what?'

'You like him?'

'Sure.' It was Megan's turn to shrug. 'I guess.'

'You *guess*,' Bashir repeated, clearly not fooled. 'I don't need to read your mind to see you like him a *whole* lot.'

She stepped past him, pulling herself up and into the astrogation chair, leaving the petals folded down while they still talked. 'He wasn't like I thought he would be.'

'Which is?'

'A blowhard, I guess . . . full of himself. But he's not. In fact, he's almost ridiculously charming.'

Bash's expression grew fractionally more sober. 'Still,' he said, 'you probably aren't the first pretty girl he's made feel that way.'

By the time they were halfway through their six-month voyage in search of the Wanderer, the *Beauregard*'s crew of four had fallen into patterns of behaviour that only rarely saw them all meeting at the same time. Megan found herself spending more and more of her off-duty hours with Tarrant, while Bashir disappeared for long hours with Sifra, the two of them poring over the *Beauregard*'s nova drive. Sifra, it now turned out, had trained as a drive-specialist.

Megan and Bash, however, maintained their customary habit of taking meals together on those occasions when neither of them was required in the astrogation chair. They spent long hours talking about all the ways they would spend their newfound wealth, once they returned home.

'You know, it hit me that even if they parade us in triumph down the streets of Ladested,' said Megan on one such occasion, 'any time we step outside of Alliance territory, we'll be targets. There'll always be someone from the Accord gunning for us.'

Bash stopped, a spoonful of broth halfway to his mouth. 'You mean like arrest us, for taking the *Beauregard*? Then we'll just have to head the other way,' he said, gesturing with the spoon as if to indicate the entirety of the universe beyond the hull. 'There's a whole galaxy out there, Megan.'

'Yeah, I guess.'

Bash sighed and finally put his spoon down, then sat back with both hands resting on the table. 'Okay,' he said, 'what is it?'

'What?' said Megan.

'Whatever it is you're thinking of saying to me, could you please just hurry up and say it?'

She pursed her lips. 'Okay, fine. But this is between you and me, right?'

Bash cast a long gaze around the deserted refectory. 'Sure. I promise I'll keep my voice down, in case anyone's listening.'

'Funny.' She sucked her lips for a moment. 'Okay, it has to do with the Wanderer.'

'Are you *still* digging through all that stuff? Even thinking about it all makes my brain ache.'

'There's just . . . something not right about some of it.'

'Not right how?' he asked.

She put down her own spoon and pushed her bowl to one side before leaning towards him. 'Do you remember,' she asked him, 'what Gregor told us before we set out? He said that Otto Schelling's research staff found out that both the Atn and the Shoal had prior contact with the Wanderer. That's how they managed to locate it in the Calafat-Holt Cluster.'

'Sure,' said Bash. 'What about it?'

'Do you know the name the Shoal had for the Wanderer?'

Bash shrugged, playing again with his spoon. 'I guess there's no reason to think they'd give it the same name the Meridians did.'

'They called it,' she said, 'the Marauder.'

He raised his eyebrows. 'Sounds ominous.'

'Doesn't it? I mean, why give it a name like that?' she asked. 'Doesn't it suggest something . . . well, dangerous?'

He sighed. 'I don't know. I guess maybe. How sure are you it's an accurate translation?'

'Well . . .'

'You did the translation yourself?' he asked.

'I had to,' she replied, a touch defensively. 'I downloaded some learning modules. We don't have any experts in alien languages on board.'

He looked thoughtful for a moment. 'Have you talked to Gregor or Anil about this?'

She hesitated. 'Not yet.'

'Why not?'

'Because I'm increasingly sure some of the data's been redacted. There are large chunks missing.'

Bash shrugged. 'Maybe they only gave us the highlights. Or maybe there was stuff they just didn't think we needed to know. Does it matter?'

'I've spent a lot of time going over what those researchers dug up on Alyeska, and what I've found are huge gaps, not just little ones. This isn't the kind of thing you'd notice just by casually browsing, but when you run a really deep analysis you find big, fat, glaring omissions. Look.'

She scrunched her hand into a fist, and when she opened it again, there was a tiny, glistening ball of light spinning silently just above her palm, visible only to herself and Bash. She slid her hand out from under it, then batted it towards Bash, who closed his own hand around it. She waited, sucking down some more of her broth, while he absorbed the information.

'See?' she said, after his eyes had focused on her once more. 'At first it was just a suspicion, then I became sure of it.'

Bash sighed and gave her a weary look. 'Megan, did you ever think about just *asking* them about the missing data?'

'I did, but . . .'

'But what?' he asked. 'What exactly are you afraid of?'

'Well, what if they *are* deliberately keeping something back from us? What if there's a reason the Shoal called it the Marauder instead of the Wanderer? Why would they want to keep anything like that back from us?'

'Or maybe, now that you're tight with Tarrant, you don't like the idea that he's been keeping something from you.'

Megan glared at him.

Bash chuckled, reaching out to put his hand on her arm. 'Okay then, supposing you're right. I'm not saying that maybe we shouldn't ask questions, but if they've really been hiding something we should know about, then, under any normal circumstances, maybe that's something we *should* be concerned about. But these aren't normal circumstances. Sometimes there are things you need to know and things you don't need to know. If they're not telling us something, then maybe there's a good reason for it.'

She stared at him, appalled. 'We need to know *everything*, Bash, or how the hell are we going to know how to deal with whatever we end up finding out there?'

'Look,' said Bash, his tone getting defensive, 'Tarrant and Sifra are both of them good men. Remember I was stuck on that moon along with him – with Tarrant, I mean – and the rest of the survivors from the *Chesapeake*, waiting for a rescue we nearly convinced ourselves was never coming. He's the kind of man you'd follow through the gates of hell, because you know for damn sure he'd lead you back out again.'

'I know it sounds stupid,' she said quietly, 'but something still just doesn't feel right.'

He shook his head. 'The time to worry, Megan, was before we even set out. Now we've just got to deal with the cards we've been given, and do the best we can. With this much riding on the four of us, I don't see either of those guys holding anything back from us if we really needed to know it.'

'I'm still going to talk to him,' she muttered. 'And if he doesn't tell me, then . . .'

'Then what?' Bash asked, with a slight smile.

'I don't know,' she said, 'but I'll think of something.'

And yet something still kept Megan from confronting Tarrant. She tried to tell herself it was because Bash was right and she was just overreacting, that whatever reason there might be for some of the material being redacted, it was almost certainly a perfectly reasonable and mundane one. Chunks of incomplete records from some archaeological dig did not, after all, amount to a conspiracy.

But she knew there was another, more pertinent reason for her failure to act. At some point she had crossed a line and fallen, very, very hard, for Tarrant.

Bash was right in one respect; she was far from being the first girl who had fallen for Tarrant's undoubted charms, and she had hoped that awareness would help her maintain a certain emotional, if not physical, distance. But they were a long way from home, with a long way to go still and a long way back again, with none of the companionship and support of the *Beauregard*'s usual complement of crew. Under the circumstances, maintaining that distance proved to be much harder than she'd thought.

She told herself that her nagging doubts meant nothing. The alternative explanation, after all, might be too much to bear.

Over the following weeks, the Calafat-Holt Cluster expanded towards them with each successive jump they made, until they had finally passed inside it. Megan spent long hours in the astrogation chair, the hard radiation baking the ship's hull like warm sun directly on her skin, and the stellar dust flowing past the ship's electromagnetic envelope like the kiss of a summer breeze.

And yet there were other things that concerned her, too. There were unusual readings emanating from the cargo pod that had come aboard the *Beauregard* just before their departure from Kjæregrønnested, but Tarrant refused to let her check it out in person, saying he'd prefer to take care of that personally.

'Are you *hiding* something in that cargo pod?' she finally asked him on one occasion.

'No,' he said. 'But we do have some materials on board which are vital to negotiating with the Wanderer.'

'Shouldn't I know what they are?'

He had looked at her oddly. 'Don't make me say no, Megan.'

She subsequently hated herself for not pushing harder. And the next time they made love, she did so with a furious passion, her desire mingled with anger at herself for being so weak.

'You don't like it when people get too close, do you?' Tarrant remarked to her, some time later, when they were just a few weeks out from the target system.

At that time, the ship was coasting at a steady velocity between jumps. The two of them floated together in a recreation sphere, the sweat still drying on their skin. Handholds and harnesses designed to overcome the physical limitations of zero-gravity sex floated around them like the fronds of deep-sea flora.

'What do you mean?' she asked.

'I mean that sometimes your mind is clearly elsewhere: either running the ship or staring out at the stars.'

'I've never done that,' she argued, feeling slightly offended. 'When I'm with you, I'm with *you*.'

He assumed a slightly more conciliatory tone. 'All I'm saying is, it's as if you're holding yourself back – like you're afraid of getting too close.'

'That's because I am,' she said, gazing back at him frankly.

He smiled but broke eye contact. 'All right,' he said, moving to grab an item of his clothing floating within reach, 'here's another question. Why don't you ever talk about your past?'

She let out a sigh. 'Because I don't *like* talking about it,' she said, snatching some of her own clothes out of the air.

'But . . .'

'Wasn't that the big selling point of the Three Star Alliance,' she asked, 'that you get to leave your past behind? Nobody cares who you were or what you did before you got there.'

'But Bash knows, doesn't he?' he prodded, but she didn't answer.

Over the next week, Tarrant conducted a series of long, private discussions with Sifra about what they would do once they reached the target system, and so he and Megan saw less of each other than usual. In a way, she was relieved, because she was frightened he might try again to get her to talk about her past – and even more frightened of what she might tell him.

She dug deeper than ever before into the Wanderer data. By now she had read all the summaries and detailed analyses put together by Kjæregrønnested's data-archaeologists, and had begun working directly on some as yet untranslated Meridian records. She constructed her own linguistic and mathematical algorithms based on their findings, using her heuristic circuits to process the information. She hoped thereby to find some way of closing the remaining gaps in the data.

To her surprise, she found much more than she could ever have anticipated.

TWELVE

Gabrielle

2763 (the present)

Karl ignored Gabrielle throughout the short voyage that followed, after leading the Freeholder with whom he had been having a discussion down the passageway traversing the boat and out of earshot.

Unsure what to do with herself, Gabrielle took a seat on a narrow bench, where she could feel the vibrations from the vessel's engine as it carried them towards the bank of the river. The sense that something was very wrong kept growing inside her, particularly the way Karl had looked at her, as if she were nothing more than a distraction or a nuisance, rather than the woman he loved . . .

Stop being ridiculous, she told herself. There was almost certainly a perfectly good explanation for all of it. She had just helped him commit mass murder, after all. Both their lives were at stake now, and not just hers. She could hardly expect him to behave the same way, under such circumstances, as when they were alone in her bedchamber.

And yet that voice full of doubt kept shrieking at her from somewhere deep inside her own head. *What about the tidal wave? Or the way he looked at you when he called you an 'angel of death'. And why are there Freeholders here? And . . .*

She shut the voice out and tried to activate her Tabernacle link, in the hope of distracting herself. To her shock, she discovered that she could not access it. She had no way of finding out any more information about the impact Abramovic had described, or the resultant tidal wave.

She reached up and touched the back of her neck, where Karl had injected her with what he had called an 'inhibitor'. Supposedly it made tracking her via her implants impossible, and she wondered if it might also be the reason why she was unable to access the Tabernacle.

There was little to do, then, but pass the time staring out of a porthole, though she was barely able to see anything beyond the surging waters outside, and the dim outline of hills growing ever nearer. She eventually caught sight of an antiquated-looking jetty extending from the shore. The rhythm of the turbines soon changed subtly and, after another minute or two, the boat bumped gently up against the wharf.

One of the Freeholders reappeared from the passageway, handing Gabrielle another, better-quality jacket and a new breather mask. 'Put these on,' he instructed.

She slipped on the new gear, while the Freeholder pulled a mask over his nose and mouth, quickly checking that the seal was effective. Once she was ready, with her mask on, he yelled back along the passageway that he was about to open the hatch.

The rest, including Karl, then reappeared and pulled on their own breather masks, while their compatriot cracked the external hatch. Karl himself went out first, then gestured for her to follow him. She only did so with increasing reluctance. There was little she could do under the circumstances but comply, at least until Karl gave her some kind of proper explanation of what was going on.

Waves slapped hollowly against the underside of the dock as Gabrielle climbed out onto the jetty. She spotted a decrepit-looking emergency shelter nearby on the shore.

The voice of doubt manifested itself again, this time louder than before. *He's been working with the Freehold.* They must, she realized, have been the ones holding Mater Cassanas's son prisoner all this time.

Hard as it was to believe, the only conclusion was that Karl was acting as a double-agent. He must have been funnelling information back to the Freehold the whole time he had been in the employ of the Demarchy. Despite his supposed successes in locating their hideaways, she had heard Abramovic and others complain bitterly that no matter how much firepower they threw at the Freehold, they always managed to pop up somewhere else, and stronger than ever.

And no wonder, since Karl himself had most frequently led these supposedly punitive expeditions against the Freehold, when he wasn't busy safeguarding her.

The men around her all glanced up, and she followed their gaze, at the same moment hearing a dull roar from above. A dropship was descending towards them from out of the night sky, with drive-fields flickering around its hull. For a moment she thought they had been caught, and that the approaching craft was an Accord patrol come to return her to the Demarchy.

Karl and his Freeholder companions, however, watched the craft's descent with equanimity. Once the dropship had settled down onto the hard frozen soil, half a dozen metres away, Karl took charge of Gabrielle once more, tugging her towards the craft as light spilled out from its interior.

Gabrielle felt a sudden, powerful instinct urge her not to get on board the craft. She tried to shake herself loose from Karl, but his grip only became tighter.

'Move,' he snapped, dragging her forward. It was the first word he had said to her since picking her up and throwing her into the river's freezing waters.

One of the Freeholders followed them. Karl paused at the drop-ship's ramp and turned to him. 'It's all up to you from this point on, De Meer,' he said. 'The impact wave should hit before very long.'

De Meer nodded, and slapped Karl on the shoulder. 'You've been a good friend to us, Tarrant. Maybe we finally have a chance at getting back everything we lost.'

Tarrant? Gabrielle stared between the two men in confusion. Why had De Meer addressed Karl by that name?

Karl nodded towards the boat bobbing gently in the starlight. 'Can you get away before the wave arrives here?'

'We have our own air transport waiting nearby,' De Meer replied. 'We'll be able to watch Dios drown from above.'

Karl laughed at that, and the two men embraced as if they were old comrades. Gabrielle thought suddenly of the tens of thousands of pilgrims who had converged on Dios for Ascension Day. Then De Meer turned without another word, and went to rejoin his companions who were waiting by the dock.

'Inside,' said Karl, his expression hardening again as he turned back to her.

Gabrielle stared at him. 'That name, he called you . . .'

He grabbed her by the shoulder, nearly throwing her into the dropship. The hatch closed behind them, and Gabrielle swallowed hard as the airlock rapidly cycled through. The inner door opened and he pushed her into a bay where a man was waiting, wearing a jumpsuit similar to her own.

'Get her inside a medbox,' instructed Karl, pulling off his breather mask and pushing her towards the other occupant, 'before hypothermia sets in.'

The man saluted him. 'You'll need attention too, sir,' he said, stepping up beside Gabrielle. 'And the sooner the better, once we're out of here.'

'I want to know why that man called you Ta—'

Karl whirled towards her, grasping her by the jaw. 'Now, you listen to me,' he hissed, leaning in close, 'things are going to be very, very different from now on. What I say, you do. Is that clear?'

She hated herself for nodding wordlessly, but she had never been so frightened, not even back on board the Grand Barge while waiting for the right moment to kill a roomful of people.

Karl gestured with his chin towards the waiting crewman. 'Briggs here is going to put you in a medical unit for a while. Until we get to where we're going, Gabrielle, you're going to keep your mouth shut and do whatever the hell you're told.'

THIRTEEN

Gabrielle

Briggs led her to a tiny medbay, where he left her to strip off her coveralls before she climbed into the warm embrace of a medbox.

She remembered using such machines in her youth, when she had first received her machine-head implants. Cilia-like feelers attached themselves to her skin as she lay back inside it, punching barbiturates through her skin even before the lid had fully closed over her. In the moments before consciousness slipped away, she felt the craft shudder as it lifted up.

The next thing Gabrielle was aware of was the sound of the medbox unsealing itself with a soft hiss. She had a sense that some hours had passed. She now sat up slowly, blinking in the harsh glare of the overhead lights.

She experienced a falling sensation, but everything around her looked still and silent. *We must be in orbit.*

She had never been off-world before and yet, despite being unfamiliar with the sensation of weightlessness, she discovered it was not unpleasant. She recalled learning, long ago, that the DNA of the earliest human colonists had been tweaked in order to optimize their chances of surviving the rigours of space travel. That meant she would never feel space-sick.

Climbing out of the medbox, she found the same oversized coveralls she had been wearing when she first boarded the dropship. Once she had tugged them back on, she realized that her boots were gone, replaced by a pair of slippers with soft, rubberized soles better suited for onboard life.

She wondered who was piloting this craft, and if they were a machine-head like her. There was something intoxicating about the idea of controlling an entire vessel through one's mind, but when she reached out and tried to interface with the control systems, she quickly found they were inaccessible to her.

Damn Karl and his inhibitor.

Moving with the extreme caution of the inexperienced, Gabrielle pulled on the slippers, then gently pushed herself towards the medbay exit. Being in motion felt like flying. She then carefully made her way along a claustrophobically narrow corridor that followed the curve of the craft's hull, until she came to an open hatch wedged between banks of instruments and bracketed conduits, and heard voices on the other side.

She climbed through the hatch and found herself inside what she guessed must be the cockpit or bridge. She noticed more instrument banks angled over and around a number of acceleration couches, and a Tabernacle projection floating just below what she took to be the ceiling.

Karl was seated in one of the couches, which had been adjusted so that he could look straight up at the projection. There was no sign anywhere of Briggs. She saw Karl make subtle gestures with his fingers, to which the projection responded by first rotating one way and then the other, before suddenly fading to be replaced by some new set of data.

Gabrielle looked more closely at the images, and saw great floods of water flowing around the roots of a canopy tree. She saw whole buildings and enormous vehicles bouncing and spinning in the tempest.

Karl glanced briefly towards her, then continued flicking through more images.

'What is that?' asked Gabrielle, now afraid to get too close to him.

'I tapped into an Accord news feed,' Karl replied, twitching his hand towards the projection as he spoke. 'Take a look at this.'

The images changed, the projection expanding until it filled nearly the whole of the cramped cockpit.

This time, instead of a canopy tree, she saw floodwaters surging around towers and the shattered ruins of buildings. It was clearly a drowned city, but Gabrielle didn't recognize it as Dios until the camera view panned around to show the Ship of the Covenant. The buildings, walls and bridges that had once surrounded it had all now been swept away.

She put her hand to her mouth, the breath stilled in her throat.

The camera view then shifted to take in more of the surrounding landscape. The docks were entirely submerged. Gone were the grand towers, capped by silver and gold minarets, that had stood at the Gates of Dios to greet pilgrims as they arrived. Further inland was yet more devastation, a flattened wasteland of debris where once had been homes and places of work, of worship and of entertainment. In their place were surging black waters filled with the bodies, she realized with a deep and absolute certainty, of countless pilgrims.

She felt her gorge rise and swallowed hard. Dios had almost literally ceased to exist.

She stared at Karl. 'How . . . ?'

'An impact,' replied Karl, 'just like Abramovic said. The news feeds are speculating over an unidentified asteroid.'

Gabrielle shook her head. 'That's not possible – not in this day and age. The Accord would have seen it coming. *We'd* have seen it coming. We have orbital defences.'

'Unless,' said Karl, 'you have friends in the outer system who can make sure no one sees it coming. Or at least not until it's much, much too late.'

The view had shifted to the waters still spreading inland, hundreds of kilometres from the shores of the Ka, and sweeping away towns and villages. The waves looked as if they might easily rise to a hundred metres in height.

'I don't believe you. That's impossible. *Someone* would have known.'

He laughed, and looked back over at her. 'I can't make up my mind if you're wilfully blind or just stupid, so let me explain it so you can understand: the Freehold has had agents working on this for years. Don't get me wrong: it took a hell of a lot of planning to circumvent the security networks and get the right people into the right positions, but it's not impossible. Or are you really going to deny the evidence of your own eyes?'

She felt a sharp stabbing pain in her palms, and realized she had been digging her fingernails into them. 'Why?' she asked, her voice sounding harsh to her own ears.

The man she had known as Karl Petrova, but who in reality was some stranger named Tarrant, looked at her as if she had asked the dumbest question in the world. 'Because it was necessary,' he said.

'You didn't do this for me,' she protested. She stared again at the projection, and saw bodies caught in an eddy. 'Nothing could be worse than thinking that . . . *this* could have had any connection with me.'

His expression grew hard. 'Your hands are just as dirty as mine, Gabrielle. After all, you were happy to kill Thijs and the rest in cold blood.'

'Yes, but they . . .' The words choked off in her throat.

'*Deserved* it?' he laughed. 'Of course they did.'

'But all those people in Dios, all those pilgrims . . .'

'. . . are the same people,' said Tarrant, 'who helped eject the Freehold from Redstone. The Freehold settled this world long before the Demarchists or anyone else turned up. Now, it seems, the tables are turned once again.'

'So what do you need me for, if all you wanted to do was destroy the Demarchy?'

Karl laughed again. 'Destroying the Demarchy was just a way of distracting the Accord long enough for me to get you away from there and make it look as if you're dead.'

She suddenly felt a depth and intensity of loathing towards this man – this *stranger* – that she had previously reserved only for Thijs. 'You really think I could still love you after . . . after . . .'

'Don't be a child,' he snapped, pulling himself out of his couch, his expression coldly devoid of emotion. 'You're an asset, nothing more.'

Gabrielle stared at him, mute, then wrapped her arms around herself as if suddenly cold. *An asset, nothing more?*

'No.' She shook her head. 'Take me back. I want to go home.'

Tarrant snorted with derision. 'Port Gabriel doesn't exist any more.'

She forced back the tears she could feel welling up. She was determined not to lose control in front of him.

'What happened to Dios was necessary,' Tarrant continued. 'Even killing Thijs and his friends wouldn't have been enough to enable us to escape for certain. We needed a bigger distraction, one that would convince people we must have died along with everyone else.'

She launched herself towards him, beyond reason now, a noise that was barely human escaping her throat. Everything he had ever said to her, every word whispered to her in the depths of the night, had been little more than elaborate lies.

Tarrant avoided her onslaught with ease, grabbing hold of both her arms and twisting them behind her back until she screamed from the pain. 'Now you have a choice,' he said. 'Unless you decide to be cooperative, I can put you back in a medbox and leave you there until I need you. We're going to meet with some old friends of mine, and then we're going on a trip, Gaby. A long one.'

'I hope they catch you,' she hissed, still struggling to free herself from his grasp. 'I hope the Accord finds you and cuts you into little pieces for what you've done.'

Tarrant laughed. 'The Accord? And what the hell do you think would happen to you if their soldiers got hold of us? The best you could hope for is that they'd hand you over to the Demarchy, but it's much more likely they'd just try to find some way to merge you with the Ship of the Covenant themselves.'

She twisted in his grasp, the movement sending them both into a slow spin in the zero gravity. 'They wouldn't do that,' she said, aware of the uncertainty in her own voice.

'The Accord badly needs the data that the Demarchy was about to extract from you. It has come to rely on it, so don't make the mistake of thinking it would treat you any better than Thijs would have done. It'd use you for what you actually are: a made thing, a clone.'

'I'm pregnant,' she whispered.

Tarrant released one of her arms and used his other hand to yank her around until she faced him.

'What did you just say?' he demanded, sounding furious.

'Are you deaf?' she spat at him. 'I said I'm *pregnant.*'

A range of emotions flickered across his face. 'Why the hell didn't you tell me before now?'

'I guess I couldn't find the right moment,' she sneered.

His face darkened with rage, and for a moment Gabrielle thought he might strike her.

'You stupid little whore,' he muttered under his breath instead, before letting go of her. She pushed herself away from him, and moved towards the hatch.

'You *stupid* little whore,' he shouted after her again. 'How long has it been?'

'Almost four months,' she told him, and saw his eyes drop towards her waist. 'It's just starting to show.'

She saw him doing the calculations in his head. She'd give birth in another two months, shorter gestation periods being another benefit of long-ago DNA tweaking by her colonist ancestors.

'I suppose this changes all your plans, doesn't it?' she said, enjoying what felt like a fleeting moment of triumph.

His eyes were bright and hard as he stared at her. 'No, not really, Gabrielle,' he said. 'It doesn't change a damn thing.'

FOURTEEN

Megan

2751 (twelve years before)

When they were no more than a half-dozen jumps from the target system and the Wanderer, Megan called an emergency meeting.

She waited for them on the command deck. Sifra was the first to arrive, red-eyed and yawning, closely followed by Bash, who studied her curiously but said nothing. Tarrant was the last to appear, a bulb of hot coffee in one hand. Megan had made an excuse not to spend the previous night with him.

'Whatever this is about,' Sifra grouched, 'it had better be really damned important.'

Megan stalked around the base of the astrogation chair, rubbing her hands together as the others took seats by various consoles, swivelling the chairs to face towards her.

'It has to do with the Wanderer,' she said, finally stopping her pacing, her body turned rigid with suppressed anger. 'But mostly it has to do with certain details, Gregor, that you omitted to mention before we left Kjæregrønnested.'

Tarrant gazed back at her coolly. 'What details?'

'Details that were deliberately redacted from the research material you passed on to me and Bash.'

<What exactly are you up to, girl?> Bash fired at her.

<Never you mind.>

Tarrant, unaware of this private communication, nodded expressionlessly. 'Go on.'

'I didn't say anything at first, because I thought maybe there was a reason why some of that material had been redacted. I thought perhaps the missing details weren't that important. But then I took a look at the source texts – the original Meridian data, from which Schelling's researchers first extracted the details regarding the Wanderer – and fortunately all the source material was provided as well.'

Her muscles felt sore and achy after a long and mostly sleepless night relieved only by intermittent and angry dreams. She glanced briefly at Tarrant, who gazed back with an innocent expression that brought her anger flooding back. 'I decided to have a go at translating those source texts myself,' she continued, 'after downloading the expert knowledge necessary to manage it. I had to do a lot of backwards engineering to try and figure out how your researchers built their translation algorithms but, once I had, I realized the missing details were still there, in those source texts.'

She now stepped a little closer to Tarrant, not even trying to hide her contempt. 'That was a mistake on your part, Gregor, thinking I wouldn't dig deep enough actually to translate the Meridian records myself. I could hardly believe what I discovered, but the real breakthrough came when I cracked the encryption on those low-energy transmissions you've been secretly sending back to the Three Star Alliance.'

Tarrant's eyes widened, his cheeks flushing with anger.

<Megan, what the hell is going on?>

<Not now, Bash. Just let me talk.>

'You had no right to intercept our communications,' said Tarrant. He hadn't moved from where he sat, but he held himself totally rigid.

Megan smiled humourlessly. 'We do have a right to know how much danger we're putting ourselves in, Gregor. Even though each of your messages consisted of no more than a few kilobytes of data, the energy cost of sending them through the tach-net array all the way back to Kjæregrønnested was enough to catch my attention. You covered your tracks, but not quite well enough. I dug around until I found older messages buried in a systems cache, full of all kinds of surprising little details you've been keeping from us. Imagine my surprise when I discovered we weren't the first ship from out of Kjæregrønnested to encounter the Wanderer.'

Tarrant's expression was unreadable, but Sifra glared at her with undiluted hatred. Bash, meanwhile, simply looked appalled.

Tarrant started to say something, but Bash put up a hand, cutting him off.

'What ship?' asked Bash.

'A deep-space research vessel from Al-Jahar,' said Megan, 'called the *Kelvin*. It was ordered to divert from its course more than a year and a half before we set out. Alliance researchers had located the Wanderer with their probes, and since the *Kelvin* was already on a deep-space exploratory mission, and the only ship available at short notice, it got sent to investigate. But after it arrived, the Wanderer nearly tore it apart before its crew managed to jump it back out of range.'

Bash stood up, his expression thunderstruck, and stared at Tarrant. 'Is this true?' he demanded.

'And, according to those records I translated,' said Megan, 'the same thing happened to the Shoal. They approached the Wanderer and it attacked their ships – except *they* called it the Marauder, and with good reason. It was powerful enough all on its own that they were forced to retreat, and it refused to negotiate with them except on its own terms – ones that were apparently unacceptable to the Shoal.'

'But what about the Meridians?' asked Bash. 'And the Atn? They encountered the Wanderer long before the Shoal did, and it didn't attack *them*.' Doubt flickered across his face. 'Did it?'

Megan shook her head. 'No, it didn't attack them, and I still don't know why. But there's no way we can proceed without knowing *exactly* what we're going to be dealing with – not if there's any chance the Wanderer might try and attack us as it did the *Kelvin*.'

'You're getting this all wrong,' said Tarrant. 'Of course there are some inherent risks in an expedition like this, the same as there are in any such, and we've already assessed those risks. But you're talking as if we're going out there without any game plan whatsoever. Besides,' he continued, 'last time I looked, *I* was the one in charge around here.'

'Maybe,' said Megan through clenched teeth, 'we should put that to a vote.'

'All right.' He raised both hands in a conciliatory gesture. 'The fact is that we were going to have to tell you the truth about the Wanderer soon enough.'

Bash moved closer to him. 'What the hell was the point of keeping us in the dark in the first place?'

'As Megan says, the records show that different species had different experiences when they approached the Wanderer. Sometimes it reacted aggressively, sometimes it didn't.' The way he was talking, he sounded almost reasonable. 'We're not clear on the reasons for this discrepancy,' Tarrant continued, 'but we've made reasonable preparations, given what happened to the *Kelvin*. That much you must understand.'

Bash drew in a sharp breath, his eyes full of betrayal. 'You still haven't answered my question.'

'Maybe it's because Bash and I wouldn't have wanted to come out on this trip if we'd known – is that it?' asked Megan. 'We're just *one ship* up against something that sent even the Shoal running, so what the *hell* do you imagine is going to happen to us?'

'We have,' Tarrant ground the words out one by one, 'certain *advantages* that the *Kelvin* didn't possess.'

Megan nodded as if he had answered a question. 'The anti-matter weapons in the cargo, is that what you mean? The ones that came on board with that final shipment just before we left Kjæregrønnested?'

Sifra finally stood up, uncoiling rapidly from where he sat. He made no move towards her, but something in his expression sent a shiver through her.

'All right,' said Tarrant, also standing, 'maybe we *should* have been more straight with you, and I'm truly sorry we weren't. But we were in one hell of a hurry to get away before we lost our chance to take command of the *Beauregard*. Our mission objective still hasn't changed, and there's just as much at stake as there ever was. We weren't sure how you'd react if you knew the whole truth so, yes, we held some details back.' He let out a sigh and fixed his gaze on Megan. 'We should have told you sooner than this,' he said. 'I'm sorry we didn't.'

'And maybe, if that's all there was to it, I might have been okay with that,' said Megan. 'But I haven't even got to the worst part yet.'

'Megan,' said Tarrant, a hint of warning in his voice.

She turned to Bash. 'Remember the Accord's justification for the embargo, and why it threatened war against the TSA? It claimed we were retooling our nova drives into offensive weapons.'

'Except that was all bullshit,' said Bash, 'because they never found any.'

'I seriously wish that was true.' She stared hard at Tarrant and Sifra. 'But it's not. The Schellings built nova mines – as many as a dozen, all of them stockpiled at different locations throughout the TSA. Enough of them to start a whole new Nova War and wipe out half of the Accord, if they wanted to.'

'No.' Bash turned to stare at Tarrant and Sifra, his fingers flexing by his sides. 'That's impossible.'

'It's detailed right there in their secret communiqués,' she said, and pushed the data over towards him. 'Take a look.'

Bash's eyes lost focus for a few seconds as he glanced through the data, his expression becoming more and more angry.

'Is this true?' he demanded, looking from one man to the other.

'No,' said Tarrant.

'Yes,' said Sifra, 'it's true.'

Bash swore under his breath.

'What the fuck else were we supposed to do?' demanded Sifra. 'The TSA has to be strong, has to be able to protect itself. Just because we have those weapons doesn't mean we'd ever need to use them. They were a bargaining tactic, nothing more – a way to force the Accord to treat us as equals.'

<They're both crazy,> Bash sent to Megan. <How the hell did we never notice before now?>

'Let me tell you something,' said Megan. 'If there's one thing that scares me, it's nova mines. When the Accord claimed we had them stockpiled, I didn't believe a word of it. Nobody did, as Bash just said, because they couldn't find any evidence. I didn't believe that anyone amongst the First Families could possibly be so stupid. You can't build weapons like that and just hope they're never going to be used. It's putting billions of lives at risk.'

'Then we'll agree to disagree,' said Sifra. 'You've already been paid. Therefore, in the meantime, there's no reason not to get the hell on with this expedition.'

'You sorry bastards.' Bash shook his head. 'Don't you get it? She's telling you it's over.' He caught Megan's eye. 'I think maybe the best thing we could do now is turn this ship around and go the hell home.'

'I agree,' said Megan. 'You all lied to us – not just the two of you, but the First Families as well. And, for pity's sake, Gregor, were you seriously going to try and *blow up the Wanderer* with those anti-matter missiles stored in the hold?'

'Consider them a worst-case negotiating tactic,' he said, his face like stone.

'You know what?' She glared at him with contempt. 'If this is what the Three Star Alliance stands for, I don't want any part of it. Not any more.'

She turned and moved towards the astrogation chair. Before she had taken more than a few steps, a hand grabbed hold of her shoulder, yanking her around hard. She found herself face to face with Tarrant, his face twisted and furious.

'We are not turning back,' he said.

Megan tried to break loose. 'That's not your decision to make any more.'

Bash stepped forward, pushing Tarrant away from her with enough force that he stumbled and fell against the broad flat base on which the astrogation chair rested.

Bash moved to stand over Tarrant, his fists clenched. 'With the greatest of respect, sir,' he said, 'if you lay one finger on her again, I'll hit you so hard you won't come out of a medbox for a year and a day.'

'The *Beauregard* isn't going anywhere I don't want it to,' Tarrant said with menace. 'I have the systems override for the ship, and I can lock either one of you out of that chair at any time I want.'

Megan did not see Sifra moving towards Bash until it was too late; never noticed that he had pulled on a pair of dark gloves, whose fabric was threaded through with fine silver filaments.

These were, she realized belatedly, nerve-induction gloves. A long time ago, someone had used a pair on her, too, and it was not an experience she was likely to forget.

Sifra laid his gloved hands on Bash, who let out a terrible cry of anguish, his back arching as he reached up to try and tear Sifra's hands loose.

Megan ran forward to help him. 'For God's sake, Sifra, don't—'

Sifra reached out with one hand, grabbing hold of her by the wrist. She screamed, her teeth clenching as pain washed through her in a white-hot tide.

Sifra soon let go of her and she scrabbled back out of his reach. Then he released Bash, who slumped to the floor, unmoving.

'Stay the hell back,' Sifra shouted after her. 'I swear to God, Megan, I'll kill him now if you move.'

Tarrant went over to kneel by Bash, and Megan saw that a beautifully worked knife had appeared in one of his hands. The blade began to shimmer. Meanwhile, Bash's skin had turned an unhealthy shade of grey, and he looked as if he was having trouble breathing.

'Gregor, please.' She swallowed hard. 'Whatever you're thinking of doing, don't.'

'I want you to understand something very important,' he said, bringing the blade very close to Bash's throat. 'We'd prefer to have both of you alive but, if you don't give us any choice, we'll see how we get by with just one of you. So you can either cooperate or watch him die, understand?'

'You're out of your mind.'

'You've just threatened a mission critical to the TSA's continued survival, something I'd willingly die for. Tell me, Megan, are *you* prepared to die for your principles?'

Megan said nothing.

'That's what I thought,' said Tarrant, removing the blade from the vicinity of Bash's throat. 'There will be no turning back. Once we're back home, you're free to go where you want, do what you want, but until then you belong to me. Both of you.'

She saw Bash stir. <Bash? Can you hear me?>

<Sure.> He lay still, with his eyes closed.

<I think they're going to kill us once we're done doing whatever it is they brought us out here for,> she sent. <I think that was always their plan.>

<I think maybe you're right,> Bash sent back. <But if we bide our time, maybe we can think of something.>

'Fine,' she said, in a voice clipped and cold. 'If that's how it's going to be, we'll pilot you the rest of the way, and back again. But, after we're home, promise me I never have to see either of your fucking faces ever again. Are we clear?'

'Entirely.' Tarrant nodded tautly. 'But there are going to be some changes. I need to be sure you won't make any attempt to compromise our mission.'

Megan closed her eyes for a moment and swore under her breath. 'So what did you have in mind?'

'You'll each keep taking your shifts in the chair, but whichever one isn't on active duty is going to be held under guard. I'm limiting your external access to either the chair, or the ship's onboard net. Myself and Anil will take turns in guarding you. And if either one of you tries to sabotage this mission again, the other one dies immediately.'

Megan forced herself to nod.

'I know you don't want to hear this,' said Tarrant, 'but I'm genuinely sorry about how things have worked out. You should never have gone prying into business that wasn't yours, Megan.'

Megan stepped past them both to help Bash stand up, holding him under the armpits.

<Come on,> she said. <I'm taking you down to the medbay.>

<I'm sorry, Megan,> he sent. <I'm sorry I got you into this whole—>

<Just shut the hell up and put one foot in front of the other.>

'Bash,' Tarrant called after them. 'I hope one day you'll maybe understand that we did what we had to.'

'With all due respect, sir,' said Bash, without looking round, 'go fuck yourself.'

FIFTEEN

Megan

Sifra followed them to the medical bay and waited there at the entrance. Megan made a point of ignoring him while she helped Bash get undressed. She pushed up the lid on one of the medboxes and held it open while he crawled inside, before sealing the lid over him. After that she pushed her way past Sifra and cracked open the neighbouring box.

'You sure you need this?' asked Sifra. 'My gloves don't cause any physical damage.'

She paused, one hand on the open lid of the medbox. The skin over her knuckles, she saw, was shiny and bone-white. 'We're machine-heads,' she said in a monotone. 'For all I know, you've damaged our implants.'

'I'm not sure that's—'

'Don't you understand?' she yelled, her control suddenly slipping. 'If you ever want to find your way home, you'd better make sure your pilots are kept in good condition. Because if you did any serious damage to us, you might want to get used to the idea of spending the rest of your fucking life on this ship.'

Sifra's demeanour turned even more hostile. 'Fine, then, get the hell on with it.'

'I don't want you in here while I'm getting undressed,' she said. 'You can go and wait outside.'

He shook his head. 'I'm not letting you out of my sight for one—'

'Goddammit,' she screamed, 'I want you out of here!'

Sifra's nostrils flared, and for a moment she wondered if she had pushed him too far. The last thing she wanted was for him to use those gloves on her a second time.

'Fine,' Sifra spat. 'You've got two minutes.'

'Five,' she said, as he stalked back outside.

She undressed quickly, climbing inside the medbox and pulling the lid down over her.

She kept trying to think of some other way she could have handled things, but however she played it out in her head, it kept coming out the same way.

She felt something gently prick the skin of her arms, back and legs. Bash was right, she thought, in those last moments before she lost consciousness. They'd find some way to get through this, somehow.

Whatever it took.

A few days later, Megan found herself back inside the astrogation chair, while Bash was spending yet more time in a medbox. He had needed four or five consecutive sessions so far, since Sifra's gloves had apparently caused more extensive damage to his higher-level functions than Megan had anticipated. She had required a few additional spells in the medbay herself.

She realized that Bash needed to be seen by a specialist back home, but out here the best that could be done for him was the auto-medicinal equivalent of applying a splint. And that meant she would have to do double-duty on the command deck until he was ready to resume his duties.

At least Tarrant had shown the good grace to vacate their shared quarters by the time she had returned from the medbay. They were now within a few light years of C-H45k – their target system, and the Wanderer's hiding place. Just from the drain on the ship's plasma stores, she knew that Sifra and Tarrant had been sending more messages back to Otto Schelling.

The two of them kept their promise, each taking turns to watch her carefully. They also made a point of being conspicuously armed at all times. But she could still hide herself away inside the astrogation chair's petals, the only place on board the *Beauregard* she felt remotely safe any more.

She had been there, the day before, when the *Beauregard* had suddenly come under the focus of a powerful and highly directional tach-net signal emanating from somewhere deep inside the C-H45k system.

According to Sifra, the Wanderer had followed the same strategy before, broadcasting a faster-than-light hailing signal towards the *Kelvin* once it had come within a few light years. She had thought immediately of the legends of Sirens calling ancient Greek ships to their ruin on treacherous rocks, but said nothing.

Sifra arrived on the command deck just then, parking himself in front of a console and thus disturbing her solitude. He glanced towards the folded petals of the astrogation chair.

Any luck deciphering that signal? he asked, as if nothing had changed on board.

She pictured her fingers wrapped around his throat. <No,> she replied. <It pretty much defies analysis. If it wasn't for the coordinates piggybacking on the signal, I'd have said it was background noise, simply static.>

Are you sure that's not what it is?

<Any communications technology sufficiently advanced relative to our own is going to produce signals that are indistinguishable from noise as far as we're concerned. It's like trying to pick up a standard tach-net signal using an analogue radio.>

Sifra nodded. *Other species previously managed to figure out how to talk to it.*

<We really need the kind of specialists they have back on Kjæregrønnested. They'd have been able to work something out.>

Well, said Sifra, *that's the reason for all the back and forth with Kjæregrønnested. Want to hear what they've come up with?*

She gritted her teeth. <Go on.>

He made a sweeping gesture across the top of his console, and in response more images appeared within her personal datascape. What she saw looked like an exercise in pointillistic chaos – thousands of multi-hued dots arranged in no initially discernible manner, but recognizable as Meridian text.

<What is all this?>

He touched the console and some of the dots began to pulse with light. *See the way the highlighted figures are arranged in a specific pattern? They found the same string of data in Shoal records concerning their own, later, encounter with the Wanderer. I want you to run an analysis on the signal and see whether there's any correlation.*

It took mere moments to find the exact same pattern buried within the millions of petabytes of data currently being beamed towards them. Despite everything, Megan felt a rush of elation.

<You're right. There's a correlation.>

Our guess is that string is some kind of handshake protocol the Meridians – as well as the Shoal – used to identify themselves to the Wanderer.

<So what now?>

We want you to incorporate that string in a microburst transmission and send it back to the Wanderer. If we get some kind of an acknowledgement, we'll know whether we're on the right track or not.

<That's going to drain even more power from the *Beauregard*'s reserves and delay our arrival. You've already used up a lot of our energy stores with all those tach-net transmissions to Kjæregrønnested.>

<We can live with a short delay.>

It took her a while to compile a return transmission incorporating Sifra's handshake string. The message was large and complex enough to drain the batteries by nearly ten per cent when she sent it off in a single tach-net burst.

As soon as this was done, Megan severed her link to the ship's primary systems. The petals slid back into the base of the chair as she stood up for the first time in some hours, rolling her shoulders and stretching her neck to try and unkink it. Sifra, thankfully, had long since left.

Bash walked on to the command deck just as she was stepping down from the chair. He was closely followed by Tarrant, wearing his pistol holstered by his side.

<I think it's long past time you took a break,> sent Bash, glancing towards her. He looked a lot thinner than he had done just a couple of days ago, and there were dark circles under his eyes. <How about letting me take a turn?>

<Are you sure it's not too soon? I can still—>

<Goddammit, woman, I'm not crippled. You've been sitting in that chair for near as damn three straight days now. Go get some sleep.>

She nodded, and stood aside as Bash pulled himself into the chair without even meeting her eyes. The petals slid back up and around him.

<Hey,> Megan sent. <Are you going to be okay?>

<I told you to go and get some rest.>

<If you want to talk about—>

<Sometimes, Megan, much as I love you, I reckon you talk too damn much. Did you know that?>

Megan stared at the closed petals for a moment, then found her way out of the command deck.

SIXTEEN

Megan

Megan slept for twelve straight hours before she awoke with a chill on her skin. She had dreamed of floating in darkness, listening to a voice that was like nothing she had ever heard before. It had been indistinct, as if she was hearing some muffled conversation through a wall.

Then the memory of the past few days came crashing back down on her. She lay there with her eyes still closed, wondering where she could find the will to survive the coming days, and where to . . .

An idea came to her.

She dragged herself out of her cot, still thinking it over. She was due to relieve Bash, and she knew that if she didn't get moving soon, Tarrant would come looking for her. And the thought of him walking into her quarters was more than she could stand.

She stumbled over to the tiny kitchenette, dialling up a cup of coffee and a bowl of porridge laced with as many neuro-enhancement supplements as she could persuade the ship to give her without making it think she was aiming for a deliberate overdose. While she ate, she linked back into the ship's data-net, her mind still churning over the possibilities.

For the first time in a long while, she started to feel excited.

She discovered that Bash had been keeping busy. Maps of the target system were arranged everywhere around his datascape, including images of all of the inner planets.

<You awake, baby?> he said, sensing her electronic presence hovering nearby.

<More than I really want to be.>

<Your neurochemistry just spiked. What the hell have you been doing to your brain?>

<Keeping myself happy so I don't become a basket case,> she replied. The enhancements were kicking in, making her feel as awake as if she'd just plunged herself bodily into a pool of ice water.

<There are limits to how much you can screw around with your internal chemistry, you know.>

<None of your business,> sent Megan. <Listen, I had an idea, a crazy one, maybe, but I think it's worth at least discussing.>

<Uh-oh,> sent Bash. <Should I be worried?>

<First, is there any way they could tap into our private comms and hear what we're saying?>

<I doubt it. Only way is by accessing higher-level ship's functions through the chair, and you can't do that unless you're a machine-head. That's probably one of the few advantages we have over those two sons of bitches.>

<Then let's make the best use of it we can. Look . . . maybe we don't need the *Beauregard* to get ourselves home, Bash.>

<What the hell are you talking about?>

<The lifeboats.>

He laughed. <Those are short-range boats, Megan. They don't have nova drives.>

<But there's nothing to stop us modifying one of them.>

There was a significant pause before he replied. <Modify it how?>

<We take the *Beauregard*'s nova drive and install it in one of the lifeboats. We'd have to make modifications, a lot of them, but—>

<Wait just one goddamn minute. How the hell do you propose to get the nova drive out of its mounting, then install it in a lifeboat that's not much bigger than itself, all without Sifra or Tarrant even *noticing*?>

Megan felt her face grow hot, but forged on regardless. <We make the modifications to the lifeboat using the engineering section's dedicated fabricators. They're running on automatic most of the time, anyway, producing replacement drive-spines, hull com-

ponents and all the rest of the stuff the ship needs to keep itself functioning. If we programmed them to make modifications to one of the lifeboats, there's really very little chance they'd get to know about it.>

<That still doesn't tell me how you fit an entire nova drive inside a lifeboat.>

<We trigger a core dump, and eject the nova drive into space. Then we launch the lifeboat, grab the drive, and we're on our way home.>

<This,> sent Bash, <is what happens when you juice your own brain chemistry with wild abandon.>

<I know what I'm talking about,> she retorted. <We can do this.>

<Megan, even if we can pull this off, it's going to take us near-as-damn half a year to get home. A lifeboat just doesn't have the resources to keep either of us alive that long.>

<So we engineer the lifeboat to incorporate medbox technology. We fly most of the way home in suspended animation.>

He was silent again for a moment. <I can think of a hundred more objections,> he said eventually.

<You asked how we'd integrate the drive into the lifeboat. We build a cage to contain it. And with the lifeboat having such a tiny mass, it's going to take a lot less power and a lot less time between jumps. We can make it back home a hell of a lot faster than a ship massing as much as the *Beauregard* does.>

<Okay, fine, I can see you've thought this through. But there's still the question of opportunity. You can't just trigger a core dump. It's an emergency manoeuvre designed to remove a nova drive from a ship in order to prevent its capture. It needs the permission of the registered senior crew before the command deck AI will accept it. And right now, that means Tarrant.>

<Unless those two have been hurt,> she said, <or killed, or can't communicate with the pilot. Or if the ship's integrity has been severely compromised. The Wanderer attacked the *Kelvin* without warning. If it attacks the *Beauregard* as well, that's when its systems can trigger a core dump and push the nova drive outside the hull.

But we need to have the modified lifeboat ready to go the moment the Wanderer makes its move.>

<*If* it makes its move,> sent Bash. <*If* the ship's integrity is damaged. *If* both Tarrant and Sifra, by some miracle, fail to notice what's going on. Do you see how much of a long shot all of this is? *If*, *if*, and *if*.>

<Got any better ideas?>

<Hell, no. And just thinking about all the things that could go wrong makes me want to shit my pants. So when do we start?>

<You're serious?>

<It's either that or sit here in the dark watching the universe go by and playing with my dick.>

She laughed. <You have to be kidding me.>

<Oh, like *you* haven't ever done that. Rather be doing something than nothing, baby. And if we're going to get screwed, might as well try and screw them back, right?>

<I already checked out the specs for the lifeboats,> she said, a grin spreading across her face. <We'll leave that pair of assholes to the Marauder, or the Wanderer or whatever its name is, and get the hell home.>

<Let me run some numbers, before you take over from me in the chair,> sent Bash, <and you can check them over once you've finished parboiling your brain in happy juice. If we're going to do this, let's make sure we do it *right*.>

He signed off. Megan picked up her coffee and found it had turned cold. She knew Bash didn't really believe the plan could work. And maybe he was right. But he was also right when he had said it was better than doing nothing.

She still hadn't lost her sense of excitement. She would *make* it work.

The next few days, prior to their final jump into the system, were only outwardly uneventful. Bash ran some simulations and used them to develop a set of custom modifications for the lifeboats, without Tarrant or Sifra becoming any the wiser. Before long, the engineering deck's fabricators were stripping down a lifeboat in preparation for rebuilding it.

Megan meanwhile prepared the way for the core dump that would eject the *Beauregard*'s nova drive into space. The mounting within which the drive nestled sported a cluster of miniaturized drive-spines, making it a self-contained starship in its own right. Following an emergency core dump, it could, if necessary, jump to any one of a number of pre-programmed destinations, in order to evade capture.

But if the Wanderer didn't attack, she and Bash were going to have to figure out something else. She wondered if it might be possible to provoke the Wanderer in some way, but, given that they still didn't know how to get it even to respond to them, the chances seemed remote.

'You can't even get the Wanderer to acknowledge our signal,' she said in exasperation, later that day, as she stepped back down from the chair to find Tarrant waiting for her. 'Except I got the distinct impression that the *Kelvin*'s crew found some way to talk with it before it attacked.'

Tarrant had been sitting with one booted foot up on a console, turning a Freeholder knife this way and that under the deck lights. 'That's correct,' he replied, without looking up.

'So what happens when we get there?' she asked. 'How *are* you going to talk to it? Shouldn't you have told us that by now?'

He gave her a thin smile. 'It'll all be taken care of soon enough,' was all he said.

Five days after its crew's violent confrontation on the command deck, the *Beauregard* finally ramped up for a long jump into the target system, with Megan occupying the chair. Sifra's idea of using Meridian hailing codes had failed to provoke any kind of response, which left her wondering what the two men would do, should the alien entity still prove unwilling to communicate at closer range.

Then the stars around the *Beauregard* changed abruptly, and new data from the external sensors began flooding into her datascape. She pushed most of it to one side, for the moment engaging solely with the incoming visuals.

She floated in space, her virtual body immune to the cold and radiation. Great billowing clouds of gas obscured the star itself, the colour of the clouds ranging from deep red to brown and yellow. Somewhere at the heart of those clouds lay a single massive star comprising more than twenty standard solar masses, its outer layers stripping away as it entered its last few million years of life.

According to the *Kelvin*'s initial survey, a few tiny rocky worlds orbited the giant, but this close in, and with so much interference affecting their long-range sensors, it was nearly impossible to acquire accurate readings on anything. The gas and dust clouds were so dense that the Wanderer could be hiding almost anywhere amongst them and indeed, if it weren't for the original beacon signal to home in on they might never have been able to figure out where within the system it might be.

As hiding places went, thought Megan, there could be few better.

One of those worlds was a pockmarked and airless wasteland with a largish moon, about a thousand kilometres in diameter, around which the Wanderer currently orbited.

Once she'd run a standard all-systems check following the latest jump, Megan returned to the short-range visuals that the *Kelvin* had recorded during its closest encounter with the Wanderer. Something kept drawing her back to those pictures of twisted, root-like limbs extending from a central mass that measured at least a couple of kilometres across. They never failed to make her skin crawl. The Wanderer looked more like a wind-tossed seed coated in barbs than the product of some ancient civilization.

She zoomed in on the image, noting yet again the peculiarly granular quality of the Wanderer's hull. It looked as if it had been smashed into tens of thousands of pieces, then carefully glued back into a misshapen whole.

Something brushed against her thoughts.

Something alien.

She swallowed hard and opened her eyes to the pitch darkness inside the chair's folded-in petals. She felt suddenly claustrophobic, as if something was lurking in the dark unseen.

She sensed Bash coming online. <Hey. Did you feel that just now?> he asked.

<I thought you were asleep.>

<I *was*, until a couple of seconds ago.>

<You mean that sense of . . . of . . .>

<As if I was being watched,> he replied. <Near as damn wet myself. You swear you felt that, too, and it wasn't just me having some insanely vivid dream?>

<No,> she sent. <I felt the same thing. That's exactly what it felt like. Maybe it's just interference from those gas clouds.>

Bash's response was full of scorn. <Tell me how the fuck solar interference causes something like that.>

<The only alternative is that it's the Wanderer.>

<I don't see anything else around here that could be the cause of something like that, do you? I'm looking at the transmissions log right now. There's no sign of any kind of message coming from it, but we both experienced something that I'm pretty sure only a machine-head could understand or experience.>

<So?>

<So maybe,> sent Bash, <the Wanderer is trying to talk to *us*. Specifically, you and me.>

Megan felt her eyes widen, her hands gripping the armrest of her chair. <But why not the others?>

<All the evidence is that the Wanderer is some kind of machine intelligence. So, if I were to hazard a guess, I'd say maybe it reckons *we're* machines too – because of our implants.>

Megan?

She pulled up a visual encompassing the command deck and saw that Tarrant had just entered. *Anil just alerted me that the Wanderer's beacon signal cut off just now, without any warning. Can you confirm that?*

She made a quick check and saw he was right. The beacon signal had indeed cut off within just the last minute or two.

<I can confirm it, but I can't tell you why it happened.>

Then there's one other thing I wanted to ask you, he said.

<What?>

Whether either you or Bash have experienced anything unusual since we arrived in-system.

<I'm not sure what you mean,> she replied carefully. She opened up the channel so Bash could listen in.

When the Kelvin *was here, its two pilots proved to be* – Tarrant appeared to be searching for the right words – *sensitive, in some way, to transmissions coming from the Wanderer.*

<Holy shit,> said Bash. <Is he talking about what I think he's talking about?>

<What kind of transmissions?> she asked.

<This would be a lot easier, Megan, if you just told me yes or no.>

<All right, yes, we both felt something. We're not sure what it was.>

Well, then, we need to talk about it, he said, stepping back towards the exit. *I want you to come down to the ship's lounge in half an hour, and join me and Anil. Tell Bash to come as well. We need to talk about what we do next.*

<Aren't you going to escort me there with a gun to my head?> she sneered. <What exactly are you up to?>

I like to think we've achieved some kind of mutual understanding, he replied, pausing by the exit. *I like to think force is no longer necessary. And the reason I want you both there is that we have an idea about how to avoid the* Kelvin*'s fate.*

<He's up to something,> sent Bash. <I can feel it.>

<Even if he is,> sent Megan, a sour taste in her mouth, <there's not a great deal we can do about it.>

<How long before that lifeboat is ready?>

She smiled to herself. His earlier scepticism seemed to have faded entirely. <At least another couple of days,> she replied. <If we divert any more resources than we already have to the modifications, they're going to start noticing.>

Megan? said Tarrant. *Don't delay.*

<Why not just tell me now?> she asked. <Why do I need to go anywhere just to be told something?>

It's not a request, said Tarrant, his voice edged with anger. *Let's at least be civil. Half an hour, Megan, no later.*

Knowing they had a plan in place made it easier for her to be civil. <Fine,> she replied. <We'll see you then.>

SEVENTEEN

Megan

2763 (the present)

Three days after she and Bash had been forcibly taken aboard the system transport *Liberia*, now decelerating on its final approach to Redstone, Megan prepared to make her escape.

Throughout the journey, Luiz and Sifra had returned only rarely to the dropship in which she and Bash were held prisoner, and then only to let them eat and visit the head. It was fine by Megan, since it gave her endless opportunities to work out how to subvert and tap into the core programming of the two bead-zombies more thoroughly.

The control systems for both zombies had proved to be a rat's nest of encrypted routines and command protocols, any one of which might alert Sifra or Luiz to the fact that they were being interfered with if she wasn't extremely careful. But, two days into the journey, she had finally managed to get one of them to unstrap itself and climb out of its acceleration couch. She remained, as ever, cuffed at the wrists and strapped into her own separate couch.

The sight of the creature under her direct control had made her weep with joy, but she knew the right time to make her escape was once they got into orbit above Redstone.

That meant, unfortunately, she was going to have to stay where she was for just a little while longer. So it was with considerable feelings of regret that she had the same zombie climb back into its acceleration couch and strap itself down.

Just another couple of hours, Megan, she told herself. *Then we're the hell out of here.*

Luiz picked the worst possible time to enter the dropship's cockpit.

'What the hell . . . ?' he said, staring at Megan. She was out of her couch, and already working at getting Bash free.

Luiz floated just inside the cockpit hatch. One of the zombies floated nearby, one hand threaded through a ceiling grip. The other was still strapped into its couch.

She froze as Luiz reached inside his jacket and withdrew his torch gun. 'I don't know how the hell you managed it,' he said slowly, 'but you're going to get back in that couch right now. Do you understand me?'

'I don't think that's such a good idea,' she said, edging away from him.

Luiz's eyes roved around the cockpit, until they settled on the couch where the bead-zombie had been seated until a few minutes before. He glanced at the other zombie beside him, as if seeing it for the very first time.

'I want you to tell me,' he said, 'what the *fuck* you've been up to.'

They were his last words.

Megan switched the freed zombie to lethal mode and gave it a target. She watched as it unsheathed its sword and, in a single liquid motion, drew the razor-edged blade across Luiz's windpipe.

The Freeholder's limbs fluttered and jerked as he died. Globules of his blood floated in the zero gravity, misting the air red. It was impossible to avoid as it spread throughout the tiny cabin. After a moment the dropship's monitoring systems finally realized something was wrong and activated a pump that sucked out the tainted air, rapidly replenishing it from the emergency tanks.

That got rid of most of the blood floating in the air, but it was also the worst possible thing that could have happened just then. It meant an alert had gone out to Sifra. And that meant he would soon be on his way back to the dropship – and vessels such as the *Liberia* offered a distinct lack of hiding places.

Not to mention that she still hadn't figured out how she was actually going to get off the *Liberia* and down to Redstone without being stopped . . .

Focus, damn you.

She kneeled by Bash and touched one hand to his now blood-stained cheek. 'I'm sorry, baby,' she whispered. 'It's going to be hard enough getting away from here without having to lead you by the hand the whole way.'

You don't have to worry about me, she imagined him saying. *You just need to take care of yourself.*

'But I still need to take care of you,' she said, and felt tears running down her cheeks. 'Everything got so fucked up, ever since I managed to find you again, but I'm going to come back for you, okay? And, when I do, I swear I'll never let you out of my sight, not ever again.'

His eyes stared at nothing, his face expressionless.

She stood then, looking down at him. *Somehow I just keep abandoning you, don't I?*

She edged over to Luiz's corpse, which had come to rest against an instrument bank, and carefully pulled the torch gun from his hand. It was sticky with his blood, but then everything in the cockpit was sticky with his blood. She wiped it on her jacket, then pocketed it on her way out. She forced herself to stop off at the head to see how bad she looked, and stared at her reflection in the mirror. She was caked in blood, like something out of a nightmare. She got the water running and frenziedly splashed it on her face and hair, scrubbing with her hands until she had washed off the worst of it. Then she stepped back out into the passageway and yanked open random doors and lockers until she found a pair of spare overalls that just about fitted.

She went back to the head and changed quickly before checking herself again. She still looked like a disaster but, with luck, she didn't look as if she'd just killed someone.

Working her way to the external hatch, she discovered to her vast relief that it was secured with only a default access code. It was a moment's work to get it open.

She then pulled herself along the docking extension that connected the dropship to the *Liberia*'s interior, and soon emerged into a brightly lit passageway stretching for some distance fore and aft. Here and there up and down its length, she could see any number of entrances leading to other docking tunnels. There were even signs and advertisements telling her where on the ferry she could find a place to eat or sleep.

Making her way over to an observation window, she found herself looking down at the surface of Redstone for the first time in a very long while. The sight generated a variety of conflicting emotions within her, few of them good.

Things would have been so much simpler if she had been able just to steal Sifra's dropship outright and take it down to the surface. But a cursory examination, once she had freed herself, showed the craft's guidance computers to be remotely slaved. Sifra would therefore have had no trouble assuming command of it remotely.

That meant she had to find some other way of getting herself down to the surface.

She walked quickly, putting some distance between herself and the dropship, terrified that she might literally run into Sifra on his way to see what the alarm was about. He was without doubt already hurrying back to investigate.

She spotted a figure coming towards her and slowed down, her whole body tensing. As the figure came closer, she saw it was only a member of the *Liberia*'s crew. The man came to a halt, staring aghast at her as she drew closer to him. Clearly her attempt at cleaning up had been less successful than she had thought.

'Hi,' she said, as brightly as she could manage. 'I'm kind of lost and I need to get downside as soon as possible. I've got business in Aguirre and . . . well, I'm really in a hurry.'

'A hurry?' he said. 'Are you . . . are you with the relief teams?'

'Relief teams?' she echoed.

'The surgical teams,' he said, his expression growing ever warier. 'I assume you're from that emergency medical unit they set up in Bay Five?'

She had absolutely no idea what he was talking about.

'Exactly.' She nodded with as much enthusiasm as she could humanly muster. She spread her hands, looking down at herself before flashing an apologetic grin at him that said, *Well, will you look at the state of me*. 'I'm with the relief teams, but I need to get back down there and . . .'

He nodded, visibly relaxing and gestured back the way he had come. 'There's a shuttle just docking that's brought in more people. If you make it there in the next couple of minutes, you can hitch a ride back down.'

'Thank you!' she said as cheerily as possible, and headed in the direction he had indicated, trying hard to think of where the hell she could go next, once she hit ground-side. It wasn't as if there was anyone down there who could help her, or who could . . .

Sarbakshian.

How could she have forgotten?

She felt a grin spreading across her face as she continued along the passageway.

EIGHTEEN

Megan

By the time Megan landed on Redstone less than an hour later, she had already managed to contact Sarbakshian and arrange a place to stay; somewhere, he assured her, where nobody would be able to find her.

On getting down to the surface, she found the spaceport in utter chaos. Redstone, she was beginning to understand, had recently suffered some kind of major disaster. Under the circumstances, it wasn't hard for her to slip away from the gaggle of relief workers whose shuttle she had joined, drawing in her wake a trail of puzzled or downright suspicious glances. But it was only when she managed to access the Tabernacle for the first time that she understood the enormity of what had happened here.

The bolt-hole Sarbakshian had located for her turned out to be an apartment near the centre of Aguirre, a city neighbouring the spaceport. She showered for a solid hour, meanwhile scraping up every detail she could about the disaster from local news feeds, before falling into a dead sleep and only waking again late the next morning.

She concocted some breakfast from the dried ingredients she found in a kitchen cupboard, then walked, stiff-legged and groggy, to a window seat. It offered a view across the pastel-coloured rooftops of the Rook, as this particular district of Aguirre was known.

This city's proximity to the spaceport meant it had become a melting-pot of different cultures and species over the centuries. A

Bandati hive-tower stood on the Rook's western perimeter, while further inland a small colony of Skelites occupied a subterranean warren that emitted a never-ending haze of industrial fumes from surface vents. This was a logical base of operations for a *sans de sezi* dealer like Sarbakshian, and Megan had her own reasons for wanting to keep a distance from the Demarchy.

Staring out of the window, it was hard to believe anything had happened at all. Aguirre was a long way from the Demarchy, and so had avoided the direct effects of the flood. A series of hundred-metre waves had smashed into the Demarchy's coastal regions, reaching far inland and destroying countless settlements, large and small. The death toll was reported to have reached the tens of millions, exacerbated by the fact that so many thousands of pilgrims had been making their way to Dios to celebrate Ascension Day.

Speculation on the cause of the disaster was increasingly focused around a rogue mining shipment from the outer system, which had apparently gone astray before plunging through the atmosphere at several thousand kilometres an hour. It had not, however, been anywhere near large enough to cause such terrible damage, so there were suggestions that it could have secretly contained an anti-matter core.

Certainly no one seemed to believe it was all an accident. *Someone* had brought this about, just as Avilon – and Sifra – had arrived in 82 Eridani, with uncanny timing.

Ever since encountering Luiz, Megan had wondered just what connection Sifra and Otto Schelling might have forged with the Freehold. Because if anyone stood to benefit from a catastrophe like this, it would be the latter.

Megan hit Aguirre's streets swaddled in warm padded clothing, her face hidden behind a stylish breather mask. She jumped on a tram that creaked its way through dusty streets, its barely functional AI squawking out the names of each district they traversed through a damaged grille. Everywhere she looked, she saw people piling goods into the rear of vans and trucks. There were long queues on the main roads out of the city, and a constant stream of ground-to-air vehicles lifting up above the rooftops.

Megan sat back anxiously and glanced around the tram, realizing that, apart from herself, it was deserted. She watched some of the vehicle's peeling flicker-posters, which displayed stylized animations of menacing figures adorned with Freehold tattoos placing bombs in public places or slaughtering busloads of children with equal enthusiasm. It wasn't hard now to guess what Aguirre's citizens were running from.

She disembarked on the furthest edge of the Rook and made her way inside a single-storey building, also owned by Sarbakshian. Passing through a pressure field that separated the native atmosphere from that inside, she peeled off her mask and found herself in the nondescript foyer of what purported to be a trade and economics consultancy. It was completely deserted, and there was a fine layer of dust evident on the single desk it contained.

As instructed, she made her way down a dark and dank staircase at the rear of the foyer, until she reached a security door at the bottom. Light flickered in her eyes for a moment, and then the door swung open with a gentle click.

Megan passed through a second pressure field: the air was now warm and moist and slightly perfumed. She looked around, seeing that the entire lower level was open plan in layout. Pillars supporting the building above were artfully concealed behind clusters of ivy, while grass crunched beneath her boots. One or two tiny yellow birds fluttered from the branches of potted trees. She could almost have been in one of the cloistered gardens of Morgan's World. The illusion was marred, however, by a number of crates stacked here and there, with their contents spilling out.

She felt sweat beading on her forehead and pulled off her heavy coat before making her way towards a set of divans arranged around a low table at the centre of this open space. Arrayed on the table were tiny silver bowls filled with what passed for delicacies on Redstone.

Sarbakshian himself, looking tired and grizzled, sat on an upholstered chair to one side of the table, the invisibly narrow band of a data interface pressing against his long and unkempt hair. He waggled a finger towards one of the divans, without even looking at her; his attention was clearly focused elsewhere.

She took a seat and waited until the man finally pulled off his interface, dropping it onto the table between them with a sigh. He leaned back, pressing the heels of his hands against his eyes for several seconds, then dropped them back in his lap before giving her a smile.

'Long day?' she asked.

'Like you wouldn't believe,' he replied, in a monotone. 'Everyone's getting out.'

'I noticed. Why?'

He eyed her with an expression of disbelief. 'You're kidding me. The Freehold is on the way here. They want Redstone back.'

'No, I haven't heard anything about that. I mean, there were some rumours floating around the Tabernacle, but . . .'

Sarbakshian laughed unpleasantly. 'Rumours? More than rumours, my dear. People know exactly what's going down. Now that the Demarchy's been effectively wiped out, it's only a matter of time before a bunch of crazy tattooed Freehold bastards turn up here in Aguirre, armed to the teeth and claiming ownership. And once they've finished with the Sacerdotal Demarchy of Uchida, their neighbours, the River Concord States, will be next.'

'Do you really believe that?' she asked, her tone clearly sceptical.

'Does it matter?' Sarbakshian shrugged sadly. 'I go where the business is, and Aguirre is fast turning into a ghost town.' He tapped the fingers of one hand against an armrest, studying her carefully. 'You know, I was more than a little surprised about the way you turned up here without any warning. I'd already heard a rumour you were retiring.'

She thought for a moment. 'It was more that I decided to take a career break.'

He looked amused. 'And do drug smugglers *take* career breaks?'

'This one does.' She licked her lips. 'Look, I can't thank you enough for everything you've—'

He waved a hand. 'We've got a lot of history between us, Megan, and even criminals like you and me have to trust someone. You asked for help, and I gave it, but that doesn't mean it's free.'

'I know I owe you.'

'Yes,' he agreed. 'And also for the information you asked me to get.' He made a practised gesture in the air. '*Especially* for that.'

Glyphs appeared in the air by his hand, and Sarbakshian reached out to touch one of them. It quivered momentarily before expanding to reveal several screeds of data.

'Regarding your friend Anil Sifra,' said Sarbakshian, 'his dropship is still docked with the *Liberia*.'

'That's *all*?' she shook her head. 'I'm paying you to tell me *that*?'

'Look, everything's changed since the flood. The Accord has investigators operating all over Aguirre. It knows it's been caught napping, and badly, so when it's not dealing with the disaster, it's trying to limit other kinds of damage – primarily political. That means it's watching people like you and me very, very closely. I have a contact on the *Liberia*, but common bribery isn't working nearly as well as it did just a couple of days ago.' He squinted as if in pain. 'And, much as I hesitate to sully our friendship with such a mundane and lowly matter, there does regretfully remain the matter of recompensing those very individuals who are taking it upon themselves to watch over your friend at considerable personal risk.' At this, he pressed one hand over his heart, and flashed her a grin.

Megan regarded him coolly. 'I already told you, I'm good for it.'

Sarbakshian nodded and waved the glyphs away. 'We'll discuss that more in a moment. First, however, I would very much like to know if you intend to kill this man Sifra.'

'I'm not sure that's any of your business, Sabby.'

'But it *is* my business,' he insisted. 'Sifra is well known, since he's closely linked to the former TSA's First Families. Those are very powerful people, Megan. If they were to realize I aided you in killing one of their own, who would be able to protect me from them? You?'

She stared at him in disbelief. 'You didn't forget that I'm a machine-head, did you? You do understand I have a pretty good idea of just how much firepower you've got stashed all around this lair of yours? Not to mention those three men who followed me here after I disembarked from the tram.'

For a moment, Sarbakshian looked startled, but he recovered quickly, slapping his knee and laughing loudly in a manner that was only slightly less than convincing.

'However, I'm not going to pay you in money,' she declared, 'but in knowledge.'

Sarbakshian's expression clouded. 'What the hell are you talking about?'

It was her turn to make a gesture in the air. She wafted a tiny glowing star towards Sarbakshian, who caught it with ease. He glanced at her impatiently, then glanced down at his open palm. Data flowered around him.

She watched as he sorted through the contents of the data package she had just given him, examining first the technical data and then the financial projections. She knew how he had been a communications engineer in a previous life, and so would immediately understand what he was looking at.

When he finally waved it all away, some minutes later, he wore a rather dazed expression.

'There's no way to maintain that level of coherence,' he said hoarsely, 'over that kind of distance, using tach-net communications technology. It simply isn't possible.'

'You'll be able to license that data towards the development of a new generation of tach-net nodes, with minimal to zero signal loss and at a fraction of the current cost, reaching all the way across the Accord. It'll be the start of a second revolution in faster-than-light communications technology, and you won't have to waste your time just scrabbling for a living on this pissant world or any other, Sabby.'

He shook his head in bewilderment. 'What the hell are you doing smuggling *sans de sezi* when you have access to something like this? You could be richer than the Schellings, or even the Besters.'

'I don't like to attract attention,' she said. 'And if I myself tried to use that information to make money, I would most definitely get the wrong kind of attention.' She leaned towards him. 'Put it this way: I've been saving it towards a rainy day, for a very long time.'

He shook his head. 'There's something about you that's always intrigued me, Megan Jacinth. You're the proverbial mystery wrapped inside an enigma. You came out of nowhere . . . I have no idea where you even got your implants.'

She looked at him, surprised. 'You've been looking into me?'

'I look into everybody,' he said. 'I trust people, but I'm no fool. I don't rely just on gut instinct. I had the feeling that one of these days I was going to find out something surprising about you, but never anything like this. Why me, Megan? And why now?'

'For one thing, it's going to take years before that data starts paying out, and I can't wait that long.' She took a deep breath before continuing. 'I need a ship, Sabby – one that can keep me alive for months, preferably years. You're the only person I can think of who could possibly find me one at short notice.'

He began to chuckle, the sound dying on his lips when he noticed her expression. 'Oh, my God,' he said. 'You're serious.'

'And it has to be equipped with a nova drive,' she added.

His smile faded entirely. 'Now I do know you're crazy. You just can't *buy* a ship like that.'

'Back in the old days,' she said, 'the Three Star Alliance had a couple of small, nova-equipped scout ships used for exploration and mapping. One or two of them are still missing, since the Accord's never been able to find them.' She paused for effect. 'But in fact I know they're being used to transport *sans de sezi* all across the colonies.'

Sarbakshian paled. 'How could you know about . . . ?'

'Except the cost of maintaining them was too high,' she continued, 'not to mention the fact that they became so hot to handle that you and your partners couldn't even offload the damn nova drives they contained.' She shrugged. 'Did I get any of the details wrong?'

Sarbakshian looked haggard and defeated suddenly, shrinking into his seat. 'I should kill you,' he muttered.

'You could,' she agreed. 'But you won't, because you'll assume I've made arrangements for everything I know about those missing ships to be transmitted to the relevant authorities if I don't check in at a certain time and place.'

'I have people who could torture that information out of you.'

'I know you, Sabby. You don't work that way. You never have. And you've been looking for a way out of this business for a long time. Or so you told me the last time you talked me into bed, back on Corkscrew.'

She saw all the fight go out of him.

'Fine,' he said, waving one hand. 'The ships were a dreadful investment – one of my worst. They nearly bankrupted me.'

'So do we have a deal?'

'Yes, damn you. We have a deal.' Sarbakshian's gaze dipped momentarily towards her chest. 'We'd make a wonderful team, you and I. You have the body of an angel, and the mind of a hungry snake. Maybe if you stuck around . . .'

'I wish I could, Sabby. But I owe a favour to another old friend.'

Sarbakshian shook his head and leaned over the table, to pick up a pitcher full to the brim with a pale liquid that smelled faintly of flowers. 'Then, unless you're really in a hurry, how about a drink to old times?'

'Sabby.'

Megan watched him, with her head propped up on one elbow, as Sarbakshian coughed violently and rolled onto his back, swallowing with evident difficulty. Although the bedroom was dimly lit, she could see that when he opened his eyes they were rimmed with red, while his face was pale and bloodless. There was no sign of the lusty energy he'd demonstrated just a few short hours before, when she had allowed him to believe he was seducing her.

'God damn you, look at you,' he said, staring at her. 'How does *anyone* drink that much and wake up without a hangover?'

'Another benefit of being a machine-head,' she said. 'Full functional control of the diuretic system, the increased ability to process alcohol – so no hangovers.'

He thought for a second. 'So were you only faking becoming drunk last night?'

'You'll never know,' she said, and nodded past him. 'I woke you up because you have an alert, and it looks like an urgent one.'

Sarbakshian twisted his head the other way to see a pale red globe floating by his bedside. He reached out and touched it, and it vanished like a soap bubble. Whatever it was must have been private, because she could see nothing more. 'It's your friend Sifra,' Sarbakshian grunted. 'He's on the move. His dropship's just departed the *Liberia*.'

Megan pulled herself out of the bed and looked around for her clothes. 'Any idea where he's heading?' she asked, finding and pulling on her underwear.

'I had someone put a tracking device on that ship of his, and it's heading east.' Sarbakshian frowned. 'Well, well.'

'What?'

He turned and looked at her. 'It's heading for the Montos de Frenezo. He seems an interesting fellow, your Sifra.'

'About what you're thinking,' she said, 'I don't know the answer.'

'What was I going to ask?'

'Whether he had anything to do with what happened to the Demarchy. If I knew, I swear to God I'd tell you. But right now I have to go.'

She hunted around until she found her top, and pulled it on. She looked down at him, still sprawled amidst tangled sheets. 'There's just one more thing I need from you, Sabby.'

He chuckled. 'After last night, I'm ready to say yes to just about anything.'

*

If Sarbakshian regretted making that offer before hearing just what it was she wanted, he did a good job of hiding it.

An hour later, Megan boarded his personal jump-car and started checking its systems. It wasn't machine-head compatible, but required only a minimum of manual intervention. All she needed to do, Sarbakshian told her, was tell it where she wanted to go. Manual control was entirely optional. Megan would have preferred something a little more interactive – something she could genuinely *control* – but, for all that, it was a surprisingly roomy beast.

It was also, she knew, his pride and joy: its lines sinuous and curving and sleek, almost verging on the organic. But beneath that sporty exterior lurked the guts of a powerful machine designed to keep its occupant from being shot out of the sky.

'Okay, Sabby,' she murmured, as she found her way into the tiny cargo area at the rear of his jump-car, 'let's see what you've got tucked away in here, shall we?'

She soon found the bulkhead he'd told her to look for, feeling around its side until she found the hidden switch. A concealed door then clicked open, revealing a veritable arsenal of weaponry. She saw long-range neural disruptors, pocket-sized hunter-seeker drones with k9-enabled neural networks that could identify individual human targets according to their scent, a rack of zero-kickback high-powered rifles, and a small cache of throwaway energy weapons suitable for a dozen uses – after which they could be used as grenades.

Not bad, she thought, *not bad at all.*

When you say you're going away for a long time, he had said to her in the moments before her departure, *you make it sound as if you don't mean to come back at all?*

She had pressed a finger to his lips, but his frown hadn't quite disappeared. She knew what he was thinking: that, wherever she was going, she wasn't expecting to come back alive. Otherwise, why hand him so much potential for wealth?

She activated the vehicle's primary systems and took a moment to check up on Sifra's recent movements. His dropship had indeed landed deep in the heart of the Montos de Frenezo, half a world away from Aguirre.

The next time we meet, Anil, she said to herself, *it's going to be on my terms.*

NINETEEN

Megan

2751 (twelve years before)

Megan stepped down from the astrogation chair twenty minutes after Tarrant had demanded the presence of herself and Bash in the ship's lounge, meanwhile wondering why the Wanderer's signal had cut off so unexpectedly.

She felt a growing sense of unease as she made her way down through several decks to reach the lounge. When she met Bash half-way, they continued together in silence. She felt a sharp pang of regret as she remembered her first meeting with Tarrant and Sifra in the same lounge, several months before.

They arrived to find Tarrant sitting on a couch facing the entrance, a large aluminium case resting by his side. He stood up and pointed what looked like some kind of gun directly at Bash.

Megan heard a soft hiss of air, like a suddenly indrawn breath.

'What the hell . . . ?' exclaimed Bash.

She turned to see him examining a tiny, sliver-like dart protruding from his chest. He reached down to pluck it out, then tipped forward, with his knees folding under him.

The door closed behind them. She turned, startled by the sound, to see Sifra advancing towards her, wearing his nerve-induction gloves. He had obviously been waiting just out of sight behind the door itself.

Sifra grabbed hold of her before she had a chance to react. It was as if molten lava flooded across her skin. Her legs gave way and she hit the floor, a liquid warmth spreading round her groin.

She saw Bash lying unconscious nearby, and felt a depth of terror she hadn't experienced in many years.

Sifra deactivated his gloves, then, with Tarrant's help, dragged her over and dumped her on another couch.

'Get the inhibitor,' said Tarrant.

She willed herself just to reach out and take hold of his throat, to wrap her lean, strong fingers around the neck of her former lover and squeeze, and yet her muscles refused to obey her. She watched helplessly as Sifra opened the silver case Tarrant had brought with him. He withdrew a device of some kind, pressing its muzzle against the base of her skull. There followed a sharp stab of pain that brought tears to her eyes.

Sifra stepped away from her, allowing Tarrant room to tug both her wrists behind her back and secure them with a plastic tie. All the while, she struggled feebly, but to no avail.

The two men stepped away and grabbed hold of Bash, dragging him up onto the couch that Tarrant had been sitting on when they entered.

'You aren't one half the man people think you are,' she managed to gasp at Tarrant. 'Not one hundredth. And I hope I die and go to hell, just so I can be on the reception committee when you finally get there.'

'Nobody's dying,' said Tarrant. 'In fact, the inhibitor I just injected you with is going to help keep you alive.'

She twisted her head from side to side as if she could shake the damn thing loose. 'What the fuck is an "inhibitor"?'

'Something that should keep you safe from the Wanderer.'

'Keep me *safe*?'

Tarrant gave the cord securing Bash's wrists an experimental tug, then nodded as if satisfied, before coming to stand before her with hands on hips. 'There are some other things we didn't tell you. When the *Kelvin* was here, the crew tried communicating with the Wanderer by conventional means.' He shook his head. 'It didn't work. Sifra tried again, on our own approach, but he got the same results. But what you don't know, Megan, is that the Wanderer was somehow able to communicate with the *Kelvin*'s crew through their two machine-head pilots, but in a way we still don't really understand. Unfortunately, the two pilots didn't come too well out of the experience.'

Megan felt a terrible sense of dread. 'What are you talking about?'

Tarrant squatted before her, so his face was level with her own. 'Right after the *Kelvin* got within hailing distance of the Wanderer,' he said, 'they found one of their pilots lying unconscious in his quarters. He never regained full consciousness and, less than a day later, the other pilot suffered what initially appeared to be a seizure. Unlike the other guy, he *did* regain consciousness, and it rapidly became clear the Wanderer had found a way to speak to the *Kelvin*'s crew through them.'

She realized that in a strange way she had been expecting something like this. Even after Tarrant's dreadful act of betrayal less than a week before, there had been some part of her that still believed his actions were caused by a misguided belief that the ends justified the means. Now she understood he was in fact a monster more terrible than she could have ever imagined.

'In some way,' Tarrant continued, 'the Wanderer was able to communicate with the pilots directly, via their implants, but something about that experience blew half their synapses. The first pilot died after a couple of days, without ever waking up; the other suffered such bad epileptic attacks that they had to sedate him.' He shrugged. 'And that was the moment it chose to attack.'

'So how did they get away, with their pilots compromised?'

'They managed to revive the surviving pilot long enough for him to jump them to safety. He wound up dead of a brain embolism just days after they arrived back at Kjæregrønnested. And that,' Tarrant concluded, 'is why we shot you with an inhibitor. It should keep the Wanderer from taking control of your higher-level machine-head functions, the way it did with the *Kelvin*'s pilots. We're going to need you well enough to get us back home, once we're done here, after all.'

'You didn't shoot one into Bash. Why not?'

Tarrant returned her look without saying anything.

'No,' she said, struggling to pull her wrists free. '*No*.'

'Now, listen,' he said, standing up once more, 'there's too much at stake not to have to make some sacrifices. We need to talk to the Wanderer; we need to get it to share data with us, like it did with the Meridians, if we're to have any hope of salvaging the Alliance. And since you're the better pilot, that means Bash has to be our sacrificial goat.'

He walked back over to the open aluminium case, and pulled out a tangle of black rubbery-looking cords all connected at one end. They looked to Megan like poisonous snakes joined at the tail.

'Use me,' she whispered, 'not him. Let *me* talk to the Wanderer.'

He shook his head. 'If things don't work out as well as we're hoping they will, we might find ourselves in need of those exceptional piloting skills of yours.'

'Please, Gregor,' she begged, 'don't do this!'

He ignored her, kneeling beside Bash and carefully arranging the snake-like cords across his skull, with the join positioned at the back. Sifra stood behind Bash, holding Bash's head steady while Tarrant worked. Each cord ended in a broad, flattened pad that adhered to the skin of Bash's head.

'Now let's wake him up,' said Tarrant, stepping back.

Sifra nodded, lowering the back of Bash's head onto the couch. Then he walked over to Megan and dragged her into an upright seated position on her own couch, before stepping around behind her and placing both of his gloved hands on her shoulders.

Megan tensed, her breathing constricted, as she watched Tarrant remove a pressure-hypo from the silver case and touch it to one side of Bash's neck.

The unconscious man jerked in response, then drew in a deep, shuddering breath, his eyes flickering open. He blinked and looked around him, his gaze turning baleful when it finally settled on Tarrant.

'What the hell is going on here?' Bash demanded. 'First you shoot me, then you—'

'Bash, I want you to listen to me very carefully,' interrupted Tarrant.

'Fuck that,' said Bash, twisting from side to side as he attempted to pull his hands free of the plastic ties. He started pushing himself up on to his feet, his mouth becoming a grimace of anger.

<You have to get free,> Megan sent to him. <You mustn't let them—>

She saw Bash glance towards her. Then Sifra activated his gloves, and Megan screamed. The pain wasn't as bad as before, but it was still bad enough. She twisted wildly, but he had a tight hold on her. She tipped forward, vomiting between her knees onto the floor of the lounge.

The pain kept coming.

'What the hell are you *doing*?' she could hear Bash shouting. 'Don't you understand you're going to fry her implants?'

'I'm using a low setting,' said Sifra, from behind her. 'Too low to cause any permanent damage to her implants. But I can make up for that by maintaining the pain for hours, Bash, or even days. However long it takes to get you to cooperate.'

'Please,' said Bash, his voice cracking. 'Let her go. Just stop this.'

'As soon as you stop resisting us,' said Tarrant, 'he will.'

'Shit. Fine.' Bash sat back down, his face pale and sweating. 'Stop the fuck now. *Now*.'

Suddenly, the pain was gone. Megan collapsed back onto her side, her breath wheezing and her teeth chattering.

'What the hell is this thing you've got on my head?' said Bash.

'Should we go ahead now?' said Tarrant, glancing at Sifra.

Sifra nodded. 'All ready.'

Tarrant made a gesture, and a virtual control panel shimmered into existence next to him. He reached out and began tapping at it.

'Has this got something to do with the Wanderer?' asked Bash. 'Because if you're . . .'

Bash fell suddenly silent, as if he was trying hard to listen to something.

'What is it?' asked Tarrant. 'Do you hear something?'

Bash looked up at him uncertainly. 'I don't know, but maybe. Why don't you tell me what you—?'

'Open it up as far as you can,' Sifra interrupted him. 'Link him into the main tach-net array and let's see what happens.'

Megan hated herself, in that moment, for not shouting at Bash to get to his feet, to make a run for it, to do anything he could to stop this happening. But she knew what would happen if she did, and nothing frightened her more than the thought of those gloves touching her again.

She watched, helpless and filled with self-loathing, as Bash's expression slowly changed to one of amazement. He grinned, then laughed, shaking his head from side to side.

'Tell me what you see,' said Tarrant.

'I . . . don't know how to describe it,' said Bash. 'It's as if I can hear a million voices all talking at once, but I can't make a single one of them out. I can't make any kind of sense out of any of it. I . . .'

Bash jumped so suddenly that Tarrant stumbled back from him. Bash's eyes bulged in their sockets, his jaw clenching in a deathly grimace. Then he slumped against the couch and began to shake with a dreadful, high-pitched keening emerging from the depths of his throat. Megan watched in horror, her heart aching to see him in such terrible distress.

'Watch he doesn't swallow his tongue,' said Sifra, his tone calm and unaffected.

'He's wide open,' said Tarrant, glancing at the virtual panel. 'His vitals are spiking all across the board.'

'Then ramp him down, for God's sake,' snapped Sifra. 'Let's not blow every circuit in his brain before we've even had a chance to talk to the damn thing.'

'You're killing him,' Megan rasped, her terror of Sifra and his gloves momentarily forgotten. 'Goddamn you, Gregor . . . you're killing him!'

Tarrant made an adjustment and Bash's fit came to a sudden and spontaneous end. His chest heaved like that of a drowning man gasping for air, his eyes unfocused and staring wildly.

'He looks as if he's trying to say something,' said Sifra.

Bash's mouth opened wide, his tongue flicking around his teeth. His eyes rolled in their sockets in a way that sent a shiver up Megan's spine; his head twisted from side to side, first slowly, then quickly, then slowly again.

When his gaze finally settled on her, it felt to Megan as if she was looking into the eyes of a complete stranger. As if he was possessed.

Bash began to thrash, twisting wildly as if again trying to break free of his plastic restraints.

'Belle's tits,' said Tarrant, wrapping an arm around Bash's shoulder in an attempt to keep him still. Sifra pulled off his gloves and hurried over, struggling alongside Tarrant to keep Bash firmly on the couch.

Bash finally stopped thrashing about and fell back again, breathing loudly through his nose. His eyes revealed no hint of human intelligence. Tarrant and Sifra stood back cautiously, waiting to see if he'd jump up again.

'I think that's it,' said Tarrant. 'Now we see if we've established a bridge.'

'What the hell are you talking about?' demanded Megan.

Tarrant looked over at her. 'You're about to talk to the Wanderer, via Bash.'

'I don't understand what you're—'

'I told you that one of the *Kelvin*'s pilots went into a coma and never recovered. But his co-pilot, before he died, found he could communicate with the Wanderer through the unconscious pilot's implants, by linking mind-to-mind with him. We think that's the reason he survived longer, because the Wanderer wasn't tapping directly into his own implants.'

'Whereas what Gregor shot you with inhibits your higher-level implant functions,' added Sifra, pulling his gloves back on and coming to stand beside her once more. 'The device on Bash's head boosts his. All we need you to do is link to Bash, and see what you get. Got that?'

Megan nodded tightly, unable to take her eyes away from Sifra's hands.

'Okay,' said Tarrant, reaching out once more to the virtual panel hovering beside him. 'I'm now going to patch Bash through the comms array. Tell me if you hear or feel or sense anything at all.'

As Tarrant adjusted something, Megan felt her skin begin to prickle. She had the sudden sense that there was someone else standing immediately behind her, where Sifra had been. Yet he was there right in front of her, watching with evident fascination.

It took an enormous amount of willpower not to look behind her to see if something was there that shouldn't be.

'Anything?' asked Tarrant.

'Not yet.'

<Bash?>

No reply, but the link appeared to be functioning optimally.

In the next moment, she had the inescapable sense of being *noticed* by something cold and alien, and utterly unlike anything she had ever come into contact with before.

<Bash, are you there? Can you . . . ?>

NOT YOU ARE NOT THEY WHO SAIL DEPTHS

Megan gasped as a torrent of sensory information came racing towards her across the link with Bash. A welter of alien sensations assaulted her, and for a moment she was lost in the flood.

She cut the link, with cold perspiration beading her skin. She noticed Tarrant and Sifra staring at her.

'What happened just now?' asked Tarrant.

She shook her head. 'I don't know. I'll try again.'

'Is there anything at all you can describe?'

She thought for a moment. 'Imagine looking up at the stars,' she said, 'and seeing the sky rip open and an enormous eye stare down at you.'

The two men exchanged uncertain glances. 'Try again,' instructed Tarrant.

<Who are you?> she asked. <Are you on board the Wanderer?>

WE SEEK THE LEAF THAT FLOATS ON THE RIVER OF LIGHT THAT FALLS THROUGH THE SKY

The voice was Bash's but the words were nonsensical, the rush of accompanying sensory data so vast and deep that she felt in danger of being swamped by it.

The leaf that floats on the river of light, she thought. *That falls through the sky.*

Somehow, she knew this river of light was the Milky Way. And the leaf was their own ship, the *Beauregard*.

Something else came flooding across the link. She found herself assailed with yet more sensory information she could hardly begin to comprehend. She felt pain in her lungs, as if she were drowning in this flood of data.

It was too much.

The *Beauregard* disappeared from around her, as she found herself adrift in a timeless void full of chaos and noise, her every sense under assault.

And all of this was coming through Bash's implants, yet further filtered through the inhibitor Tarrant had put into her. What the hell must it be like for Bash, then? How could he possibly live through something like this and stay sane?

She slowly began to understand, to thread some meaning through the sheer noise. There was a message there, coming from the Wanderer.

Once she understood that, she began to laugh.

She opened her eyes to find Tarrant leaning over her, with his hands on her shoulders. She lay on the floor next to the couch, her wrists still secured behind her back.

'You had a fit,' said Tarrant. 'How are you feeling?'

'Water . . .' Her voice was hoarse and brittle. 'For God's sake, please give me some.'

To her surprise, Sifra obeyed instantly, darting towards the kitchenette in the far corner of the lounge and returning moments later with a bulb of water. He knelt by her as Tarrant helped her into a sitting position, and held the bulb towards her so she could take a sip. She sucked at it greedily, then fell back against the side of the couch, coughing violently.

'Well?' asked Sifra.

'You're in so fucking deep,' she said, 'you have no idea.'

Sifra's expression turned angry. 'What the hell are you talking about?'

She cleared her throat and remembered the message the Wanderer had conveyed to her. 'You came all this way to get something from it,' she said. 'But we're only here at all because of what it wants from you.'

'So what does it want?' demanded Tarrant.

'Our nova drive,' she said. 'It doesn't care about anything else.'

Both men stared at her in blank surprise.

'It knows all about the Magi ships, and about how they came to our galaxy.' The Shoal Hegemony, before it wound up ruling much of the galaxy, had stolen the secret of faster-than-light travel from the Magi ships, before destroying most of them. 'It knows the nova drives come from caches like the one at Tierra.'

'And it told all this to you?' asked Tarrant.

'Not exactly – not in anything I'd call words. It was more like taking in an expert memory dump: suddenly I know things I didn't just moments before.'

Tarrant rubbed at his face and glanced at Sifra. 'We've been so blind,' he said.

Sifra stared back at him in stupefaction. 'How so?'

'Think about it,' said Tarrant. 'That damn thing's been sailing around the galaxy all this time at sub-light speeds, but not out of choice. Once it saw the *Kelvin* and then us jump into this system, it was obvious to it that we had a means of travelling faster than light.'

'That's got to be why it attacked the Shoal,' said Megan, 'but not the Meridians.'

'Because they didn't have FTL technology?' suggested Sifra.

Megan nodded. 'It wants a nova drive so it can get to wherever the hell it is it's planning on going.'

'But why attack at all?' said Sifra. 'Why not just negotiate for a nova drive in return for the information we're looking for?'

'Imagine how dangerous it would become if it could travel at superluminal speeds,' said Tarrant. 'That thing out there repelled the Shoal, for God's sake. How much chance would the Three Star Alliance, or the Accord for that matter, have against it if it decided to turn on us?'

'So why the hell doesn't it just go and find itself a Maker cache, since that's where all the faster-than-light drives come from in the first place?' said Sifra.

'It's a big universe,' replied Tarrant. 'Especially if you're stuck with traversing it at sub-light speeds. Besides, nobody knows how many more caches there are left, not after the Shoal Hegemony spent millennia destroying as many of them as it could.' He shook his head. 'My guess is that a cache is exactly what the Wanderer's been looking for all this time, but we can't afford to risk giving it what it wants until we have at least some idea what it's ultimate intentions are.'

'Then we need to get the hell away from here,' said Megan, 'before it decides to take our nova drive away from us whether we like it or not.'

Sifra moved towards the exit.

'Where the hell are you going?' demanded Tarrant.

'To prep the anti-matter missiles,' said Sifra, stopping by the door. 'We can launch them into their own separate orbit. That way it'll understand exactly what's going to happen if it tries to attack us.'

'And, for all you know, it's likely to assume that we're attacking it the moment we *do* launch them,' said Tarrant. 'And maybe that's all the excuse it'd need. We need to try and talk to it again, to see if there's something else we can use to try and get it to deal with us.'

'You can't put Bash through all that again,' protested Megan. 'You saw what happened. It nearly killed him.'

Tarrant stared at her, his expression hard. 'No, Megan, we'll keep trying until we get some kind of result.'

TWENTY

Megan

Tarrant kept to his promise. Over the next week, Megan was forced to undergo more attempts at communicating with the Wanderer, using Bash as a go-between – or a 'bridge', as the two men chose to refer to it. And gradually, as the hours and then days passed, she learned to communicate with it, after a fashion.

More and more, 'Marauder' struck Megan as a far more apt name for the alien vessel.

By now, the *Beauregard* had performed a slingshot manoeuvre around the star, still on its way to the moon around which the Wanderer orbited. The violence of the solar wind emanating from the system's Wolf-Rayet star caused endless problems with the external sensor arrays, making it nearly impossible to get accurate readings about anything outside the ship itself.

They then climbed into acceleration berths for the braking procedure that would place them into orbit around the moon, which, along with its parent world, had grown to become a visible disc. Before long, they slipped into orbit around the moon, and then back into zero gravity. The Wanderer was now visible to the naked eye, orbiting much closer to the tiny world's surface.

It rapidly became clear from Megan's communications with the Wanderer that what little had so far been gleaned from the Alyeska digs represented only the beginning of a much larger story.

The Wanderer had, she discovered, been drifting through the Milky Way for the better part of two million years, and perhaps even longer. It was the product of a machine-civilization it called the

Core Transcendence, that had once resided close beside the supermassive black hole at the heart of the galaxy.

Two million years earlier, the Makers had arrived at the centre of the galaxy, challenging the Core Transcendence's dominance. She saw their black-hulled ships, constructed on a scale to beggar comprehension, swooping through the star systems scattered throughout the black hole's accretion disk. Their passage warped the physics of space-time, shattering worlds.

Megan herself suffered more fits, and worse ones. One time, she woke inside a medbox only to discover, upon emerging, that she had blacked out after her last bridging session. Tarrant showed her a recording of her body spasming, blood running from her nose, as Tarrant and Sifra dragged her into the medbay.

But what happened to her was as nothing compared to the effects of the procedure on Bash.

The physical changes in him, after just a few days, shocked her. He continued to lose weight at a tremendous speed, and when he moved at all, it was with the feeble and shaky gestures of a very elderly man. Indeed, every step he took appeared to involve great and ponderous effort. Whenever he spoke, it was in monosyllables, and there were times when he clearly had difficulty remembering who she was.

'They're trying to *what*?' exclaimed Tarrant, when she gave her latest report.

Having spent the better part of three hours interrogating the Wanderer, Megan now had difficulty forming words. 'I think what it's saying,' she rasped, 'is that the Makers are trying to redefine the laws of the universe. They've converted entire star systems at the core of the galaxy into gigantic computers, transmuting them on the subatomic level. For some related reason, they needed access to the black hole at the galaxy's centre. The Core Transcendence tried to stop them encroaching on its territory, and the Makers just . . . wiped them out.'

'But why?' asked Tarrant. 'What purpose could there possibly be in all this?'

She coughed and massaged her eyes vigorously with the heels of her hands. 'They think there's something hidden beyond our universe, and therefore if they change the rules by which this universe operates, they can gain entry into that greater reality.'

Tarrant appeared clearly unsettled. 'You're talking about them in the present tense. Are you saying they're still around?'

She nodded tiredly, wanting nothing more now than to go to sleep. 'They're still around, all right, and building something around the black hole itself. But what it is, I couldn't even begin to guess.'

She let her eyes slide shut for just a second, and she was rewarded with the flat of a hand striking her on one cheek. She gasped from the shock, and reopened her eyes to see Sifra leaning directly over her.

'You need to stay with us,' he snapped, before turning to face Tarrant. 'This is all very interesting, but it sure as hell isn't what we came here for. We need, instead, to focus on getting hold of practical information.'

Megan laughed wearily. 'What does it take to make you understand?' she said. 'It's not going to provide *anything* unless it gets our nova drive in return.'

Sifra gave her a scowl. 'Then make it very clear that we'll destroy it if it refuses to negotiate. Maybe it'll start to see reason once it understands what's at stake.'

'And what if it attacks us?'

'Then we jump out of range,' said Sifra. 'It's not as if it can follow us, after all. The *Kelvin* may have been taken by surprise, but it's not going to catch us out the same way.'

That was it, then, she thought hopelessly. They were going to keep forcing her and Bash to link to the Wanderer until they both died or were left permanently brain-damaged.

It was too late for Bash anyway. He had soon stopped speaking altogether, and when she sat by him and took his hand and tried to talk to him, he just stared blankly past her as if unaware either of her or of his surroundings.

She had to act soon, before she herself wound up the same way.

Fourteen hours later, Megan was woken up in her quarters by strobing alerts. She linked into the ship's net, to find the *Beauregard* had suffered multiple impacts to its hull.

Even in zero gravity, and knowing how much was at stake, it proved an effort to pull herself out of her bunk. She was exhausted from blackouts, fits and long hours of wrestling with the Wanderer.

<IdentMeganJacinth ### BeauregardPrimaryAI>

—Identified.

<Specify source of impacts>

—Source of Impacts: large object +>123km distance [ident: Wanderer].

—Multiple impacts hull sections 13a/25b/178sigma6.

<Restate protocols for emergency drive core ejection following loss of senior commanding personnel>

—Core dump requires fifteen-minute countdown rescindable at any time by senior personnel/≤70% Hull Integrity.

<What is current hull integrity?>

—Current hull integrity 87%, borderline optimal but dropping.

<State current status of senior personnel.>

—All senior personnel accounted for.

If the hull's integrity dropped to critical levels, in other words, she'd be able to trigger an emergency core dump and capture the nova drive before it had a chance to engage its automated jump circuits.

She got dressed quickly, while keeping her link active. The modifications to the lifeboat were complete. If she was ever going to find some way of escaping, it had to be now. She didn't otherwise think she could survive long enough for the next opportunity.

Tarrant opened a link to her. *Megan. It looks as if we've run into trouble. We need you in the astrogation chair.*

<I hate to say I told you so, but . . .>

This is only a temporary setback. Get up to the command deck and see if you can get us out of range.

<I'm still locked in my quarters. You need to let me out first.>

Sifra should be with you at any moment.

Sifra arrived shortly after, looking harried as the door to her quarters slid open. Instead of the gloves, he was carrying a more conventional weapon, which looked as if it had come out of one of the engineering deck's fabrication units. She hoped he hadn't been paying too much attention to anything else in that part of the ship.

She stepped out into the corridor. 'Get moving,' he said, gesturing with the gun.

She was ushered to the right, Sifra following close behind. More symbols indicating an alert appeared around them just as the ship shuddered with insane violence. A pressure field popped into existence a couple of metres away from them, indicating that a loss of pressure had taken place elsewhere within the *Beauregard*.

Sifra looked around wildly, his attention distracted from her for a moment as he tried to figure out what was going on. That was all the time she needed.

Without thinking about it consciously, she reached up, took hold of an overhead hand-grip and swung herself around so that her boots impacted directly with Sifra's belly just as he turned back towards her. His gun went flying, caroming off the walls and spinning away down the length of the corridor in the zero gravity.

The same impact sent her sailing in the opposite direction. Her heart was beating wildly, the adrenalin surging through her veins making her forget all about the myriad aches and pains assailing her body.

She managed to bring herself to a halt just as Sifra crashed into a far wall. Megan thrust herself back along the passageway towards him, barrelling into him before he could step out of her way. He doubled up, and she anchored herself with another ceiling grip before she slammed the back of his skull against a steel flange protruding from the wall behind him.

He screeched in pain and fury, then she rammed his head against the flange a second time.

This time, Sifra went limp.

She pressed her ear against his mouth and listened. He was still breathing – not that it mattered. She rifled through his pockets and laughed with delight when she found exactly what she was looking for: a systems override card, operable for the whole ship. Tarrant would have a similar card, but just one was all she needed.

She tucked it into a pocket, then went in search of Sifra's pistol, shortly finding it near where the pressure field had appeared. Just holding it in her hand made her feel considerably more confident.

<Gregor,> she sent. <The hull's been breached near to our current location. We're stuck down here unless you can get the forward doors to release.>

Where's Anil? Is he there?

<He's unconscious. He smacked his head off something – we got hit by bad decompression, and we both took a tumble before the pressure fields kicked in. You need to come down and help me with him.>

She waited long, tense moments before Tarrant finally replied. *Fine, I'm on my way down.*

She tried swallowing, but her throat was completely dry. Just from his tone of voice, she'd been able to tell he didn't believe a word of her story.

She swam through the air towards the nearest drop shaft, guiding herself along with occasional deft touches to strategically positioned handholds and ceiling grips. She then pushed herself up to the very top of the drop shaft, and waited there with her back pressing against its ceiling.

Just a few metres below her feet was the entrance to another passageway, beyond that part of the ship containing the command deck. Keeping Sifra's gun aimed firmly towards it, she waited.

It didn't take long before Tarrant came barrelling into the drop shaft, twisting around sharply so that he hit the opposite side of the shaft with one shoulder. He glanced wildly around until he spotted her, then tried to bring his own pistol to bear on her.

Megan shot first, having the advantage, and hit Tarrant in the shoulder. The recoil slammed her against the ceiling with painful force. The impact, meanwhile, sent Tarrant spinning down the shaft and away from her, cannoning off the walls as he went. A trail of blood arced through the air behind him.

She pulled herself back through the passageway that Tarrant had just emerged from, making her way towards the command deck as fast as she could. Once there, she pushed Sifra's override card into a slot on the primary command console. Its display shimmered and changed as she locked into the ship's AI.

<Requesting top-level command of primary navigational systems.>

—Top-level command cannot be granted without permission of senior crew members or a report of null status of same.

<Confirmed, dammit. Anil Sifra and Gregor Tarrant are injured and unable to command. The ship is under attack.>

The ship shook around her, even more violently than before.

—Warning. Hull integrity has dropped to mission-critical levels. I am issuing automated remote alert signals.

<I know that! Give me control or we're finished.>

—Primary navigational control is granted.

She had full control of the *Beauregard*; it was now hers to do with as she pleased.

Don't screw this up, she told herself. *Not when you've got this close.*

She tapped back into the ship's net in time to receive a message from Tarrant. *I'm coming for you, Megan. Do you hear me? I'm going to take a long time to kill you.*

<The ship's mine, Gregor. You're not going to be doing anything.>

She climbed into the astrogation chair, the petals quickly folding around her. The external monitors revealed that something had melted a deep gash into several hull plates, triggering catastrophic depressurization across three of the decks. Things were a lot worse than she'd realized.

Something dark flew past the *Beauregard*, gone almost as soon as it had appeared. Bright light flared towards the aft, revealing multi-legged *things*, like something out of her worst nightmares, which began cutting through the hull plates directly over the engineering section.

Where the nova drive was.

God damn you, Tarrant snarled. *I'll kill you, do you understand me? I'll flay you alive while Bash watches.*

She brought up a visual, and saw that Tarrant had found and pulled on an emergency pressure suit, his face white and bloodless behind the visor as he made his way back along a passageway towards her. She brought a hull-section door slamming down, blocking his way.

<Bash is dead,> she sent back. <He was dead the moment you hooked him up to that machine of yours.>

It was a truth she had not permitted herself until now. For a moment, grief threatened to overwhelm her. She was abandoning him, after all; leaving him here to die. That he had been reduced to little more than an ambulatory corpse made no difference to the fact that it was the hardest thing she would ever do.

I knew you were lying, you stupid little bitch. I knew you'd done something to Anil. Take a look outside the ship.

She checked the externals and saw that he had launched the anti-matter missiles. But how could he have . . . ?

You might have taken Anil's override card, but that still doesn't give you sole control over everything aboard this ship, including the missile-launch systems. And once I've dealt with the Wanderer, Megan, I'll deal with you.

Megan watched as the missiles receded with astonishing speed, heading towards the Wanderer, which was clearly boosting its way towards the *Beauregard*. No more than a few seconds later, light bloomed out from the Wanderer, throwing the moon's every crater and valley into brilliant, stark contrast. Filters kicked in, showing the Wanderer glowing a deep orange that shaded into yellow. Parts of it began to break off, drifting away from the main body. She watched, stunned. Surely it couldn't be killed so easily?

She switched her view back to the *Beauregard*, where the strange alien machines she had seen earlier were still trying to dig their way through the hull.

It'll be your turn soon, she heard Tarrant bellow.

She set the modified lifeboat to prepare for immediate launch, then stepped down from the chair, its petals folding back into its base.

<Trigger emergency core dump *now*.>

—Acknowledged. Core dump in three hundred and sixty seconds.

She made her way back out of the command deck and down a different drop shaft. Following a route that would allow her to work past Tarrant, it took her long, precious minutes to get to the engineering section and the modified lifeboat hidden inside it.

She found it prepped and ready for launch. Part of its hull had been replaced by a hollow cage almost as large as the lifeboat itself. Her heart nearly broke when she saw the pair of life-support units integrated into its hull.

She pulled herself inside one of these units, the opaque lid closing over her almost immediately. For one brief instant, she was in absolute darkness. Some part of her thought: *This is what it feels like to be buried alive.*

She pushed the thought away as soft lights came on within the unit. She pressed her hands against the inside of the lid and noticed they were shaking. She felt on the verge of hysteria. The sooner she got under way, the sooner she could sink into blissful unconsciousness.

She linked through to the command deck and triggered a launch sequence. She watched through the onboard surveillance systems as two massive hull plates swung open immediately below the lifeboat, revealing blackness beyond.

The cradle opened, releasing the lifeboat, which moved rapidly away from the ship. After a moment the lifeboat's thrusters pushed it further away from the *Beauregard*, at an accelerating speed.

She switched to the lifeboat's own sensor arrays in time to see light blossom all along the *Beauregard*'s belly as emergency explosive charges blew through several hull plates. The nova drive came tumbling out seconds later, accompanied by a storm of shattered electronics and escaping air.

She ordered the lifeboat to give chase.

Megan? Do you hear me?

It was Tarrant again.

You think I'm finished, but I'm not. I've come through worse and survived. I'll kill you a thousand different ways, over and over and—

She cut the connection before he could finish.

It took a good fifteen minutes to rendezvous with the rogue nova drive, which had stabilized sufficiently to cease spinning and match course with Megan's lifeboat. The cage to the rear of the life-support units opened wide, like the leaves of a flower spun from silver mesh, closing around the drive as it was manoeuvred into position.

Megan worked feverishly, running a systems update that allowed the drive to integrate with the lifeboat's low-level AI. Once that was completed, crude drive-spines dotted around the lifeboat's hull flickered with eerie lightning, sucking energy out of the interstellar void.

The stars shimmered and changed. Megan laughed, pounding the interior of her life-support unit with her fists. But the laughter turned to sobs, with tears cascading down her cheeks.

She forced herself to take deep, even breaths, then activated the cryonic circuits. She was now going to sleep for a long, long time, but get home she would. And when she awoke under some different star, with the familiar chatter of human worlds filling the comms circuits, she would remember Bash and ask his spirit to forgive her – before she set about picking up whatever pieces remained of her former life.

TWENTY-ONE

Gabrielle

2763 (the present)

A few hours after Gabrielle, the Speaker-Elect of the Sacerdotal Demarchy of Uchida, had been taken on board a dropship by the man she had known as Karl Petrova, but who was in truth some stranger named Tarrant, she felt the ship begin to rumble around her.

She had run from Tarrant after telling him she was pregnant with his child, and hidden herself within a storage locker in another part of the dropship. She had curled up in a ball in the zero gravity, her eyes still full of the images Tarrant had shown her – of vast waves spreading inland through the Demarchy, crushing everything and wiping whole cities and towns out of existence.

He was, in some way she did not yet understand, responsible for this devastation. That made her, in a sense, an accessory to the worst of all imaginable crimes.

This thought was more than she could bear, and she determined to find an airlock and throw herself out into the vacuum without a suit – or hunt for something sharp enough to cut through the tender flesh of her wrists. But, even as she entertained these thoughts, another part of her felt a deep determination to go on living so as to resist whatever Tarrant had planned for her, with all her might.

Tarrant came and searched her out, after a while.

'You have a choice,' he declared, staring down at her. 'Either you ride back down in the cockpit with us, or you'll go back inside the medbox if you don't behave yourself.'

If you don't behave yourself. As if she were still a child.

She blinked away angry tears, her hand reaching instinctively to protect her belly. 'But if I spend too much time inside a medbox, mightn't it hurt my—?'

'I already told you I don't care about that,' he snapped, gripping the frame of the doorway one-handed.

Gabrielle wondered what kind of man he had been before becoming the one she had known as Karl Petrova. Had he a family, perhaps, or children? She found that difficult to imagine.

'I'll behave,' she said quietly, unable to keep a slight edge out of her voice. 'Where are we going?'

'Back down to Redstone, before very long.' He seemed stiff, reserved, as if holding something back. 'Somewhere a long way from Dios, in fact, around the other side of the world.'

'To meet more of your Freehold friends?'

'Clean up and get yourself to the cockpit,' he demanded, stepping back out of the storage cupboard. 'And don't be long. I don't want to have to come looking for you again.'

Gaby found her way to the dropship's head and studied herself in the tiny mirror. She looked like a wreck: her skin was puffy and bruised, her hair a tangled mess from its immersion in the icy river water. She dug around inside several of the drawers until she found a disposable comb, along with a pair of scissors.

She picked up the scissors, studying them beneath the head's unforgiving light. They were small, cheaply fabricated, but sharp. How easy it would be, she thought, to draw their razor-sharp edges through the soft tissue of her wrist . . .

No. She felt a flare of anger, both at herself and at Tarrant. In a way, that would feel like letting him win.

She put the scissors back down, then tried to pull the comb through the knots in her hair. It proved to be a hopeless task and she stared at her reflection in despair. She looked like some discarded rag doll come to life, wrapped in the folds of oversized coveralls. How could she have fallen so very far?

She ran some water, which formed a wobbling globe as it emerged from the tap, then dipped her hands into it, in the way she had seen people doing via the Tabernacle, before moistening her eyes and cheeks. Pressing a button below the mirror activated a device that sucked the remaining moisture away.

She picked up the scissors and began to work them through a clump of hair, cutting it close to her scalp. The strands came away easily, and she stared at her reflection once more, remembering how long and lustrous her hair had been. But that had been another person, another life.

She kept on cutting, thrusting each severed clump of hair into a chute marked DISPOSAL. It whined briefly before sucking them away.

Slowly, a new person emerged in the mirror: boyish in looks, with hair curling around her ears and sticking up on top in spiky clumps. The grooves and lines of her implants were much more visible than before, making her appear somehow strange and alien.

With each whir of the disposal unit, another chunk of her past life was sucked away: Thijs, Karl Petrova, all those petty little restrictions she had endured, the oppressive weight of Mater Cassanas's watchful gaze (was the old woman even still alive?). On finishing, she looked again at that unfamiliar reflection and thought: *This is the face of a murderer. This is the face of a woman whose greatest love committed genocide.*

But, instead of seeing a stranger, she felt as if she were seeing herself clearly for the very first time.

She made her way back through the ship to the cockpit, seeing as she entered that the man named Briggs was now seated on another couch, surrounded by such a density of projected data that he was almost invisible behind it all.

Tarrant's eyes widened slightly when he saw what she had done to her appearance, but he recovered quickly. 'You took your goddamn time,' he snarled.

I'm sorry, she almost said, but checked herself.

As she climbed into an unoccupied couch, several virtual panels appeared around her, demonstrating how to secure herself properly. Then she glanced over at Briggs and saw that some of the projections surrounding him were maps of various terrains, mostly containing snow-capped mountains and deep river valleys. She recognized these images as the Montos de Frenezo: a part of Redstone that was particularly mountainous and extremely inhospitable, even compared to the rest of the planet. But it had the advantage – from the Freehold's point of view – of being riddled with caverns and caves and uncountable hiding places. This was the base whence they struck out against the Demarchy, as well as the other Uchidan states.

Other views showed Redstone's horizon gradually losing its curvature, the deep black of orbital space sliding out of view as the dropship descended. The entire craft shivered around her as it bit once more into atmosphere.

It wasn't long before Gabrielle again felt the familiar tug of gravity. The views around Briggs had changed again, now showing clouds punctuated by occasional sharp-edged mountain ridges.

They banked, dropping through the cloud layer and heading towards a broad valley lying between two taller peaks, their slopes littered with ancient scree. The dropship shuddered violently as its drive-fields reduced its rate of descent prior to a final landing.

The craft around her quivered one last time as it dropped onto frozen and stony soil, its bulkheads creaking and pinging as if in protest.

Tarrant quickly and expertly released himself from his restraints, then turned to point towards her. 'Out.'

Briggs had unbuckled himself almost before the dropship had settled into place, data still rippling around him as he lifted himself out of his couch by grasping hold of the two straps dangling overhead. He gave Tarrant a brief nod, then exited the cockpit while Gabrielle was still struggling with her own restraints.

Tarrant grew impatient waiting, and quickly and expertly

unfastened her. Gabrielle glanced past his shoulder at the video feeds showing the outside of the dropship, which were still running above Briggs's couch. She saw half a dozen ancient-looking trucks, two-storey affairs possessing tractor wheels, now approaching them along the valley floor. They had been painted to match the mottled reddish-browns and whites of the mountains and, even from a distance, it was clear that they had been repaired and re-repaired many times.

'What now?' she asked, standing.

'Follow Briggs,' he said, gesturing to the open hatch.

They found Briggs waiting for them at the airlock, already clad in cold-weather gear and with a breather mask strapped in place. Tarrant quickly followed suit, then supervised Gabrielle as she did the same.

When they finally stepped out onto the ramp, she saw the morning sun had barely risen over the peaks towering above them on either side. The sight of them made her catch her breath. The trucks she had seen through the cockpit monitors had rolled to a halt nearby, while several bearded Freeholders with hard eyes and old-fashioned breather masks stood waiting.

One of the Freeholders came over and took Tarrant in a bear hug, clapping him soundly on the back.

'Ah, it's been a long time, Cuyàs,' said Tarrant.

The man Cuyàs turned to look at Gabrielle. 'This can't be her, Gregor,' he said, his accent sounding thick and guttural to her ears. 'All this effort, just so you can kidnap some girl?'

'Remember, it's what's in her head that counts,' Tarrant replied.

Cuyàs grinned. 'I'll admit I had my doubts, Gregor. But I've never seen anything so astonishing in all my life. We didn't just hurt the Demarchy – we near as damn *destroyed* it. And we never could have managed it without you.' He looked around. 'However, we should not tarry here. We need to go before the orbital platforms zero in on us. Let's not fuck up, this close to our final victory, eh?'

With that, he turned to his men – Gaby could see at least a dozen of them, all heavily armed, their eyes scanning the nearby peaks – and barked a series of commands. Several of the men darted past them to board the dropship.

'We have a camp not far from here,' said Cuyàs, nodding towards the nearest of the trucks. He snapped his fingers at two of the remaining soldiers, and jabbed a finger at Gabrielle. Two of the men trotted forward, each taking hold of one of her arms and pulling her along after Tarrant and Cuyàs, as they made for the truck.

'And my friends?' asked Tarrant (*Gregor* Tarrant, it seemed, for Gabrielle had not failed to notice the Freeholder addressing him by that name). 'Are they here yet?'

Cuyàs shook his head. 'No, but they should be arriving from orbit shortly.' He glanced again at Gabrielle. 'Can we be certain the Accord won't come looking for her?'

'The Grand Barge is by now a pile of kindling spread all up and down the Ka River,' Tarrant replied. 'We took care of Thijs and the others first, in case they might have had a chance of getting away before the waves hit. Anyone mounting a rescue operation is going to assume she's dead, along with everyone else on board. When do you intend to begin the main assault?'

They came to a stop by the designated truck. 'We've had units spread all through the hills bordering the Demarchy for a good while now. And some have already started to push deep into their territory, now the waters are beginning to recede. The rest of us are currently mobilizing, and we should be moving en masse in just another few days. In the meantime we've been picking off a few scattered Demarchy troops and outposts – not that there's much fight left in the few who survived.'

'Well,' said Tarrant, 'sounds to me like you should be able to walk right in there.'

'Except,' Cuyàs pointed out, 'we still have the Accord to deal with, which remains my greatest concern.'

'The important thing to remember,' said Tarrant, 'is that they don't give a damn about the Demarchy. All they care about is that

Magi ship and whatever information it may have locked away inside it. Remember to keep your forces at a distance from it – don't do *anything* that might give the Accord reason to think you might cause a problem for it. Then there should be a relatively smooth transition of power.'

'And yourself?' asked Cuyàs. 'Are you going to stick around for the fight?'

Tarrant laughed and shook his head. 'No, I'm going off-world. I don't think it's at all likely I'll be back.'

Cuyàs nodded, something glinting in his eye. 'Perhaps that's for the best.' He glanced again at Gabrielle. 'And the girl?'

'She goes with me.'

'Amazing to think some mere child could be so important.' Cuyàs's eyes flicked back to Tarrant. 'Or that the contents of her mind could be so enormously valuable.'

Gabrielle sensed a new tension in the air, which made the muscles of her belly tighten in fear. Cuyàs was making a point of not looking at her. *He's thinking of taking me away from Tarrant*, she thought.

'Perhaps I should remind you,' Tarrant stepped closer to Cuyàs, his voice low and dangerous, 'that Otto Schelling will be here shortly. *If* anything were to go wrong, or if there were to be any . . . *disagreements*, then I feel sure he would be more than happy to provide the Accord as well as the surviving Uchidan states with the precise coordinates of your primary bases of operations.'

The two men glared at each other above fixed smiles. Then light flared from behind them, and Gabrielle turned to see the dropship from which they had just disembarked lifting up and accelerating into the sky.

The tension broke, and Cuyàs laughed. 'That's what I like about you,' he said, grinning. 'You're a snake, Gregor Tarrant, and too damn smart for your own good.'

Tarrant took hold of Gabrielle's arm, guiding her up a ramp and into the rear of the truck, where she took a seat on one of the two facing benches. A couple of the Freeholders meanwhile climbed into the front cabin, where Tarrant joined them, chatting with them briefly as the truck ground into motion.

'He was going to take me from you, wasn't he?' said Gaby, her voice full of scorn after Tarrant had stepped back through, to take a seat opposite her.

'You heard what I said. He knows it would be over for them. He was just testing to see how far he could push me.'

'You don't feel even an ounce of regret for everything you've done, do you?'

'It's a fact of life that innocent people get hurt on the path towards a greater good, Gabrielle. I really wish it was otherwise.'

He actually believes that, she realized. And there was nothing she could do or say that would change his mind or cause him to see things any differently.

She stared out of the window of the truck, thinking of the life growing inside her belly, and wondered if she would live long enough to ever see its face.

TWENTY-TWO

Megan

Megan boosted Sarbakshian's jump-car high into Redstone's stratosphere, the force of acceleration crushing her back into her seat. The pressure relented as the landscape became more curved, until finally the car reached low orbit and she became weightless.

She watched the dawn chase the night across the planet's northern hemisphere. Even from this altitude, the damage done to the Demarchy was clearly enormous. Great brown and grey streaks mottled the entire west coast of the continent on which the Demarchy lay. The lights of cities and outlying settlements speckled the globe everywhere but along that coast. She dreaded to think of what it must be like for the few survivors wandering through the ruins down there.

She began thinking about what lay ahead. The Tabernacle was rife with speculation about just when the Accord would send heavy forces into the Montos de Frenezo to strike back against the Freehold forces hiding there. She had, at most, a few days to track Bash down and get him out before that entire mountain range became one huge battleground.

Redstone revolved beneath her, the Demarchy slipping into night while another, craggier continent came into view. The jump-car began dipping downwards, shaped-fields flickering into life all around its hull as it roared on through the upper reaches of the atmosphere.

Less than two hours after departing Aguirre, the vehicle was cruising just a few hundred metres above a gorge in the foothills of the Montos de Frenezo. A river lying to the east sparkled blue and white.

Alerts began to flower around Megan, warning her that she was entering an Accord restricted zone. She swept them away, focusing instead on the dusty jagged peaks ahead. She was now fewer than a hundred klicks from where Sarbakshian's tracer told her that Sifra's dropship had only recently touched down.

Something appeared then on the jump-car's radar, about a hundred and fifty kilometres south-west of her current location. Whatever it was, it was clearly too small to be carrying passengers.

The radar display floating before her blinked and changed. The blip was now only a hundred and thirty kilometres away, and closing in on her fast.

She felt her brow prickle with sweat. That had to mean it was a missile of some kind. Possibly it had been launched automatically, but almost certainly it belonged to the Freehold.

She tried to see if she could pick up echoes from its internal circuitry, something that might allow her to gain access to its control systems and divert it. But when that didn't work, she wasn't really surprised. Weapons and bombs had actually become dumber and cruder over the past few centuries, making them proof them against such attempts at remote intervention. The best she could hope for was to outrun it.

The blip jumped again. Suddenly it was a great deal closer, altering its course slightly to match hers, and still closing.

Definitely a missile, she thought. However fast Sarbakshian's pride and joy might be, the missile was clearly a lot faster. She could try and outmanoeuvre it, but the g-forces required would render her unconscious, possibly even kill her.

That left her with a simple choice: land now or die.

The blip moved once more. It was now just ninety kilometres away.

She pushed a map of the mountain range into the air next to her, doing her best to stay calm and not panic. She saw a glowing dot that represented Sifra's dropship, while another dot represented the encroaching missile.

She felt a jolt of shock when she realized just how fast it was closing. Seventy-five kilometres . . .

Sixty-five . . .

Sixty . . .

She was beginning to wonder if she would have time even to land before it hit her.

She brought the jump-car right down until it was skimming just above the ground. Meanwhile the gorge had disappeared behind her, the jump-car nosing over jumbled peaks, and dipping down again as it followed the course of a winding river valley.

The valley walls began to widen and become less steep, merging with the foothills of a tall and particularly forbidding-looking peak rising to the East.

Megan searched frantically for some place flat enough for her to land. The missile was now only twenty-five kilometres away, and she could almost feel it nosing up behind her.

There. She spotted a flat pebbled area to the north-west, where the valley twisted to one side. She set the jump-car instantly to land, its propulsion fields flickering as it lost speed.

Fifteen kilometres. Megan realized she was holding her breath.

She pulled herself out of her seat and ran into the hold, locating the secret bulkhead door and hauling out as many of Sarbakshian's weapons as she could. She threw them through the doorway leading into the cockpit.

Ten kilometres. She looked up front and saw dust blowing up around the windshield, as the jump-car settled onto the hard-frozen soil. She dumped the armful of weaponry she held and scrabbled for her cold-weather gear, fumbling it on as fast as she could, before pulling up the hood and fastening it at the front. She searched around for her breather mask, and for one terrible, lurching moment, was unable to find it. Then a cry of relief when she realized she had folded it up earlier and stuffed it in one pocket of her jacket.

Five kilometres, and closing fast. This wasn't at all how she'd imagined things would pan out.

She hit the emergency release button on the car's hatch. It swung open, air gusting outwards. She had a rifle slung over one shoulder, and several of the short-use beam weapons stuffed into any available pocket that wasn't already jammed full of ammunition. Lastly, she grabbed up a rucksack she'd at least had the foresight to load with a couple of bottles of water and some survival rations, and threw it down onto the barren grey soil, before jumping down and snatching it up again.

She started to run, her legs pumping as fast as they would go. All she had to do now was get clear in time and—

Something picked her up and sent her hurtling against a boulder. White light flared all around her, followed by a wave of intense heat. She rolled onto her front, gloved fingers digging into the half-frozen soil . . . and felt darkness steal over her.

When Megan finally regained consciousness, she saw that the sun had moved a considerable distance further across the sky.

She stared around in a daze for some moments, then struggled to push herself upright. Something in her shoulder hurt like hell, particularly if she tried turning her head to the right.

Checking the inbuilt interface on her cold-weather gear, she found that its built-in heating circuits had kicked in automatically. It was the only reason she was still alive.

Megan struggled to her feet by leaning against the boulder next to her, before taking a look around. Her breath rasped loudly inside her breather mask. A trail of dark smoke rose into the sky from a mass of tangled wreckage that was no longer recognizable as the jump-car.

Damn it, she thought.

She searched around until she found the rifle she'd taken from the vehicle, then found her rucksack lying nearby and strapped it back on.

Her first thought was to put as much distance between herself and the wreck as possible, in case someone was already on their way to check for survivors. That meant getting as far away from the crash site as she could manage, regardless of the multitude of aches and pains afflicting her.

By the time Megan reached the crest of a hill, just ten minutes later, she was utterly exhausted. She tried to access the Tabernacle, but was unsurprised to find she couldn't, having already been warned that the Freehold jammed anything more advanced than analogue radio within range of their hideouts.

Glancing around the slopes below the hill, there was nothing to be seen but desolate terrain, stretching out to the horizon. She knew her circumstances were hopeless: lost in an utterly inhospitable environment and surrounded on all sides by fanatical and murderous Freeholders. But she had to keep moving, or give up any hope of staying alive.

Eventually she started to make her way down the other side, looking east along the length of a valley, in the same direction she had been flying before getting shot down. It was somewhere in that direction that Sifra's dropship had landed.

The walking got a little easier after another half-hour, but for all she knew it might take days to reach the dropship – assuming it was even still there, by the time she reached its landing point.

A small voice in her head urged her to give up. Sifra surely wouldn't have landed in the middle of nowhere; he'd have aimed for one of the Freehold's main mountain bases, which meant Bash was by now almost certainly under the guard of God knew how many murderous lunatics adorned with neck tattoos.

As the sun kept moving across the sky, she stopped frequently to rest. Whenever she glanced behind her, she could still see a rising column of smoke from the downed jump-car. It didn't look that far away at all.

Give up, that same small voice kept insisting. *Find a way back home.*

But she couldn't do that. Not with so very much at stake.

The valley walls grew steeper, with narrow, rubble-filled ravines branching off to each side. A little while later, she came to a halt, seeing a column of dust rising up ahead.

With a start, she realized that it came from a line of trucks making their way in her direction. She stood and watched numbly as one of the vehicles broke ahead of the pack, bouncing its way straight towards her.

She licked suddenly dry lips. They had clearly spotted her. Tiny black dots, which had been hovering above the convoy like fireflies swarming above a campfire, were now moving in her direction as well: drones, and almost certainly hunter-killers at that. Against them, the weapons she carried would be worse than useless.

Megan glanced around frantically, noticing a dense thicket of desiccated jug-leaf bushes spreading all across one side of the hill. She darted towards them. They wouldn't provide much cover, but it might be enough to fool the drones for a few minutes until she could figure something out.

She pushed her way in deep amongst the tangled bushes, their dry branches scratching viciously at her exposed flesh. From there she saw a dark shape flying immediately overhead, before it doubled back again. A mechanized voice said something unintelligible; by the sound of it, the drone's speech circuits were shot to hell.

Through the dense tangle of bushes, she could barely make out the dark shape of the machine, but from its movements she guessed it must be zeroing in on her, most probably by detecting her heat signature.

She aimed the rifle and fired. The drone spun in the air for a moment, then darted away.

Megan made a break for it, snow and dirt puffing around her ankles as she dived from cover. To lighten her load, she deliberately left her rucksack, containing its vital supply of water and food, among the bushes. She knew she'd be dead in no more than a day or two out in the open without her supplies, but maybe if she could get away from those drones and trucks, she could double back after nightfall and retrieve them.

She slid and half fell or half ran down the hillside, aiming for one of the ravines. Some of the boulders filling each ravine were the size of houses, but there were enough gaps between them to let her find her way through – and there would be no way for the trucks to follow her.

A second drone now overtook her, dropping in height as it slowed and turned back towards her. Lenses suspended beneath its body zeroed in on her face. She raised her rifle again.

Before she could take aim and fire, something hit her hard in the back, and sent her crashing to all fours. She rolled onto her side and saw that a third drone had come up on her from behind. Vortexes of dust went spinning up from the ground beneath where the two drones now hovered, stationary.

Her breath rasping harshly, the back of one shoulder icy-cold and numb where something had struck it, she listened helplessly to the sound of heavy treads crunching over icy soil as a truck pulled up nearby. She heard its doors opening and slamming shut, followed by the sound of footsteps coming closer.

A shadow fell across her, and Megan looked up into the familiar face of Gregor Tarrant, only partly hidden behind a breather mask.

'I used to dream of a day like this,' he began, his voice strangely distorted. 'I used to think about all the ways I could kill you. But now I think I just feel sorry for you. Megan, what the hell are you doing all the way out here?'

'Fuck you,' she rasped. 'I left you for dead. You should have stayed that way.'

She glanced past him, towards the truck, where two men, both clearly Freeholders, had also disembarked. They stood on either side of a girl, in her early twenties perhaps, her eyes wide and visibly frightened above her breather mask. From the way the two men held her, she was clearly a prisoner of some kind. The tufts of roughly cut hair sticking out from her scalp could not conceal the fact that she was also a machine-head. Megan instantly tried to link to her but found that she couldn't.

There was something hauntingly familiar about the girl, and after a moment it hit her. She had seen the girl's face regularly via the Tabernacle's news feeds. Here in front of her stood the Speaker-Elect of the Demarchy of Uchida . . .

Just as Megan herself had once been, until she found a way to escape.

TWENTY-THREE

Megan

The two Freeholders left the other girl in Tarrant's care while they hauled Megan up from the ground, before carrying her into the back of another truck that pulled up next to the first. They strapped her into a seat in the rear and climbed into the front cabin.

The truck reversed, then turned to rejoin the rest of the convoy, which had meanwhile come to a halt. Every time the vehicle bumped over a rock, a spike of agony shot through Megan's injured shoulder.

Seeing Tarrant again was one thing. Seeing him in the company of the supposedly deceased Speaker-Elect was something she was having trouble either processing or understanding.

Megan watched through a window as they bounced along the valley floor. The convoy got under way again and, after another hour, they began to make their way down through a narrow gulch, following the course of a dried-out riverbed before finally arriving at the base of a high cliff, above which mountainous slopes became lost in misty clouds.

A huge tented shape sat on the floor of the riverbed, immediately beneath a broad overhang of the cliff. It was only as the truck drew closer to this vast canvas shroud, painted the same colours as the surrounding landscape, that Megan could see the stanchions of a dropship peeking out from underneath. She guessed immediately it was the one that Sifra had used to transport her to Redstone.

The truck continued past the dropship, following a trail leading into a wide passageway carved out of the mountainside right beneath the overhang. The passageway angled downwards, its interior illuminated by a long sequence of lights strung from the arched roof, and eventually dwindling out of sight. A subtle shift in the pitch of the truck's engine noise told Megan they had passed through a pressure field.

The truck continued through a number of caverns, some natural and some clearly drilled out of the bare rock, before coming to a halt in a low, wide tunnel that clearly doubled as a makeshift hospital. A few dozen canvas cots had been arranged in rows against a wall, along with – of all things – an actual operating table, surrounded by trays of surgical instruments and bits and pieces of ancient-looking equipment. The two Freeholders left Megan in the charge of a single watchful guard and a gaunt, elderly-looking man who told her he would tend to her wounds.

She pulled off her breather mask as she perched on the edge of a cot while the doctor – at least, she *assumed* he was a doctor – examined her shoulder. She sat with folded arms concealing her breasts, her shirt lying by her side, till he informed her she had nothing more than a sprained shoulder and some severe bruising. It seemed the drone had used gel-capsule bullets, good for incapacitating people while leaving little in the way of actual physical damage.

He pushed an ice compress against her shoulder, then gave her some bitter liquid to drink before telling her to catch some sleep. The guard then cuffed one of her wrists to the rail of the cot and left her there.

At least they weren't going to kill her instantly. That had to count for something, even if she suspected that Sifra was behind this decision. He had made it clear, after all, that he still had need for both herself and Bash.

Studying the ancient scars on the hands and face of the Freehold doctor, it had occurred to Megan that if the man had ever visited a body clinic, he hadn't been back there for a very long time indeed. It wasn't really until her guard cuffed her to the cot, giving her an opportunity to notice that one of his ears consisted of little more than scar tissue, that she understood how little access these people had to modern medical technology. All they had were primitive, half-forgotten surgical and medicinal techniques that spoke of dreadful deprivation.

She glanced towards the nearby operating table and shuddered to think of what they might have done to her if her injuries had been more serious.

Megan awoke some hours later, to hear the distant booming and hissing of what might be machinery, or equally well some subterranean river coursing through the bowels of the Montos de Frenezo.

Someone nearby cleared his throat, and she stifled a grunt of shock when she saw Tarrant sitting on the edge of a cot next to her own.

'Hello, Megan,' said Tarrant. 'Long time no see.'

He had changed since she had last seen him: any fat on his face had diminished with age, leaving him hollow-cheeked and hungry-looking. But his eyes remained just as startling as on their first encounter aboard the *Beauregard*.

'Gregor,' she acknowledged haltingly. 'Come to gloat?'

There was no sign of her guard or anyone else. They were all alone.

'Anil made the mistake of underestimating you when he left you alone on that dropship,' he said, then shook his head slowly. 'He won't make that same mistake again, and neither will I. The only thing keeping him from killing you is his loyalty to the General.'

'That girl . . .' said Megan. 'The one who came out of the truck with you . . .?'

'Is none of your business,' Tarrant replied. He stood up and came to stand beside her, reaching down to stroke her cheek with one finger. She flinched away.

'Do you know, Megan,' he said, 'how very easy it would be for me to kill you right now?'

She squirmed as far away from him as she could get, given she still had one hand cuffed to the cot's metal rail. 'You had something to do with what happened to the Demarchy, didn't you?' she asked him. 'That's why you're working with the Freehold. You're even more of a murderous, deceitful, untrustworthy son of a bitch than I thought.'

'Mr Tarrant can't take all of the credit for the Demarchy,' said another voice, coming closer.

Megan twisted the other way to see a man with bristly white hair approach from out of the shadows. Anil Sifra and several heavily armed Freeholders followed in his wake.

'As a matter of fact,' the white-haired man continued, as he came to a halt before her cot, 'it took dozens of people working in unison for over two years to bring about the events of the past few days.' He nodded towards Tarrant. 'That's not to say that Gregor's role wasn't vital.'

'You're Otto Schelling,' Megan said, realizing. 'You disappeared along with a bunch of nova mines, right after strenuously denying they ever existed.'

Schelling gazed down at her. 'I prefer to be addressed as *General* Schelling. You've caused me more trouble than I could have believed was possible, Miss Jacinth. You wouldn't be alive right now if not for the fact we still have a use for you.'

'Worse luck,' said Sifra tonelessly.

'What the hell are you talking about?' said Megan.

'Gregor,' said the General, 'get someone to uncuff her from that cot, would you?'

Tarrant gave him a tight-lipped glance. 'Sir, it's too much of a risk having her here. We don't need her, and it's better all round if we find some other way of—'

'You've already made your objections abundantly clear,' snapped Schelling. 'Now do what the hell you're told.' He gave Megan a brittle smile. 'And then we can find somewhere comfortable to continue our conversation.'

*

Two heavily armed Freeholders led her downslope, with Sifra, Tarrant and General Schelling taking the lead. They passed a cluster of digging machines that stood quiescent amidst piles of rubble, before turning into a cathedral-sized cavern made eerily beautiful by patches of bioluminescent algae clinging to its walls and ceiling.

They were heading, she realized, towards a huddle of prefab buildings erected in the centre of the cavern. Standing on a platform next to one of these buildings was a huge industrial-scale fabricator that looked both newer and in far better condition than anything else she had seen since entering the Freehold base.

Tarrant led her inside one of the buildings, while the soldiers waited outside. She found herself ushered into a small bare room, followed by Schelling and Sifra.

'Are we secure in here?' Schelling demanded, as Tarrant pushed the door shut.

Tarrant nodded. 'It checks clean for listening devices, General. Our hosts won't be able to listen in.'

Megan wondered what they had to say that they didn't want even the Freehold to overhear.

'Good,' said Schelling, stepping over to a small table in one corner and picking up a bottle. He poured a splash of its contents into three glasses, before handing one each to Tarrant and Sifra. Then he turned to Megan and gestured with his own glass towards a chair set against the wall. 'Sit,' he said.

'I'd rather stand,' said Megan.

'You can either sit,' said Schelling menacingly, 'or I can ask Anil to work you over with his gloves. He's still very upset about the state you left his dropship in, you know. So the choice is yours.'

Megan stared at him for a moment, then sat down.

'Gentlemen,' said Schelling, turning to the others and raising his glass. 'To a job exceedingly well done. I almost can't believe it went as well as it did.'

They drank, but Tarrant still looked troubled. 'Sir . . .'

'I know I've kept some things from you while you've been stuck here on Redstone, Gregor,' Schelling interrupted him, 'but there were good reasons for it. If we'd told you we were intending to bring Jacinth here to Redstone, you might have tried to stop us.'

Schelling next turned to Megan, raising his glass to her too. 'Although I must say it was very kind of you, Miss Jacinth, to deliver yourself to the exact place we were intending to bring you anyway.'

The muscles in Tarrant's jaw worked noticeably for a moment before he replied. 'Sir, myself and Anil were stuck on that goddamn wreck for two years – *two fucking years* – before rescue came. All because of her,' he said, jabbing his glass in Megan's direction. 'You cannot expect me to ignore that fact.'

'Gregor,' said Schelling, 'you've been a sterling example to us all, but you need to put some things behind you. You have to see our goals clearly. It's what lies ahead of us that matters now.'

He turned again to Megan. 'A while back, I initiated a research programme to try and re-establish communications with the Wanderer through Mr Bashir, once it became clear he was still linked to it in some way.' He shook his head. 'Unfortunately, the results were less than positive.'

'So Anil told me already. You murdered a bunch of machine-heads in the process.'

Schelling ignored that remark. 'All of which makes your own ability to communicate with the Wanderer via Bashir, without losing either your mind or your life, somewhat unique for reasons we do not as yet understand. The question for us now is, can you repeat the trick?'

'What we really need to know,' said Sifra, his eyes bright and cruel and alert, 'is what the hell makes her so different from the rest?'

'The last thing I want,' said Megan, 'is to do anything to help a bunch of genocidal murderers.'

'Anil seems to believe you were planning on paying a visit to the Wanderer yourself,' said Schelling.

'Anil is a delusional psychopath who threatened to burn Bash's face and limbs off if I didn't tell him exactly what he wanted to hear,' she retorted sharply. 'I'll bet he didn't mention *that*.'

Schelling's face remained impassive, but she saw the fury in his gaze as he turned to look at Sifra, who struggled to remain silent.

'Sir—' said Sifra.

'We'll talk later,' the General interrupted sharply. 'For now, shut the hell up.' He turned back to Megan. 'Your job will be to negotiate with the Wanderer on our behalf, via Bashir.'

'Go to hell,' said Megan.

Schelling smiled thinly. 'It's not that we require your cooperation, Miss Jacinth. It's just that it would make life easier.'

Megan stared off into a corner of the room, as if dismissing him.

Schelling shook his head and sighed as if washing his hands of her. 'I think this is where you come in, Anil.'

'With pleasure,' said Sifra, pulling on his gloves and stepping towards her.

Megan jumped up from her chair, but Sifra caught her by the arm, drawing her in close as if embracing her. She tried to scream as the pain hit, but the sound stalled in her throat.

She blacked out for a few seconds. When she came to, she was slumped on the floor, dazed and sick, her heart pounding. Sifra stood over her, his heavy-lidded eyes full of anticipation.

'Anil can keep this up indefinitely until you decide to cooperate,' said Schelling, staring down at her. 'There's too much at stake here to waste on niceties. Do we have an understanding?'

'Yes,' she said, her voice barely above a whisper.

Schelling nodded. 'The Three Star Alliance, Miss Jacinth, has been reduced to little more than a vassal state of the Accord – thanks largely to you. Conquered, with barely a shot fired. We could have turned things around if we'd succeeded in dealing with the Wanderer. This, then, is your opportunity to make up for your past crimes.'

The floor felt cold and hard beneath Megan's splayed fingers. 'The Wanderer attacked us,' she said, twisting her head round to stare up at him. 'It was never going to deal with us. All I did was take advantage of what was already inevitable. All it cared about was acquiring the *Beauregard*'s nova drive. Don't you understand that?'

'Indeed I do. Which is why the next time we go out there, things will be different. For one, we're taking along one of those nova mines you mentioned a moment ago. The Wanderer might be able to survive an anti-matter detonation, but I suspect the same couldn't be said as regards an exploding star.'

Schelling gave her a supercilious grin. 'Not to mention,' he continued, 'that we have remote probes in place showing the Wanderer is still engaged in a process of self-repair that began immediately following your last encounter, making it especially vulnerable. I suppose it's a sign of just how badly we hurt it that it's still hiding in the same star system, instead of fleeing into interstellar space.'

'What do you think the Accord is going to do to you and the Freehold,' she asked, 'once it figures out that you helped the Freehold commit genocide against the Demarchy? Do you really think it's going to just stand by while you fly off on yet another expedition?'

'We'll make sure it doesn't find out. And even if one day it does, with luck it'll be long after the Alliance finally has the chance to achieve its full potential, without outside interference.' He took a sip of his drink. 'Recent findings on Alyeska make it clear that the Meridians advanced far more within a few generations of encountering the Wanderer than we previously suspected. With power like that, the Three Star Alliance can, under my command, become the Hundred Star Alliance – and perhaps, one day, the Thousand Star Alliance. The Accord will fade into memory, just like the Consortium before it.'

Megan pulled herself back into the chair with unsteady arms. None of the three men made a move to help her. 'I saw the girl,' she said. 'I recognized her. She's the Demarchy's Speaker-Elect. What does *she* have to do with any of this? Or do you lot just kidnap religious leaders for the hell of it?'

'Because,' said Schelling, 'we need to have something actually to offer the Wanderer, don't we?'

'Sir,' said Tarrant, struggling to keep his voice level, 'she does *not* need to know about—'

'Shut up, Gregor,' said Schelling. 'If she's going to negotiate with the Wanderer for us, she needs to know exactly what it is we have to offer. And we'll negotiate those terms before we even depart Redstone, Miss Jacinth.'

Which means, thought Megan, *that Bash is almost certainly somewhere close by*. 'Then tell me about the girl,' she said.

'We took her on the eve of Ascension Day,' said Schelling. 'I'm assuming, since you know who she is, that you're aware of the significance of that day?'

'It's when the Speaker-Elect goes to the Magi ship in Dios,' said Megan, struggling to control her deepest emotions. 'The one the Demarchy likes to call the Ship of the Covenant.'

'And then,' said Schelling, his voice assuming a mocking tone, 'if things had gone to plan, she would have ascended bodily to Heaven, in front of a select group of witnesses who would testify to that fact.'

Sifra snickered quietly from the other side of the room.

'Or at least that's the official explanation,' Schelling continued. 'Gregor posed undercover as the girl's personal guard for some years, and thus uncovered the truth. It turns out that this process of "merging" with the ship in reality wipes the Speaker's personality and replaces it with that of a woman called Dakota Merrick. Are you at all familiar with that name?'

'She recovered the first Magi ship,' Megan replied, in a monotone.

'Somehow, sometime in the past, presumably before it crash-landed on Redstone, Merrick's mind became absorbed into the Ship of the Covenant. All the Speakers – including the girl Gabrielle that you saw – are her genetic clones. They are identical except for their minds, which develop naturally, and their physical appearance, which is surgically altered from Speaker to Speaker to prevent anyone outside an inner circle within the Demarchy discovering the truth of what they really are. Are you following me so far?'

Megan made herself nod, despite her mounting sense of horror.

'The girl is of no value as she is, so we ourselves are going to take her to Dios, and to the Ship of the Covenant. That would have been impossible for us if the Demarchy still existed, but now the ship is unguarded, we should have total control over the bonding process. Once it's complete, and the girl's mind has been replaced by that of Merrick, she'll be able to act as a bridge via which the Wanderer will be able to access directly the vast quantity of data believed to reside within every Magi ship still in existence.'

'So all this,' said Megan, 'wiping out the Demarchy, tricking me into coming after Bash, killing all those people – it was all just so you could kidnap that girl and "give" her to the Wanderer?'

'Precisely.' Schelling nodded. 'Of course, by then she'll have Merrick's mind, but we plan to transport her there sleeping inside a medbox.'

'You're insane. Why the hell do you think the Wanderer gives a damn about the Magi ships?'

'When you first communicated with the Wanderer,' said Schelling, 'you told Gregor about a war between the Makers and the Core Transcendence, the very civilization responsible for creating the Wanderer. Do I have the details right?'

'So far,' agreed Megan.

'The Magi ships were created as weapons to be used specifically against the Makers, meaning that the Magi and the Core Transcendence shared the same adversary. Surely it's reasonable, then, to think that the information contained within the Ship of the Covenant – or indeed any Magi ship – might prove to be of immense value to the Wanderer?'

Megan was entirely aware how much sense this all made. If not for the inhibitor Tarrant had once shot her with back on the *Beauregard* – and which she had long since had removed – the Wanderer could easily have done the same with her, using her as a direct conduit to the memory banks of any of the surviving Magi ships. And now Schelling and his cronies were going to give that girl to the

Wanderer for the exact same reason, precisely like ancient priests offering up a sacrifice to some volcano god.

'All right, fine,' she replied. 'It makes sense. But why do you even need to take her all the way out there? Bash can be used as a bridge from anywhere, can't he?'

'Bash might be linked directly to the Wanderer,' Schelling replied, 'but Speaker-Elect Gabrielle is not. Therefore, before the Wanderer can make use of her as a conduit into the minds of the Magi ships, we have no choice but to physically transport her to it. After we've merged her with the Ship of the Covenant, of course.'

Megan laughed, the sound echoing faintly through the cave system. 'You fucking idiots,' she said, 'haven't you learned anything? As soon as you're in range of it, it's going to do its damnedest to steal your nova drive. I've seen directly into the mind of that thing, Schelling. It's going to tear your ship apart and kill everyone on board the moment you show your faces.'

Schelling's face coloured. 'I've been as polite with you as I can, Miss Jacinth, but only because you're useful to us. And not because I want your opinion, now or ever.' He glanced at Sifra. 'Is the bridge nearby?'

'We have a specialist checking him over just now,' Sifra replied. 'He's healthy enough, physically anyway, and his implants appear to be at optimum. There's no reason not to start immediately.'

The bridge. Megan tasted something sour in the back of her throat. They couldn't even allow Bash the decency of calling him by his own name. With just that single word, they had managed to remove his last trace of humanity.

'Then we'll do just that,' said Schelling, turning towards the door.

TWENTY-FOUR

Megan

A couple of guards led Megan back out into the main cavern, then into one of the other prefab buildings it contained. She saw two men in the vestibule busily uncrating several medboxes that were clearly brand new. One had already been powered up, its interior glowing softly from within its semi-opaque lid.

These must, she realized, have come from General Schelling himself, as a gift for their Freeholder hosts. The same must also be true of the fabricator she had seen earlier.

They led her further into yet another room. Megan felt her heart skip a beat when she saw Bash seated in a high-backed chair, with virtual panels floating to either side of him.

A device had been fitted on his head that, like the one Tarrant and Sifra had used all those years before, looked like a tangle of black snakes. It was, she recalled, their way of controlling and monitoring Bash's link with the Wanderer.

The elderly doctor who had treated her earlier was leaning over Bash, shining a light into first one eye and then the other. Bash stared blankly ahead during the whole procedure. The doctor nodded to Schelling as he, Tarrant and Sifra entered the room, before stepping past them and heading out of the door.

Tarrant moved up to one of the virtual panels and activated it.

'Miss Jacinth,' said Schelling, indicating a stool against the wall opposite where Bash sat, 'if you will.' He studied her for a moment. 'You *are* going to cooperate, aren't you?'

'Do I have a choice?' she asked.

Schelling studied her pointedly. She sighed and placed herself on the stool.

'You must make it absolutely clear to the Wanderer that the girl is a bridge directly into the mind of a Magi ship,' he told her, 'and therefore to everything they know about the Makers. We'll make an exchange: the girl, and remote access to the Magi ship at Dios, for whatever it gave to the Meridians. Oh, and, Miss Jacinth . . . ?'

Megan eyed him expectantly.

'We have a specialized AI hooked up so as to monitor the dataflow,' Schelling continued. 'We'll be recording everything you say to the Wanderer for future analysis. So if you had any plans to communicate with the Wanderer for your own reasons, don't. Because, I promise you, we'll know.'

'We should start now,' said Tarrant, making a final adjustment. 'He's all ready.'

Megan rested her elbows on her knees, letting her head fall into her hands and taking a couple of deep breaths.

'Whenever you're ready, Megan,' said Tarrant.

She opened herself up, shifting her mental focus into her personal datascape – an artificial void, generated by her implants, that contained doors through which she could access data by whatever means it was made available to her. She pushed her mind towards the door beyond which lay Bash.

She didn't have to wait long for something to happen. For, all of a sudden, she felt that very same sense of an alien presence she had first experienced years before on the *Beauregard*, when they had first jumped into the Wolf-Rayet system where the Wanderer hid. Schelling, the cavern, Redstone . . . all of that was gone.

She floated in silence and darkness, without any sense of her own body. The presence she had sensed changed . . . and became something more familiar.

Something that was not the Wanderer.

A whisper in the dark, which might have been her name.

No, she thought, it couldn't be.

Bash?

Then that familiar presence was gone, replaced by something far more terrifying. There was a sound like moons grinding together, and in the next instant Megan found herself again confronted by the black-and-grey bulk of the Wanderer. Its multitudinous branches seemed to reach out to grasp for her, as if she had somehow crossed tens of thousands of light years in one single, cataclysmic leap.

She tried to scream as a barrage of alien thoughts and sensations flowed into her mind, but she no longer had a voice, or lungs, or even a body.

LOOK for the FOR THE move between MOVE BETWEEN STARS we WE search SEARCH FOR

The tide grew stronger, becoming a torrent of nonsensical data that threatened to overwhelm her.

THE magi MAGI star dwellers THE STAR DWELLERS FIRE that WASHES over OVER

<I have something to trade.> It was like whispering into a tornado, but somehow, she knew, the Wanderer could hear her. <My information in exchange for yours.>

The barrage seemed to lessen somewhat. She steeled herself, then opened up wider, telling it about Gabrielle and the Ship of the Covenant.

There was no reaction, no response. It was like shouting into the wind. The Wanderer's attention began to slip back into the abyss, and she fell, tumbling away.

She opened her eyes to find she had collapsed onto the floor, sweating and shaking and severely dehydrated. Her stool had tumbled on its side next to her.

'Well?' demanded Schelling, standing over her with a look of impatience. 'Did you manage to get a reply?'

'Not exactly. I thought you were recording everything?'

'Yes, but—'

In that moment, she heard a sound like none she'd ever heard before, coming from the other side of the room.

From Bash.

She peered over at him. They all did. He was leaning forward in his seat, with eyes staring and mouth hanging open, a deep bass rumble emerging from somewhere in the depths of his throat like a protracted death rattle.

'Mmm . . . *magi*.' Bash's mouth stretched itself wide, his tongue roving around the interior of his mouth as if unfamiliar with its contours. His eyes rolled in his head.

'Mmm . . . *machine*. For. Move. *Mmph*. Moving between. *Stars*,' he grunted, with apparently enormous effort, before falling back against his chair.

'What the hell?' said Schelling, turning to look questioningly at first Sifra, and then Tarrant. 'You told me this man was brain-dead.'

'That's not him speaking,' said Sifra, his eyes locked on Bash. 'It's the Wanderer.'

Bash started to shake, grinding his teeth together so vigorously that the sound made Megan's own jaw ache.

'There's something wrong with him,' declared Tarrant, with one eye still on the floating panels. 'His brain's all lit up as if he's suffering a *grand mal* fit, and his heartbeat's showing severe dysrhythmia. We need to stop this now, or he's going to suffer a seizure, or a heart attack, or both.'

'Not yet,' said Schelling. 'Maybe this is our best chance finally to talk to the Wanderer directly.'

Schelling stepped closer to Bash, who let out a piercing animal shriek that stopped him in his tracks.

'Listen to me,' Schelling addressed Bash. 'We've got something we know you want – information about the Magi and also about the Makers. Tell me if you understand me.'

For the first time, Bash's eyes actually focused on Schelling. Something about his expression sent a chill through Megan: it wasn't human.

'Mmmm-*machine*,' said Bash. 'For moving between. *Stars*.'

'Do you understand what we're offering you?' said Schelling. 'Information about the Magi and the Makers.'

Bash's expression morphed rapidly from childish delight to terrible pain. 'Magi,' he grunted. 'Yes.'

'And in return, we want whatever it is you gave the Meridians.'

Megan covered her mouth. It was all too horrible to have to see Bash like this.

'Mmm . . . ust come,' said Bash. '*Come*. Here.'

'It still hasn't agreed to anything, General,' Tarrant remarked quietly.

'Yes, I'm aware of that,' Schelling snapped, then he turned back to Bash. 'We won't come to you unless you agree to our terms first. And if you try and hurt us again, we'll destroy you. Do you understand? We will destroy you utterly.'

'Yes,' Bash replied. 'I understand.'

'And our terms?' said Schelling, almost shouting now. His skin was flushed, and damp with perspiration. 'Will you give us what we ask for in return?'

Bash ducked his chin down almost to his chest. Ye . . . mmph . . . *yes*.' He jerked upright, his eyes rolling upwards until only the whites were visible. All of a sudden his muscles unclenched and he slumped forward, sliding off the chair.

Tarrant ducked around, catching hold of him before Bash landed on the floor.

'He's gone into cardiac arrest,' shouted Tarrant. 'We need to get him in a medbox immediately.'

Megan pushed past Schelling and Sifra, took one of Bash's arms and draped it over her shoulder, then helped Tarrant drag him back out and along the corridor towards the medboxes they had passed earlier. Tarrant held on to him while she cracked the lid of one of them open, then they both lifted him inside before closing it again.

'Dear God,' said Schelling, stepping up beside them. 'I have never in all my days seen anything like that before.'

Sifra arrived at that same moment. 'Nor me either. The damn thing's never talked to us *directly* before.'

Schelling turned to Megan. 'You've just proven your worth, Miss Jacinth,' he said. 'If I hadn't seen that with my own eyes, I wouldn't ever have believed it.'

Megan nodded wordlessly, feeling too tired to care what he wanted to say.

It's all over, she realized; everything she had fought for. She had managed to escape from these people, then all too easily walked back into their arms. Perhaps, she thought, she deserved nothing better than whatever fate waited for her now at Schelling's hands.

Before long the guards returned to lead her back out and across the courtyard, the bioluminescent algae clinging to the roof of the cavern still shining down on them. It felt wrong, somehow, to witness such beauty under such dreadful circumstances.

Megan's despair only increased as they locked her inside a windowless room. Despite her fatigue it took her a long time to fall asleep, and when she finally did, curled up in a foetal position on the floor, she dreamed of that moment she had been reborn, on an examination table, over twenty years before.

TWENTY-FIVE

Megan

2742 (twenty-one years before)

Megan remembered her first ever breath with razor-sharp clarity. She had opened her eyes, her last memory being that of dying, and found herself strapped to a table. Half a dozen faces, all of them entirely unfamiliar, stared down at her with cold and calculating gazes.

She had died when a star, in its final death throes, had torn apart the Magi ship she had piloted to the very edge of the galaxy, in the hope of finding some way to halt the Nova War then threatening life throughout the Milky Way. Her search had led her to a Maker Swarm, a cloud of interlinked alien machines whose sole purpose was to prevent the rise of other interstellar civilizations, only for it to cripple and then destroy her precious ship.

As she lay immobilized on that table, she knew herself only as Dakota Merrick. She did not yet know that her thoughts and memories now occupied the body of a young woman who had, until only a few hours before, been the Speaker-Elect of the Demarchy of Uchida.

One of those gazing down at her – a fresh-faced young man who introduced himself as Thijs – took it upon himself to explain to her, in precise and laborious detail, exactly how she had come to be where she was – and what they wanted from her. She had actually died, he explained, more than two centuries earlier, and had subsequently been resurrected by yet another Magi ship. And if she wanted to live for more than just the next few hours, she would do exactly what was required of her.

She had died. Then somehow the same Magi ship that had transported her to the Maker Swarm had, in its last moments of existence, transmitted her memories and thoughts to others of its kind. And one of those others had subsequently come to crash, burned and crippled, here on Redstone.

If she only cooperated, Thijs explained, she would be allowed to live. Failure to cooperate, however, would cause her to be tortured until she divulged the information they wanted – information she could already sense looming large in the data-repositories of her machine-head implants.

As she had stared up at those callous and overfed faces, she knew deep down in her gut that they were lying to her. They had no intention of letting her survive, whether or not she cooperated. They had brought her back to life just so they could murder her all over again once she was no longer of use to them.

She had refused to cooperate, in the strongest terms possible. She kicked out with one foot, catching one of them under the chin. He staggered away, clutching at his throat. It then needed all of the rest of them to hold her down on the table.

She watched, helpless, as the one called Thijs stepped over to a trolley carrying a variety of instruments, some of them razor-sharp, arranged in neat rows on its surface. He had lifted one up, and it glittered as it caught the light.

A dreadful eternity passed for her on that examination table.

After a few hours, they left her still strapped to it, bruised and bleeding and half mad, with the promise that they would return soon. And, when they did, Dakota knew she would tell them anything and everything they wanted to know.

And then, she also knew with equal certainty, they would kill her.

She lay there for a long time, whimpering and sobbing beneath the mercilessly bright lights, until she heard the sound of approaching footsteps, a steady rhythm like the ticking of a clock measuring out the last seconds of her life.

But the young man who stepped through the door of the chamber moments later was not one of her torturers.

'Esté,' said the stranger, his face full of alarm and shock as he stepped further into the room. He dropped a heavy backpack onto the floor next to the examination table on which Dakota lay strapped. 'Esté, what have they *done* to you?'

He hurriedly undid the straps holding her down, then reached out his fingers to her cheek. Despite herself, Dakota flinched from his touch.

He frowned and withdrew his hand. 'I came for you,' he said. He wore a military uniform of some kind. 'Just as I told you I would.' His eyes passed over her bruised and torn flesh, as if seeing her injuries for the first time. 'But I never imagined *this* . . .'

She sat up carefully, unsure of how she should respond to him or what she should say. Glancing past him, she saw to her dismay that someone else had now entered the cell behind him. It was a girl with large, dark eyes, her head cleanly shaven, and wearing a plain paper smock identical to the one Dakota wore.

She returned her gaze to her would-be rescuer. Whoever this young man was, she felt sure he was suffering from a case of mistaken identity. She was in no mood to correct him, however.

'Esté?' she echoed, as he helped her down from the table. She found it difficult to stand at first, and had to grab hold of the edge of it with both hands. 'That's my name?'

He frowned, his expression now becoming deeply confused. 'What the hell are you talking about? It's *me*, Malcolm, and we need to get you out of here.'

'I'm having trouble remembering things,' Dakota said carefully.

He put both hands on her shoulders and stared into her eyes. 'Esté, for God's sake, you don't seriously mean to say you don't *remember* me?'

Esté, she realized, must be the name of the Speaker-Elect – the girl who had formerly occupied this body. And this man Malcolm, she guessed, had been her lover. Somehow, either one or both of them must have discovered the truth about what would happen to her once she became merged with the Magi ship.

Or rather, she suspected, they had uncovered *part* of the truth as it had been explained to her by Thijs. It was obvious that Malcolm had no idea that the process Esté had undergone mere hours before had driven all of her thoughts and memories into oblivion.

She stared at Malcolm with a mixture of pity and horror, wondering how she could possibly tell him his sweetheart was gone forever, and that someone else entirely now resided within her skull.

But if she did, she reminded herself, he might not feel so committed to rescuing her.

'Yes. I remember,' she said, reaching out with one faltering hand to touch his cheek. 'Malcolm, it's just . . . the things they did to me make it hard to think straight.'

He stared at her for another long moment, then kneeled by his rucksack, pulling out clothes, a pair of boots and some breather masks.

'Get dressed,' he said, handing her the garments and one of the masks. 'We don't have much time.'

The clothing proved to be a uniform similar to Malcolm's own, and was clearly tailored for a male wearer. She tore off her paper smock and hurriedly pulled it on. The uniform hung loose on her, but it proved a great deal warmer than the smock.

She glanced up towards the girl standing shivering by the door, looking dejected and frightened.

Malcolm turned to the girl, too. 'Get on the table,' he told her. 'And, remember, tell them nothing.'

She nodded and stepped forward, taking care not to even look in Dakota's direction. She climbed wordlessly onto the table and lay back, as Malcolm secured her ankles and wrists with the same straps used before.

'What's going on?' Dakota demanded. 'What the hell are you doing to her?'

'She's our decoy,' he replied. After securing the final strap, he grabbed hold of Dakota's wrist and pulled her towards the door. 'They've been sending guards to check on you every half-hour, so we need to go now, before they return.'

Dakota reached up and touched her own scalp for the first time, only to discover, with a shock, that she was just as bald as the other girl.

'My hair,' she exclaimed, 'what happened to it?'

'They shaved it off, remember?' he said. 'To "facilitate the bonding process"?'

She studied the girl again, looking so young and so very frightened. 'We can't just leave her here like this,' she said. 'They might—'

'Her family's been very well compensated,' interrupted Malcolm impatiently. 'She's not here against her will.'

'But she's not even bruised or scarred,' said Dakota. 'Surely they'll figure out what you've done, the moment they see her?'

'The guards are simply expecting to find a bald girl strapped to a table,' snapped Malcolm. 'Thijs himself won't be returning for at least another hour, and that's all the time we need. Now *hurry*!'

'No, wait,' she said. 'We can't—'

'For God's sake, Esté,' he exploded, raising his voice for the first time. 'We discussed this already and we agreed. It's either you or her, except she gets a choice in the matter. Now come *on*.'

She felt too weak to resist as he dragged her out of the room and along a passageway. They descended several flights of steps before arriving at an airlock, next to which lay the bodies of two men in uniforms identical to Malcolm's own. One of the men had a dark stain spreading across his chest, while the head of the other seemed to be twisted at an odd angle.

Dakota studied Malcolm with new respect as he hauled the airlock door open, and she wondered what kind of woman Esté must have been to inspire such fierce, and deadly, devotion.

Inside the airlock, a pair of cold-weather jackets and matching over-trousers hung on hooks. They quickly pulled them on.

'Here.' Malcolm handed her a thick, knitted cap, which she looked at questioningly as she took it from him. 'To help keep you from being recognized,' he explained, then nodded to her head. 'And to hide those.'

Dakota reached up again to feel the bumps and contours of the implants beneath her scalp. Clearly Esté had been a machine-head as well. The cap, when she put it on, fit warm and snug around her ears. She next pulled on her breather mask and followed Malcolm out into a crisp, cold night.

Glancing behind, her gaze moved up along the broad curve of a Magi ship's hull, looming above the building from which they had just emerged. It looked like some vast leviathan of the deep, washed up from unknowable depths and towering over everything beneath it.

She looked further to see that the ship actually leaned against the broad face of a cliff. Dozens of other buildings circled the base of the ship like watchful guardians, and were interlinked by a tangle of metal walkways and stairways.

Turning the other way, she saw a three-metre-high wall, illuminated by tall arc lights, standing perhaps a hundred metres away. She followed it with her eyes and realized that it ran all the way around the Magi ship itself and the various buildings surrounding it.

Malcolm pulled her in the direction of a row of half a dozen structures close to a gate set into the perimeter wall. They were moving so quickly that Dakota, with legs shorter than Malcolm's, almost had to break into a run to keep up with him. As they came abreast of what she now recognized as warehouses, Malcolm drew her towards a vehicle parked in the shadows between two of them.

It consisted of little more than an open chassis mounted on a set of bulbous wheels. A man in the driver's seat, his face half hidden by a breather mask, nodded a greeting to Malcolm.

Malcolm pushed her into a bucket seat in the rear before climbing in next to the nameless driver. 'Strap in,' he instructed her, 'in case we have to make a break for it.'

The car slowly drove out from between the two warehouses, then headed straight for the gate. Two large steel-plate doors slid apart automatically at their approach.

Sirens began to sound through the night air, echoing off the face of the massive cliff. The sliding doors suddenly came to a halt, then began to close again, fast.

'*Go*,' yelled Malcolm, grabbing his companion's shoulder. The vehicle shot forward, accelerating hard. It spun to a halt on the other side of the gate, having only narrowly avoided being sliced in two.

'Close,' said Malcolm's friend grimly. Malcolm merely nodded, looking shaken.

They got under way once more, rapidly picking up speed. They were soon racing downhill along a nearly deserted access road, with the sound of sirens still wailing behind them. At the bottom of the hill, a city brilliant with light stretched out before them. Beyond it she could just make out the dark expanse of a mighty river or ocean.

Something buzzed overhead, shining a light down onto the road ahead. Their driver reacted by swerving violently into steep undergrowth, sending the vehicle crashing and bouncing down a vertiginous slope at such speed that Dakota felt sure it would flip over and crush them beneath its weight. Instead they bounced out onto a switchback road level with the rooftops of what looked like residential buildings situated near the base of the hill.

The driver swerved again, and suddenly they were passing along a narrow street. Dakota saw businesses and homes on either side, the machine that had buzzed them – probably a drone of some kind – now lost in a haze of light and noise.

The driver wove through another series of tight turns, before taking them down a steep ramp leading underground. Passing through an atmospheric containment field, they entered a brightly lit space that was broad and big and busy enough to constitute a whole subterranean city in itself.

Dakota pulled her mask down and breathed in air that tasted of sweat and smoke and a thousand other flavours that made her very, very glad still to be alive. After the freezing temperatures of the

Redstone night, this underground community felt shockingly warm. She even began to sweat under her heavy coat.

Malcolm's friend had barely slowed down. They careened along a thoroughfare with a bustling open market on either side, huge stone-and-steel pillars supporting the city streets above ground. Dazzlingly colourful images shifted and morphed above a warren of stalls and businesses.

'Put your mask back on,' said Malcolm, looking back over his shoulder. She saw he was still wearing his own breather mask. 'It'll reduce the chances of you being recognized, especially with all these pilgrims around. And besides, we're not staying down here much longer.'

She pulled the mask back up, just as the car ascended another ramp, passing once more through a pressure field as they emerged on the surface. At that moment, Dakota caught sight of industrial docks situated just a few blocks away.

They began driving much more slowly, merging with any other traffic. The streets and squares were crowded with an enormous number of people, tens or perhaps even hundreds of thousands of them jostling together. She decided these must be the pilgrims Malcolm had mentioned.

The two men turned to each other, laughing and grinning. 'I've got a safe house ready for both of you,' explained Malcolm's friend. 'You can hide there for the next couple of days at least, but after that they're going to be searching for you through every inch of the city. Fortunately, having all these pilgrims around makes it easier to smuggle both of you out, once we've made arrangements.'

'Something's different about you, Esté,' remarked Malcolm, turning to study her closely. 'I can't figure out what it is, unless they hurt you a lot worse than I feared they might.'

She reached out and took his hand, which was draped over the back of his seat. 'Thank you for saving me,' she said, with as much earnestness as she could muster, which wasn't hard. 'I owe you my life, Malcolm, but you shouldn't have used the girl like that. It was wrong.'

Malcolm's face clouded. 'She was nothing,' he said, his tone suddenly terse. 'A nobody. Besides, she's almost certainly dead by now. You should put her out of your mind.'

What kind of girl were you, Esté, that you fell in love with a man like this? She could hardly believe that someone who shared identical genes to her could ever fall for such a callous man. She wondered what Malcolm would do to her once he realized who and what he had rescued.

'Tell me one thing,' said Dakota. 'That girl, what was her name?'

'For God's sake, Esté, what does it matter?'

'Please,' she said, fighting to keep the tremor out of her voice. 'I really want to know.'

Malcolm looked away and shook his head, his nameless companion grinning with apparent amusement.

'Jacinth,' Malcolm finally said. 'Her name was Megan Jacinth. Satisfied now?'

Megan Jacinth. She silently shaped the two words in her mouth.

The car was slowing as it came to a crowded crossroads, and Dakota now saw her opportunity. She reached down and unbuckled herself from her seat while Malcolm was looking the other way, then threw herself sideways out of the vehicle just before it began to accelerate once more.

She rolled to a halt on the roadway, then pushed herself upright, feeling dizzy. She had been lucky not to break her neck, but she didn't want to stay around Malcolm or his friend any longer than she had to.

Up ahead, their car had come to a sudden halt.

'Hey!' Malcolm shouted back at her, his face turned white with fear and tension. All around them, people were staring, and they had begun attracting all the attention he'd warned her they had to avoid. 'What the hell do you think you're doing?' he yelled.

She started to run, pushing through the crowds of curious onlookers. She felt hands grab for her, curious voices shouting in her wake, but she determinedly shook them off, fighting her way in deeper amongst the crowds, frantic to put as much distance between her and Malcolm as possible.

Finally she emerged into a sidestreet, feeling cold and terrified and exhausted, with no idea of where to go or what to do next. So she simply put one foot in front of the other, and kept going, until she had got herself thoroughly lost in the depths of a city that she hadn't even known existed during her previous life.

Thus she wandered for hours, warm air exiting from her breather mask and rising up into the night. Her stomach rumbled from increasing hunger. She constantly kept a wary eye out for anyone wearing a uniform like Malcolm's.

Just by following the crowds, and listening to snatches of conversation around her, Dakota learned that the pilgrims would come to Dios in such numbers that the city authorities were obliged to construct vast temporary accommodations solely to house and feed them. She followed one group of people who looked as if they knew where they were going, heading into an enormous prefab hangar filled with welcome heat and light. There, she quickly discovered food and drink for the taking. Better still, nobody questioned her, or asked where she came from.

Dakota saw numerous posters featuring a girl in ceremonial robes, and she realized with a shock that these must be images of the Speaker-Elect – of *herself*. The images did not, however, look anything like she remembered herself, and she guessed Esté's appearance had been surgically altered at some point in the past.

She continued staring at the poster until she felt dizzy, feeling as if she had woken up into some kind of endless waking nightmare. Despite the humid warmth within the hangar, she kept the woollen cap on, and the hood of her coat pulled over her head. She also took particular care not to meet anyone's eyes or let herself become involved in conversation.

After standing in a queue for nearly an hour, sweltering beneath the hood and the heavy overcoat, she was finally handed a plastic tray laden with food. Then she made her way down the long rows of mass-fabbed bunks and squeezed into one next to a wall. There she ate silently, always keeping an eye out for anyone who looked as if they might be searching for her.

She presently overheard a conversation about an Accord military base located a few hundred kilometres further inland. She had no idea what the Accord was, but it was easy enough to infer from what she could hear that it offered a real chance for her to get off-planet and as far away from the Demarchy as she could go.

This was a slim enough straw to grasp at, but it seemed to be all she had. So, with a full belly, she drifted off to sleep, trying hard not to think about what the next day might hold.

The following morning she made her way alone along a canal bank, as dawn crept up behind the Magi ship, stranded on its hill. She had seen armoured patrols racing along main roads, and uniformed soldiers setting up roadblocks, but it was clear that the soldiers out in search of her were overwhelmed by the sheer flood of pilgrims.

Unlike the streets, the canal appeared to be unguarded. She encountered boats racing by occasionally, but they were easy to hide from.

She followed the canal, away from the river, until she reached the city limits. The inland continent spread out before her, a far-off range of mountains visible beyond a vast river plain. As it got dark again, she made her way back to the main road, rejoining the masses of pilgrims now making their way out of the city on foot, and heading towards another of the municipal shelters nearby. That night, she fell asleep on coarse matting, her coat thrown over her head and shoulders, and surrounded on all sides by thousands of warm bodies.

When the old woman sleeping next to her asked what her name was, she said it was Megan, though still carefully keeping her face hidden.

Out of sheer desperation and the urge to put as much distance as possible between herself and the city, she managed to talk her way on board one of a flotilla of vehicles provided to carry several hundred pilgrims at a time to the settlements further inland. It proved surprisingly easy. Whatever security checks were in place, it was clear they were struggling just to cope with the sheer number of people on the move.

The flotilla she chose was accompanied by an armed escort of peacekeepers, who were affiliated to the Accord. She had asked careful questions, teasing significant details out of the few other passengers she risked talking to. It soon became clear that the Accord served more or less the same function as had the Consortium, back in the days when she had last been alive. The peacekeepers were from the military base she had heard of earlier, and were apparently on the lookout for Freehold insurgents trying to make their way over the mountains to the north-east.

It thus slowly dawned on Dakota that the Freehold was no longer the dominant military force on Redstone. It seemed it had lost its long struggle with the Uchidanists, and the vast majority of Freeholders had since decamped to new colonies, while only a fanatical few remained behind to fight for what they still saw as their rightful homeland.

She kept the knitted cap pulled down tightly over her ears as the convoy trundled across the broad inland plains, crossing bridges and parallel series of canals, the mountains growing closer and taller as they drove on through the night.

It was a few hours before dawn when Freehold guerrillas opened fire, from the shelter of a ditch, on the flotilla of peacekeepers escorting them.

The sound of gunfire filled the air, while energy weapons seared her eyes with after-images that took long minutes to fade. Then she heard the dull thud of a detonation, and saw the windows of her transport implode, allowing Redstone's poisonous atmosphere to come rushing in.

The lights went out. Dakota struggled through the dark as people all around her fought to find their masks, or escape through the shattered windows of the transport, or both. Fortunately, the mask given to her by Malcolm still hung around her neck by its cord.

She could hear those people who hadn't yet been able to find their breather masks struggling for breath as Redstone's native atmosphere flooded in. She managed to pull her own mask over her mouth and nose, then clambered through a window, tumbling out and onto the verge.

It came to her with a horrible shock that most of the people she had been riding with were going to die. The transport's heating systems had been faulty, and even while she had slept, she still wore the heavy coat Malcolm had given her. If it hadn't been for that, she would probably have frozen to death within minutes.

She felt a desperate urge to stay and help the pilgrims, but she could see little in the darkness, and with a battle under way all around them, she knew the most she could hope for was to save herself.

The ground shuddered beneath her feet, as a great cloud of ash and fire rose up into the sky from further along the road, revealing the silhouettes of other transports. The sound of the explosion followed a moment later.

Leaving the highway behind her, she ran out onto the night-darkened plain. Before long her ears were filled with an eerie, ghost-like silence.

She was far from alone, however. Once her eyes adjusted to the darkness, she could just about make out dozens of men and women, some of them carrying young children, their eyes tired and frightened above hastily retrieved breather masks. They were all similarly trying to put some serious distance between themselves and the convoy before any more shells struck. Any who hadn't managed to retrieve their masks were most likely dead by now.

Some instinct drew them all towards the relative shelter of a canopy tree that stood half a kilometre or so from the highway. Its trunk soared eighty metres above their heads, with multiple layers of veined shrouds spreading out from its highest branches like an umbrella. The air here was fractionally warmer because the thermal energy the canopy trees tapped via their deep roots, combined with their sheer size, allowed them to engender their own microclimate with its own unique flora and fauna.

They gathered in their dozens amongst the tree's blade-like roots, many clinging to each other out of terror or, more likely, the need to stay warm. From there could be heard the distant boom and hiss of artillery, and the thunder of orbital energy weapons discharging into the foothills a hundred kilometres away.

An hour passed, and then another, and her coat's heating elements began to run out of juice, the cold slowly digging deeper and deeper into Dakota's unprotected flesh. She heard someone sobbing loudly, and glanced over to see a shadowy form crouching over another that lay ominously still and silent.

Unless help came very soon, she realized, a lot of these people were going to die.

After another couple of hours, the fighting seemed to become more sporadic, until finally there was only the hiss of the sleeting rain blown under the tree's canopy.

Some hours after dawn had broken, a dropship with Accord markings finally settled onto the hard soil just outside the tree's protective canopy. It wasn't until Dakota heard excited cries from the people around her that she felt convinced it was not a hallucination.

From the dropship emerged figures in armour that flickered and shifted, so that those wearing it immediately faded into the surrounding landscape. She heard them calling to each other, though their voices were rendered identical by the processors built into their helmets. Soon they began moving amongst the pilgrims, some equipped with stretchers, while others wrapped the shivering survivors in sheets of reflective material before guiding them towards the waiting dropship.

One of the peacekeepers eventually approached Dakota and helped her get to her feet. He pushed up the faceplate of his environment-skinned helmet, leaving only the lower half of his face hidden behind a partial breather mask.

This man had the gentlest eyes Megan had ever seen, though his protective gear did little to hide the fact he possessed the body of a well-muscled bear.

'What's your name, honey?' he asked, his voice as warm and deep as a river despite the electronic distortion of his breather.

'Megan,' she replied.

He nodded and unravelled a strip of foil from the long roll he carried, before carefully wrapping it around her shoulders.

The woollen cap slipped from her head and she swore, reaching down to fetch it back. She looked up again at her rescuer and froze in alarm, knowing what he was seeing: the tell-tale furrows and all-too-regular patterns of bumps beneath her recently shaven scalp.

'You're a machine-head,' he observed quietly. 'I never heard of Uchidan machine-heads.'

She shook her head. 'That's not what it is. It's . . . it's a kind of faith implant. All Uchidans have them, didn't you know?'

'Don't bullshit me,' he said, though sounding not in the least angry. 'I know a machine-head when I see one.'

Reaching up, he fiddled with the clasps on his helmet and lifted it off. Megan saw how his hair was cut close to the skull, revealing a scalp covered with identical subcutaneous patterns: a machine-head.

'Who are you *really*, girl?' he asked her, tilting his head quizzically.

'I already told you my name,' she said, defiance creeping into her voice. But he laughed and shook his head, as he replaced his helmet.

'You running away from something, Megan?' he asked softly. 'I won't tell anyone if you don't want me to.'

Tears began rolling down her filth-streaked cheeks, and she ground her fingernails into her palms. 'Please don't take me back there,' she begged him. 'Please. They'll kill me. They'll . . .'

'Hey, now,' he said, gripping her by the shoulder and leading her back towards the dropship. 'Ain't nobody going to hurt you now.'

'You say that,' she half whispered, 'but you can't possibly know.'

He looked beyond her, past the canopy tree and back towards the direction of the city, in silent thought.

'Baby,' he said finally, returning his gaze to her face, 'if there's one thing to be said about old Bash, it's that he *always* keeps his word.'

TWENTY-SIX

Gabrielle

2763 (the present)

After they disembarked from the dropship that had brought them back down from orbit, and after she was loaded into a truck driven by Freeholders, Gabrielle had spent long hours staring out at the Montos de Frenezo as the vehicle made its way amidst endless foothills, followed by a convoy of other trucks.

Tarrant had long since made his way through from the rear compartment to talk to the two Freeholders sitting up in the front cabin, and Gabrielle had gradually dozed off, until a sudden increase in speed jolted her awake. When she glanced outside again, it was to see a narrow trail of greasy smoke rising high into the sky.

The truck had changed direction, clearly headed towards the same smoke trail. When she had looked out through the rear, she could see the other trucks still following them. The terrain became rougher, requiring numerous detours to avoid scree and scattered boulders.

After another hour or so, they had passed over a low hill when the truck accelerated again. It bounced violently over stony ground, although they were still nowhere near the source of the smoke.

At that moment, she pressed her face to the glass in time to see someone running as if pursued by all the demons of hell. Black shapes – drones of some kind – darted through the air, rapidly converging on the figure before it collapsed. Gabrielle wondered if a ship might have crashed, and this was a survivor struggling to avoid capture by the Freehold. Perhaps, she thought hopefully, the Accord had already begun a counter-attack.

The truck came to a halt not far from where the figure lay. At first Gabrielle thought it was dead, then saw the figure's limbs moving weakly. Despite the bulky clothing, instinct made her sure it was a woman. A drone hovered directly before the figure, its recording lenses focused on her.

She heard Tarrant's voice clearly from the cabin up front. 'Son of a bitch,' he exclaimed.

Then there was a sound like the slamming of a fist against the ceiling of the truck.

'Son of a *bitch*!' he repeated, louder this time.

As he made his way back through, he looked to Gabrielle like someone who'd just seen a ghost. She watched him unlock the two rear doors of the truck, freezing air rushing inside as they swung open.

The two Freeholders quickly followed him outside, without either of them giving her so much as a glance. Gabrielle adjusted the seal on her mask and followed them out of the truck, curious despite herself.

As their eyes met, the other woman had stared at Gabrielle with an expression of bleak despair mixed with astonishment. Gabrielle had the strangest feeling that she knew this woman from somewhere, yet she felt sure she had never set eyes on her before.

Before long the new prisoner was lifted up and bundled into the back of one of the other trucks, while Gabrielle was guided back to her own. Soon they had caught up with the rest of the convoy, Tarrant again choosing to ride in the company of the Freeholders.

Some time later, the trucks had traversed a wide expanse of flat ground to reach the steep hills surrounding the base of a mountain, much of its bulk hidden behind clouds. They continued onwards until they came to a high cliff, in front of which sat what appeared to be a dropship hidden beneath a shroud the colour of the surrounding landscape. The trucks kept going, entering the mouth of a long, sloping passageway at the base of the cliff that appeared to extend deep beneath the mountain. This, she guessed, must be one of the Freehold bases that Tarrant had supposedly been so skilled at smoking out on behalf of the Demarchy.

The truck turned through a series of side-passages before stopping briefly to let Tarrant disembark, then continued on, finally coming to a halt outside a row of prefab buildings lined up against a sloping cave wall. The two Freeholders led Gabrielle inside one of these buildings, before locking her inside a room furnished only with a cot and a chemical toilet. The cot smelled of sour sweat and unchanged sheets.

She peered out through the single barred window in time to see the truck disappearing back the way it had come.

Without sight of the sun or any hint of the world outside, the following hours seemed to stretch into an eternity. There was little for her to do but stare out of the window, watching pallet-laden trucks drive past from time to time, which reminded her of something said during Tarrant's conversation with Cuyàs, about the Freehold preparing for a full-scale invasion of the Demarchy.

Perhaps, she thought, they were getting ready to abandon this complex.

She soon gave up avoiding the malodorous cot, which at least offered the advantage of not being quite as freezing cold as the cell floor. To begin with, she pulled one sleeve of her jacket across her mouth and nose, in an attempt to block out the stink, but when that didn't work she tried sleeping with her breather mask pulled on.

Long hours later she woke with the uncanny sense that she was being watched. She sat up with a start, her heart thudding, at the suspicion that she might no longer be alone in that locked and silent room. Yet a glance confirmed she was mistaken, while the great cave beyond the window was silent.

She could see nothing from the barred window, and it suddenly occurred to her that the complex might already have been abandoned, leaving her here to die alone beneath the mountain . . .

<Gabrielle.>

She gasped and stared wildly around, one hand still gripping a bar of the window. There was no one there, and yet she *knew* she had heard a voice.

It took her another moment to work out that the voice was coming through her implants. Someone was trying to communicate with her remotely, and was managing to do so despite the device Tarrant had injected into her neck. The voice was male, with a deep and resonant warmth to it that somehow soothed her jangled nerves. It certainly did not sound like the voice of someone intent on doing her harm.

'Who are you?' she spoke tentatively into the air.

<You need to get out of there,> said the voice. <Go over to the door, Gaby.>

Gabrielle hesitated, then did as she was instructed. The door had no visible handle of any type, and she had already tried pushing it open, to no avail. The lock was clearly electronic.

To her amazement, it swung quietly open at her approach. She stared outside at the far wall of the cave in astonishment.

'How did you do that?' she demanded. 'Who are you?'

<I need you to come and find me, Gaby,> said the voice. <I've been lost out here for a long, long time, and I can only stay for a little while. So believe me when I say you need to hurry.>

Gabrielle swallowed hard, and stepped out onto the sloping floor of the cave. When no one challenged her, she scanned up and down the length of the cave, seeing that it was entirely deserted. Downslope lay only darkness.

<Go up, Gaby.>

'What if someone sees me?' she whispered.

<I can see you through their cameras, but they can't – not for now, anyway. Get moving, girl.>

She pushed her breather mask into one pocket of her coat and headed upwards to where the cave accessed a tunnel drilled out of the rock. Overhead lights shone down on rows of parked trucks and racks of equipment.

<Now go left.>

She halted. 'I'm not going anywhere until you tell me who the hell you are,' she whispered loudly. 'How do I know you're not working for Tarrant? And just where are you sending me?'

<You can call me Bash,> said the voice. <I'm a friend. You can trust me.>

She held her ground, even though her heart was hammering in her chest. 'That isn't enough,' she said. '*Why* are you helping me like this?'

<I've been fighting a war>, said Bash. <I've been far away, in places you couldn't even begin to imagine. I'm so close to figuring out just what it is the Wanderer's been hiding all this time.>

'What war?' she hissed, peering ahead of herself as she proceeded further along the tunnel. *And what the hell is the Wanderer*? Up ahead she could see what looked like the entrance to another cavern. 'Are you talking about the Freehold?'

<Find Megan,> said the voice. <She'll know what to do.>

'Who? Who's Meg . . . ?'

The voice – and the presence – faded at the same moment that a sliver of knowledge suddenly materialized in the back of Gabrielle's mind, as if it had always been there. Somehow she *knew* where to find Megan – whoever she was.

An increasing sense of excitement gripped her. Was this the same woman she had seen knocked down by a drone? She wanted to know who this person was, and how she had so badly disturbed Tarrant. Gabrielle had an intuition that the woman might even be able to answer some of her questions about the man she had once known as Karl Petrova.

She found herself at the mouth of a cavern, its walls speckled with green and blue light emanating from some kind of fungi. Towards the centre of the cavern lay clustered a number of buildings. Megan, she felt sure, was inside one of them.

Gabrielle walked as quietly and quickly as she could towards them, keeping a watchful eye out. On her right tarpaulin-covered stacks of machinery rose far above her head, while on her left stood a row of partially disembowelled trucks.

She heard the sound of footsteps, reverberating from the cavern ceiling, and approaching from somewhere on the other side of the stacks. She crept on towards the last truck in the row, before crouching in the narrow space between one of its treads and the cavern wall.

The footsteps came to a halt. 'Control,' said a man's voice, 'the security net's still down. Any idea when it'll be back up?'

She waited and listened.

'Well, if it's localized,' said the same man after a pause, 'I'll take a look and see if I can figure something out from this end.'

Gabrielle hardly dared breathe. He sounded as if he was just right around the other side of the truck.

'Okay,' he said, after another pause. 'Soon as I've checked that out, I'll check on the girl Tarrant brought in. Sound good?'

The man again fell silent. After a minute, Gabrielle risked a glance around the rear of the truck.

She saw the back of a man's head. He was wearing the familiar grey-and-white fatigues she had seen on other Freeholders. He had opened up a virtual console, most of it taken up by what looked like a map of the caverns. He had a rifle over one shoulder, and various tools arranged in sheaths on a multi-pocketed waistcoat.

If he was on his way to check up on her, she might have only a couple of minutes before he raised the alert.

A crowbar lay on the ground next to the truck, along with some oily rags and a pile of what looked like spare parts. She reached down and picked the crowbar up.

One end of it accidentally banged against the side of the truck, the sound immediately echoing across the cavern.

She froze with one hand over her mouth, her heart beating like thunder.

She could hear the guard breathing loudly. He had to know someone was there.

She listened. Just silence. But surely he *must* have heard . . . ?

She forced herself to take her hand from her mouth and, gripping the crowbar with both hands, risked another glimpse towards where the guard had been standing.

He was gone.

'Get up,' said a voice from immediately behind her. 'And drop that fucking—'

She turned, swinging wildly. His rifle was aimed straight at her head, but the crowbar caught him hard in the knee, and he collapsed against the truck treads with a howl of pain.

She stood up and swung the crowbar again and again. He slipped to the ground, limbs twitching. She struck again . . .

And again.

When he finally stopped moving, she let the crowbar clatter to the ground. Then she turned away and vomited.

It hadn't felt like killing Thijs or the rest of them back on the Grand Barge. It had been different. And worse.

She wiped her mouth clean and forced herself to pick up the dead man's rifle before continuing on her way.

The buildings seemed deserted, and yet her machine-senses drew her inside one of them and along a corridor, before stopping at one specific door. It felt . . . right.

As the door slid open at her touch, she peered inside and recognized the woman who had caused Tarrant so much consternation. Slumped on the floor, with bandages visible beneath her shirt, she stared up at Gabrielle in utter disbelief.

'How the hell did you get in here?' the woman demanded weakly.

'I . . . I don't know,' replied Gabrielle helplessly. 'You're Megan, I think? Bash told me to get you out of here. My name's Gabrielle, and I—'

'I know who you are,' she declared, then dragged herself upright and came closer. 'But what was that you just said – about Bash?'

'He . . . he told me to hurry. That we didn't have much time.'

Megan's face creased in blank astonishment. She pushed past

Gabrielle and made her way back along the corridor and out into the main cavern. Gabrielle followed, unsure what she was supposed to do next.

'That rifle –' Megan suddenly turned back to her – 'where did you get it?'

'From a guard.'

The woman cocked her head. 'And what happened to him?'

'I . . . he's dead.'

The woman's eyes narrowed, as if re-evaluating her. 'You shot him with that thing?'

Gabrielle swallowed. 'No, I . . . hit him with something.'

'That's a heck of a thing for anyone to do, let alone . . .'

The woman halted mid-speech. *Let alone a girl like you*, Gabrielle knew she had meant to say.

'I didn't have any choice,' said Gabrielle, her voice rising. 'He was going to kill me. I . . .'

'Okay,' said Megan, putting a hand on Gabrielle's arm, her voice soothing. 'Okay. I get it.' She gestured to the rifle. 'Tell me – do you know how to use that thing?'

Gabrielle swallowed. 'No, not really.'

Megan waggled the fingers of one hand. 'Then give it to me.'

'Are you sure?' said Gabrielle. 'You look like you've been hurt—'

'Just give me the goddamn rifle,' she snapped. '*Now.*'

Gabrielle unslung the rifle and passed it over. Megan lifted it up to study a reading on one side of the barrel. 'It's only half charged,' she said. 'The guard you killed. Did he have any spare battery units on him?'

Gabrielle opened her mouth, then closed it again. She clearly hadn't thought of that. 'I don't know what they even look like.'

'Well, this is only good for a couple of shots anyway,' said Megan, sounding doubtful. 'Damn thing's so primitive it doesn't even have active sighting.'

'What's active sight—?'

'Forget it,' said Megan dismissively, slinging the rifle over her own shoulder. 'Now I want to be absolutely clear about this: when you say Bash sent you, do you mean he actually *spoke* to you?'

Gabrielle frowned. 'Yes,' she said. 'Well, I mean I heard a voice through my implants. And he said his name was Bash.'

Megan stared at her once again. 'I don't like being lied to,' she said quietly. 'So tell me again. What did he say his name was?'

'Bash.'

Gabrielle was dumbfounded to see tears glistening in the corners of the other woman's eyes. 'And he told you to find me?'

'But who *is* he?' asked Gabrielle.

'A friend of mine,' said Megan. 'We need to look for him.'

'But I don't know even know where to start.'

Megan regarded her dubiously. 'You didn't seem to have much trouble finding *me*.'

'Yes, but that was different,' said Gabrielle.

'How?'

'Look . . . I don't know *how* I knew where you were, but I just knew.'

'Like the knowledge had just been dropped into your head, like something you'd always known? Was that what it felt like?'

'I . . . yes,' said Gabrielle. 'How . . . ?'

'You're a machine-head,' said Megan quietly, 'which means you're supposed to know about these things. But I'm beginning to think you must have led a pretty sheltered existence.' She nodded towards one of the neighbouring buildings. 'Best place to start is the last place I saw him.'

Megan led the way with quick, determined strides. 'What happens if we manage to get out of here?' asked Gabrielle, following her inside. 'We're thousands of miles from anywhere.'

'Whatever happens,' whispered Megan, 'it's got to be better than what they've already got planned for us.'

Megan unslung the rifle and signalled for silence as they came to one particular door, before nudging it open with the toe of her boot.

There was a sharp exclamation from within, and Megan quickly stepped inside.

Gabrielle waited outside. After a moment there was a single flash of light from within, followed by a strained grunt.

'Get in here,' Megan yelled.

Gabrielle found Megan standing over the crumpled form of an elderly Freeholder with a scarred face and a smouldering hole in his chest that still flickered with flames. The smell of cooked flesh made her gag, so she hurriedly reached for her breather mask and pulled it back on.

There was another man in the room, tall, dark-skinned and emaciated. He was seated in a high-backed chair surrounded by complicated-looking equipment, and merely stared past them with an unfocused gaze.

Megan's breath shuddered as she slung the rifle back over her shoulder. 'I didn't like doing that,' she muttered.

'Why?' asked Gabrielle.

'He fixed my shoulder.' Megan stepped towards the man in the chair. Gabrielle wondered if he was mentally impaired or perhaps paralysed.

'C'mon, Bash,' said Megan, undoing the straps holding him in the chair. She slid one hand behind him, and the other under his arm, and tried to get him to stand, grunting with the effort. After a few seconds he slowly stood up, still demonstrating no apparent awareness that they were even there.

Gabrielle's mouth flopped open. '*That's* Bash?' she exclaimed. 'What's wrong with him?'

Megan regarded her wearily. 'Something that's going to take a really long time to explain.'

'But he *spoke* to me . . . in my head.'

'Then you might be interested to know,' said Megan, 'that, apart from one recent occasion that's going to give me nightmares for the rest of my life, he hasn't said one damn word to anyone else in well over a decade.'

It took Gabrielle several moments to absorb this. 'But . . .'

'You know what,' said Megan, looking over at her, 'how about we cut the fucking questions until we get out of here? And you can start to help by getting hold of his other arm.'

Gabrielle did as instructed and, not without some difficulty, they steered him out of the room and into the main cavern.

'Those trucks over there,' Megan panted, 'let's see if one of them's working.'

Gabrielle pulled her breather mask off again, and waited beside Bash while Megan investigated the cabins of three separate trucks in turn before finding one that seemed to her satisfaction. She waved down to Gabrielle from the driver's window, and Gabrielle guided Bash aboard the rear compartment. She was careful not to look anywhere near the dead guard's body lying close by.

Megan climbed through to the rear and helped her get Bash strapped into one of the compartment's benches. A baby, thought Gabrielle, would be less helpless. It seemed impossible that the voice she had heard – so warm, so certain – could possibly have originated from this vacant-eyed and shambling shell of a man. Megan found a packet of disposable breather masks and strapped one over Bash's face before taking another for herself. Gabrielle followed suit, then pulled her own mask back on.

Megan paused as Gabrielle followed her through the connecting hatch to the main cabin. 'Maybe you should ride in the back with Bash.'

'No.' Gabrielle shook her head adamantly. 'I'm tired of being driven around places without having any idea what's going on. I'll sit up front with you.'

'Look, I really think . . .'

'We can stay here and argue all day,' said Gabrielle, staring defiantly at the other woman, 'or we can try and get out of here.'

Megan held her gaze for a moment, as if testing her resolve, before nodding with a sigh. 'Fine.'

She had only just managed to get herself strapped into the seat next to Megan before the truck surged forward, bouncing up the slope and towards the connecting tunnel.

'If you have some kind of a plan in mind,' said Gabrielle, as they swerved at a sharp turn and into the tunnel, 'I'd really like to know what it is.'

'When they brought us here,' Megan hunched forward, 'there was a dropship parked right outside the entrance.'

'I saw it, too.'

They barrelled on past the cavern where Gabrielle had been locked up, before executing another ninety-degree turn into an entirely different part of the underground complex. 'Well,' said Megan, peering ahead, 'that ship should be the best and fastest way out of here.'

'But what if it's not there any more? Or—'

'It'll be there,' Megan snapped.

A siren began to wail, low and sonorous. Gabrielle was surprised that it had taken them so long to notice that all three of their captives were making a break for it.

Megan responded to the siren by driving even faster. They were heading up a long incline now, faint daylight seeping down from above and filtered through the atmospheric containment field.

Gabrielle saw some figures emerge, gesticulating wildly, from behind a huge stack of crates. Before she could shout a warning, something blew out their windscreen.

The truck swerved and crashed to a halt. Gabrielle stared down at the broken glass covering her lap, then looked over at Megan. 'Are you all right?'

Megan nodded, breathing hard. 'You?'

'I think so.'

'Didn't get hit,' said Megan. 'That's the main thing.'

She worked the truck's controls. It reversed, then shot forward and back on up the incline, picking up speed.

'Get down,' Megan yelled, 'and stay down.'

Gabrielle ducked and heard the sound of gunfire. Voices doplered past, then the truck juddered slightly as it collided with something. More shots followed in their wake. The light up ahead of them seemed painfully bright after so long down in the dimly lit caverns.

Megan pushed the rifle into Gabrielle's lap. 'I need you to shoot anything that moves,' she explained.

'But I've never used a gun bef—'

'You said you wanted to ride up front, Gabrielle,' Megan shouted, 'so make yourself useful. Just point the damn thing and pull the trigger. It's easy. You don't have to even fucking hit anything, just so long as it makes them think twice about getting in our way.'

Gabrielle nodded, her throat going dry, and grasped the rifle awkwardly in both hands. She squinted over the rim of the windscreen.

Up ahead, just on this side of the containment field, she saw a figure climbing into a truck just a moment before it moved to block their way.

Megan didn't even slow down.

'Wait,' protested Gabrielle. 'You can't—'

'No choice,' Megan grunted, swerving at the very last second, aiming for the narrowing gap between the truck and the tunnel wall.

They almost made it. Almost.

Gabrielle shrieked, twisting to one side to try and protect her belly and the child within. Megan sideswiped the other vehicle, and they came to a sudden halt that propelled them both forward in their restraints. The other truck had jammed them up against the wall.

Gabrielle glanced at the driver of the other vehicle, now visible in his cabin. He looked in worse shape than either of them. The front of his vehicle had crumpled up from the impact, while blood oozed from his forehead. He slumped to one side even as she watched, and it looked as if he was having trouble breathing.

'I need you to go through to the back and unstrap Bash,' shouted Megan. 'Leave the rifle with me. We're going the rest of the way on foot.'

Gabrielle got herself free of her seat and climbed back through the hatch, dropping down into the rear compartment and quickly unbuckling Bash. If he'd suffered as a result of the impact, she had no way of telling. She got the side door open and guided him outside to where Megan was already waiting, staring back down the slope with the rifle in her hands.

'Bash isn't dressed for the cold,' warned Gabrielle, as they guided him towards the containment field. 'He could freeze to death in minutes.'

'Once we're through the field, we can get to the dropship in a minute flat,' said Megan. 'Maybe even less. So come on.'

The temperature indeed plummeted sharply the moment they passed through the containment field. It was snowing outside, great drifts of it building up beyond the cave entrance. Bash instantly tensed up, his eyes looking wide and startled above his disposable mask. They both tugged him onwards, one on either side, until he began to walk faster, his whole frame trembling from the terrible, debilitating cold.

They were halfway to the dropship when they heard shouts from behind them.

'Keep him moving!' yelled Megan. 'We're nearly there!'

Up ahead, a man appeared from around one of the dropship's stanchions. He aimed a rifle at them, and immediately a shot echoed through the frozen air.

'Get inside as fast as you can!' yelled Megan, dropping to one knee and aiming her rifle. 'And keep your goddamn head down!'

Gabrielle dragged Bash towards the already lowered ramp of the dropship, which was surrounded by pallets and lifting gear. Light flashed and she saw the Freeholder stagger back from the stanchion, bright flames erupting from his chest.

Something whined past Gabrielle's ear just as she reached the ramp. She glanced back towards the tunnel entrance, and saw more Freeholders gathered there, some of them kneeling just inside the containment field.

'Are you *trying* to get yourself killed?' shouted Megan, running up beside her and tugging Bash into the craft. 'Get him inside!'

Bash stumbled up the ramp between them, while more gunshots filled the air. Megan then hit something on a wall and the ramp began to close behind them.

'Over here,' barked Megan, before dragging Bash towards a door that hissed open at her approach. 'Get him inside.'

On the other side of the door was an elevator that looked as if it doubled as an airlock. It rose quickly, depositing them at the entrance to the cockpit. The air felt furnace-hot after spending just a minute or so in the open. Bash's hands felt as cold as ice, and he was shaking.

'Get him strapped in,' instructed Megan, while pulling herself into a couch. Primary-coloured virtual panels materialized all around her. 'We need to get this thing off the ground as fast as we can.'

Gabrielle coaxed Bash into one of the other couches, which, like much of the rest of the cockpit, was stained and streaked with red. By the time she finished strapping him in, the floor beneath her feet had begun to vibrate.

'Your turn,' said Megan.

Gabrielle threw herself into another couch, and felt an invisible weight pressing down on her even before she had finished securing herself. A glance at the screens that had flickered into being all around Megan confirmed that they were already a good distance from the ground.

'That's not good,' Megan muttered.

'What isn't?'

'One of those idiots hit something vital. I'm not sure this thing is going to take us as far from here as I was hoping.'

Sour acid flooded into Gabrielle's belly. 'Then what do we do?'

'Hope for the best,' said Megan, as the dropship boosted upwards.

TWENTY-SEVEN

Reaching low orbit a little over ten minutes later, Megan wondered if she should have been more honest with the girl about just how much trouble they were in. High-priority alerts floated all around her and, based on what those were warning her of, there was a real risk they might simply fall out of the sky. And every minute they stayed up, the more certain that became.

They clearly weren't going to make it to high orbit. Or anywhere else, for that matter.

'There's been a change of plan,' she muttered grimly. 'We're going to have to put down, and soon.'

Gabrielle's nose wrinkled in a frown. 'Is it really that bad?'

'Could be worse,' Megan grunted.

Until we hit the ground, anyway.

More alerts appeared nearby, and she hoped to hell Gabrielle didn't know what they meant. They were now arcing high over the Montos de Frenezo, with the coast of the Great Barren Sea clearly visible to the south.

The question now was, where could they land? The systems-failure estimates dashed any hopes of their reaching even Aguirre.

She pulled up a map that showed the locations of various settlements scattered all across the plains to the west of the Montos de Frenezo. They still had a chance of reaching one of those. One or two were apparently research outposts staffed by off-worlders from other parts of the Accord. One of them might offer some means whereby they could get back to something resembling civilization, if not actually off-world.

A glyph appeared directly before her, flashing an urgent red and accompanied by a message: MULTIPLE BREACH ALERTS. CONTAINMENT SYSTEM FAILURE IMMINENT.

'Gabrielle?' said Megan, her voice high and tight. 'I want you to unbuckle and go to the rear of the cockpit. There's an orange cabinet there. See it?'

Gabrielle twisted round in her restraints. 'Yeah. I see it.'

'There should be survival gear in there. Maybe even some rations if we're lucky. Dig out anything and everything you can, because I think we're going to need it.'

Gabrielle's face was stiff with fright, but she undid her restraints and did as she was asked, without saying anything further. She dug out several breather masks and numerous items of cold-weather gear, along with some freeze-dried rations.

'Maybe you'd better come straight with me,' said Gabrielle, returning to her couch. 'Are we going to make it?'

'I don't know,' Megan admitted. 'I can get us down, but I can't guarantee it's going to be a soft landing. At least there's a settlement we can aim for.' She twisted round to look over at her companion. 'Look, I don't want you to get worried or anything, but if it does come to the worst – and I hope that it won't – I need you to take care of Bash for me and try and get him to safety. Can you do that?'

Gabrielle, in that moment, looked even younger than Megan knew her to be. 'I guess,' she said, sounding less than convincing.

Had Esté been anything like this girl, wondered Megan? So pale and thin and young? Had *she* herself?

'I'm just talking outside contingencies here,' she continued. 'But I'm going to tell you what you need to do to get off Redstone. That's what you most want, right?'

Gabrielle nodded. 'More than you'd believe.'

Oh, I'd believe, all right. 'You heard of Aguirre?'

'Sure,' said Gabrielle. 'It's a city in the River Concord States.'

'I have a friend there,' said Megan. 'A man by the name of Sarbakshian. He owes me . . . a lot. Go to him and he'll get you off-world. Can you remember that name?'

The girl nodded. 'No problem.'

'You're sure?'

'I'm sure.' She nodded, then her expression grew more uncertain, her hands straying towards her belly. 'Listen, Megan, there's something I need to tell y—'

'Later,' said Megan, more abruptly than she meant to. 'We're on our way down again.'

The forward array indicated dense cloud layer below, and it looked like a storm was building up, north of their destination. By now the mountains had slid out of sight around Redstone's curving horizon, and the craft had identified a number of potential landing spots close to the settlement.

Megan thought about how different everything was going to be for Gabrielle from now on. She'd need to get as far away from Redstone as she could – preferably after getting some major facial surgery in a body shop, as Megan herself once had, to reduce the chances of her being recognized. And then there was the question of finding her a new identity, and somewhere to call home.

Nothing that Megan hadn't done herself.

She realized then that she wanted Gabrielle by her side when they did finally leave Redstone. She hardly knew the girl yet, but the fact remained that, in a sense, they were family. Her and Gabrielle, and Bash.

She laughed quietly to herself. *One hell of a fucked-up family you've got there.* A runaway and a walking vegetable.

'We're putting down in another couple of minutes,' warned Megan. 'Brace yourself, Gaby. Bad weather's coming in before long, and I can't make any promises about this being an easy landing.'

'I'm pregnant,' Gabrielle finally announced.

TWENTY-EIGHT

Megan stared at her, thunderstruck. 'You're *pregnant*? For how . . . ?'

'Four months,' said Gabrielle.

Four months? And they both came from short-birther stock, meaning that Gabrielle had perhaps no more than another two months before she'd give birth.

Not long at all, in other words.

'Okay,' said Megan, bringing up a series of menus and studying them with a feeling of hopelessness. 'I guess that does change things.'

She wondered who the father was, and just prayed it wasn't Tarrant.

The ship's computers had recalculated their best options for landing before the anti-matter-containment systems overloaded, based on the changing weather conditions and the topology of the local landscape. It showed her an area of flat terrain adjoining a small body of water – a lake, although it was barely large enough to qualify as such.

The dropship shook again as it hit turbulence during the final minutes of their descent. The drive-fields were now barely keeping them aloft.

Megan kept her eyes on the feed from the external sensors, as white-dappled hills flashed by below, and she got a visual sighting of the lake-shore ahead. She manually tweaked their course slightly and then, before she was really ready, they were dropping towards the ground at a shallow angle.

The drive-fields flickered, then faded forever. Their angle of approach steepened, and Megan realized they weren't going to make it all the way to the actual shore.

They slammed into the lake, sending a fountain of water high into the air. She heard Gabrielle scream as the cockpit lights died, to be replaced a moment later by red emergency overheads.

The dropship yawed and rolled to one side. For a heart-rending moment, Megan felt sure the craft might capsize altogether, but then it partly righted itself before listing back the other way.

She checked a screen and saw that part of the hull now rested on silty gravel beneath the water's surface, just a few metres shy of the shore.

'Gabrielle, you okay?'

'I . . . I think so. Are we down?'

'Yeah,' said Megan, pulling her restraints off, 'but I don't think we're in the clear yet. Not until we get the hell off this ship.'

She climbed out of her couch and struggled to stay upright on a deck sloping at thirty degrees. She held on to the back of the couch and lowered herself until she was positioned next to Bash. It was hard to see clearly in the dim light, but he looked as if he'd come through their crash-landing in one piece.

'You're going to have to help me get him out of here again,' she called out to Gabrielle. Her eyes were adjusting now, and she could see the other woman climbing out of her couch. Given everything she'd been through, thought Megan, and not to mention her condition, the girl was holding up a lot better than might have been expected.

Then, staring down at Bash's calm, unchanging features, she remembered her disbelief when Gabrielle claimed he had sent her to find him.

I know you're in there, she thought. *I don't know what's going on in that head of yours, but I'm more sure than ever there's still some part of you that's aware I'm here.*

What truly hurt, however, was that after everything she had gone through to find him, Bash had instead chosen to speak to Gabrielle.

Megan was surprised to experience a brief flurry of jealous resentment.

He should have spoken to *her*, dammit.

Gabrielle picked her way carefully down to Bash's couch. 'Come on,' urged Megan. 'We've got to get him off this tub before it blows.'

'Blows?' Gabrielle shook her head in puzzlement. 'Where the hell *are* we?'

The dropship shuddered around them, only settling deeper into the soil of the lake bed. 'We landed in the water, just short of the shore.'

'So we're still okay, right?'

'No, we're not.' Megan shook her head. 'Sifra obtained this dropship from the Freehold. It's fuelled with anti-matter, held inside a containment system which is supposed to be just about indestructible, but in fact this thing's a heap of junk.' *And damn Sifra for taking one of their dropships*, she thought. *We could all have been killed before we even got to Redstone.* At least he hadn't left his damn bead-zombies on board for her to have to deal with. 'You saw how rundown and broken everything back there was, right?'

Gabrielle nodded.

'I think that maybe some of that shooting at us pushed the core containment systems towards a possible breach,' Megan continued. 'We need to get off this ship as fast as we can, and as far away as we can, before it gives out entirely. Now, get a hold of Bash and be ready to move quickly, okay? There should be an emergency escape hatch just outside the cockpit, so we can climb out from there.'

Gabrielle nodded mutely, her expression still dazed.

It seemed to take them much too long to free Bash from his restraints and drag him out of his couch. The steep angle of the floor, plus the fact that the dropship rolled slightly from time to time, made the job far harder than it should have been. But they finally managed to half lift him over to the cockpit hatch.

After only a couple of minutes, both women were panting with exertion. 'I'm pretty sure,' said Gabrielle, in between gasps, 'this isn't the activity recommended for expectant mothers.'

With a lot of cursing and muttering, they managed to guide Bash out through the hatch and into the cramped passageway beyond. Megan next located the escape hatch just about where she'd expected to find it.

Gabrielle disappeared back inside, returning with a bag stuffed full of the rations and with some cold-weather gear for Bash. They both dressed hurriedly, then worked together to get him dressed suitably and a mask over his face. By the time they were done, Megan's skin was slicked with perspiration.

She tapped a code into a panel next to the emergency hatch, and a small red light began to blink: slowly at first, then more rapidly.

'Stand well back,' warned Megan. 'Cover your eyes – and his, too.'

Gabrielle did as she was told, tugging Bash back away from the hatch. They crouched a few metres back along down the passageway, feet braced expectantly against the sloping deck.

Explosive bolts blew the hatch loose, filling the air with acrid-smelling smoke and leaving their ears ringing. Freezing cold air rushed in even as the pressure equalized.

Megan was first out through the hatch. She crouched on the broad curving surface of the hull, feeling the ship roll very slightly beneath her, then leaned back in.

'Get one of his arms up to me,' she called down.

She heard the sound of cursing as Gabrielle shoved Bash directly beneath the hatch and then lifted one of his arms up towards her. Megan secured a good solid grip on his hand.

'C'mon, Bash,' she muttered, trying hard not to topple back through. 'Climb the fuck up for mommy.'

Bash's pupils contracted in the bright daylight, his other arm hanging uselessly by his side. Megan fought back a sudden wave of despair. What if they couldn't get him out? What then?

'Climb, damn you,' she cried, finally losing her temper. 'Get the *fuck* up here, you son of a bitch. You were able to talk to her, so don't stand there pretending you don't fucking understand me!'

She could feel now she was close to losing it. She'd had too little respite from a constant struggle for survival over the past several days. 'Up, damn you!' she yelled. 'Climb up!'

In that same moment Bash blinked, then she saw him reach up with his spare hand, his fingers tightening around the hatch's coaming.

Her heart began to thud. *He heard me.*

She held on to him, pulling and grunting with the sheer effort. Gabrielle was doing her best to help him climb up, but the space was too tight and the angle too difficult for her to be of any real use.

The muscles in Bash's arm flexed, and he rose up and through the hatch. Megan grabbed hold of his shoulders as he emerged, and let out a cry of delight.

'That's my baby!' she yelled, putting all her strength into hauling him the rest of the way out. It felt like delivering the world's largest child. He was soon crouching on the hull, staring mindlessly off towards the horizon, while Gabrielle also climbed out.

'Shouldn't we get out of here?' she said, her face shiny with perspiration.

Megan nodded, then carefully began to work her way down the smooth expanse of the hull to where it curved into the water below.

'I think I can jump down from here,' she said over her shoulder. 'It doesn't look too deep.'

She slid a little further, then gravity took over, and she began to slide, her feet and hands skittering helplessly. She fell through the air for a brief moment, then landed feet-first in the freezing cold water barely a second later. The water came up to her waist, deep and cold enough to make her teeth chatter. 'Bash next,' she called back up.

'*How?*' Gabrielle yelled back, in exasperation.

'Just . . . give him a goddamn push, okay? He's like a cat. He'll land the right way up.'

I hope.

Bash came sliding down the hull a moment later, his feet and hands trying and failing to find purchase on the surface. He landed with an almighty splash, then came upright, shaking his head like a dog and sending off a spray of water.

Gabrielle was next, letting out a small shriek of shock as she dropped, rear end first, into the water.

'Move,' yelled Megan, pointing towards some low hills nearby, dotted with snakehead bushes. 'That way.'

Without further discussion, they each took hold of one of Bash's arms – which was starting to feel like the most natural thing in the world to do.

Gabrielle glanced back at the dropship as they splashed their way on to the shore. 'Are we really in that much danger?' she asked, her teeth chattering as violently as Megan's.

'Remind me again: how much do you know about anti-matter containment systems, Gabrielle?'

'Nothing.'

'Then you're going to have to take my word for it that we don't want to be *anywhere* near that thing when it blows.'

They left the shore behind and pushed on between the bushes, scraping past curling black branches with bulbous tips. 'Just a little bit further,' urged Megan, knowing it would be just too ironic if they got blown to smithereens this close to being home free.

They soon came to a narrow pass between two hills: a steep-sided gorge with a trickle of water descending towards the lake from higher ground. The bushes became less dense, and the going therefore marginally easier, except they had to keep stopping to untangle Bash from clawing branches.

Just as they reached the far side of these hills, the sky behind them suddenly flared white. This was followed a moment later by a roar that shook the ground right beneath their feet.

Gabrielle stared back the way they had come. 'Was that . . . was that the dropship?'

Megan squeezed her eyes shut to eliminate the after-images. She could still see the outline of the hill rendered in bright, pulsing colours.

A pall of smoke rose high into the air and some of the bushes at the gorge entrance were burning merrily, now sending up their own plumes of acrid smoke.

'Yeah,' said Megan, 'that was the dropship.' *And my second crash-landing in just a couple of days.* It occurred to her that they were all likely to be affected by residual radiation, so the sooner each of them could get inside a medbox, the better.

Gabrielle's face had turned completely white above the rim of her breather mask, having not realized until now just how much danger they had been in. 'How much anti-matter was in that thing?' she asked shakily.

'A pinhead's worth,' said Megan. 'And that's all it takes.' She reached inside her coat and adjusted the heating elements, turning them all the way up. She saw Gabrielle do the same first for herself, and then for Bash. Before long, all three of them were billowing clouds of steam, as their jackets dried them from the inside out.

'We should get going,' announced Megan. 'But before we do, there's something I've been meaning to ask you. Did Tarrant do anything that might prevent you communicating mind-to-mind?'

Gabrielle only looked confused. 'I don't understand.'

'We're both machine-heads,' said Megan. 'That means we can talk privately via our implants. Like you did back there with Bash, right?'

Gabrielle thought for a moment. 'Before we came here, Tarrant shot something into my neck, some kind of machine. He called it—'

'An inhibitor?' Megan interrupted.

Gabrielle nodded. 'How did you know?'

'There are ways of telling,' said Megan. 'Like the bruise on the back of your neck. And the fact I just tried and failed to communicate with you through my implants.'

'Oh.' Gabrielle instinctively reached up to touch her skin there.

'Soon as we find a medbox, we'll make getting rid of that thing a priority.' She glanced up towards the horizon. 'Sunset is still a couple of hours away, and that settlement we were aiming for is a good twenty kilometres from here. We should try and cover as much ground as we can before then. We don't want to stick around here one second longer than we have to.'

Gabrielle nodded. 'Sure.' She stepped over and touched her fingers to Bash's elbow. Megan watched, astonished, as Bash followed her lead with surprisingly little prompting.

'Has he spoken to you again since you came looking for me?' asked Megan, sensing a touch of bitterness in her tone.

Gabrielle appeared not to notice it. 'Not a peep,' she replied.

Megan nodded and swiftly stepped over to take Bash's other arm. 'You up for a long walk?' she asked.

'Sure,' said Gabrielle. 'Beats getting shot at.'

An hour later, they could still see the same dark plume of smoke spiralling high into the evening sky behind them.

For a while, they followed what looked like an animal trail, exhaustion reducing both women to silence. The land on one side of them dropped away into a deep crevasse, at the bottom of which Megan could see a river churning. There were hills up ahead that looked likely to prove a challenge, but a cluster of canopy trees stood closer, just a few kilometres away and rising tall above the surrounding landscape. If they became too exhausted, or the weather deteriorated, they could at least shelter there for a while.

The sight of these trees reminded Megan of the first time she had ever met Bash, and she glanced sideways at his broad features, wishing she could share this same memory with him. Somehow it felt almost as if she'd come full circle.

She ignored the tiny voice in the back of her head that was whispering how they could get to the settlement so much quicker if they just left him behind.

In fact it took nearly six hours of walking, including a number of detours, to reach the nearest of those canopy trees. In the meantime, they had covered seven or eight kilometres at most.

Megan called a halt as soon as they were under cover. She noticed Gabrielle staring up at the tree's immense canopy, her eyes roving up the length of the massive trunk to its apex. If this girl's life had been as sheltered as she suspected, it was entirely possible she had never before seen one close up.

They sat wherever they comfortably could amongst the roots, taking the weight off their legs with joint groans of satisfaction. Gabrielle pulled Bash down into a sitting position beside her, then leaned back and closed her eyes, for long enough that Megan thought she must have fallen asleep. But then finally Gabrielle lifted her head once more, and looked in her direction.

'Tell me,' said Megan, 'exactly how Bash communicated with you, back in those caves.'

Gabrielle shrugged. 'It's like I told you. I heard his voice inside my head.'

Megan frowned. 'That's what doesn't make sense. Why could he communicate mind-to-mind with you, while I couldn't?'

'I had wondered about that,' Gabrielle admitted.

'Did he say anything else?' she asked. 'Apart from telling you to find me, that is?'

She nodded. 'He said he's been fighting some kind of war.'

Megan stared at her. 'A *war*?'

'It didn't make any sense to me either. He talked about something called a wanderer. He said it was hiding something.'

Megan felt the breath catch in her throat. She forgot about her exhaustion, the pain in her feet and the throbbing in her bandaged shoulder. She looked over at Bash – poor, sightless Bash – and felt a shiver of awe mixed with fear.

'Anything else?' she asked.

'He said something about being lost for a very long time, and that he could only stay for a while.' Gabrielle shook her head. 'I can't even begin to tell you what he might have meant.'

Megan felt her cheeks growing moist, and wiped the tears away before they could freeze solid on her skin.

'Does any of this mean anything to you?' asked Gabrielle.

'I feel crazy for saying it but, yes, it does.' Megan scratched at the dirt with one boot, waggling and stretching her toes until the pain felt slightly duller. The fit of her breather mask was not quite perfect, and it had chafed her skin as they walked away from the lake. She drew in a breath, then lifted the mask from her face for a moment, sliding her hand under and scratching at her cheek for one long, luxurious moment before dropping it back into place.

'I already know who *you* are,' she said to Gabrielle. 'But I think it's time you know who *I* am.'

The girl regarded her uncertainly, as the wind rustled the feathered canopy overhead. 'I had wondered, obviously.'

'I was the Speaker-Elect before you, Gabrielle.'

Gabrielle stared at her uncomprehendingly. 'I . . . I was about to say that's impossible, but for some reason I believe you.' She laughed nervously. 'I don't know why I do, but I do.'

'Why?'

She peered at Megan for a moment, then looked back towards the lake, now lost somewhere over the far horizon. 'The official story I heard was that there had been an attempt to kidnap the Speaker-Elect before me, which was why they made Karl – I mean, Gregor Tarrant – my bodyguard. But he told me once that he had heard other stories, that the girl before me somehow escaped, with help, and that the official story was just a cover-up. But he couldn't find any proof and decided it was just a rumour, and nothing more.'

Megan felt her blood chill. If Tarrant had kept digging further, he might eventually have worked out who she really was.

'It's slightly more complicated than that,' she said.

She told Gabrielle about her flight through Dios with Malcolm – and how she had no memories of her previous life in the Demarchy. Gabrielle's eyes widened and her skin turned even paler than from just the cold.

'You don't remember *anything*?' asked Gabrielle.

'Not a thing. I know that her – *my* – name was Esté, but that's all.'

'So what they were going to do to me . . . they had already done to you. And now you have all Dakota Merrick's memories?'

'Yes, but I'm not her,' Megan replied, a touch defensively.

'But you *are* her, aren't you? We're both genetically identical to her, so if you have her memories as well, then . . .'

Megan shook her head adamantly. 'That still doesn't make me her. She died centuries ago. I have no . . .'

No responsibility for the things she did or the decisions she made, she had almost said.

'Who *is* he, really?' asked Gabrielle, changing the subject. 'Gregor Tarrant, I mean. Before we escaped, I knew him as Karl Petrova. What does he even *want* from me?'

'He wants an opportunity to merge you with the Ship of the Covenant himself, then give you to the Wanderer so it can use you the same way Tarrant wants to use Bash – as a means to an end.' She went on to tell Gabrielle about her first encounter with the alien entity, and the circumstances whereby Bash had been reduced to a near-vegetative state.

'That's so terrible,' said Gabrielle, her eyes downcast, once Megan finished the whole story.

'Gabrielle, I have to ask . . . is Tarrant the father of your child?'

Gabrielle lowered her gaze to the stony black ground at her feet, then nodded. 'I feel such a fool.' Her hand folded over her belly. 'All the time, he was telling me such ridiculous lies, and I believed him because I wanted to.'

'Are you sure you want to keep it?'

Gabrielle darted a surprised glance towards her. 'It didn't do anything wrong,' she said. 'It's all I have left . . . as Bash is all *you* have left.'

'Come again?'

'That's the reason you came to find Bash, isn't it? Because you care about him.'

'One of the reasons,' Megan admitted. 'That, and the fact that Tarrant will dispose of him as soon as he gets what he wants from the Wanderer.'

'Was he . . . was Bash your lover?'

'No. No, he wasn't,' said Megan. 'But I've never felt closer to anyone else in my life. He . . . saved me, Gabrielle. He's family now – the only one that ever really meant a damn to me, and the only one who knew the truth about who I really am.' She shrugged. 'I guess you're right: he's all I've got left.'

'And when this is all over?' asked Gabrielle. 'Do you think you can cure him, fix him?'

'Until you told me about him speaking to you in some way, I didn't think that was possible. But if I could just get him to talk to me the same way he did with you . . .' She shook her head, unable to keep the pain out of her voice. 'I'm going to take him with me myself, to the Wanderer, and make my own deal with it.'

Gabrielle looked at her with alarm. 'Why?'

'When I . . . when *Dakota* died, she was hunting something called a Maker Swarm. It's like a cloud of machines, in their millions, all capable of travelling at light speed, and all utterly inimical towards other civilizations. That's what's heading our way, and I have to try and find a way to stop it.'

Gabrielle stared at her, then shook her head, looking away.

'I know it's a lot to take in,' said Megan.

The girl shook her head. 'You have no idea.' She frowned. 'Why can't the Magi ships just go and do something about the Swarm themselves?'

'They were designed not to be able to function – to carry out actions – without having a controlling intelligence, a pilot. It was a way of preventing them from evolving into just as much of a potential threat as the Swarms themselves. It means they cannot act autonomously. So they alerted me – someone who's effectively part-Magi and who understands the threat – knowing I'd then have to act. We're forever connected to the Magi ships, you and me. We were made by them, in a sense.'

'You make it sound as if we're not really human,' the other woman remarked.

'I'm not sure that we *are*, to be honest. I think the ships had some way of knowing where the Swarm was, and which way it was heading, and let me know.'

'Then why is it coming here?' asked Gabrielle.

'I told you how Dakota died when she was visiting a Maker Swarm halfway across the galaxy. Before it killed her, the Swarm learned things from her about us – about humanity.'

'What does it want with us?'

'The Swarms are programmed to prevent the rise of any advanced interstellar civilizations. If they'd ever discovered that the Shoal Hegemony had bucked the trend for as long as it did, they'd have tried to destroy them, too. But the Hegemony is gone, and now it's the Accord which is growing into a true interstellar civilization. Unfortunately that makes us a target, and that's why I need to fly out to the Wanderer and negotiate with it. I believe it knows something that could help us stop the Swarm before it arrives.'

'How can you be sure the Wanderer will help you, after what it did before?'

'I can't. But I'm pretty sure it isn't going to turn me down once it knows what I have to offer.'

'And what's that?' asked Gabrielle.

Megan hesitated, and realized she had been on the verge of telling her the truth of what she intended. But before she could say anything more, Gabrielle looked past Megan, her eyes growing suddenly wide. She scrambled to her feet.

'Look,' she pointed. 'Over there, coming this way.'

Megan stood up, realizing she could hear a faint rumble somewhere far off in the distance. She looked in the same direction as Gabrielle, and saw multiple pairs of headlights coming their way. She could even hear the sound of heavy treads crunching across ice and rock.

She glanced at Gabrielle and thought about telling her to run, but knew it was already too late.

Whoever had found them – whether it was Tarrant, or someone else – there was nowhere left for them to hide.

A high-built truck pulled to a halt just a short distance away, looking far newer than anything Megan had seen in the Montos de

Frenezo. Gabrielle stepped up beside her, taking a tight grip of her hand.

Light played across them, almost blinding them.

'Hey there!' a voice shouted in an accent that didn't sound at all as if it came from Redstone. 'We saw that dropship going down. Were you on it?'

'Yes, we were,' Megan called back, raising a hand to shield her eyes from the brilliant light. 'Who are you people?'

'Thank God,' said the owner of the voice, coming closer. Megan saw it was a woman, short and round and swaddled in brightly coloured survival gear. 'We were pretty sure there weren't any survivors, but then we saw your tracks heading this way. How many of you are there?'

'Just three,' replied Megan as the woman stepped up close to her.

'Hey, Lloyd!' the woman shouted, turning towards the trucks behind her. 'Kill those goddamn lights. You're blinding them!'

The lights dimmed. 'Martha Stiles,' announced the woman, holding out a gloved hand towards Megan. 'We're based fourteen or so klicks from here, and you guys look like you could really use a hot meal.'

'More than you could even begin to imagine,' was Megan's heartfelt reply.

TWENTY-NINE

Even with the trucks, it still took a couple of hours to get back to the settlement on the far side of the hills.

Low, grey-coloured domes loomed out of the encroaching night as they pulled to a halt. Several of Stiles's fellow workers had clearly waited up for their return, and they proved to be friendly but eager to find out just what had happened to the dropship.

Stiles shooed them away, then guided the three newcomers into a building which proved to be a communal refectory. By now, Megan had worked out that Stiles must be in charge of this research base, and her suspicion was confirmed when the woman told her, over hot coffee and freshly baked *char siu*, that she was project director for a long-term study of the canopy trees. They were trying, she explained, to find some way to adapt the same techniques the trees used to create their self-contained microclimates, as part of ongoing research into terraforming low-viability worlds.

Over the past several days, however, work had taken a distant second place to watching the news about the disaster that had struck the Demarchy. Most of her staff, Stiles explained, were in fact absent – called away to aid in the various relief operations springing up and down the coast to deal with the few survivors. And, given that a clash between the Accord and the Freehold seemed inevitable, Stiles had been spending much of her own free time holding remote conferences with her funding body about whether they should all stay put or pack up and go home before things turned really nasty.

When Gabrielle pulled down her hood, revealing her freshly cropped hair and the traces of circuitry visible beneath the skin, Megan felt suddenly certain that Stiles knew exactly who she was. But, rather than saying anything, she merely glanced knowingly at Megan.

'And what about your friend?' asked Stiles, turning to study Bash. Megan had guided him to a seat and helped him eat one of the heated buns. 'I can see you're all machine-heads, but is there a reason why he doesn't speak?'

By now, some of Stiles's staff had joined them at the table. 'That,' said one of them, 'is a persistent vegetative state, if I ever saw one.'

'He's brain-damaged,' Megan admitted, and then improvised: 'I'm not sure who he is, or how he got that way.' She flashed a taut smile. 'It's a long story and I'm sure, after all that driving, you really don't want to—'

'Nonsense,' said Stiles, her gaze hawklike. 'Why don't you start from the beginning?'

Megan sighed inwardly and gave herself up to the inevitable. 'I work as a commercial pilot for the AM refineries in the outer system,' she began, then nodded at Gabrielle, whom she had introduced as her niece Beth. 'Beth lives – well, *lived* – in Port Gabriel. I myself was in orbit when the floods hit.'

'You were in Port Gabriel at the time?' said a young woman sitting next to Stiles, now staring at Gabrielle. 'Shit. And you *survived* that?'

'She managed to make it to higher ground,' Megan said quickly.

Gabrielle nodded uncertainly, glancing from Megan to Stiles. 'Yeah,' she said. 'It was pretty bad.'

'She managed to get word to me that she was okay,' said Megan. 'I was on an orbital station at the time, so I managed to borrow a dropship and fly down to pull her off.'

'And your friend?' asked Stiles, nodding at Bash. 'Where did he come from?'

To Megan's surprise, Gabrielle spoke up. 'We found him just wandering on his own in the middle of all the devastation, out in the middle of nowhere. We don't have any idea how he got there. He hasn't said one word yet to either of us.'

Megan eyed Stiles uncertainly, now quite convinced the woman didn't believe one word of their increasingly elaborate story.

'So where were you flying to, when you crashed?' asked a plump-looking man. 'You're a heck of a long way from the Demarchy out here.'

'We were on our way back into orbit when something went wrong with our fuel containment,' said Megan. 'We tried to send out an alert for help, but the comms traffic was overloaded.'

'That's true,' muttered the girl next to Stiles. 'The Tabernacle's been severely hit all over. A lot of communities are completely cut off.'

'We had no choice but to come back down,' Megan finished. 'We were in serious trouble.'

'And I guess you didn't have much choice about *where* you put down,' said Stiles, her face impassive. 'Am I right?'

'That's exactly it,' said Megan, mentally damning the woman for toying with her. 'And I can't even begin to tell you how deeply, hugely grateful we are that you came out there and found us. We owe you our lives.'

'Well, you're damn lucky we found you when we did,' said Stiles. 'A storm system's been building up for a couple of days north of the Frenezo range, and it looks like it's heading this way.'

'I think I can handle a bit of bad weather,' said Megan stubbornly.

Stiles shook her head. 'You're not from here originally, are you?'

'No, I'm not,' Megan admitted.

'This is more than just some wind and snow we're talking about,' said Stiles. 'When blizzards hit at this time of year, believe me, nothing moves – and not much flies either. Wind speed can top two hundred and thirty kilometres an hour out here in the middle of nowhere. And on top of that, starting tomorrow, half of Redstone's going to be a no-fly zone for anything except Accord gunships, troop carriers and ground-to-orbit ambulances. What that means is that you can figure on being our guests here for at least the next week – if not quite a bit longer.'

Megan nodded. 'Again, thank you. But there's one other thing we need to talk about. Beth is pregnant.'

Stiles looked shocked. 'That's the *first* thing you should have told us,' she said. She turned towards Gabrielle. 'How long, sweetheart?'

'Four months,' said Gabrielle.

'Short or long-birther?' asked Stiles.

'Short,' Gabrielle replied.

Stiles nodded. 'You're well past the midway point, then. You picked a hell of a time to get pregnant, young lady.'

At least Stiles had the tact not to ask about the father. Megan had already stretched the limits of her creativity in inventing a story for the three of them.

Stiles spread her hands flat on the table and look around at her co-workers. 'Okay, then, down to business. As I said, half our people are away, working in the refugee camps, so you'll have your pick of quarters to use so long as you're here.'

'Again, I just want to—' Megan started to say.

'Hold it.' Stiles raised a hand. 'You don't need to keep thanking us; it's not as if we'd just leave you out there.' She nodded towards Megan's still-bandaged shoulder. 'We should check over all three of you, not just Beth. And as for Mr Mute, I don't know what we can do for him. He's a machine-head, which means he's on a registry somewhere, so one way or another we'll eventually figure out who he is. But, until then, we don't have the equipment for scanning neural hardware or anything like that.'

'Beth is the priority,' agreed Megan, looking pointedly at Gabrielle. 'But we're all going to need treatment for radiation damage, at the very least.'

'Well, we're not doctors, but we do have a medbox. Beth, if you could go with Lucy –' Stiles turned to the young woman seated next to her – 'and she'll show you where our medbay is.'

'Come on,' beckoned Lucy, pushing her chair back.

Gabrielle gave Megan one last, long look before following Lucy out of the refectory. Her eyes were rimmed with dark blotches due to fatigue, and Megan could see how much the events of the past few days had taken out of the younger woman. If the sheer emotional impact hadn't hit her yet, it soon would. Growing up knowing you would have to die so that a stranger could occupy your body was one thing. Surviving long enough to discover you had a cloned twin old enough to be your mother constituted a whole new level of fucked-up.

'I think it's about time you got some sleep, Megan,' suggested Stiles, standing up. Those members of her staff that had joined them rose also, as if they had been waiting for a cue. 'You can take your turn in the medbox tomorrow, as soon as we're sure your niece is going to be okay. After that we can talk some more.' She glanced at the plump young man. 'Mike, could you find Megan somewhere to sleep?'

'Sure thing,' he replied.

Stiles took Megan's hand and shook it. 'I must say,' she said, studying the bandages visible beneath Megan's shirt, 'whoever patched you up did a very good job.'

'It's been quite a couple of days,' said Megan.

'Oh, I'm sure it has,' Stiles agreed, her gaze piercing.

Megan undressed carefully in the quarters Mike had found for her, then cautiously peeled the bandage away from her shoulder. Standing before a full-length mirror, she turned this way and that, studying the vivid yellow and purple bruises covering her shoulder and a good part of her upper back.

Admit you've been lucky, she told her reflection. But she still couldn't quite bring herself to relax, even now, as she wasn't sure yet whether Stiles was really a friend. The story she had managed to concoct for the woman's benefit, on the spur of the moment, sounded less and less convincing in retrospect the more she thought about it.

She next stepped into the tiny shower cubicle and used its limited supply of hot water to wash as much of the blood and sweat from her skin as possible. Then she dried herself and crawled into the single narrow bed, passing into unconsciousness just moments after her cheek touched the pillow.

The next morning, Lucy came and fetched Megan for her turn in medbay. The baby, it turned out, was doing fine despite everything they had been through, and Gabrielle had been moved into her own quarters, next to Megan's.

Lucy left her alone in the medbay, promising someone would check up on her in the next couple of hours. She closed her eyes as the lid of the medbox folded down over her. Nanocyte-rich gel flooded the tank, cooling and numbing her skin so that she hardly even felt the gentle prick of microscopic needles.

When she emerged from the tank half a day later, the bruises had faded considerably. The machine's diagnostics informed her she had suffered relatively minor cell damage, no more than might be expected of someone who spent much of her life in space. She washed off the gunk, then dressed in the fabricator-printed overalls Lucy had left out for her.

She found Stiles waiting for her in the corridor outside the medbay with a tray of coffee and food. 'Right on time,' said Stiles, leading Megan back to her quarters. 'I'd like to have a little chat, if I may.'

Stiles herself took the single available chair, while Megan made do with perching on her bed with a bowl of porridge. 'You're looking better than you did last night,' observed Stiles, flashing Megan a taut smile over the rim of her mug.

'Thanks,' said Megan, worried about what might be coming next.

Stiles blew gently on her coffee, clearly gathering her thoughts. 'Let's get straight to the point,' she said, as she looked up. 'I'd swear on my left tit that girl you brought with you is the Speaker-Elect of the Demarchy. I wondered if maybe you'd kidnapped her, but it's clear she's not accompanying you under any kind of duress. And that whole story about your friend, the mute, wandering alone through the ruins . . . ?' she snorted. 'I'll give her this, she's got imagination.'

Megan studied the other woman's expression and realized there was going to be no fooling her. 'You're right,' she said. 'I didn't kidnap her.'

'So –' Stiles regarded her candidly – 'are you going to tell me who you really are, and how the hell all three of you wound up out here?'

'That depends,' replied Megan. 'Are you going to send Gabrielle back to the Demarchy?'

'That's her name?' asked Stiles.

Megan nodded.

'Well, see, that's the thing,' said Stiles. 'Technically, sending her back is my legal duty. On the other hand, I don't much like the Demarchy, or all that bullshit about girls ascending to heaven after becoming one with that damn ship. I don't know what they do with them for real, whether it's kill them or hide them away or just lock them in some deep hole somewhere – but I don't approve, put it that way.'

'So you're saying you'll help us?'

'That depends on what it is you want help with, doesn't it?' Stiles remarked drily. 'Whatever your story really is, I'm betting it's a damn sight more interesting than that little tale the pair of you concocted last night.'

'What I said about her not being kidnapped is only half the truth,' admitted Megan. 'The reality is, she was kidnapped by the Freehold . . . and so was I, and so was Bash.'

She noticed Stiles's blank expression. 'That's his name,' Megan explained, 'the one who can't speak.'

'Just to be clear,' asked Stiles, 'your name really *is* Megan?'

'It is, yes.'

'Okay, go on then.'

'To cut a long story short,' Megan continued, 'we managed to steal a dropship and make our escape, but the ship was already damaged when we took off from the Montos de Frenezo. That's when we had to take it down towards the lake.'

'So why did they kidnap you?'

'In Gabrielle's case, it's because she's extremely valuable to them.'

'They want to ransom her back to the Demarchy? Is that it?'

'Not exactly,' said Megan, then surprised herself by telling something like the truth. 'They want her because she's a key to information stored inside the Ship of the Covenant's memory banks, and there's no other way to get hold of it.'

She watched Stiles absorb this.

'And you?' asked Stiles. 'Where do you and your other friend fit into all this?'

Megan opened her mouth to explain, then she grinned and shook her head. 'Well, you can ask all you want,' she said, 'but that's something I'm keeping to myself. Sorry.'

'Then at least tell me how your friend Bash ended up brain-damaged? Is that connected to all of this in some way?'

'It is. And his vegetative state is because of something done to him by the same people who kidnapped Gabrielle. He's my oldest friend, Miss Stiles. I . . . couldn't just leave him with them.'

'Call me Martha,' said Stiles. 'Must have been hellishly difficult, leading him all the way from the lake to that canopy tree. He can't even walk a couple of paces without someone guiding him, can he?'

'No,' Megan agreed. 'No, he can't.'

Stiles sighed and put her coffee on the floor between her feet, before sitting back.

'I'm going to do something really stupid, and trust you,' she declared. 'The only alternative is throwing all three of you back outside, but I'm not going to do that. Want to know why?'

'Go on.'

'I saw how well you cared for him – for Bash. I saw the way you handled him. Call it gut instinct, but something about you made me feel sure you were a good person, even if you were being more than a little economical with the truth.'

Megan hardly knew what to say. 'I . . . thank you, but I think you should be aware that the Freeholders are going to be looking for us, and for Gabrielle in particular.'

Stiles thought for a moment. 'Thanks for the warning, but I don't know how likely that really is, since the dropship's a total write-off. For all they know, you three got killed in the explosion.'

Megan nodded. 'I won't deny I was kind of hoping they might think that.'

'I'll admit we managed to find your trail,' Stiles continued, 'but only just, and the storm that's coming in is going to obliterate it pretty swiftly. Now, why don't you tell me just what it is you have planned for Gabrielle, once you're finally gone from here?'

'I'm going to take her somewhere safe, and a long way away from Redstone,' said Megan with heartfelt conviction. She leaned forward. 'You know, we *could* leave right now. If you gave us some transport, we could be out of your hair forever.'

Stiles shook her head. 'Forget it. With the current no-fly restrictions, your only way out of here is overland, and we're hundreds of kilometres from the nearest settlement – not to mention that the storm's going to hit any minute now. And besides, your friend Bash still needs to take his turn in the medbox.'

'Then I want to ask you a favour, Martha . . . maybe a big one. I badly need to get to Aguirre so I can arrange safe passage off Redstone for all three of us. But I can't do that if I take the others with me.'

'You heard what I said, didn't you? It could take you weeks just to get to the nearest settlement.'

'I can't afford to waste any time,' insisted Megan.

'Can't do it.' Stiles shook her head and sighed. 'We need every resource we've got, including all the trucks. Best bet for you is to wait here until the storm season has passed and, if the no-fly restrictions are over by then, we can get you back that way.'

'Maybe now's not the best time to ask—'

'No, Megan,' said Stiles firmly. 'We'll help you, and that's only right, but I'm not just going to hand over one of our trucks to you when you're still unwilling to tell me exactly who you are. And if it wasn't for Gabrielle, and what I think might happen to her if she did return to the Demarchy, maybe things would have worked out differently. But my decision is final, do you understand?'

'Yes.' Megan nodded. 'I'm sorry if I seemed pushy.'

'That's fine,' said Stiles, standing up now. 'It's just that, with half this damn planet going up in flames, I'm beginning to wonder if coming here was really such a good career choice.'

'It might be all over by next week.'

Stiles smiled. 'Do you really believe that?'

Megan chuckled. 'No, not at all.'

'I should get the medbox prepped for Bash,' declared Stiles, stepping towards the door. 'Look, this is all for the best. Okay?'

Megan nodded. 'Okay,' she said, with as much feigned sincerity as she could muster.

The storm came down a day later, blanketing out the sun and spreading a dim twilight all across the landscape. Megan could hear the howl and shriek of the wind through the walls of her quarters.

The Tabernacle was barely functioning, if at all, though experience told her that the Accord had probably shut down most of the network to try and prevent the Freehold using it for military communications. The Accord's own military comms nets were unhackable, even to a machine-head like herself, so all she had any access to were news feeds about the latest relief efforts, most of which were currently focused on Port Gabriel. The weather there had worsened considerably, hampering all recovery attempts.

The storm continued blowing all through the next day, and then the day after that. Some more news trickled in: half the planet was now in lockdown under new martial restrictions – despite strong protests from the River Concord States, a rival Uchidan nation that had long shared a bitterly disputed border with the Demarchy. In her mind, the howl of the wind became an indrawn breath of suspense, as if the whole of Redstone was waiting for the Accord to begin its counter-attack.

She dropped in on Bash late one night, when she knew the rest of the outpost was asleep. Megan had put him in the quarters opposite hers and Gabrielle's, to make it easier for them both to look after him. He needed to be fed, washed and regularly guided to the toilet.

She found him sitting on the edge of his bed, hands cupped in his lap, and wearing the fabricator-printed pyjamas she had dressed him in earlier. It was feeling slightly chilly, so she turned up the room's thermostat, then tugged some of his blankets up around his shoulders.

Next she returned to the door and locked it, since the last thing she wanted during the next couple of hours was to be disturbed.

She sat beside Bash, placing a hand against the side of his head, feeling the rough furrows and bumps just beneath his hair. 'Okay, Bash,' she said, her voice barely above a whisper, 'you and I are going to see if we can talk to the Wanderer.'

She closed her eyes, cleared her thoughts and prepared to open a mind-to-mind link with him.

'You're going away, aren't you?' said Gabrielle, a few days later, after easing herself on to a stool next to Megan in the refectory and absentmindedly rubbing at the back of her neck. Megan had made good on her promise to herself to see that Gaby's inhibitor was removed from her neck and destroyed. Over just the last few days, the girl's belly had started to round out at a speed Megan found terrifying.

Megan stared at her, startled, before glancing around the room. There was no one else within earshot. 'What the hell makes you think that?' she hissed.

'I can read people better than you think,' replied Gabrielle. 'You just look . . . furtive, the way you creep around, as if you're trying to find a door you can escape through.'

'That doesn't mean—'

'I saw you,' said Gabrielle, 'sneaking out of the garage the other day. The one where they keep all the trucks.'

'Okay, fine. I was going to tell you,' said Megan.

'Does Martha know about this?' asked Gabrielle.

'As long as you're not going to tell her, no, she doesn't,' said Megan. 'Would you?'

'No. No, I'm not. But you know she's going to be seriously pissed off if you steal one of her trucks.'

'I can't help that,' said Megan. 'I have to do what I have to do.'

'But what about us – me and Bash?'

'You're safer here,' said Megan. 'Especially given your condition. And as for Bash . . .'

'Yeah, I know,' said Gabrielle, glancing towards two members of Stiles's staff, who were the only other occupants of the refectory, seemingly deep in conversation with each other. 'I've already got a really good idea of how hard it can be with Bash in tow. I *want* to go with you, very badly. I don't want to just be sitting here waiting to see what happens next. And I don't really feel safe here, or anywhere else on Redstone, not so long as I know that Tarrant or any of the rest of them might still be trying to find us.' A flicker of uncertainty crossed her face. 'But you *are* coming back for us, aren't you?'

'Of course I damn well am.'

'Yeah, I figured.' Gabrielle smiled faintly. 'So, where exactly are you going to go?'

'There's an Accord outpost about four hundred kilometres west of here. I still have sufficient pilot accreditation that I can maybe persuade them to let me hitch a flight on a military ship to Aguirre.'

'Aguirre? That's where you told me to find that man Sarbakshian.'

'That's right,' said Megan. 'He's still the one I'm relying on to get us off Redstone.'

'And then what?' asked Gabrielle. 'We all live happily after?'

Megan hesitated.

'Because I was thinking,' said Gabrielle, 'about what you told me the other night. About how you first met Tarrant, and Sifra, and what it is you all want from the Wanderer and why you want to fly out there to it. While you were explaining all that, I got this feeling from you that maybe you didn't think you'd be coming back alive.'

'That's ridiculous, Gaby. I have to come back. I'm no use to anyone dead.'

'But the Wanderer is dangerous, *very* dangerous – that's what you said.'

Megan nodded slowly. 'That's true. I did say that.'

Gabrielle reached out and touched Megan's hand as it rested on the table. 'Back in Port Gabriel, I used to look in the mirror every day, once I knew what they wanted from me. All I saw was the face of someone who was waiting to die. You've had that same look on your face ever since I met you.'

Megan sighed, and rested the fingers of her other hand on top of Gabrielle's. 'Look, I'm not out to get myself killed. You know that. But you also know I couldn't live with myself if I didn't go out there and find some way to stop the Swarm.'

'I just . . .' Gabrielle swallowed, with apparent difficulty, her eyes downcast. 'I don't know if being clones, or whatever it is we are, makes us sisters or maybe something else there isn't really a word for.' Her eyes came back up to meet Megan's. 'But you're the nearest thing I'm ever going to have to a real family.' She reached down with her free hand and cupped her increasingly protuberant belly. 'Apart from her.'

Megan's eyes dropped towards Gabrielle's stomach. 'What makes you think it's a girl?'

'The medbox told me.'

Megan shook her head and grimaced. 'When I think of the things Tarrant did to the both of us . . .'

'Just promise you'll be back,' said Gabrielle. 'That's all I want to know from you. You have to, Megan, because I don't want to lose you just when I found you.'

Megan felt something welling up deep inside her. She had worked so hard, for so very long, to hold her emotions in check; and now this girl – this *child* – threatened to overcome that carefully maintained balance.

'Of course I'll be back,' she said, meaning it with every ounce of her being.

THIRTY

A week later, once the worst squalls had died down, leaving relatively clear skies, Megan broke into the base's garage with the intention of stealing a truck.

She had already scouted out the three vehicles parked there. She had heard stories from one of Stiles's staff about people sometimes getting stuck out in trucks for weeks or even months on end before they could be rescued, and for that reason all three vehicles were kept stocked with up to half a year's flash-frozen rations. Drinking water could be obtained by scraping snow and ice from the ground and running it through the filtration system. As far as power and heating went, the trucks ran on miniature fusion packs that'd last near as damn forever. Even if she got lost or stranded, she'd be able to survive.

Megan had meanwhile discovered, through casual chat, that Stiles had come to Redstone following the death of her teenaged daughter from a prolonged illness. She now had a sense of why Stiles was so willing to help them, and Gabrielle in particular.

She waited until night had fallen before quietly making her way along one of the sealed passageways connecting the base to the garage. All she needed to do was cycle the air out, board one of the trucks and ease it outside. By the time she was gone, it would be too late for Stiles or anyone else to stop her.

So she was more than a little chagrined to find Stiles already there, waiting for her.

'Martha,' said Megan, dropping her rucksack by her feet. Stiles stood right beside the immense treads of the nearest truck but was, so far as Megan could tell, unarmed.

'I figured you'd pick about now to make a run for it,' said Stiles, coming forward. 'Weather's getting better . . . but you know that's temporary, right? Another couple of days and it'll come down even harder than before.'

'It doesn't matter,' said Megan stubbornly.

Stiles sighed and gave Megan a pitying look. 'You should know that even if you're not willing to tell me anything about yourself, Gabrielle's a different matter. The two of us got talking, though I'm still not sure whether I quite believe everything she said.'

Megan stared at her. 'Does that mean you're going to try and stop me?'

'I'm not sure there's anything I could really do to stop you taking one of these trucks if you really wanted to,' said Stiles, 'and besides, this isn't a prison. Gabrielle told me you were going to try and make it to Aguirre, so you could try and arrange safe passage for all three of you off of Redstone.'

'That's all true,' said Megan.

'You know,' said Stiles, 'you strike me as the kind of person who attracts trouble, even if you're not looking for it.'

Megan shrugged. 'Sounds like a pretty fair assessment of my whole life so far.'

Stiles stepped closer. 'Didn't you consider just telling me the truth earlier, about why you needed to leave?'

'I didn't think you'd believe one word.'

'You're right, I wouldn't have, but hearing it from Gabrielle is another matter. I do believe her, but that's at least partly because of who she is. And that's one reason I'm letting you go – because you need to find some way to get her off Redstone.'

'I will,' Megan promised, then hesitated. 'So what are the other reasons?'

'All the people in this station are my responsibility,' said Stiles. 'I care about them – really, genuinely care about them. They're smart, dedicated people, and my hope is that the further away from here you are, the better chance the rest of us will have of avoiding any of that trouble.'

'It's Gabrielle they want,' said Megan, 'not me.'

'Yeah, well.' Stiles shifted her balance. 'We both know she isn't going anywhere, the state she's in, but you'd better swear on your life you're coming back for her.' Then her tone became angry. 'Tell me I'm not just a stupid old fool who's being too goddamn trusting.'

'You're not, Martha. I swear, on my life, I'll be back for them both.'

Stiles looked at her hard for a long time. Then she shook her head and muttered something under her breath, before turning to the truck beside her.

'Don't try and keep pushing on once the weather turns bad,' she said, slapping one hand on the side of a tread. 'That's the main rule. Find somewhere low and sheltered, and stay put if or when it worsens. The onboard AI is preprogrammed to locate shelter when things get rough, so more than likely all you'll need to do is sit back and let it do its thing.'

Megan nodded slowly. 'Stay put for how long?'

'As long as it takes,' said Stiles. 'Head out too soon, while the weather's still bad – and, believe me, it will get very, very bad – you could get yourself killed. Got all that?'

'Okay,' said Megan.

'Just remember,' Stiles added, 'I'm not doing this for your sake. It's for Gabrielle's. Got that too?'

'Got it,' said Megan.

Stiles came towards her and pulled Megan into a brief hug. Then she turned and walked towards the door leading back into the base.

'Now get the hell out of here,' she called over her shoulder, 'before I come to my senses.'

At first, Megan thought she might have an easy time of it, but the clear skies evident on the morning of her departure proved to be little more than a temporary lull in an ongoing tempest.

Towards the end of her first day of driving, Megan came to the banks of a river that the truck's AI assured her was shallow enough to ford. She sat there for a while, staring out through the windscreen at the primordial tempest sweeping past in front of her, and guessed that, with the Tabernacle's satellites out of commission, the truck's maps probably hadn't been updated since several days before the storm hit.

She reversed back the way she had come for a couple of kilometres, the vehicle bouncing and shifting from side to side as it made its way over rough and broken terrain, then drove upriver until evening fell. Eventually she found a point where the river was just about shallow enough that she could finally get the truck across. After that, she had to drive all the way back downriver again, so she could get back onto the optimal route that the truck had picked for her. Before long she was driving into the foothills of mountains that looked like a smaller version of the Montos de Frenezo.

The journey brought her the visceral realization of just how very sparsely inhabited Redstone really was. Most of its major population centres clustered around the equatorial coastal regions. Beyond that lay only a few scattered outposts amidst a windblown and icy wasteland. It would be all too easy for her truck to break down and get buried in snow within hours.

She parked in the lee of a canopy tree's roots, and woke up again to darkness. At first she thought she had been roused in the middle of the night, but on investigation it proved to be already late morning. The storm had returned, filling the landscape with a rising howl and blanketing out the sun. She took a chance and drove on for a few hours, until the truck flashed a warning that she needed to find shelter as fast as possible.

The wind kept building in force until the truck rocked on its suspension with such violence that Megan feared it might be blown over, regardless of its size and squat, bulky shape. The storm howled unceasingly like a demon out of hell, striking terror into Megan's heart.

Sleet and snow came down in vast billowing clouds that reduced visibility to just a few metres. The truck finally identified a possible hiding place in a steep-sided arroyo lying to the north. She gave up trying to steer manually and let the truck itself take over, and it finally found shelter less than half an hour later.

There she stayed for more than ten days. Occasionally she thought about ignoring the truck's strident warnings as soon as she suggested possible escape routes to its AI, but one look out of the window at the howling chaos beyond the windscreen was always enough to give her second thoughts. And she had not forgotten Stiles's warning either.

Much of her time was spent sitting in the truck's front cabin, a mug of hot coffee cradled in her hands as she stared out at the black sky. As a distraction she tried reading – the truck had a database of several million volumes – but nothing would stick in her mind. All she wanted was for the storm to be over.

When it finally abated, the truck started to dig its way out of the vast drift that had by then filled the arroyo. Its treads slid and slipped around on compacted snow as it fought its way free like some huge and ponderous beast emerging after a long hibernation. At one point Megan had to get out with a shovel and dig away some of the compacted snow herself, setting about it with a furious energy. She had been stuck on board the truck now for just about as long as she had spent at Stiles's outpost, yet she had covered no more than three hundred kilometres – with another hundred to go – before she could reach the Accord military outpost that was her destination. Once it was freed, after long hours of effort, the truck carried her along the narrow gorge that was the only possible route through the mountains, only to find the way blocked by a landslide that, again, did not show up on the truck's increasingly outdated and useless maps. Megan stared through the windscreen at boulders the size of houses, piled on top of one another, and felt a depth of frustration and anger such as she had never known she was capable of feeling.

The only way to circumvent the landslide was by driving back the way she'd come, for a good hundred kilometres or so, then head either north or south to skirt around the furthest edges of the mountain chain. But such a journey would take her thousands of kilometres – and long weeks – out of her way.

Or, instead, she could walk the rest of the way. Just because the truck couldn't go any farther, didn't mean she herself couldn't.

She thought hard about the potential risks, for if she got hit by another storm as bad as the one she'd just lived through, her chances of survival were not likely to be good. But getting to the Wanderer and back – even assuming she was successful in her mission – would take her half a year, and by then the Swarm would be getting dangerously close to the Accord. Time was fast running out.

The truck had emergency gear stowed in the back, including an inflatable tent, several high-quality breather masks, some portable water and air filtration systems, not to mention the emergency rations. It was indeed a risk, but one she decided she had to take.

She set out at dawn the next morning, beneath a bright and clear sky. She had uploaded a map of the terrain to her implants, and fixed for the truck to transmit constant weather updates to her in case the weather did decide to get bad again.

Two days after she set out, it did, and she had to fight her way through a wind threatening to carry her off bodily, until she at last found a narrow ravine. She pitched the tent in the most sheltered part of it and settled in to wait.

Six more days passed before Megan finally emerged beneath clear skies, feeling grimy and cold and slightly unhinged. Her breath smelled foul inside her breather mask and her skin itched beneath clothes she hadn't been able to take off for a week.

She reached the military outpost a whole two weeks later, only to find it deserted, and half the buildings bombed out from some kind of attack.

She crept cautiously across a landing field on which sat the still-smoking remains of a dropship. At one point she came across the body of a Freeholder lying in the shadow of a huge storage shed, his kill-ratio tattoos vivid above the collar of his white-and-grey camouflage. After that, she moved with even greater caution. Even if the Freehold had moved on, it might have left gun-drones behind to guard the place.

Megan made her way inside one of the buildings and found only death. In an auditorium she discovered rows of corpses, their wrists tied behind their backs and neat holes drilled through the backs of their heads.

She pictured a night raid in which Freehold saboteurs had destroyed the dropship on the landing field, while others worked at neutralizing the perimeter defences and jamming all communications. Then she thought of Otto Schelling, and the vast resources such a man could provide.

Enough, perhaps, to equip an entire army.

Wandering on, she came eventually to the garage block. It contained more than a dozen vehicles, all of which appeared to have been sabotaged. But they included a bus that looked in slightly better condition than the rest and, having worked on it for a couple of hours, Megan managed to get its internal diagnostics running. After that, she was able to pinpoint the damage: a circuit board controlling the fuel systems had been ripped out, along with some other vital engine parts.

Locating a machine shed stocked with a fabricator, miraculously undamaged, she then managed to program it to produce some of the replacement parts, before finding somewhere to sit down and chew on a protein bar.

A couple of hours later, she had acquired some shiny new engine parts and a replacement circuit board.

As the bus powered up on her first try, Megan pressurized its cabin and pulled off her breather mask for the first time in a very, very long time. The canned air inside the vehicle tasted sweeter than spring blossoms.

After shutting the bus down again, she found her way into an empty dormitory block equipped with bunks and showers. After standing under a hard spray of hot water until her skin was raw and pink, she stepped out, dressed and then studied herself carefully in a mirror. The image confronting her was one she hardly recognized: positively gaunt, and with her clothes hanging loose on a bony frame.

More than a month and a half since setting out on Stiles's truck, and it felt as if an eternity had passed.

Megan finally reached Aguirre just four days later, only to find that the Freehold had already paid the city a visit. After passing through half a dozen Accord checkpoints in the city's outskirts, she joined a long tailback of traffic that then took hours to work its way through. At one point an Accord trooper carried out a cursory search of her bus, before waving her on.

By now she had picked up some idea of what had happened since her last visit here. Over the course of a week, waves of guerrilla fighters had struck periodically, flying low over the mountains and hills in stealthed gliders, and working in small isolated teams according to some prearranged plan. This series of carefully coordinated attacks had caught the overstretched Accord forces unawares. To make things worse, they had dressed themselves in the same heavy outdoor coats and breather masks worn by Aguirre's own citizens, making it nearly impossible to tell friend from foe.

Sarbakshian's place, when she finally reached it, turned out to have been demolished some time during the fighting. After poking half-heartedly through the still-smoking debris, she eventually found a body so badly charred that it was impossible to tell whose it might once have been.

So much for her nova ship, then.

Megan wandered on for a while until she came to a municipal garden dominated by a miniature canopy tree rising higher than most of the buildings surrounding it. She dug amidst its roots and pulled out a sprig of flowering lizard-tails with red and green blooms, then headed back to the ruins, laying her tribute on the chest of the cindered corpse.

'Goodbye, Sabby,' she said, under her breath. 'You were a son of a bitch in more ways than one, but I still liked you better than most.'

She next returned to the apartment Sabby had loaned her, to find it undamaged. Entering the bedroom, she sat staring around her and feeling as if she'd lived an entire lifetime since she'd last been here. She stripped off her clothes and showered until the water sputtered and suddenly cut off, then she dug fresh garments out of a drawer, before gratefully binning the stinking rags she'd worn for all too long.

Finally she crawled into bed and slept, without dreams, for the next sixteen hours. Nevertheless, when she woke late the next evening, it was with a new plan almost fully formed in her mind.

It was something, she realized, that she should have thought of long before now.

The next day, Megan departed Aguirre for what she knew was the last time. News remained sparse and unreliable. There were conflicting stories that other cities belonging to the River Concord States had been seized by Freehold forces apparently intent on warring against all of Redstone's Uchidan nations, and not just targeting the Demarchy. There was no way of verifying any of these reports, however.

Exiting the city, she guided the bus onto a highway that led to Dios, a long way further down the coast. Aguirre itself was built on a plateau and, as the road gradually wound its way down to sea level, the more evident the damage resulting from the floods became. In fact, it looked as if a hand as wide as the sky had reached down and swept the land clean of most signs of human habitation.

When she reached another checkpoint on the border between the Demarchy and the River Concord States, the Accord troops staffing it made it abundantly clear she would be allowed to go no further.

The Freehold, it was explained to her, had turned the whole of the country beyond into a war zone. Thanking the checkpoint guards good-naturedly, she turned her bus around, and drove back the way she had come for a good ten or twenty kilometres, until she found a side road she'd spotted earlier. Before long she was on her way back towards Dios by a different route, this time encountering no more checkpoints.

At one stage she passed through what her maps assured her was a provincial town, but all she could see was waterlogged wreckage and ruins. Every now and then she came across small convoys of civilian vehicles, heavy bundles strapped on their roofs, heading slowly in the opposite direction. Small shanty towns had sprung up around the roots of a few canopy trees that had managed to survive the devastation. Some of the refugees she passed stared with disbelief as she drove by, heading in what they clearly considered to be the wrong direction.

Some hours later, as the sky darkened into dusk, she pulled up next to an Accord military convoy that appeared to have been destroyed in an attack. There were corpses scattered everywhere, and trucks and rover units reduced to piles of twisted wreckage.

Driving for a short distance back the way she had come, she kept a nervous eye on the landscape all around, then parked for the night in the shelter of a building that had been flushed out during the flood. Every now and then, before she fell fast asleep, she spotted the sleek shapes of Accord military cruisers cutting through the clouds overhead.

She woke once, in the middle of the night, to see beams of light playing across the horizon, then heard the distant thunder of heavy artillery. The flash of orbital beam weapons lit up the clouds from beneath as they struck at some unseen target on the ground, and more than likely, she thought, they were firing at whoever had destroyed the Accord convoy.

After that, she drove a lot more cautiously. Once, after catching sight of figures far off in the distance, she halted the bus and climbed up on its roof with a pair of binoculars to grab an enhanced video image. She saw men dressed in grey-and-white Freehold fatigues, weighed down under equipment and weapons. They were, she saw with relief, heading in the opposite direction to her. Clearly they hadn't seen her.

She decided to wait out another night, then resumed her journey. By now, perhaps no more than another day's drive from Dios, she could see the twisting, sinuous shape of one of the Ka's major tributaries snaking off towards the west.

Setting out the next morning, she came across the site of another battle: the ruins of buildings were still smouldering, and there was a greater variety of corpses this time. Most of the Freehold dead sat inside appropriated civilian vehicles, and only their neck tattoos identified them as enemy soldiers, since they were dressed in civilian clothes. The craters pitting the road all around them might have been caused by grenades or mines, or both.

Hearing a noise, she glanced up to see, above the curving expanse of a shattered biome, a half-dozen gun-drones locked in battle with an unseen enemy somewhere on the ground.

It occurred to Megan that driving a bus into Dios was likely to attract entirely the wrong kind of attention. She pulled the vehicle to one side of the road and slept again until nightfall. Then, shouldering an ultra-light rifle she had brought with her from Sarbakshian's apartment, she set out to cover the rest of the way on foot.

Over the next couple of days, Megan continued through low-lying mounds of weed-entangled rubble that were all that was left of what had once been Dios's satellite towns. She slept during daylight in some of the better-preserved ruins, wrapped up in a survival sleeping-bag, with her rifle close by her hand. She avoided moving during the day, and paralleled the roads from a distance, hiding whenever she heard the sound of approaching vehicles.

Before dawn one morning, she crested a hill on the outskirts of

Dios, and found herself looking out across the mouth of the Ka River. Few of the city's slender towers had survived the floods, and the stink of decay and death came to her strongly on the breeze. The sheer scale of so much tragedy now overwhelmed her.

She hid in the remains of an apartment building until nightfall, then made her way through rubble-strewn streets that were not entirely deserted. She occasionally caught sight of guerrillas moving in groups of two or three, chased by or chasing flocks of Accord gun-drones. She hid a couple of times, waiting for over an hour each time before daring to venture back out into the open.

It was nearly dawn by the time Megan reached the Ship of the Covenant. All the structures that had once surrounded it – the research labs, the dormitories and barracks – were gone, entirely swept away.

Her heart began beating harder and harder as she made her way to where the ship had come to rest against the shattered ruins of a skyscraper. Beyond an occasional flash off in the distance, or the occasional sound of gunfire far off across the ruins, she saw and heard nothing. The ship appeared to be entirely unguarded.

She stepped into the shadows, where the Magi ship's hull pressed deep into the soil, then fell to her knees, opening up the machine part of her mind to the crowded intelligences she could already sense buried within. She could hear their murmuring voices, the gathered memories of a million long-dead civilizations.

They were waiting for her as they had always done – for the woman who had once been Dakota Merrick.

She got up and pulled off a glove, then reached out to touch the great ship with her fingers. The hull had a slight give to it, almost like living flesh, a fact that had never failed to surprise her in that other life.

The hull dimpled where she touched it, growing rapidly deeper and wider and forming deep shadows within. She waited, tense, as a tunnel formed before her, extending deep within the body of the ship.

Light appeared from the depths of that tunnel, glowing softly. She hesitated at the threshold.

Only then did Megan finally offer the ancient vessel her terms – and, to her surprise and pleasure, it agreed to them.

THIRTY-ONE

Gabrielle

Back at the research outpost, Gabrielle awoke to the sounds of gunshots and screaming.

Evie was also awake. Her tiny hands, as small and delicate as flowers, brushed Gabrielle's face, her pink nose twitching as her eyelids parted.

She began to cry.

Gabrielle sat up, her heart pounding in her chest. Evie began to cry louder.

At first she thought the sounds were coming from somewhere outside, but after a moment she realized they were coming from *inside* the building.

In that instant, she knew Tarrant had found her.

'Hush now,' she said to the tiny girl in her arms, all wrapped up in swaddling clothes, and rocked her gently in her arms. But it was no use. Evie could clearly sense her mother's fear.

Gabrielle slid out of bed and stepped over to the door of her quarters. It was just a little after dawn, and Paul and Jen were usually up first and into the refectory, before heading out to take whatever measurements Martha expected them to take, returning late each evening.

She listened, hardly able to breathe, and heard a voice.

It sounded like Sol – Sol with the hawklike nose, whose over two-metre frame was permanently stooped. He seemed to be pleading for his life.

Gabrielle heard someone mutter something, followed by a

gunshot so loud and so near it might as well have passed through her own head. She let out an involuntary moan of fear and pressed herself up against the wall, next to the door, sliding down it until she was sitting on the floor. Evie screamed, as Gabrielle clutched her to her chest.

They had just killed Sol.

She looked around the room that had been her home for the past couple of months. Barely any time at all, really, but she already had so very, very many memories. The people here were utterly unlike anyone else she had ever met: kind and thoughtful and full of joy, with stories and gossip and friendship that made Gabrielle want so very badly to experience life a long way away from chilly Redstone. It was all a far cry from the cloistered existence she had known back in the People's Palace.

Martha Stiles had become something like a mother to her, far more than Mater Cassanas ever had been. She had set the outpost's fabricators to printing out special obstetrics equipment, then, with the aid of the medbay's AI, had taken Gabrielle through every step of the birthing process. And when Martha had first laid the tiny baby against her breast, just a few days ago, Gabrielle, her damp hair still stuck to her forehead, had finally felt the last vestiges of her old life slip away.

Evie had been the name of Martha's daughter, and when she had told Gabrielle the story of her child, and the illness which claimed her life, the name had somehow fitted. The first time Gabrielle had spoken to the tiny bundle in her arms, the baby smiled and let out a sound that was half gasp, half cry of delight.

Gabrielle shuffled, on her knees, across the floor of her room and squeezed herself into the tiny gap between the bed and a wall. Evie grasped at her mother's face with her fingers, but she had stopped crying for the moment at least.

Gabrielle remained there waiting until the door finally swung open. Evie's father entered, dragging Martha Stiles after him, one side of her face so badly swollen that one eye had almost closed. Her mouth was stained with blood.

'I'm sorry,' said Martha huskily. 'They threatened to kill even more of our people if I didn't tell them where you were.'

Tarrant meanwhile said nothing, his face an emotionless mask.

A Freeholder guerrilla wearing fatigues stepped up behind him. 'Find Anil Sifra,' Tarrant turned to him, 'and tell him to come here.'

With a nod, the guerrilla went on his way.

Tarrant's gaze drifted down towards the tiny bundle clutched against Gabrielle's shoulder.

'Her name's Evie,' Gabrielle told him boldly, then watched as a clutch of emotions went to war across the man's face. Perhaps there still was something human left within him after all.

He then let go of Martha, thrusting her towards another man with a scraggly blond goatee who had at just that moment appeared in the doorway. She guessed this newcomer must be Sifra. Gabrielle kicked out and screamed as Tarrant stepped forward, reaching down to drag her out of her hiding place.

Evie began crying, much louder this time.

She didn't have the strength to resist as Tarrant took Evie from her grasp and lifted the child to his shoulder. Then Sifra stepped forward, and struck Gabrielle across the face with the back of his hand, before grabbing hold of her and dragging her into the corridor outside.

They hustled her and Martha along to the refectory, passing Sol's slumped body on the way. Half his head was missing, and the wall behind him was liberally spattered with his blood.

The rest of the outpost staff were already gathered in the refectory. Tables and chairs had been pushed to one side, and they had been forced to kneel with their backs to a wall, their hands resting on top of their heads.

She could hardly bear to look at those white and terrified faces. The bodies of two of them already lay in the centre of the room, seemingly shot at point-blank range.

This carnage, she realized, was all her fault. If she and Megan hadn't sought refuge . . .

Three Freehold guerrillas kept watch over the prisoners. They were dressed in grey-and-white camouflage, with breather masks hanging from straps around their necks, and all of them armed with rifles. Bash stood amongst them, restrained by a light grip on his upper arm.

No matter where she went, she seemed to find herself surrounded by death.

'You didn't need to do this,' she reproached Tarrant, her voice a hoarse whisper and her whole body trembling. 'You didn't need to hurt any of them.'

'They were trying to hide you from us,' snapped Sifra in clipped tones. 'Now tell me exactly how the hell Jacinth managed to steal the Ship of the Covenant.'

She stared at him in utter confusion.

'Speak up, Gabrielle,' ordered Tarrant. 'She must have told you what she was going to do.' Evie gurgled quietly against his shoulder, one of her hands touching his neck.

'I swear I don't have any idea what you're talking about,' she replied, completely baffled. 'She left here to find help, that's all I know. That's all *anybody* knows.'

'She's lying,' snarled the man with the goatee.

'No, Anil,' said Tarrant, without taking his eyes off her. 'Just look at her. She doesn't have a damn clue what we're talking about. None of them does.'

He stepped closer to the frightened woman. 'Megan was sighted in the immediate vicinity of the Ship of the Covenant, just shortly before it lifted up from Dios. I had people tracking her from the moment she entered the city, and they watched her actually go *inside* the ship. How could she do that, when so many other machine-heads have failed during all the centuries since that thing landed?'

'It must be because—' Gabrielle started to say, almost automatically, then she stopped mid-sentence.

'Must be because *what*?' demanded Sifra.

She shook her head. 'Nothing.'

Sifra was now looking dangerously unconvinced. He unholstered a pistol, then gestured towards the kneeling row of terrified scientists. 'Bring one of them over here,' he ordered a guard.

Gabrielle felt sick with dread as a young man whose name was Josh was dragged into the centre of the room, then pushed down onto the floor next to the two corpses. He had soft, dark eyes, and she had often noticed him sitting quietly in the gene lab, studying endless virtual projections of organic molecules. He knelt on the floor with his hands on his head, issuing high-pitched, panicked gasps as Sifra pressed the pistol against the back of his head.

'Start talking,' Sifra said to her, his voice strangely calm. 'If you don't tell us *right now* what you were about to say, your friend here dies. It's your call.'

'I wasn't going to say anythi—'

The sound of the gunshot cut off the rest of her words. She stared, speechless, at Josh's slumped form – and the dark red crater where the back of his head had been.

'Well?' demanded Sifra, gesturing towards the remaining prisoners with his pistol. 'How many more of them do I have to kill before you start talking?'

Gabrielle stared at Sifra, seeing only Thijs wearing a different skin. They were the same man, really: calculating, vicious, and ultimately weak.

'No,' she said quietly. 'You want me to break down and tell you everything, and then you're going to murder every last one of us, regardless. So why should I tell you anything?'

Sifra stared at her impassively, his fingers flexing around the grip of his gun. Gabrielle felt a strange calm come over her. She knew she was going to die; she had already accepted it. *At least this way it's my choice.*

'Fine,' Sifra said at last. He beckoned to Tarrant, still cradling Evie against his shoulder. 'The kid – give it to me.'

Tarrant stared at him uncertainly.

Gabrielle felt her sense of calm melt away as quickly as it had appeared. 'Gregor,' she said, 'no.'

Tarrant was clearly experiencing a deep internal conflict, and for a moment she thought he might refuse. But then he lifted Evie away from his shoulder and handed her to his colleague.

'No,' said Gabrielle again, and began moving towards Sifra.

Hard, rough hands seized hold of her from behind.

'Bring her over here,' said Sifra, carrying the child over to the far end of the room, and laying her down on a small table by the entrance.

A guard dragged Gabrielle over beside him. Sifra had reversed his pistol in his hand, so he was now holding the butt over Evie's tiny, fragile head.

'Time's up,' said Sifra. 'Start talking.'

Gabrielle struggled to breathe, her lungs aching with a kind of pain she had never experienced before. She didn't want to believe what was happening was real, or that she was really here.

'Just tell him what he wants to know,' Tarrant grated, stepping up behind her.

'She's your daughter,' she croaked, twisting round to face him. 'How could you let him *do* something like this?'

Instead of answering, he looked away.

'Well?' asked Sifra, raising his pistol a little higher.

'Megan Jacinth isn't her real name,' Gabrielle finally said, in a rush. 'She was the last Speaker-Elect before me. They made up the story about a kidnap attempt to hide the fact that she had managed to escape on her own – but not until after she'd merged with the Ship of the Covenant.'

Sifra and Tarrant stared at each other.

'Bullshit,' said Sifra, raising his pistol again as if about to bring it smashing down.

'Wait a minute,' said Tarrant, putting out his hand.

Sifra halted.

'How do you know all this?' Tarrant asked her. 'Did Megan tell you?'

'She's making this up,' Sifra was shaking his head. 'Don't seriously tell me you believe her?'

'I want to be clear about this.' Tarrant was staring at Gabrielle. 'You're telling me Megan is also a clone of Dakota Merrick?'

Gabrielle nodded.

'Gregor, what are you . . . ?' began Sifra.

Tarrant turned to regard him with a look of triumph. 'Think about it for a moment,' he said. 'It obviously makes sense.'

'How?' demanded Sifra.

'If Megan escaped from the Demarchy *after* merging with the ship,' said Tarrant, 'then she must also possess Dakota Merrick's thoughts and memories, right?'

Sifra lowered his gun, suddenly looking less certain.

'It explains so much, doesn't it?' Tarrant continued. 'Otherwise how could she get on board the Ship of the Covenant so easily, and simply fly away with it?'

Sifra's eyes grew wide in realization. 'Nobody but her could ever make sense of the Wanderer,' he murmured. 'Nobody could get Bashir to respond the way she did, let alone survive the experience.'

'All that time, the one thing – the one *person* – we needed to get the Wanderer to deal with us was right there on the *Beauregard* along with us,' said Tarrant. 'And we never even suspected.' He shook his head in disbelief and laughed. 'I don't think it's too much of a jump ahead to guess where she's headed. She's clearly after the same damn thing we are.'

'Okay, fine,' said Sifra. 'You're right, it *does* make sense. But it still leaves us with a problem: how do we get the Wanderer to deal with us if we don't have Megan – or Merrick or whatever her damn name is?'

Tarrant's gaze settled once more on Gabrielle. 'I was wondering the same thing, but then it hit me.'

Sifra followed the direction of his gaze. 'What?'

'Anil, we have *her*,' he said, pointing at Gabrielle. 'Remember, she has the identical DNA to Megan.'

'So?' asked Sifra.

Tarrant made an exasperated sound. 'Think about it. They're both linked in some way to the Ship of the Covenant. They're both machine-heads. Maybe that means she can do the same things with Bashir that Megan could.'

'You want to use *her* to talk to the Wanderer?' said Sifra, looking uncertain. 'You think it could work?'

'It's got to be worth a shot, hasn't it? We'll take her and Bash up to orbit, then we'll run a trial experiment with them.'

Sifra nodded, his expression speculative. 'You're right. We've got nothing to lose, anyway, have we? But she's not bringing that brat of yours on the ship with her, Gregor.'

Oh no, thought Gabrielle. *Oh, please, no*. They were about to kill Evie.

Tarrant stared at Sifra, his expression unreadable. 'I'm not sure that's necessary—'

'Your job,' said Sifra, 'was to infiltrate the Demarchy and bring out the girl. Getting her pregnant wasn't part of it. This is your mess, Gregor, and you're going to have to . . . clear it up.'

Tarrant glanced at her briefly, then back at Sifra. 'There must be an alternative,' he said.

'*Alternative?*' Sifra hissed. 'Don't waste any more of my time.' He stabbed a finger towards Stiles and her staff, still kneeling at the far end of the refectory. 'I want you to *take care* of them while I fetch Bashir back to the dropship.' He turned to the Freeholder still gripping Gabrielle's arm. 'Think you and your men can handle that?'

The man nodded. 'No problem.'

'I'll see you shortly, Gregor,' said Sifra. 'As soon as you've settled matters here.' He signalled to the guard left in charge of Bash. 'Bring him along.'

The guard nodded, and led Bash back out of the refectory in Sifra's wake.

The one in charge of Gabrielle turned to Tarrant, and nodded towards the prisoners. 'Should we . . . ?' he asked, in a low voice.

Tarrant nodded stiffly. 'Do it,' he murmured quietly. 'Don't give them any warning – there's a lot more of them than us, and I don't want to take the chance they might try and rush us. But leave Stiles alive. I still want to talk to her.'

Gabrielle tried to pull free of the guard's grip. 'No,' she protested, 'you can't. They haven't done anything. You—'

Tarrant responded by first unclipping his own pistol, then pulling Gabrielle close to him, covering her mouth with one hand while pushing the barrel of his gun against her cheek with the other.

'Shut up,' Tarrant snapped at her, his expression furious. 'For once in your fucking life, just *shut up*.'

She continued struggling as the guard stepped away from them to join the other one covering the research staff with his rifle. They conferred briefly, then both raised their weapons to unleash a volley of shots before their prisoners could have a chance to react.

Gabrielle finally tore herself free of Tarrant's grasp and swept Evie up from the table. She then pressed her face against the wall as the sound of killing filled the air.

Finally the noise abated, leaving only a terrible silence that clawed at her innards.

'Sir?' she heard one of the guards say.

'Bring Stiles over here,' said Tarrant. 'Gabrielle, turn around now. You and me and Miss Stiles are going to have a little talk before we leave here.'

When she didn't respond, Tarrant grabbed her by the arm and yanked her round to face him. She saw Martha, looking dazed and bruised and pale with shock, standing between the two remaining soldiers.

'Sir,' said one of the two men, 'my understanding was that we shouldn't leave *any* of them alive.'

'I'll take care of it,' said Tarrant, indicating his pistol. He jerked his head towards the door. 'Now go.'

The two men regarded him uncertainly.

'I said *go*,' Tarrant repeated, in the same voice she had heard him use to his troops back in Port Gabriel.

As soon as they had departed, Tarrant turned his attention back to Stiles. 'You're in charge here, right?'

'Yes,' Stiles managed to reply, her voice still sounding ragged and hoarse. She swayed a little, her gaze slightly unfocused.

'Gabrielle, give her the baby,' instructed Tarrant.

'No. You're going to—'

'No, Gaby, I'm not going to kill either of them.'

'But—'

'Martha, right?' he turned to Stiles.

She nodded.

'Can you take care of the child if we leave her here with you?' he asked.

Martha looked as if she wasn't sure she'd heard him correctly. 'I . . . yes.' She nodded. 'Yes, I can.'

'Good.' Tarrant nodded as well. 'Now, Gabrielle, before Sifra comes back to find out why all this is taking so long . . .'

'There must be—'

'There's no other way,' he said sharply. 'Now give her the goddamn baby before Sifra realizes what I've done.' He took a deep breath, forcing a smile. 'This'll be our secret, understand?'

Gabrielle nodded automatically. Moving like an automaton, she handed Evie over to Stiles, who accepted the baby with disbelief clearly written across her face.

Gabrielle no longer resisted when Tarrant took hold of her arm once more. He paused at the entrance to fire two shots into the refectory floor, in quick succession.

The last Gabrielle saw of Martha, she was still standing amidst the bodies of her friends and colleagues, Evie clasped tightly in her arms.

THIRTY-TWO

Megan

Megan had no memory of anything that might have taken place after boarding the Ship of the Covenant. Instead, without the memory of transitioning from one place to another, she found herself on another world.

Or rather, she found herself on the virtual representation of a world that had existed aeons before, in another galaxy; a dream, spun by an ancient machine intelligence specially in order for it to communicate with her. Back in her previous life, when her name had been Dakota Merrick, she had wandered through countless such worlds, preserved within the matrices of this ship and others, interacting with the shades of creatures that had passed away long ago.

Such as the one standing before her now.

She stood near the middle of a vaulted hall, and a Librarian – an anthropomorphic representation of the collective intelligences within the Magi ship – stood before her, with its face lost in shadows.

When it spoke, the creature's voice sounded strangely flat, despite the expanse of space around them. 'You asked us,' it said, 'whether we would take you to the Wanderer.'

'And you said you would.'

'That decision is contingent on our first having full possession of the facts. May we ask how much you yourself know about the Wanderer?'

'I know it's all that's left of a civilization called the Core Transcendence that was wiped out by the Makers. It's been wandering the galaxy ever since, looking for something that can help it destroy them. Sometimes it runs into other spacefaring species, and trades information with them if it's feeling peaceable. I know it's been searching for a Maker cache, so that it can get hold of a nova drive.'

'And as for yourself, you believe the Wanderer can help you destroy the Maker Swarm that is currently bound for this part of the galaxy. Why do you think that?'

'Because it managed to destroy a Maker Swarm at least once before.'

'And it told you this?'

'The first time I encountered it, yes.'

'And you kept this information to yourself?' asked the Librarian.

She felt her skin colour. 'Who was I supposed to tell? Nobody knew who I really was . . . I mean, who I had been,' she corrected herself.

'And it hasn't succeeded in destroying another Swarm since?'

'How could it, without a superluminal drive? It got lucky one time when a Swarm came to investigate it, and the Wanderer managed to destroy it before it could jump out of range again. But a strategy like that is unlikely to work more than once, and the dying Swarm would almost certainly have broadcast a warning to others of its kind.'

'Which does explain why the Wanderer is so very desperate to acquire its own nova drive. And yet you yourself clearly think it would be a bad idea if it did. Why?'

She gathered her thoughts before replying. 'Look, there's always been something inimical about the Wanderer during all of our communications – something cold. You and all the Magi ships share the same goal with it, to destroy the Makers – but your underlying programming also demands that you preserve intelligent life throughout the universe. The Wanderer doesn't care about life anywhere else, since all it wants is revenge, regardless of the consequences.'

It occurred to her then that Tarrant and Sifra were not so very different from the Wanderer in that respect.

'In short,' the Librarian concluded, 'you mistrust the Wanderer's motives. Its past aggression suggests it could prove harmful to your own civilization, were it to come into possession of a nova drive. You should know, then, that we agree with your assessment. Which begs a further question – what could we possibly hope to gain by taking you to it?'

'All you've ever really done is engage in skirmishes with the Swarms, without ever once striking at the Makers themselves . . . and yet, finding some way to destroy the Makers is central to your purpose. The Wanderer thinks you already have the key to fulfilling that purpose buried so deep in your memory banks that you don't even know it's there.'

'How could the Wanderer possibly know if that was the case?'

'I re-established contact with it some weeks back.' It had taken her the whole of that long night, locked in Bash's quarters back at the research outpost, to establish an effective bridge to the Wanderer. 'It turns out that the Core Transcendence once had contact with the Magi, a very long time ago.'

'We have no record of this,' said the Librarian.

'Are you sure about that?' She stepped slightly closer. 'I remember what it was like to wander through all those worlds that every one of these ships has preserved inside it. Tens of thousands of worlds and cultures spread over hundreds of thousands of years and more. How do you know that precisely just the information you need isn't already buried somewhere inside your memory banks?'

'This is possible,' the Librarian agreed. 'Do you know when this meeting might have occurred?'

'Nearly two million years ago,' she replied.

'The time of the very earliest Magi cultures?'

Megan nodded. The history of the Large Magellanic Cloud was one of constant expansion and contraction, of different civilizations and species coming to the fore at different times. Each successive civilization had built on the ruins of those that preceded it. 'And it's also at just about the same time,' she continued, 'that the Core Transcendence first encountered the Makers here in *this* galaxy. The Core Transcendence sent an expedition out to the Large Magellanic

Cloud to contact those early Magi in order to try and find out if they knew of a way to fight the Makers.'

'And?' asked the Librarian.

'And they came back empty-handed,' she said. 'But not without having learned that this early Magi culture supposedly had a means of preventing the Makers from expanding any further – one that's been lost ever since.'

'I presume,' said the Librarian, 'there's a reason why they came back empty-handed?'

She spread her hands. 'That's just it. I don't know why they did. All I know is that, according to the Wanderer, all this time there's been a way to stop the Makers – to wipe them out forever. But the ancestors of the people who built you didn't want to share it with the Core Transcendence.'

'And this leads you – and the Wanderer – to believe that the means you refer to remains buried somewhere within the collective memories of the Magi ships.'

'It's possible, isn't it?' she asked. 'God knows, we need at least to try. But unless you can locate that data yourself, we're going to have to try something drastic.'

'Such as?' asked the Librarian.

She held her breath for a moment. 'Such as letting the Wanderer have direct access to your memory banks.'

'Do you really think that would be wise,' said the Librarian, 'given the Wanderer's apparent tendency towards the unpredictable?'

'It's a question of priorities,' replied Megan. 'If you don't do this, the Swarm will reach human space, and we've got no way to repel it. Your programming will prevent you from allowing this to happen – and that's why you found a way to warn me, by letting me know the Swarm was on its way.'

She paced back and forth before the Librarian, cupping one fist with her other hand. 'How long has it been?' she demanded. 'More than a hundred and fifty thousand years, since you and the rest of the Magi ships came to the Milky Way? And you haven't even come close to fulfilling your core programming. If the Wanderer is telling the truth about there being some way to destroy the Makers, then this could be your chance for a final, all-out victory against them.'

The darkened silhouette's head moved slightly to one side. 'And yet you chose to arrange your own expedition rather than approach us once we informed you of the Swarm's approach. You were going to offer yourself as a bridge to the Wanderer, and allow it to access our memory banks. Why, when you could simply have come here and made use of this ship?'

'How?' she asked. 'What was I supposed to do – just stroll in past the Demarchy's security? Until the flood swept everything away, that would have just got me killed. Not to mention that my first memory, after dying somewhere on the other side of the galaxy, was of waking up in a torture chamber in which *you* helped to put me, and who knows how many others. Why the hell would I trust you after that? Not to mention that for all I know you're still too crippled to fly.'

'We would have found a way to circumvent the Demarchy's security operations once we knew you were on Redstone,' said the Librarian. 'As to your other concerns, you should remember we had no control over what the Demarchy chose to do with you or any of the other clones, once your original memories were restored. In truth, we had every reason to expect that, given your innate resourcefulness, one or more of you would have found a way to escape. And you and Gabrielle did manage that, eventually, although it took rather more lifetimes than we had originally anticipated.'

She stared at the Librarian, thunderstruck.

'Let me ask you something in turn,' said the Librarian. 'If you didn't trust us before, what brings you to trust us now?'

She shook her head. 'Well,' she said, her tone calmer now, 'I guess the fact is I'm all out of any other ideas.'

'You should know,' said the Librarian, after a short pause, 'that this ship is not so crippled as it might appear. We have already lifted off from Redstone, and we are even now accelerating to jump velocity.'

She stared at the creature in astonishment. 'How . . .?'

'Taking off at this particular time is admittedly risky,' the Librarian explained, 'given that this ship is still not fully repaired, and therefore remains in a weakened state. But it is, as you yourself have made clear, a necessary risk.'

'No,' she said. 'We can't leave, not yet. I need to go back for Bash first . . . and Gabrielle.'

'That won't be necessary,' said the Librarian. 'They are both currently on board a ship called the *Damien Ingersoll*, which is owned by Otto Schelling.'

Megan felt all the blood drain from her face. 'Are you sure?'

'Entirely, yes. The *Ingersoll* broke orbit shortly after we escaped Redstone's gravity well.'

'How do you know they're on board?'

'A simple analysis of encrypted data traffic proved sufficient.'

Megan swallowed. 'Gabrielle would have given birth by now. Do you – know if the baby is with her?'

'Her child's whereabouts is unknown,' the Librarian replied. 'The *Ingersoll* is clearly outfitted for a long-range expedition, so it is undoubtedly bound for the same destination as ourselves.'

'Then we need to stop them,' Megan moaned, sinking to her knees on the cold stone floor. 'What do they even need Gabrielle *for*? She's no use to them now that she can't be merged with this ship.'

'Then she may simply be a hostage,' said the Librarian. 'However, you should remember that you and she are genetically identical. It may be that, lacking you, they intend to use her to communicate with the Wanderer, through Bashir.'

Her eyes grew wide. 'They can't do that . . . can they?'

'The Demarchy created you and every other Speaker-Elect from Dakota Merrick's genetic material – and that, in turn, had already undergone considerable optimization on board this very ship. Gabrielle will almost certainly be capable of communicating with the Wanderer in precisely the same manner as yourself.'

'But if that's true,' Megan mumbled, half to herself, 'then they must know who *I* am.'

'That is yet to be ascertained. In the meantime, we should speak about the other matter on your mind.'

She stared at the alien entity in confusion. 'What other matter?'

'Your desire,' replied the Librarian, 'to recover the memories of your former life as the Speaker-Elect Esté.'

She blinked, taking a moment to comprehend what it was saying to her. 'You can do that?'

'We did not suggest that. But why is it that you so strongly reject your previous existence as Dakota Merrick?'

'Just because I have her memories,' said Megan, 'doesn't make me her.'

'Has it not occurred to you that, by living your life as if your former existence had no bearing upon it, you have made mistakes you might otherwise have avoided? I do not think Dakota Merrick, as she was, would have allowed herself ever to trust men such as Gregor Tarrant or Anil Sifra so easily, and with such dire consequences.'

Megan felt a flush of fury. The alien ship was patently digging through her mind, pulling out memories and putting them on display.

'Go to hell!' she screamed, her voice echoing through the vaulted hall in ever-decreasing waves. She was clenching her fists so hard by her sides that they hurt. 'Get out of my head!'

'By denying your former existence,' the Librarian continued regardless, 'you have denied yourself the lessons that life has taught you. Imtiaz Bashir is a good man, but perhaps not the wisest. It was wrong to have listened to him when he first brought Tarrant to meet you.'

Tears streamed down her face. '*She's* the whole reason the Maker Swarm is on its way here,' she protested, meaning Dakota Merrick. 'It would never have known the human race even *existed* if she hadn't gone out there. I just don't want to have to carry that responsibility!'

'She went looking for a means to stop the Nova War of two centuries ago – and she found it,' declared the Librarian.

Megan stared at the shadowy figure. 'What? That had nothing to do with me . . . or with her. The war was halted by some expedition—'

'There are some facts of which you are clearly unaware,' said the Librarian. 'You have been resurrected before, and it was a long way from either Dios or Redstone.'

'I have?' said Megan faintly.

'The first time was shortly after your encounter with the Maker Swarm.'

'But . . . I don't remember anything about that.'

'That other Dakota died far away from a Magi ship,' explained the Librarian. 'Hence, there was no opportunity to recover her memories directly. This is why you do not have those same memories.'

'How . . . how did she die?'

'She took part in the expedition you just mentioned, the one that brought the Nova War to an early end. She helped deploy a weapon against the Emissaries that would never have been discovered if her previous incarnation had not gone out to encounter the Swarm. Without her, the human race, and many of the species neighbouring it, would most likely have been wiped out by now.'

She stared into the shadows, thunderstruck. 'I . . . I had no idea.'

'You are not Esté,' said the Librarian. 'She died so that you might live. Her thoughts and memories cannot be recovered, and you must accept this.'

Megan cradled her head in her hands. It seemed all too much to take in.

'In the meantime,' the Librarian continued, 'we still have a new mission to complete, and our flight out to the Wanderer will take some months. That leaves you plenty of time – virtual or otherwise – to contemplate our next move. So I suggest you make the best use of it.'

THIRTY-THREE

Gabrielle

Gabrielle could think of nothing but that last glimpse of Martha Stiles, clutching little Evie to her chest.

She screamed and fought as Tarrant dragged her towards an airlock, where the two Freeholders who had murdered the outpost's staff stood already waiting. One of them seized and secured her wrists, and when she tried to struggle, the other hit her so hard across the back of her head, it left her nauseous and dizzy.

Finally they strapped a breather mask on to her, then dragged her outside into the freezing cold of a Redstone night. She hardly needed the mask, since she barely drew a single breath in the short time it took them to load her inside a waiting dropship. Once on board, she was in no position to offer further resistance.

Instead of strapping them in acceleration couches, they zipped her and Bash into padded bags that immobilized them entirely. Gabrielle felt a flood of anger when she realized that these containers were of a type designed for carrying animals into orbit.

Not long after, they transferred to a ship high above Redstone, where a woman with dark hair and a severe expression took charge of placing her inside a medbox. She returned some hours later, explaining to Gabrielle, as she emerged dripping from the medbox, that she was now on board a vessel called the *Damien Ingersoll.*

The *Ingersoll*, Gabrielle quickly learned, was a starship carrying a crew of a dozen. There was gravity on board, which indicated that they must be accelerating towards the outer system, in preparation for a jump.

Tarrant strode into the medbay while Gabrielle was still getting dressed. She cowered away, moving quickly to cover her nakedness.

'She's healthy enough,' said the woman supervising her, 'and her implants are functional. So if you want to start testing the bridge, it's probably safe.'

Tarrant nodded. 'Good work, Kathryn.' He glanced over at Gabrielle. 'Finish getting yourself dressed, then you're coming with me.'

'Where to?' Gabrielle demanded in a quavering voice. Meanwhile, Kathryn departed the medbay, leaving them alone. 'And what about Evie?'

'I thought you'd have the good sense not to mention that name.' Tarrant spoke in a harsh whisper. 'Or don't you understand the risk I took just to keep her safe? Stiles will take care of her.'

'She's your daughter,' said Gabrielle. '*Our* daughter. Doesn't that mean anything to you?'

He stepped forward and slapped her, hard. She drew in a sharp breath, and put out a hand against the wall to steady herself.

'Fuck you,' she snarled, through gritted teeth. 'I carried your child inside me. Does that really mean nothing to you?'

She waited for another blow to descend, but it never came. He just stared at her, with eyes bright and angry.

'Hurry up and finish getting dressed,' he growled finally, picking up some of her clothes from the deck and throwing them at her. 'We're only wasting time.'

A little while later, Tarrant led Gabrielle through the ship, to a room where they found Bash seated in a high-backed chair with some contraption resembling a squid made from black rubber carefully arranged on his head. Sifra was there as well, along with a third, older man she didn't recognize. This man glanced at her briefly, then motioned her towards a seat directly facing Bash.

'Sit,' he said.

Her will to resist appeared to have deserted her with the loss of

Evie. She therefore did as she was told, staring straight ahead as Tarrant secured her to the chair with some elasticated restraints. It would have been better for her, she thought, if she had simply drowned in the Ka's freezing waters.

Tarrant stood back. 'I want to be very clear about this,' he began. 'We're not trying to hurt you here. Those restraints are for your own safety while we try an experiment.'

'You want me to talk to the Wanderer? Okay, I get it.'

'You need to think of Bash as being a kind of transceiver,' said Tarrant. 'He can send and receive messages between you and the Wanderer. We need to see if you can establish the same kind of rapport through him that Megan once did.'

And if I can't, you'll toss me out into space at the first opportunity.

Tarrant seemed to be waiting for some kind of answer.

'I understand,' she said.

Tarrant nodded perfunctorily. 'Good.' He turned to Sifra. 'Let's get started.'

Sifra stepped over to her, holding a device identical to the one Tarrant had used on the Grand Barge to inject an inhibitor into her neck.

'What are you doing?' she demanded, twisting away from him as he reached out towards the back of her neck.

'Relax,' said Tarrant. 'Before we can start, he needs to install a new inhibitor.'

'I don't want—'

'It's for your own good, Gaby.'

Sifra pressed the device against the back of her neck, just above the raised flesh where her original inhibitor had been located. She tensed, clenching her jaw when she felt something like a needle punching through the skin. She'd be damned if she'd let them see how much it hurt. Sifra stepped away from her and went over to join Tarrant, who was making adjustments of some kind to a virtual panel.

The back of her neck began to throb painfully. Something about the pain fuelled her anger, making her want to throw herself at the two of them, to tear at their smug expressions with her fingernails, to rake the flesh from their skulls and listen to their screams. She twisted and strained against her restraints, but it was all to no avail.

'Let's ramp back her inhibitor,' she heard Tarrant mutter under his breath, as he moved a finger slowly across part of the panel. 'About . . . there.'

Gabrielle opened her mouth to scream obscenities at the pair of them, then glanced at Bashir and saw, with a start, that he was looking directly towards her, his gaze full of furious intensity.

Any further words died in her throat, as Bash's eyes seemed to swallow her up, drawing her inside them . . .

Suddenly she was surrounded by stars wheeling around her head. Something enormous blotted out half the universe, an infinite black horizon into which light fell forever.

She tried to scream, but by now had lost all sense of her physical body. The *Ingersoll*, Bash, Tarrant – they were all gone, lost somewhere on the far side of the universe.

And just then, when she thought she might be about to lose all hope, she sensed a familiar presence close by. It floated in the chaos like a tiny flicker of light lost in an unending ocean of dark.

Somehow she knew it was Bash.

'Gabrielle?'

She came to with a start, every muscle in her body taut, her skin slippery with sweat. Her neck felt like she'd twisted it badly, and she thought she could taste blood in her mouth. She coughed, trying to clear her throat, and tried to move, but she was still tied to the chair.

'Here,' said Tarrant, kneeling next to her and pushing something against her lips. 'Drink this.'

She swallowed, tasting cool, clear water. The foul taste on her tongue diminished.

'What happened?' she managed to ask.

'You were foaming at the mouth.' Sifra sneered from across the room, with evident amusement.

Tarrant produced a cloth, and used it to mop her mouth and cheeks. He glared briefly at the other man.

'Tell me what happened,' he pressed. 'Tell me everything you saw and heard.'

She did her best to describe everything she had experienced – all, that is, except for that brief glimpse of something she was so sure had been Bash. Something held her back from saying anything about that.

'And you're sure that's all?' he asked. 'You were under for a good hour.'

An hour? 'I thought it was just a couple of seconds,' she said, genuinely shocked. 'Did anything happen?'

She saw the three men exchange glances – and guessed something had indeed happened.

'So was your experiment successful or not?' asked the old man from across the room, sounding impatient.

'For a first time, yes,' said Tarrant, standing up again. 'She's come out of her experience better than anyone else but Megan . . . and you saw the way the bridge reacted.'

'We still haven't got anything coherent out of the Wanderer, though, have we?' insisted the old man, with a petulant edge to his voice. 'It's not talking to us now like it did when we still had Jacinth.'

'Not yet,' agreed Tarrant. He was gazing down at Gabrielle, but his mind was clearly elsewhere. 'But give it time. It knows we're on our way and, just as importantly, it knows why.'

'We'll try again,' decided the old man. 'I don't want to take any chance of it deciding to deal with that woman instead of with us.'

Tarrant glanced down at Gabrielle and shrugged. 'Looks as if we're not done with you yet.'

She stared up at him sullenly. 'I hope to hell it tears you and your ship apart once we get there. I hope to hell I get to watch you all die.'

Tarrant turned away and said nothing.

THIRTY-FOUR

Megan

The woman lived in a cliffside dwelling on a world that orbited so close to its sun that it actually passed through the corona. Through the tall and graceful windows of her dwelling, she could see great arcs of plasma thrown up from the star's surface, like fountains of fire falling back in on themselves.

Lava flowed beneath a floor fashioned from a single piece of perfectly transparent and flawless diamond, yet she felt no heat through the bare soles of her feet, nor through the windows beyond which lay graceful gardens protected by energy fields.

She had been living here for a century now, and she had long ago forgotten her name. She had lived a thousand lifetimes and more, and an infinity of worlds lay in her past and future.

When a creature appeared before her, its face wreathed in shadows, something about its demeanour struck a chord of fear in her.

'It is time for you to return,' said the creature. 'We are now almost at the end-point of our voyage.'

'I don't know who you are,' she protested, 'or what you—'

Long-lost memories then flooded back into her mind, and she remembered her name. She remembered the Wanderer, Gabrielle and Tarrant. This world on which she lived, and all the others she had visited over scores of millennia, were nothing more than shades locked in the memory of an ancient starship, like dusty photographs lost somewhere in the back of a drawer.

She sank to the floor as if wounded. None of it was real.

'No,' she gasped. 'I'm happier now. I can just stay here. You can negotiate with the Wanderer without me—'

'But you must return,' said the Librarian. 'You know that.'

She could not deny its words.

'Then give me just a little time to get ready,' she said haltingly.

She spent the next subjective century visiting worlds she had not seen for millennia. She now remembered that she had set out, long ago, to find whatever secret weapon the Wanderer believed lay hidden in the Magi ship's memory. But she had as yet found no trace of it.

As her century-long period of grace thus came to an end, the ship fashioned an actual, physical space within its body for her. It created rooms and corridors that reflected the style and appearance of craft employed throughout the Accord.

Megan finally awoke in her own body in a bed recess located inside a nondescript cabin. Her memories of subjective millennia immediately began to fade, like the half-remembered dreams they actually were.

And, while she had been dreaming the voyage away, the Magi ship had traversed very nearly fifteen thousand light years.

She finally got herself upright and ordered coffee from the cabin's kitchenette. She drank it while calling up a series of images that revealed to her the Magi ship's current location. They were deep inside the Calafat-Holt Cluster, and had just entered the very same system the *Beauregard* had voyaged to more than a decade before. They were currently decelerating from a significant fraction of light speed, and making a fast sortie of the inner worlds.

The Wanderer had meanwhile made its presence known. It had by now regained its former dimensions, and was orbiting the same small moon where the *Beauregard* had found it. Deep gouges on the moon's surface showed how the Wanderer had made further use of it as a source of raw materials for its reconstruction.

The question was, could she communicate directly with the

Wanderer without compromising her own sanity? And was it even possible to do so without Bash?

The ship itself will act as a bridge between yourself and the Wanderer, she heard the Librarian explain, from within the confines of her own skull.

She almost dropped her coffee. 'If I need to know something,' she said out loud, 'I'll just ask you, okay? Just . . . keep the hell out of my head until then.'

We understand.

The presence faded, but that sudden tension in her shoulders remained.

A small red icon suddenly glowed on a map of the local stellar region, which was floating to one side of her. She focused on this icon, and it expanded into an image of what, to her practised eye, was clearly a long-range expeditionary ship, its lengthy hull bristling with drive-spines. The *Damien Ingersoll*, Otto Schelling's ship, had jumped in-system just half a day after the Ship of the Covenant, and it was already decelerating on its long, looping inward journey.

She put the coffee down, her stomach suddenly feeling small and tight. 'We might as well get this over with,' she declared to the empty air. 'Let's see if the Wanderer's feeling chatty.'

Make yourself comfortable and we will attempt to establish a link.

Megan nodded stiffly, then glanced around to see a low, soft couch that she couldn't remember being there the last time she had looked in that direction. Had it simply escaped her attention, or had it always been there at the periphery of her vision?

Nothing here is real, she reminded herself.

She settled back on the couch and closed her eyes. 'Ready when you are,' she murmured.

This time was different. The chaos was more ordered, more comprehensible, because the Ship of the Covenant filtered out all the extraneous noise that had caused her such terrible distress in the past.

WE (you) ARE (you are) ONE (are one) IN MANY (in) ONE. WE ARE REMEMBER WE YOU (small, bright) FAST.

<We share a similar goal,> Megan sent in reply. <The destruction of the Makers.>

In truth, she did not communicate in words. The Librarian instead leeched images and concepts from her conscious and unconscious mind as soon as they formed, presenting them directly to the Wanderer and filtering them through some kind of enormously complex syntax she couldn't even begin to grasp. The experience was both uncanny and unsettling.

The Wanderer clearly remembered her from their previous encounter. The 'small, bright' ones, she soon understood, were humanity. Their lives – and the lives of all mortal creatures – were fleeting in comparison to that of the Wanderer itself, being here and gone in brief blink-and-miss-it spurts of furious activity.

WE will CONSIDER WILL (consult, contemplate) EVALUATE.

Megan opened her eyes once more and drew in a sharp breath. *What next?* she wondered.

And now we wait, said a voice in her thoughts – but she could not be sure if it came from the Librarian or from herself.

THIRTY-FIVE

Gabrielle

Back when Gabrielle had dreamed of how her life might turn out following her escape from the Demarchy, becoming nurse to a fully grown man with the self-awareness of a baby would never have entered her thoughts. But, then, neither had she imagined that the father of her child would betray and kidnap her, participate in the murder of millions and essentially attempt to sacrifice her to an alien entity of unknown provenance.

She had been kept almost entirely isolated from the rest of the *Ingersoll*'s crew throughout the long months of their journey from Redstone. On those rare occasions when she did encounter unfamiliar faces on board the *Ingersoll*, she had no idea what to say to them or how to act. The only one who had even spoken to her so far was the woman she knew simply as Kathryn, who maintained a cool and professional distance whenever she came to check on the health of both Gabrielle and Bash.

Gabrielle still dreamed constantly of her last glimpse of Evie, clutched in the dazed and blood-spattered arms of Martha Stiles. During those first long weeks aboard the *Ingersoll*, she had regularly wept until her face was blotchy and raw. But even that emotion faded after a while, leaving her feeling as if she had been hollowed out, reduced to a paper-thin shell only superficially resembling the woman she had once been; a woman that had effectively died months before and uncountable light years away.

Bash remained as incommunicative as ever, so much so that Gabrielle began to wonder if she had hallucinated the one time he had stared directly at her, shortly after they boarded the *Ingersoll*. Apart from his regular medical checks, no one else aboard showed the slightest interest in actually taking care of him. Since she and Bash were forced to share the same quarters, Gabrielle had become his nursemaid essentially by default, feeding and cleaning him and even helping him with his toilet visits.

Sometimes, when depression threatened to overwhelm her, she would lose her temper and start yelling and shouting into his unresponsive face, until self-pity or melancholia or simple exhaustion forced her to stop.

Every few days they were both led to the same room as before. Bash would be hooked up to Sifra's machine, while Gabrielle would attempt once again to establish a bridge to the Wanderer.

It proved to be a long, laborious, painful and ultimately fruitless process; despite her early success, actually engaging in anything like a meaningful dialogue with the alien entity proved to be excessively difficult. Sifra and the man who called himself General Schelling had developed a rough syntax for communication, based on previous experiments with Megan and others and, over the weeks and then months, Gabrielle first learned this syntax and then attempted to teach it to the Wanderer.

Each session left her feeling exhausted and increasingly weak. Then she would sit in silence and watch as Tarrant, Sifra and Schelling argued with increasing bitterness over their lack of progress. It was clear that the General blamed Tarrant for having allowed Megan to escape in the first place.

Gabrielle's hair had grown back quickly, till its tips now brushed against her shoulders. She no longer required restraints to keep from injuring herself during the bridging sessions with Bash. More than that, she now wanted to succeed – to give Tarrant and the others what they so greatly desired. Success, after all, meant a chance – however slim – that she might see Evie again. Whatever crimes Tarrant had committed, he had at least spared the life of his own child, and that had to count for something.

At other times, when her thoughts grew much darker, she thought of all the things she had heard said in that room, and of how it would be far more convenient for them to kill her than risk her ever repeating their remarks to anyone else.

And then, one day, months into their voyage, she had finally started to get somewhere.

Before long she was managing to establish something like real communication with the Wanderer, whereupon the three men started to argue about what they should or shouldn't say to it. Sifra kept a display running on one of his virtual consoles, showing their progress across the galaxy. One day it came as a shock to her to realize that they had reached their destination.

'It knows we've arrived,' she announced, following their next bridging session. 'But it also knows we're not the only ones here.'

'We should launch our nova mine now,' said Sifra, 'then put it into a tight solar orbit in case Jacinth's already negotiated with the Wanderer. We can't take the risk that—'

Tarrant put up a hand to stop him. 'Anil, we've already talked about this. That's Otto's decision, not yours.'

'Well, then,' said Sifra, 'there's something else we need to talk about.' He turned to look at Gabrielle. 'Megan will know by now that we're here. That means we need you to talk to her.'

'How?' she asked.

Sifra tapped the side of his head. 'You're both machine-heads – or did you forget?'

'Oh.' Gabrielle nodded. Megan had given her a few brief lessons in mind-to-mind communication back at the research base, but it had been so long since then that she had almost forgotten. 'Is that possible, with her being so far away?'

'We can route you through the *Ingersoll*'s tach-net transceivers,' said Tarrant. 'That way you should be able to communicate with each other fairly easily.'

'Our main concern,' said Sifra, 'is to stop her from stealing what is rightfully ours. Once she knows you're on board, it might give her the motivation not to do anything that might put the *Ingersoll* – and you – in danger.'

Ever since they had discovered Megan's true identity, they had all assumed she was driven only by a desire for personal profit. Some inner instinct had kept Gabrielle from correcting them.

She stared back at Sifra with a humourless smile. 'I don't think that's going to make any difference.'

'Tell her about the other option, Anil,' prompted Tarrant.

'Other option?' she demanded, looking between the two men. 'What other option?'

'A second stealthed nova mine was placed in orbit around Bellhaven's sun a few days ago,' said Sifra. 'You need to make it very clear to her about the consequences if she doesn't back off.'

'Bellhaven?' Gabrielle stared at them both in utter confusion. Bellhaven, as far as she knew, was a world somewhere on the far side of the Accord from Redstone. 'What the hell does *Bellhaven* have to do with anything?'

'It's Megan's home world,' said Tarrant. 'Or, rather, it was *Dakota Merrick*'s home world. And since they're essentially the same person, I'm willing to bet she'll do just about anything to save it from destruction.'

Gabrielle felt numb with horror. 'I won't have anything to do with it. I can't believe even you would murder an entire world just to get your way.'

Tarrant shook his head. 'It's out of my hands, Gabrielle. I had nothing to do with the decision.'

'Right,' she replied mockingly. 'So you're just following orders, is that it?'

His face flushed with anger. 'Don't try and play with me. If anything happens to Bellhaven, it's going to be on her conscience, not mine or anyone else's. So you can either do what you're told, or I can let Anil persuade you with his gloves. And, if it comes to that, I'll make sure the entire process is recorded for Megan's benefit.'

To her own surprise, Gabrielle laughed. 'It won't make any

difference,' she said. 'She won't do what you want – not ever. And you won't do anything to me as long as you need me.'

Tarrant once again struggled to hold on to his temper. 'Gabrielle, I want you to understand the situation clearly. By the time Anil is finished with you, you'll do *anything* he wants you to. You will not be the same person you are now.' He shook his head. 'The damage is more than physical; pain like that stays with you, somewhere deep inside. I don't want to let him anywhere near you, but you're not giving me much of a choice.'

'Thijs was a sadist and a monster,' she said quietly. 'But he had nothing on you, Gregor Tarrant.'

'Thijs,' said Tarrant, 'was an amateur with delusions of grandeur.' He moved towards the door. 'We'll make arrangements for you to speak to Megan later today. Please don't make things any more difficult than they need be.'

So that she could speak directly with Megan, they made adjustments to Gabrielle's inhibitor, in order to allow her carefully limited access to the *Ingersoll*'s internal net. Corridors and walls that had previously appeared starkly uniform and grey now bloomed with information and visuals that had so far been hidden from her. She could not, however, link with the primary interface, nor communicate with the *Ingersoll*'s unseen machine-head pilot.

She was now also able to follow the *Ingersoll*'s progress closely as it passed through the outer system on the way to its centre. She saw the great blooms of superheated plasma that spun off the ancient star's surface, and she found supplementary information that told her the star was dying, literally wasting away as great sheets of its body sheared off into space, generating those vast nebula clouds filling the surrounding volume of space.

The ship's computers showed her the course that the *Ingersoll* would follow, a parabolic curve bringing them within a few million kilometres of the star's bloated surface, before hurtling them back outwards once more towards the moon where the Wanderer waited.

Curiosity prompted Gabrielle to access an exterior image of the *Ingersoll*. She was thus able to see a mid-section bulge that contained the linked rings in which she and the crew resided. Something about this image made her think of a snake that had just swallowed something much larger than itself.

The thought of what she might experience were she to be given full, unrestricted access to the *Ingersoll*'s navigational systems left her with an ache deep in her belly. She promised herself that if by some miracle she survived the coming days, she would become a pilot.

They were drawing closer to their rendezvous with the star, which loomed larger by the hour in the shipboard monitors. She quickly learned that the path of a spacecraft was determined not in terms of straight lines, but rather by its movement between various orbits involving greater and lesser expenditures of energy.

Before long, the whole crew were ordered to climb into acceleration couches, in advance of the *Ingersoll*'s slingshot manoeuvre around the star. Schelling was desperate to catch up with the Ship of the Covenant, which was well ahead of them by now and already approaching a final rendezvous with the moon and the Wanderer itself. He had already ordered their nova mine to be launched into a solar orbit during the moment of their closest proximity with the star.

One of the *Ingersoll*'s security staff then came to fetch her and Bash to one of several suites specially designed with such high-g manoeuvres in mind. Tarrant and Sifra were already present and strapped into their own couches, along with several others she did not recognize, and none of whom so much as acknowledged her presence. She wondered if they had been instructed to ignore her.

For a few hours, Gabrielle's body weight grew and grew, pressing her deeper and deeper down into her couch. The ship's external sensors presented her with the heavily filtered image of the star's surface, mottled and twisted and ugly and floating against a perfect black void. The *Ingersoll*'s bulkheads sang and creaked under the stress.

Then, finally, the pressure lifted, before fading away entirely. They were now coasting on their way back out from the star.

Back in their shared quarters, Gabrielle guided Bash over to his bunk, then listened carefully for the sound of footsteps outside.

Once she felt reasonably sure they would not be disturbed any time soon, she kneeled by her own bunk and carefully lifted up one side of the mattress, feeling around beneath it with her fingers until she found the small roll of stained fabric she had long ago torn from the edge of a bedsheet.

She glanced once more towards the door, then headed over to a set of drawers fitted into a recess. She slid the lowest one out and dumped its contents on the floor, then carefully unrolled a pair of Bash's socks to reveal a narrow strip of metal, about ten centimetres in length. It had formerly been a side-runner attached to the drawer itself, and one end had been sharpened to a razor-edged point.

Removing the screws had taken her an eternity, since she had little choice but to work at them with nothing more than her fingernails. She had spent literally weeks gently prising out each of the tiny screws, one after another, until they became loose enough to remove.

With fingertips torn and raw, she had worked with the constant awareness that she might be interrupted at any moment, and more than once she had needed to slide the drawer hurriedly back into place, before making a pretence of tidying up its contents. She would then publicly chew at her fingernails in case anyone noticed the damaged tips and asked questions.

After that had come many long and boring hours of first flattening out and smoothing the metal strip, then gradually producing a sharpened point by whittling one edge against the grille covering the ventilation system.

She now wrapped the strip of sheet fabric around the unsharpened edge and tied it off. It felt too light, too insubstantial in her hands, more like a toy than a weapon, and yet beneath the overhead lights its edge glittered as sharp and deadly as she might wish. It could certainly cut a throat . . . or slice a wrist.

Could she take her own life, or even Bash's, if it came to that? She had no idea. She'd dreamed often enough of cutting the throats of Tarrant or Sifra. Could that be so hard, after poisoning a roomful of people or murdering a stranger with a crowbar?

Every now and then, she would stare at the makeshift shank clasped in her hand, and think back to the days of luxurious bed-chambers and servants. What would that other Gabrielle have thought, she now wondered, if she had ever been able to foresee what lay in her future?

She studied it for a little while longer then, as always, tucked the long metal strip back inside a pair of socks, before returning the fabric grip beneath her mattress. She did it all with the exactitude of a priestess performing a complicated but long-practised rite.

The next day, Tarrant himself came to fetch her, instead of just the usual guards.

'It's time for you to have a chat with Megan,' he declared, leading her back along the passageway. 'Make it very clear to her just how much is at stake if she interferes.'

'What about Bash?' asked Gabrielle, aware he was still asleep in his bunk.

'The guards will fetch him in a little while,' replied Tarrant. 'You don't need him for you to talk to Megan.'

'There's something I don't understand,' she said. 'Megan told me what happened to those other machine-heads when they got here. How come I'm not affected – or the *Ingersoll*'s pilot?'

'The *Ingersoll* has been refurbished with shielding specifically designed to resist the Wanderer's informational attacks,' Tarrant explained. 'You'll be safe from any such interference when you link to the Wanderer through Bash. And, if we still have any problems, we can always fully reactivate your inhibitor.'

They entered the communications suite where the bridging

sessions were carried out. Schelling and Sifra were already there, waiting for them. Gabrielle automatically took her usual seat but, for some inexplicable reason, she felt more vulnerable there without having Bash seated across from her.

Tarrant moved around in front of her. 'Remember,' he said. 'There's a nova mine in close orbit around Bellhaven's sun. So if she doesn't—'

'I didn't forget,' she interrupted him. 'Anything else?'

'Find out if she got a response from the Wanderer,' said Sifra. 'And remember, we're routing you through the navigational systems so as to let you talk to her. It's going to be a step up from what you're used to.'

'And be careful what you tell her,' warned Schelling. 'Gregor will be monitoring your conversation.'

A virtual panel appeared directly before her. 'That's your interface,' explained Tarrant. 'Pick the control access option – it's the red icon at the centre.'

She did as she was told. The icon flashed briefly, then a rippling darkness spread out from the panel to consume the entire room. Gabrielle lost any immediate sense of her body, as if her soul had been cut free of her flesh. She found herself now looking out on to naked vacuum.

She discovered she could rapidly cycle her viewpoint through dozens of different vantage points, each one flickering by with such speed that she could hardly take in what she was seeing and experiencing.

Szymurski is riding along with you, said Tarrant, as if from very, very far away.

<Szymurski?> she asked. <Who the hell is Szy—>

The Ingersoll's pilot. You're seeing everything he does, but you can't control anything. You'll be able to talk to Megan – but that's about it.

This, then, she realized, was what it felt like to have full access to a starship's senses.

<Will he be able to hear what I say to Megan?> asked Gabrielle.

Szymursky? asked Tarrant. *Yes. Why?*

<I think it's pretty likely Megan's going to ask about our daughter. I'm not going to lie about her for anyone's benefit. Do you understand?>

You won't have to, replied Tarrant, *Szymursky reports only to me, not Schelling. We're hooking you into the transceiver array now*, he continued. *If Megan's monitoring our comms traffic – and she will be – she should know just about straight away that you're here.*

Gabrielle's viewpoint changed to show the Ship of the Covenant locked into orbit around the desolate moon that lay ahead. She could also see the equally lifeless surface of the world around which the moon orbited.

<Gabrielle? Is that you?!>

<It's me, Megan. I'm here on board the other ship.>

<I knew that,> Megan replied. <Bash is there with you as well, isn't he?>

<You *knew*? But . . .> So much for the element of surprise that Tarrant had been hoping for. <You should know Tarrant is listening in to us.>

<I've been desperate to get hold of you, Gaby. Have they hurt you? And what about your baby? What the hell did they do to you after I left the outpost?>

<The baby is fine,> Gabrielle replied. <Her name is Evie.>

Megan's relief was palpable. <Oh, thank God. Where is she?>

<She's with Martha Stiles.> She decided that with Tarrant monitoring this conversation, now was not the best time to mention what had happened to the rest of the outpost's staff. <Listen . . . Tarrant wants me to tell you something. That's why he's letting me talk to you now.>

<What is it, Gaby?>

<Schelling has placed a nova mine in orbit around Bellhaven's sun. He's going to detonate it if you don't stay away from the Wanderer.>

Gabrielle realized that Megan's presence had slipped away even while she'd been talking, just like a radio signal fading in and out.

<. . . thing's happening,> sent Megan, suddenly fading back in. <I think the Wanderer might be starting to . . .>

The signal faded, then died. Gabrielle could still sense Szymurski as a distant presence.

<Megan?> asked Gabrielle in a panic. <Are you still there?>

<. . . want with Bellhaven?>

Silence fell. Then, deep in her gut, Gabrielle knew something was wrong. Very wrong.

THIRTY-SIX

Megan

The Wanderer struck without warning and, even though Megan had been prepared for such an attack, it came with startling swiftness.

She reclined on a cantilevered chair of metal and plastic with her eyes closed, in a grey-tiled communications room that probably hadn't even existed until a few moments before she entered it.

The Wanderer is aggressively testing our defences, the Librarian informed her. *It appears to be recomputing the underlying informational structure of space-time within the body of our ship.*

How is that even possible? she asked.

It has some means of temporarily redefining certain physical constants on a quantum-scale level, said the Librarian.

You're saying it can alter reality?

On a minute and highly localized scale, yes.

But why?

In order to subvert and access our memory banks, it replied.

Megan shifted her subjective experience of time until the universe beyond the ship came, from her point of view, to a near standstill. She swam through the ship's memory, and saw that great swathes of it had fallen forever dark and silent as they were consumed by the informational equivalent of a forest fire. Cancerous pockets, under the apparent influence of the Wanderer, sprang up in their place – only to be swiftly isolated and destroyed by the Librarian.

Eventually, the Wanderer withdrew its attack. Outwardly, nothing had changed; both it and the Magi ship continued their separate, apparently serene orbits around the moon.

How bad is the damage? she asked, coming back into normal time.

The ship has sustained severe damage, said the Librarian, *and is in an even more greatly weakened state than before.*

She remembered all those long hours she'd spent kneeling by Bash in his quarters, communing with the Marauder via a mind-to-mind link. *I thought it and I had an agreement.*

Our current prognosis is that it was merely testing our defences to ascertain whether we were weak enough to overcome.

It really can't be trusted, can it?

No, the Librarian agreed. *We could, if necessary, transmit your current mind-state to the nearest Magi ship, if we appear to be facing certain destruction.*

No, she replied. *That'd use up too much of your resources. Save it for the battle, if it comes.* There were other versions of her out there, after all, preserved in the memories of those other Magi ships. They could have their turn to live if it came to the worst here.

She returned her attention to the *Ingersoll*, which was clearly preparing to decelerate for its final approach to the moon. The starship was so heavily shielded against any informational attack that she could not even pinpoint Gabrielle's physical location aboard it.

<Megan! Are you there?>

<I am. You're coming through loud and clear now. What were you trying to tell me about Bellhaven?>

<Tarrant says you have to stand down. If you make any kind of deal with the Wanderer, they say they'll destroy Bellhaven using a nova mine. They . . . they know who you are, Megan . . . or who you were.>

<How did they find out?>

<It was my fault,> sent Gabrielle. <I'm sorry. I'm so, so sorry.>

<Don't be. It wouldn't have made any difference anyway. You said Tarrant was listening in to our conversation?>

<Also Szymurski,> sent Gabrielle. <He's the *Ingersoll*'s pilot.>

<Well, then, I hope they're both listening very carefully indeed, because I haven't been able to get the Wanderer to even so much as respond to me since I first got here. In fact, it just launched a failed attack on me, so there's no reason for them to be making any threats.>

<Are you sure you should be telling me this?>

<Because I'm worried about Tarrant and the others finding out? No, Gaby. I'm telling you – and Tarrant – this so you understand something very important. I only survived the attack because this ship I'm on is extraordinarily powerful. It was built by a civilization that existed for literally millions of years. If the Wanderer tries to pull the same stunt on you – and I can't see any reason why it wouldn't – it's going to feel like a tonne of concrete landing on an anthill. So make it as clear to them as you can that coming any closer than they already are will be suicide. I don't give a crap about any of the rest of them, Gaby – it's you and Bash I'm concerned about.>

<But . . . why won't it deal?> asked Gabrielle. <When I communicated with it, it said it would.>

<Hold on,> sent Megan. <You talked to it? Through Bash?>

<I . . . yes. Please don't get angry.>

<I'm not angry, Gabrielle. I just want to know that you're okay, both of you.>

<We're both fine. Or, at least, Bash is as fine as he can be.>

<Make it *very* clear to Gregor that there will be consequences if he does anything harmful whatsoever to Bellhaven – or anywhere else for that matter. Even if I don't make it back from here alive, some other version of me will find him and all the rest of his cronies, no matter long it takes.>

<Other versions?> Gabrielle was clearly befuddled. <I don't understand.>

<There's more than just one Magi ship, Gaby, and they've all got copies of my mind squirrelled away inside their memory banks. Did they tell you if they've got a nova mine on board that ship of theirs?>

<They did,> sent Gabrielle. <They've already launched it into an orbit around the sun, and they're threatening to detonate it if the Wanderer turns on them, or refuses to negotiate.>

<Then here's another message,> sent Megan. <Are you listening, Tarrant? The Wanderer is a machine. It has a single purpose: to destroy its creator's enemies. It has no sense of self-preservation, except insofar as its continued existence allows it to pursue the purpose it was programmed for. Threats just don't work on something like that. If it thinks attacking another ship is worth the potential gain, it'll go ahead and attack. That's why it attacked me, and that's why it's going to attack the *Ingersoll*: because the net gain of its getting hold of a nova drive far, far outweighs any resulting risk to itself. Got that?>

<Got that,> Gabrielle replied. <It's good to hear from you again, Megan. I just wish it wasn't under such horrible circumstances. I—>

Their connection was cut, again without warning.

Megan opened her eyes and peered around the grey-tiled room deep within the Ship of the Covenant. Something was wrong. She could sense it.

She glanced to one side and saw the Librarian standing there. There was something subtly wrong with its outline, as if it had been warped out of shape.

'What's happened?' she asked. 'What's wrong with you?'

'We were wrong,' replied the Librarian. 'The Wanderer wasn't trying to hurt us during its attack. It was distracting us, so that it could plunder data.'

THIRTY-SEVEN

Gabrielle

'Well?' asked Schelling. 'Did the Wanderer get our message?'

Gabrielle's whole body felt cramped after emerging from the sensorium, her skin slick with sweat and her jaw aching.

'I'm pretty sure it got it,' she said, hungrily sucking in air. Bash looked as if the experience had been just as rough for him as well. His head was tipped back, his mouth open and his chest rising and falling with hummingbird-like rapidity.

'"Pretty sure" doesn't cut it,' snarled the General. 'We need to be sure it understands very clearly what'll happen if it doesn't start cooperating.'

Some hours had now passed since Gabrielle's brief and interrupted conversation with Megan. Tarrant meanwhile had not reacted well to the suggestion that they should stay clear of the Wanderer, nor had he believed Megan's claim that it had refused to deal with her. As far as he was concerned, this was little more than a thinly veiled ruse designed to dissuade them.

'I think it understands just fine,' said Gabrielle, fighting to hide her irritation. General Schelling was, she had long since learned, a man used to getting his own way. 'I was very clear about the nova mine.'

'And what about the negotiations it promised?' Schelling demanded peevishly.

'I honestly don't know,' replied Gabrielle. 'I didn't get anything that felt remotely like a straight answer – or an answer at all.'

Schelling's face turned a fiery red. Tarrant stepped up beside him and put a restraining hand on his shoulder. 'Remember we're dealing with something entirely alien,' Tarrant said to him. 'You can't always make sense of how something like that might react.'

'So what do we do now?' Schelling demanded. 'Just sit and wait?'

'That's exactly what we do,' Tarrant replied. 'It's not as if we have any other choice. But at the first sign that it might already be negotiating with Megan, we'll send it off to whatever hell it has waiting for it.'

After they reached orbit above the moon a day later, she and Bash were returned to their quarters having spent some hours in acceleration couches. Entirely worn out, Gabrielle was soon fast asleep, until she felt a hand shaking her awake some time deep during the *Ingersoll*'s artificial night.

She opened her eyes to see Bash kneeling beside her bunk. At first she stared at him for long seconds, trying to absorb this new development. Finally she sat bolt upright.

'Bash – how can you . . . ? I mean, how did you . . . ?' She tripped over her own words, unable to complete a full sentence.

'I've been waiting for the right time,' he replied.

She rubbed at her face with one hand, still groggy from interrupted sleep and fatigue. 'Right time? Right time for *what*?'

'To kill the Wanderer,' he said. 'If we can.'

'I don't understand. First you're dead to the world for months . . . and now you're here actually talking to me? *What* is *going on*?'

He laid a hand over hers. 'Don't you remember what I told you?' he said. 'I've been fighting a war, but now's the time to end it. But first you have to understand some things.'

'What things?' She was sobbing now, frightened and confused.

He reached out and gently took hold of her other hand as well. 'I only have a little time – same as before. You just need to listen,' he said, his face shadowy in the dim light of the cabin. 'And listen carefully.'

'To what?'

*

In that moment, their quarters vanished from around her.

Gabrielle found herself somewhere else – not in space, exactly, but in a grey and featureless void. She could sense that her physical body lay somewhere nearby, and yet, when she turned to look for it, she saw only a confusing mass of threads that hung in emptiness, burning with light.

This tangle of threads, she somehow knew, was the *Ingersoll* itself, seen from a perspective she struggled to comprehend. Further away she could see other structures, but on a scale that defied comprehension.

Think of this as the mainframe that the entire universe runs on, she heard Bash say.

She twisted around until she spotted a tightly wound knot of light floating in the void close by her. This, she sensed, was Bash.

What happened? she cried out. *Where are we? What happened to us?*

You could call this information space, said Bash. *The thing you have to understand is that the universe is just one giant computer, computing itself. Dig down far enough into the quantum level of reality, and all that's really happening is an exchange of information regarding mass, velocity, energy – all of that, and more. The Makers want to change the fundamental rules by which all of it works. All this you see is a virtual data system created by races even older than the Makers themselves. It's threaded deep into the weave of reality, so deep you can't ever see it.*

And . . . this is where you've been? All these years?

Here and so many other places, said Bash. *When the Wanderer first entered my mind, the last time I was out here, it wanted to pick me apart, to try and understand who we are and how we work. It took my body and discarded my mind, like a landlord evicting an unwanted tenant. But I didn't die. I remained in one piece. And every now and then I sneak back into the old place for a little while, just as I have now.*

Then why didn't the same thing happen to Megan? asked Gabrielle.

She's different – just as you're different, said Bash. *The Magi changed you; made you too strong.*

Are you going to help us? Is that why you came to me just now?

I came to warn you. The pattern of light shifted slightly. *The Wanderer isn't a single unified entity, as it appears to be. It's made up of tens of thousands of individual craft, just like the Maker Swarms, except that they're all clustered together into a single body.*

So?

So, said Bash, *that fact alone makes it near as damn indestructible. As long as it can split off even a few of its components and leave them somewhere in the outer part of this system, if not even further away, it can always reconstitute itself, whatever happens in the meantime to the main part of its body. Each component contains the memories and knowledge of the whole. So even if most of it – hell, nearly all of it – was destroyed in a nova, it would still find a way to grow back to its former strength, even if it took a thousand years, or ten thousand. Time means nothing to things like that. All that means it has nothing* – nothing – *to fear from the nova mine. And, when it's ready to attack, it'll separate into its individual components, and the* Ingersoll *will be defenceless in the face of it.*

Gabrielle remembered then how the Wanderer always spoke in a clashing multiplicity of voices. *You said the Wanderer was keeping a secret, one you were trying to find?*

And I found it, said Bash. *Thanks to Megan.*

What did she do?

The Wanderer launched an attack on her Magi ship. It was a ruse, so it could ransack the ship's memory banks and find what it was looking for – and it found it.

But what is it? asked Gabrielle.

In order to help you really understand the answer to that question, I need to show you something, Gaby. That way, you'll understand what the Wanderer intends, not just for the human race, but for all life throughout the galaxy.

The void twisted around Gabrielle, and she now saw the Wanderer, surrounded by billions of blazing stars.

She was in the heart of the galaxy, witnessing events that had taken place millions of years before. She was seeing the Core Transcendence in all its terrible glory.

New data flooded into Gabrielle's implants, indistinguishable from her natural memory. The Makers, she learned, had transformed the supermassive black hole occupying the centre of the Milky Way into a kind of computer. In some way, they had used entangled pairs of virtual particles along the edge of the black hole's event horizon – the point beyond which light could never escape it – as a means of processing phenomenal amounts of data. And this, in turn, somehow allowed the Makers to dig deep into the underlying informational structure of space-time itself, and thereby alter it on a fundamental level.

It dawned on her then just what the Makers were doing. They were remaking the universe by hacking its operational constants.

Now do you see? asked Bash. *The Wanderer wants to use the* Ingersoll*'s drive to fly itself directly to the core of the Milky Way. Because the nova drive takes a ship out of normal space, it'll be able to make a kamikaze run right past the defences the Makers have erected all around the black hole.*

And then?

It'll detonate its nova drive at the point where it crosses the event horizon, disrupting the processes run by the Makers. Done the right way, it could cause a temporary but very real shift in certain physical constants, destroying not only the Makers but every living thing for up to a couple of hundred thousand light years' distance.

The whole galaxy, in other words. It was getting hard to take in.

But surely it'd take hundreds of thousands of years for a change like that to spread outwards from the core of the galaxy, even at the speed of light?

No, Gabrielle, said Bash, *it's going to be instantaneous, because the effect is propagating through information space, not through space-time as we know it. Light speed, gravity, mass – none of those mean anything here. They're all epiphenomena of information space and are therefore subject to it, rather than the other way around.*

But why do that? Why destroy all life in the galaxy?

The Wanderer isn't programmed to care about anything but killing the Makers, Bash replied. *Anything else is just collateral damage.*

The only time it ever thinks about other life forms is when they have something it can put to its own advantage.

But it still has to get hold of the Ingersoll*'s nova drive*, she pointed out. *And Tarrant and the rest aren't in any hurry to let that happen.*

It's already too late for them, said Bash.

What are you talking about?

The pattern of light representing Bash shifted and flowed. *The* Ingersoll*'s pilot is a man called Bill Szymurski*, he explained. *When Megan and I last visited the Wanderer, all those years ago, it learned a lot about how our machine-head implants work. Because of that, it was able to get inside Szymurski's head pretty much the instant the* Ingersoll *jumped into this system. He's been compromised almost from the start.*

After a pause to let that sink in, Bash continued. *And that means the Wanderer has already got effective control of the* Ingersoll. *Tarrant and the rest of his cronies have absolutely no idea just how utterly fucked they really are.*

So what do we do? she asked, horrified.

The only way now to stop the Wanderer, before it's too late, is by destroying this whole damn system.

But I'm still stuck here in this cabin.

I can get you out of there, said Bash. *But after that the rest is up to you. You need to find some way to launch the* Ingersoll*'s nova mine into the sun. Then, even if we can't kill the Wanderer outright, we can at least stop it from stealing the nova drive and sterilizing the whole damn galaxy of every last trace of life.*

Gabrielle came to with a start and realized that hours had passed. Bash still knelt by her bunk, but the intelligence had once more faded from his eyes. Instead he stared, calm and unseeing, at a bulkhead.

She glanced over at the cabin door and saw with a surprise that its light was glowing a dull green, meaning it was unlocked.

Her gaze returned to Bash. *He did this*, she thought.

Then she stepped over to the door, hardly able to believe anything would happen, and watched in numbed silence as it hissed softly open.

Standing on the threshold, she tried to think of what she needed to do next. She now understood that it wasn't the *Ingersoll*'s shielding, or even her inhibitor, that kept her safe from the Wanderer; for both she and Megan were, in essence, part-Magi – and that was all the protection they needed.

The same, however, couldn't be said either for the *Ingersoll*'s pilot, Szymurski, or for the rest of the ship with the useless shielding built into its hull.

Gabrielle decided to head for the command deck. If she was going to find the trigger code for the nova mine anywhere, it would most likely be there.

She closed the door again, and spent the next several minutes coaxing Bash into his clothes. Then she retrieved her homemade blade, winding the same piece of cloth from under her mattress around the blunt end and tying a knot to secure it. Finally she pushed it through a belt loop, where she could feel it pressing against the small of her back.

One glance at Bash told her she couldn't possibly take him to the command deck with her. Manoeuvring him in normal gravity was one thing, but now they were in orbit, the *Ingersoll* was operating in zero gravity. Getting him all the way across the ship would be excessively difficult, unless he decided to come back to life again of his own accord.

She stared at him and waited for some small sign, some flicker of awareness as before. Of course, there was none.

'I'll be right back before you know it,' she explained, kneeling beside him, then stepped back over to the door and palmed it open.

The empty corridor beyond beckoned. Playing around with the ship's data-net, even under restrictions, had already given her a pretty good idea of the *Ingersoll*'s layout.

Halfway to the nearest drop shaft, she ran into a crew member, who came to an astonished halt. He was one of the guards who usually escorted her to and from the bridging suite, and she therefore knew his name was Travis.

'What the hell?' he barked. 'How did you get out of your cabin?'

She swallowed hard and decided to try and brazen it out. 'I need to find Mr Schelling,' she replied, trying to sound more confident than she felt. 'It's urgent.'

'First you're going to get the hell back to your cabin,' he demanded. 'Then you're going to tell me how you managed to override the lock.'

She didn't move. 'I'm serious,' she said. 'You need to warn them that the *Ingersoll* isn't under their command any more.'

Travis's expression grew incredulous. 'I don't have time for this.' He moved closer, his boots making a ripping sound as he headed across the strip of sticktite that ran the length of the passageway. 'Turn around *now*,' he barked, reaching for his gun.

As he grabbed hold of her around the waist, Gabrielle pulled her homemade shank loose from the belt loop and drew it swiftly across Travis's cheek.

He yelled in surprise; the wound it left was deep and raw. His pistol spun away from him, clunking loudly against a bulkhead. She threw herself away from him, chasing after the gun and grabbing hold of it.

She twisted round, bringing it to bear on Travis just as he came sailing towards her, with hands outstretched.

The gun seared a line across the man's chest. He jerked, his arms and legs flailing, and smoke started billowing out of his mouth as his internal organs combusted.

Travis drifted up against a bulkhead, his limbs still and lifeless. Gabrielle exhaled a rush of air ending in a half-choked sob.

Pushing herself as far away from the corpse as she could manage, she stared at the weapon still gripped in one shaking hand. It felt strangely unwieldy, its grip being too large for her small fingers. She shifted her fingers to cover the coloured band wrapped around the weapon's grip, whereupon several virtual menus immediately appeared around the gun's barrel.

She let out a small gasp as the weapon's grip began pulsing and quivering beneath her fingers. It gradually changed shape, and even size, adapting itself to her grasp until it felt better balanced in her hands. Where before it had felt awkward and unwieldy, the weapon now felt as if it had been made just for her.

She pointed it towards a ceiling light further down the corridor. Lines and numbers appeared around the tip of the barrel, flashing with greater rapidity as she centred them over the fixture. Then she pushed the weapon deep into a jacket pocket, and made her way towards the drop shaft and the command deck beyond.

THIRTY-EIGHT

Gabrielle

A few minutes later, she found herself outside the command deck. Footsteps echoed from further around the curve of the corridor, coming closer.

She looked round until she saw a door marked SUPPLIES on the opposite side of the corridor; she slipped inside, peering back through the small window set into it in time to see a man with cropped blond hair entering the command deck. In the moment before the door closed again, she caught a glimpse of Tarrant.

Deciding she needed to try and talk to Megan, if she could, she found her access to the transceiver array was still active. She sent out a hailing signal and waited.

She didn't know how long she might have before Szymurski noticed her using the transceiver, assuming there was anything human left inside his skull that was still capable of noticing . . .

<. . . Gabrielle? My God, it is you, isn't it? Listen to me – the *Ingersoll* is under attack, and—>

<I know,> sent Gabrielle. <The *Ingersoll*'s pilot has been compromised by the Wanderer, and nobody on board knows about it except me. The only way we can stop the Wanderer getting what it wants is by triggering the nova mine and destroying this entire system.>

<*Trigger* it?> sent Megan. <You're kidding, right?>

Gabrielle sighed. Clearly she was going to have to explain things, even though there really wasn't enough time.

<Look, Bash came back to life, a little while back,> she began.

<He spoke to me as if he were completely normal. I mean, he was right there, Megan, in the flesh and talking to me. He's the reason I know all this.>

<Son of a *bitch*,> shouted Megan. <Are you *serious*?>

<Very. And he had news.>

Gabrielle then told her everything she knew about the Wanderer's ultimate purpose, as well as explaining further about Szymurski, the *Ingersoll*'s pilot.

<And you're serious?> repeated Megan. <He's alive in this . . . what did you call it?>

<Information space,> Gabrielle replied, feeling that she had wasted too much time already.

<God damn,> Megan muttered to herself. <We walked right into a trap.>

<Bash told me how the Wanderer attacked the Ship of the Covenant and stole the data it needed,> Gabrielle added. <And now it'll use that same information to destroy everything – just to take revenge on the Makers. I know a lot of this must sound like madness, but you have to believe me,> she pleaded.

<Oh, no,> sent Megan, <I believe you. I don't want to, but I do. Maybe I'd better tell you what I can see right now from where I am. The Wanderer boosted out of its orbit an hour or so ago, and it's heading straight towards you. According to my estimates, it'll come into direct contact with the *Ingersoll* in about another twenty minutes. Some of its components are already in place, and it looks as if they're preparing to open up the hull so it can dig out the *Ingersoll*'s drive. Whatever happens, Gabrielle, you need to get yourself and Bash the hell out of . . .>

Megan's voice faded until Gabrielle could hear nothing more than the ship's normal background hum. In the next moment, her net access failed abruptly.

She blinked, looking around the dusty supplies room, and guessed that Szymurski – or, rather, the thing controlling him – had finally cottoned on to her presence.

Ignoring the sudden clutch of fear in her belly, she slid the pistol back out of her pocket, wrapping her fingers around the grip. She was really on her own now.

Stepping back out of the supplies cabin she headed across the corridor towards the entrance to the command deck, taking a firm two-handed grip on the gun, exactly as she had seen Tarrant do on numerous occasions.

She touched the door panel with her elbow, then stepped through just as it slid open.

Sifra was inside, along with Tarrant, and also two others manning consoles whom she didn't recognize, but one was the blond-haired man she'd spotted earlier.

She took a quick glance past them towards the astrogation chair, and saw its petals were still folded up, concealing Szymurski from view.

All four of them froze on the spot as she trained the gun on each of them in turn, from her position by the door. She was conscious of breathing hard, her hands shaking with sheer terror and adrenalin.

'Gabrielle.' Tarrant spoke slowly and carefully, 'I'd like you to put that thing down before you hurt yourself.'

'I told you we should just have shoved her in a medbox,' muttered Sifra. He stood up with his hands still hovering over a console.

'Manning,' said Tarrant, 'go over and take that gun away from her.'

With a nod, the blond-haired man stepped away from his console and began moving towards her.

Adjusting her grip on her weapon, she backed away. Then she squeezed the trigger, but nothing happened.

Sifra snorted with laughter. 'She's got no idea how to even use the thing. I swear, Gregor, I—'

She squeezed again, paying more attention to the gun's control interfaces this time.

There was a bright flash accompanied by a hissing sound. Manning stumbled to his knees, one hand clasping his shoulder, his face white and his teeth clenched.

'God damn it, Gabrielle,' Tarrant shouted, 'what the *hell* do you think you're playing at?'

'Don't come any closer,' she said. 'I mean it.'

'She hasn't got it in her,' sneered Sifra.

'Go and ask Travis that question,' she said quietly.

Tarrant looked towards the remaining crew member. 'Rohloff, go and help Manning to the medbay. Myself and Mr Sifra will handle things here.'

Rohloff helped Manning upright, before leading him out of the command deck.

'Perhaps I underestimated you,' began Tarrant, as the door closed behind her.

'The Wanderer,' she said, 'has launched an attack on us.'

Tarrant frowned, before glancing towards a display. 'There's no sign of it attacking anything,' he said. 'As far as I can tell, it's in orbit exactly where we last saw it.'

'As far as you can tell,' she repeated, nodding towards the astrogation chair. 'Just ask Szymurski,' she said. 'Ask *him* if we're under attack.'

Tarrant's mask of outward calm began to slip. 'Gabrielle, nothing you're saying makes the least damn bit of sense.'

'He's dead,' she snapped. 'He's been dead almost since the moment we entered this system.'

Tarrant's face darkened. 'What the hell are you talking about?'

'Szymurski – or what used to be Szymurski – has been altering the external sensor feeds to keep you from finding out about the attack until it's too late.'

'And you know this how?'

'Bash isn't as brain-dead as you think. He knows more than you could possibly guess, such as the fact that the Wanderer's already started digging through the *Ingersoll*'s hull, to get at its nova drive. So, unless you take action right now, we're all dead.'

'I don't believe you,' said Sifra flatly. He reached into a pocket, retrieving his gloves without once taking his eyes off her.

'No, wait a second,' said Tarrant, stepping closer to the display he had been studying moments before. He activated a virtual panel, his hands moving through the projected light. 'There's something not right here.'

'What?' asked Sifra.

He looked back at Sifra, shock evident in his gaze. 'The external feeds – they've been running on a repeating loop for the past hour!'

'While you're at it,' said Gabrielle, 'maybe you should ask Szymurski to come out of his chair.'

Tarrant glared at her, before touching another panel. 'Szymurski, you there?'

'Right here.' His voice echoed across the command deck.

'The external feed,' said Tarrant. 'It's looping. We aren't getting it in real time. Why?'

'There's a software glitch in the micro-relays,' Szymurski replied. 'It's nothing to worry about.'

'God damn it,' Tarrant exploded, 'why the hell didn't you tell me? Do you have any idea how much danger you've put us in?'

'I can monitor the real-time situation just fine from here,' said Szymurski. 'Everything's quiet.'

Tarrant licked his lips, and Gabrielle saw a flicker of real fear crossing his face. 'Step down from the chair,' he said. 'I want to speak to you directly, person to person.'

Gabrielle stared over towards the astrogation chair. With its petals folded up, it looked like a sculpture of a sleeping rose wrought from steel and plastic.

Szymurski didn't respond.

Tarrant's hands clenched by his sides. 'Goddamn it,' he shouted, 'answer me!'

Still no answer.

Tarrant turned to Sifra. 'She's right. Something's wrong.'

'No.' Sifra shook his head. 'I don't believe any of this. She's lying, or bluffing. She's a machine-head herself and, for all we know, she's found some way of locking Szymurski inside his astrogation chair with no way to get out.'

Tarrant stared at him in disbelief. 'Don't be ridic—'

Something shook the bulkheads surrounding them, and in the next moment a siren began to wail.

'When you were last here, ten years ago,' said Gabrielle quickly, 'the Wanderer learned a great deal about how machine-head implants work. That's how, from the moment we jumped into this system, it was able to get inside Szymurski's head without you ever guessing.'

Sifra jabbed at a console, his face turning pale. 'I can't get hold of Rohloff or anyone else,' he said. 'The comms systems are all down.'

'All right, Gabrielle,' said Tarrant finally. 'I believe you. What do you think we should do?'

'Just what I already said. Trigger that nova mine you put in orbit around this system's sun, so it destroys the Wanderer.'

'We don't have any guarantees that we can even get ourselves out of this system before the detonation reaches us,' said Tarrant.

'We're about as good as dead anyway,' she replied. 'And, believe me, things are going to be far, far worse for the whole human race than you could possibly imagine, if that thing gets away from here with your nova drive.' The bulkheads shuddered violently again. 'I mean it, Gregor. You have to trigger it *now*.'

'Wait one minute,' said Sifra. 'I still say this is bullshit. She's tricking us.'

'Just open your eyes and ears,' Gregor rounded on him. '*Something's* attacking us.'

'Then how the hell does she know all this?' Sifra demanded, his voice shrill. 'How could she unless Jacinth's already made a deal with the Wanderer, and she's in on it?'

Tarrant peered at her intently. 'You said Bash told you all this, but how did he do that exactly? You mean he just sat up and started talking?'

'Something like that. He's capable of lucid moments, very occasionally. And he can get inside the Wanderer's mind in some way.'

'Right,' said Sifra. 'So a man with the intellectual capacity of a piece of broccoli spontaneously started having a conversation with you.' He turned to Tarrant, his expression defiant. 'Are you honestly going to *listen* to this bullshit? They're both skilled manipulators, her and Jacinth, and now they're spinning this insane story just to get us to back off.'

'For God's sake, Anil,' Tarrant exploded, 'didn't you hear something slamming into the ship? And yet our sensor arrays tell us there's *nothing out there*.'

'If what you say is true, Anil,' said Gabrielle, 'I wouldn't be asking you to destroy the Wanderer, and quite possibly kill all of us in the process as well.'

'Have you forgotten what Jacinth did to us, back on the *Beauregard*?' Sifra demanded, staring at Tarrant. 'How she tricked us?'

Around them the ship shook with even greater violence than before, as Tarrant confronted him. 'No more arguments,' he said, moving away from his console. 'We need to get Szymurski out of that astrogation chair, and put Gabrielle in his place.'

'No,' said Sifra. 'Not without General Schelling's authorization first.'

'Anil,' said Tarrant, 'I've about had it up to here with your endless whining. We can't manage to raise Rohloff or anyone else on this ship. For all we know, they're all already dead.'

Gabrielle thought of Bash, still back in their quarters, and wondered if she had made some terrible mistake by leaving him there . . . But, no, if she had brought him along with her, they might never have got past that guard. She just had to hope he would be all right.

Tarrant took a step towards the astrogation chair.

'*No*,' yelled Sifra, darting up behind him.

Gabrielle hadn't noticed Sifra pulling on his gloves. Now, before she could move, he had grabbed hold of Tarrant's arm.

Tarrant's face twisted into a death's head grimace, then he crumpled to the floor, while a thin, high-pitched whine emerged from his throat. His legs and arms twitched violently as Sifra bent over him.

Sifra finally let go of him and stood up again, breathing heavily. He then looked over towards Gabrielle, who still clasped the gun in both hands. Her arms were starting to ache mightily.

She swallowed hard as Sifra stepped closer. 'You,' he stabbed one gloved finger towards her, 'how long have you and Jacinth been plotting all this?'

'Stay back,' said Gabrielle, aware of a tremor in her voice.

'Why?' asked Sifra, bringing his gloved hands up as he advanced. 'Because you might shoot me?'

'Yes.'

'You're lucky you didn't hurt yourself the first time you fired that thing. Your second shot was just beginner's luck.' He nodded towards the weapon in her hands. 'Believe me, I can see just by looking at it that you're a lot more likely to kill yourself if you pull that trigger.'

'Don't try bluffing me, Anil. Just stay back.'

He had closed the gap between them, swinging his gloved hands from side to side so that the silver filaments glittered under the multiple lights of the command deck. Her arms were now so weary that their nerve endings felt alive with pain.

'That's far enough, Anil,' she said, forcing a little more determination into her voice.

To her surprise, he came to a halt. She had moved so far back that she was now almost up against the wall.

Sifra glanced towards the door, with an expression of relief. 'You took your time,' he said.

Gabrielle made the mistake of glancing round. It didn't even occur to her that she hadn't heard the door sliding open.

Sifra crossed the remaining gap between them in an instant.

The pain was just as dreadful as the last time he had used his gloves on her. She screamed as Sifra snatched the gun away from her.

He gazed down at her, panting and grinning. 'You know,' he said, 'if we really are under attack from the Wanderer, there's really no more point in keeping you alive.'

He aimed the gun at her, his finger already tightening on the trigger.

There was a flash of light, and Sifra jerked suddenly to one side.

Gabrielle saw his hair was on fire. Then there was another flash, and flames erupted from his mouth and nostrils.

Gabrielle scrambled away from the burning corpse, before turning to look over at Tarrant. He still lay where Sifra had left him, but with a gun gripped in his right hand.

He let the weapon clatter to the deck, then clamped his hand over his left shoulder. 'There's a manual override for the astrogation chair,' he gasped. 'You need to throw it.'

She came to kneel by him. 'What happened to the rest of the crew?' she asked.

'I don't know,' said Tarrant, his face looking grey and pinched. 'I can't feel anything on my left side. I think I must be having a stroke.'

Unable to think of anything to say, she made her way over to the astrogation chair.

'Look down at the base,' Tarrant instructed from behind her. 'There's an emergency release lever, hidden inside a panel. You need to throw it.'

She kneeled down next to the chair and searched around for a few moments. 'I see it.' She had found a small hook in one side and, when it popped out, she saw a lever within. When she pressed this, it clicked into a recess.

Gabrielle scrambled quickly out of the way as the petals unfolded from around the chair above. Szymurski was seated within, his mouth slack and eyes rolling in their sockets, and she noticed that his chin and clothes were spattered with vomit. Judging by the smell, he had soiled himself, too.

She turned to Tarrant, who was staring at Szymurski with dread. 'When I spoke to him just a minute ago,' he declared, 'he sounded fine.'

'No,' she said. 'You spoke to *something*, but it wasn't him.'

'You need to get him out of that chair,' said Tarrant. 'Can you manage it?'

'I think so.'

She stepped gingerly up on to the base of the chair, and leaned in closer to Szymurski. Like Bash, he showed no apparent awareness of either her or his surroundings. Hooking a hand under one armpit and the other around his neck, she gently tugged him forward. He slumped against her, with his drool staining her jacket, and after another few seconds he slid out of the chair.

'Leave those petals folded down,' instructed Tarrant, as she pulled herself into the vacated seat. Though he had dragged himself around so as to see her better, he already sounded weaker than a moment before. 'Just lean your head back until it touches the plate built into the headrest.'

The moment the back of her skull came into contact with the plate, menus blossomed around her.

'Before you do anything,' said Tarrant, 'you need to try and figure out where everyone else is. They should have come running here long before now.'

Occupying the astrogation chair made her feel as if she had been born to sit in it – which, in a sense, she had. Screens and menus and query options popped up the instant she thought of them.

As if it's reading my mind, she thought, then realized that was precisely what it was doing.

The chair guided her swiftly to the information she needed. 'They're all dead,' she told him, after a few moments' investigation.

He closed his eyes for a moment. 'What happened to them?' he asked, in a voice barely above a whisper.

'As far as I can tell, the life-support systems across most of the ship were disabled.' Only a few corridors and rooms immediately adjacent to the command deck, and the quarters she shared with Bash, remained pressurized. 'I think they suffocated.'

'You're telling me the two of us are the only ones still alive on this whole damn ship?'

'No,' she said, 'not just us. Bash is still alive, back in our cabin.'

'That doesn't make sense,' Tarrant whispered. 'Why keep him alive? Or even us, for that matter? Szymurski could have easily dumped the atmosphere from the command deck, and us along with it.'

The answer, when it came to her, filled Gabrielle with a sick horror. 'Because it wants me and Bash alive, that's why.'

'See if you can access the external feeds,' urged Tarrant. 'Tell me what you see.'

Images appeared at her command, showing the outer hull of the *Ingersoll.* A dozen alien-looking forms clung to the outside of the ship, just like maggots burrowing into carrion.

'I can see it,' she announced. 'The Wanderer's coming apart, separating into thousands of individual components. Some of them are currently digging their way through the *Ingersoll*'s skin.'

'It's coming *apart*?'

'It's not a single ship at all,' she explained, 'but composed of thousands of autonomous pieces – same as the Maker Swarms. It stayed all clumped together so you'd think there was only one of it. As long as any of those separate parts survive, it can reconstitute itself entirely. That means it can't be killed, Gregor.'

'Dear God.' He looked as if he was experiencing severe difficulty breathing. 'Do it, then. Blow the damn sun up. You can do it from that chair.'

She tried to comply, then found her way blocked. It took her a moment to work out what had gone wrong.

'It's been sabotaged,' she said hopelessly. 'Szymurski must have fixed it, under the Wanderer's control.'

'Come here,' said Tarrant, fumbling inside his jacket. 'That means you're going to have to arm the mine manually from within the engineering bay.'

Just as Gabrielle disengaged from the chair, she noticed one of the Wanderer's components disappear from sight as it worked its way deeper inside the hull.

It was already inside the ship, she realized. The thought of it in there alongside them made her skin crawl.

A vibration began humming through the deck underfoot, but instead of fading away after a moment, as it had done before, it grew stronger. Gabrielle could hear the sound of metal being stressed beyond its limit, a high-pitched shriek like the cries of damned souls.

She went over to kneel beside Tarrant, reaching inside his jacket pocket and pulling out the slim card he had been trying to extract.

'Take it to engineering,' he said, in a whisper that she had to strain to hear. 'There's a cradle there that the nova mine was transported in, prior to its launch. You need to find it.'

'And then what?'

'There's a slot in the cradle. Use the card to activate the arming mechanism directly. After that, it'll tell you what to do. There's also a code . . .' He coughed, then winced. 'Zero-six-nine-six-zero. Got that?'

She repeated it back to him.

He nodded. 'Nothing'll happen unless you've entered that code. Once it's in, the countdown starts.'

She slipped the card into a pocket and then pushed herself upright. Once she had armed the mine, she would have to go and find Bash. She knew there were escape pods that they could use to get to Megan.

'Gaby, I should . . .'

She looked down at him, to see his grey eyes were staring sightlessly upwards, his lips slightly parted. Whatever he might have been about to say, she would never know.

'I have to go,' she murmured to his silent body, then she exited the command bridge.

THIRTY-NINE

Gabrielle

She pulled up an offline map of the *Ingersoll* even as she exited the command deck. It showed her the location of the nearest escape-pod bay, which was close to her own and Bash's quarters. The fabricator and engineering bays were further away, located towards the stern.

The corridor beyond was lined with cupboards and storage spaces. She searched through them for a spacesuit or a breather mask, or anything else that might keep her and Bash alive while they traversed the depressurized sections of the ship.

As she searched, she became more frantic, able to feel the seconds ticking by. And yet there seemed to be nothing. But there had to be, surely, somewhere.

On hearing something clunk and scrape further around the curving corridor, followed by a kind of electronic chittering, she felt her panic grow greater.

Then she remembered those orange boxes mounted at various points around the ship, containing emergency breathers and other survival equipment.

She turned around, pushing herself away from the source of the chittering and heading towards the drop shaft. With relief, she could see two of the orange boxes mounted next to the opening.

The chittering grew closer and she looked behind her, back along the curve of the corridor, and heard the sound of metal scraping on metal.

At a yank of the cord attached to one of the boxes, it dropped open. She quickly pulled on the emergency breather found inside, then extracted another one from the second box. After that, she dropped down the shaft and passed through an emergency pressure field to get into one of the depressurized zones.

As she glanced back up, she saw something loom across the far end of the drop shaft. It possessed cutting implements that reminded her of mandibles, and a dozen eye-like sensors that rotated towards her. It began to drag its immense bulk inside the shaft, clearly intent on pursuit.

Gabrielle screamed, inside her mask, and kicked her way down the airless corridor towards Bash.

<Megan! I thought I'd lost you.>

<Most of your comms systems are down,> sent Megan, her voice sounding full of relief. <It took me a while to figure out some way to talk to you. What's happening over there?>

<Everyone but me and Bash is dead,> Gabrielle replied. According to the readout on her emergency breather, she still had air for twenty minutes, and no more. <I'm on my way to the engineering section since it looks like I'm going to have to trigger the mine from there.>

<I've brought my ship as close to the *Ingersoll* as I dare,> sent Megan. <Any closer and I can't be sure the Wanderer won't turn on me again. Once you're done, you need to get the hell out of there immediately.>

Gabrielle came to another pressure field that sealed off the stretch of corridor that had been home to her and Bash since they had left Redstone.

She pushed on through this field, then yanked her mask down: no point in wasting air she might need soon. Making her way back inside the cabin, she quickly strapped the second mask over Bash's mouth and nose, before beginning to tug him towards the door.

He came to his feet easily, drifting forward to bang into the wall next to the door. Gabrielle grabbed him around the waist and worked hard at pushing and pulling him out into the corridor, cursing silently.

Already she was sweating. There had to be a better way of doing things, she was sure.

<Megan? Listen. I'm loading Bash into a pod first, then I'll take care of the nova mine.>

Gabrielle was panting heavily from the effort. They had passed back into vacuum, and she wore her mask again, but she was using up its minuscule supply of air much too fast. It wasn't far from the cabin to the nearest escape-pod bay, but it had taken twice as long to get Bash there as she would have liked.

<No, Gabrielle, wait. Prep the mine first, then—>

<No,> sent Gabrielle. <You don't understand. To prep the mine, I need to get all the way down to the engineering section, and it's going to take much too long if I have to drag him along with me. Those – *things* – are already inside the ship, and I almost ran into one.> She hammered the palm release by the bay door, and it slid open. <I'm at a pod bay right now. I'll send Bash over first, then head for engineering. There's another pod bay down there which I can use to get off the ship.>

<Don't take too long,> Megan warned.

<I won't, I promise,> Gabrielle sent, then she manoeuvred Bash inside.

Menus and animated panels appeared around the escape pod even as she dragged him towards it. Getting it open, she shoved him inside. She was breathing heavily now, and the minutes left on her breather mask's readout were rapidly ticking closer and closer to zero.

She peered in at Bash, hoping against hope that maybe – just maybe – this might be the time for him to show some hint of his earlier awareness. She wanted, more than anything, to hear him tell her whether she was doing the right thing, or even acting like a stupid idiot. Instead, he just stared mindlessly past her.

'Goodbye, Bash,' she said anyway, from inside her breather. 'And thanks for saving my skin. Twice.'

She sealed the door and set the escape pod to launch. A red light began to strobe as the pod slid into a launching tube, but by then she was already on her way to the engineering section.

Gabrielle worked her way through the ship until she reached the main fabricator bay, which was filled with huge, industrial-scale machinery that could manufacture anything from cutlery to replacement drive-spines for the hull. The engineering section lay on the far side of this, and she made her way down a narrow aisle between the fabricators, ducking beneath feed pipes and thick bundles of cable.

The ship suddenly shook around her with sufficient force to tear one of the fabricators loose from the brackets holding it to a wall. The huge machine floated free, drifting towards her and tearing cables and pipes loose as it came. It looked as if it probably massed at least a couple of tonnes, and she scrambled to get out of its way. But the zero gravity made any movement that much harder, and she was still far from adept at manoeuvring under such conditions.

The huge machine sideswiped her, and sent her spinning. She let out a cry of pain, but at least managed to keep it together enough to avoid getting crushed between the machine and the wall towards which it was drifting.

Something didn't feel quite right with her arm, and she pulled it close to her chest as she passed into the engineering bay, looking around in the hope of spotting more of the orange emergency boxes. She really, really needed to swap her breather for a fresh one, since she had, at best, only a few minutes of air left.

Then she spotted some mounted on a wall inside the fabricator bay – just a moment before the drifting fabricator crushed them beneath its weight.

Oh, damn.

Trying to reach for a handhold with her injured arm, she nearly screamed from the pain. It felt like being stabbed with a red-hot razor.

She was now left with a stark choice. She could turn around immediately and make her way to the aft launch bay, and the escape pod there. But with the fabricator blocking her way, that would mean a long detour that would cost her precious minutes.

Or she could stay here and set the nova mine to detonate, at the risk of asphyxiating herself before she could get to safety.

She glanced at the readout on her mask, and then wished she hadn't.

Screw it. She'd known all along that she probably wasn't coming back from this trip alive.

She searched around until she located the nova mine's cradle. It consisted of a cylindrical framework covered in warning stickers.

Pulling out the control card Tarrant had given her, she hunted around until she found a slot on the cradle's underside that looked about the right size. She slid the card in, entered Tarrant's code in the menu that appeared in response, then confirmed.

Words materialized in the air. MINE DETONATION CONFIRMED. STELLAR CORE COLLAPSE IN THIRTEEN HOURS.

Thirteen hours, she reflected. Would the Wanderer be able to jump out of the system to safety before then? Only, perhaps, if it actually knew the mine had been triggered. It might not.

She thought about what had just happened. The nova mine, which had until this very moment been cruising through the corona surrounding this system's sun, had just performed a superluminal jump that took it deep inside the star's core. In the brief moment before it was reduced to a wisp of superheated gas, the exotic singularity at its heart had triggered a stellar core collapse that would consume not only the star itself, but all its planets and moons, as nearly ten billion years' worth of stored energy was released in one single, titanic instant.

Gabrielle laughed giddily to herself. *Stellar core collapse.* She had just murdered a star. How many people in history could say that?

She glanced at the readout in the corner of her breather mask, and saw that she had less than sixty seconds of air left. She pushed her way back over to the entrance to the fabricator bay, and saw that the rogue fabricator had now drifted back against the wall to which it had previously been secured. That left a narrow gap that looked as if it might be just wide enough for her to squeeze through.

And if she could manage that, maybe she could still reach the nearest escape pod.

She squeezed her way through, praying that the machine wouldn't shift again and crush her. She remembered the lessons Megan had given her back at the research outpost on how to use her implants, and she now succeeded in projecting an external array feed on the inside of her breather mask as she struggled. It showed her how the *Ingersoll*'s hull was now a blur of activity, like a corpse infested by maggots.

She then noticed a dozen or so of the alien machines dragging something out of an enormous wound torn in the *Ingersoll*'s hull. After a moment, it hit her that this was the ship's nova drive.

Her air ran out just as she reached the passageway at the far end of the fabricator bay. Sucking in her last dregs of oxygen, she wondered how long she had before she lost consciousness. Thirty seconds? Or even as much as a minute?

She pushed off hard. If she could just make it to . . .

She turned the next corner, and found herself confronted by a monster from the very depths of her nightmares. Directly between her and the escape-pod bay, she registered a churning mass of blades and struts, surrounded by blackness.

Her lungs were hurting more than she thought possible. Meanwhile, the machine-monster was busily tearing through the walls and bulkheads all around it, like a buzzsaw through soggy paper.

It suddenly turned and reached out for her. Instinct made her kick her way out of its reach, but this motion carried her up and out through the great rent it had already torn in the hull. She was now outside the *Ingersoll*, where the icy cold of deep space began infiltrating through her skin and burrowing its way into her bones.

She then caught sight of a corpse drifting close by a drive-spine. It looked as if it might be Kathryn, the woman who had once attended to her.

She tried to call out Megan's name, in the last moments before her lungs froze solid.

FORTY

Megan

<Gabrielle?>

<Gabrielle!>

Megan watched helplessly as the *Ingersoll* was torn to shreds. She also saw the nova drive being dragged out of the hull.

As its components started to drift away from what was left of the *Ingersoll*, the Wanderer began reverting to its former appearance. There was something hypnotic about the sight, like watching a sponge reform inside a tank of water after it had been segmented in a blender.

For the moment, it seemed to be ignoring her and the Magi ship. It now had what it wanted – what it had always wanted.

When she spotted an escape pod tumbling out of control, she instantly gave chase. It took her half an hour to retrieve it.

The Magi ship formed an airlock bay, and drew the drifting pod inside it. When she activated the pod's door mechanism, it hissed open to reveal Bash inside. He, of course, betrayed no awareness that Megan was even there.

Perhaps, she speculated, Gabrielle might still be alive, trapped somewhere inside the wreck of the *Ingersoll* . . .

No, declared the Librarian. *We managed to reactivate part of the* Ingersoll*'s external array, and we sighted her body drifting outside, but still near the ship.*

Megan closed her eyes for a moment, resting her forehead against the side of the escape pod.

'What about the nova mine?' she asked, lifting her head back up. 'Do we know if she . . . ?'

We detected an anomalous neutrino burst from this system's sun within the last few minutes. This indicates that the mine has been triggered, which means we have perhaps half a day before the sun turns nova.

'And Bellhaven?'

We detected no sign of a tach-net transmission being sent towards the Accord. If there genuinely is a mine around Bellhaven's star, it has not been activated.

Megan laughed from sheer relief, her hand pounding the door of the pod. Perhaps, she thought, there never had been a mine. It would be just like Tarrant to try and bluff her.

Then she thought of Gabrielle again, and the laughter caught in her throat.

'What about the Wanderer?' she asked. 'Will it be able to jump out of this system before the nova occurs?'

Unlikely, since it does not have the means to ramp up the energy levels necessary for even a short-range jump. It might be able to build new components capable of powering the drive, but not before the star detonates.

'You did it, Gabrielle,' she said softly, feeling her eyes well up with tears. She quickly stepped inside the pod before letting emotion overwhelm her completely, and began gently coaxing Bash out of it. They had a long journey home ahead of them.

All the same, they could not afford to leave without witnessing the Wanderer's destruction; only then could they be sure.

This was not the first time Megan had watched a star die, for she had personally witnessed the destruction of three during that other, previous, life.

Twelve hours after the Wanderer had ripped the nova drive out from the *Ingersoll*, the Ship of the Covenant detected a second neutrino burst from the star. In the intervening time, they had departed the moon to shelter in the cone of shadow behind the night side of the moon's parent planet. There the Magi ship could, for a short time, carry out remote observations even while the nova raged.

Bash was now lodged in his own cabin, which had appeared, newly formed, shortly after they exited the airlock bay. She had wordlessly guided him inside, finding there articles of clothing she remembered him wearing years before, and long before he lost his mind to the Wanderer.

The Librarian had recreated it all from her own memories, of course, though she did not like to be reminded of how easily it could reach inside her head.

Before long, the rim of the planet behind which they were sheltering began to burn with incandescent light as the wavefront of the nova detonation struck it. Megan saw valleys filling up with liquid fire, and the sharp-edged silhouettes of mountain peaks melting.

'Is there any way of seeing the Wanderer?' she asked. 'Can we be sure it hasn't found a way to jump out of range?'

We tapped into a visual feed from the Ingersoll*'s sensor arrays just before it was destroyed,* replied the Librarian. *You may find it interesting viewing.*

Screens appeared before Megan, showing a multiplicity of views from the *Ingersoll*'s perspective. The cameras had survived just long enough to show the star expanding in size, growing to fill the entire sky with terrifying speed.

The perspective shifted to show the Wanderer under extreme magnification, accelerating towards the system's outer darkness. It had by now fully regained its former shape. Ancillary data informed her that it had engaged in a programme of rapidly re-engineering a number of its components so as to absorb the energy the nova drive required for it to make an interstellar jump.

But too late.

She watched the wavefront of the nova strike the Wanderer. It began to come apart again, unable to maintain its integrity beneath the onslaught of superheated plasma expanding at a substantial fraction of the speed of light. The whole thing had an uncanny, dreamlike quality to it, perhaps partly because what she was seeing there had occurred in millionths of a second, and was slowed down for her benefit.

The cameras flared white, and died.

It was closer to making its escape than you might prefer to know, continued the Librarian. *There are still a few Wanderer components surviving in this system's Oort region, more than a light year out, so it can still rebuild itself, given time.*

'But how long will that take?' asked Megan.

A thousand years, more or less.

She nodded and let her shoulders sag. 'It doesn't have a nova drive any more. We don't have to worry about it again for a long time yet, if ever. I think that's good enough for now, don't you?'

She left her own cabin and made her way through to Bash's, where she laid her head on his lap and succumbed to racking sobs. She had lost Gabrielle, and now she feared Bash was gone forever alongside the Wanderer, leaving behind only this hollow, helpless shell. She was alone again.

That's not quite true, the Librarian reminded her.

In that same moment, she felt fingers brushing gently against her hair. It took her a moment to realize that she was not imagining it.

FORTY-ONE

Dakota

Over the next several hours the Magi ship listened out for those few remaining components that the Wanderer had seeded throughout the system's Oort region, but it soon became clear that they were running silent, waiting for the intruder to depart before beginning their long resurrection. To flush all of them out, and destroy them, would take decades or even centuries, the Librarian explained to Megan. Even then, there could be no guarantee of finding all of them. Besides, the Wanderer had almost certainly left components behind in other star systems it had visited, and from those it could eventually reconstitute itself.

But when that day came, the Librarian assured her, it would find other Magi ships ready and waiting for it.

The planet behind which they had sheltered from the nova inevitably began to disintegrate under the onslaught of superheated plasma, so the Magi ship made a short-range jump of half a light year. The craft's encounter with the Wanderer had seriously depleted its energy resources, and it now needed a few days to prepare for the first in a series of much longer jumps.

Megan – or Dakota, as she had once again come to think of herself – hardly needed to ask where it was taking them next. They were clearly on their way to a confrontation with the Maker Swarm.

After that first brief touch of his fingers, Bash had reverted to his familiar near-vegetative state, and remained that way despite her desperate coaxing and prompting. She returned to her own quarters, and woke later from a long and dreamless sleep only to find that Bash, and even his newly formed quarters, had completely disappeared.

She stared, dumbfounded, at the smooth expanse of wall where his cabin door had been. She then yelled out for the Librarian, demanding its presence instantly.

'We are merely attempting to repair the damage done to your friend by the Marauder,' explained the Librarian, from beside her shoulder. As ever it appeared from nowhere, as if it had been hovering just out of sight, unnoticed and unheard until it was required. 'In your past life, your body was similarly absorbed into the ship's own flesh in order to carry out necessary changes and repairs.'

'You don't do anything for nothing,' she remarked. 'And you certainly didn't ask my damn permission.'

'We didn't need to,' the Librarian replied, 'as he gave it himself.'

She stared dumbfounded at it. 'He did?'

'He well understands the necessity of the extensive rebuilding of his neural pathways that must be undertaken,' the Librarian continued. 'And, yes, it is also an opportunity to interrogate his implants for more information about the Wanderer and the Core Transcendence. We know very little about the civilization that created the Wanderer, after all.'

Bash returned a week later and she found, to her delight, that he seemed to be more aware of his surroundings than ever before. He was even able to speak a few simple words, though that clearly exhausted him, and after less than a minute his eyes would drift away from hers, staring at some unseen horizon. His full recovery, assuming the ship was successful in aiding him, was clearly going to be long and protracted. There would, she realized with sadness, be none of those sudden bursts of lucidity that Gabrielle claimed to have experienced in Bash's presence.

When he vanished a second time, she tried to suppress her anxiety over what changes the ship might be making to him, and instead distracted herself by linking into the Magi ship's external senses and watching the face of the galaxy shift and morph with each successive jump across unimaginable gulfs of space. Before long, the Calafat-Holt Cluster, in which the Wanderer had been hiding for so long, had visually shrunk to nothing.

She thought often of Gabrielle's baby, Evie, and knew her duty was to find her. Knowing that the Maker Swarm had to be dealt with first did nothing to reduce her heartache every time she thought about what might have happened to the child.

Bash this time returned to her after a period of little more than a day, and his disappearances and subsequent reappearances would soon become a regular occurrence. She could never predict how long he might remain with her on each occasion, and she fought to suppress the fear that these absences might grow longer and longer, until finally he never returned at all.

She dreamed, on one occasion, of wandering through a house where some of the rooms were left forever in darkness, while others remained brightly lit. Somehow or other, she realized upon waking, she had been dreaming about Bash. But each time he returned – and, to her relief, he always did come back – he seemed a little more voluble, a little more his old self, until eventually the intervals between his absences grew longer and longer, and then they ceased entirely.

But, as much as it gladdened her to see him restored, it was clear that something had changed in him. He was quieter, more withdrawn, no longer as effusive as he had once been. But, then, she had changed as well; death, as she had long since learned, tended to do that to a person. And for a long time Bash had been more dead than alive.

Then, just a few months away from their final encounter with the Maker Swarm, the ship detoured to pick up a passenger.

Like all its kind, the Atn reminded Dakota of a giant turtle cross-bred with a scrapheap. It now stood before them, in yet another docking bay inside the Magi ship which had not existed until moments before. Its massive wedge-shaped head swung from side to side as it regarded first Dakota, then Bash and finally the Librarian. A scratchy and abrasive sound, like a heavily distorted trumpet, eventually emanated from it.

'It says hello,' explained the Librarian, standing on the creature's other side.

'That was saying hello?' joked Bash. 'What the hell does it sound like when it's angry?'

He enunciated each word very carefully, in the manner of someone unused to exercising their vocal cords. His voice still faltered occasionally even now, and had not yet regained the quiet strength that Dakota remembered.

The Librarian regarded him with a perplexed expression, then turned to Dakota to say, 'I've prepared quarters for our guest.'

'Just to be clear,' persisted Bash, 'you're seriously telling me this thing can really stop the Swarm?'

'We believe, or at least hope, it can,' the Librarian replied, 'with the aid of data we recovered from the Wanderer regarding the means by which that entity once destroyed an entire Swarm.'

'Right.' Bash nodded, still looking far from convinced. 'A bunch of Magi ships specially designed for the purpose couldn't pull it off, but this septic tank on legs can . . . how, exactly?'

Dakota failed to suppress a grin. 'You know,' she said to the Librarian, 'you really haven't been very forthcoming on just *how* this is going to work.'

'Or about our stopping here,' added Bash. 'You *might* have mentioned it sooner than you did.'

They hadn't been told about this rendezvous until just a few days before, when Dakota had noticed, from her regular monitoring of their progress across the galaxy, that their faster-than-light jumps were becoming shorter and shorter, arrowing in on a particular region deep in interstellar space, and half a dozen light years from any star. Even when the Magi ship had matched course and speed with an Atn clade-world – an asteroid converted into a combination of living quarters and space-bound manufactory – the Librarian had been vague as to why.

'We now understand,' said the Librarian, 'the means by which the Wanderer destroyed another Swarm. By using that method, we have been running simulations to identify the optimum approach to neutralizing this Swarm, and it became rapidly apparent that our greatest chance of success in doing so lies with the Atn. We would have been more forthcoming before now but, until we felt sure of engaging the strategy with the highest chance of success, there was really very little to tell.'

'But there's still just the one of him?' Bash insisted. 'Or her. It. Whatever.'

'I'm guessing,' said Dakota, 'this has something to do with the Atn's original purpose. I mean the reason they were created.'

'Huh?' Bash stared at her.

The Librarian glanced over at him. 'A long time ago,' it explained, 'the first Atn were fashioned out of a Maker Swarm's components.'

'Seriously?' said Bash, looking between the two of them as the Atn shifted and rumbled and turned its head this way and that. Dakota wondered if it understood what they were saying.

'They were the Magi's first attempt at destroying the Swarms,' Dakota explained. 'They essentially reprogrammed a Swarm in order to hunt down other Swarms, but somewhere down the line they forgot their purpose.'

'How do you know all this, Megan?' he asked.

'From my previous life,' she said. 'I found out a lot about them from a Shoal member I met a couple of times. And it's not Megan any more, remember?'

'Right.' He nodded. 'I keep forgetting.'

Sure you do, she thought. Bash was clearly having a hard time dealing with her sudden re-adoption of her previous identity.

'The Atn essentially evolved to become a new species,' the Librarian continued. 'They were only one of many possible solutions to the problem of the Swarms – solutions including the Magi ships.'

'So why not reprogram the Atn again, and get *them* to wipe out the Swarms?' asked Bash.

'They're a sentient species,' said Dakota, 'and they possess free will. So you can't just go randomly repurposing them like that.' She cast a wary look at the Librarian. 'Please tell me that's not what you're intending to do.'

'No,' the Librarian reassured her. 'Our friend here –' it reached out to pat the alien's flank – 'is going to do something much more interesting.'

'Well, whatever the hell it's going to do,' said Bash, watching as the creature suddenly lurched towards the exit leading from the docking bay, its joints scraping and rasping with every movement, 'it's either going to be fucking spectacular or the biggest anticlimax in history.'

Once they resumed their voyage towards the Swarm, their Atn passenger immediately began a long and laborious process of rebuilding itself. The quarters created for it by the Librarian resembled nothing so much as a garage constructed by a blind man, crammed as it was with various engineering implements that moved and operated according to the Atn's will. She and Bash made a point of visiting it on occasion, watching in wonder as the Atn replaced first its limbs and then its carapace, until it resembled something chillingly close to a Swarm component. If it was even aware of their presence, it showed no sign of it.

Eight long weeks after picking up their passenger, the Magi ship came within range of a red dwarf system where the Maker Swarm had paused on its journey. They were all feeling drained by the enormous stress of waiting for the confrontation ahead, and tried to distract themselves in their own ways. Bash thus spent much of his time scanning the Accord's tach-net relays for information about home, catching up on news and, he claimed, trying to figure out what the hell to do with the rest of his life. Sometimes they talked but, when they did, she still had the uncanny sense that his mind was somewhere else.

She could hardly blame him. They were a single ship going up against something capable of destroying entire civilizations, after all, and she had seen and suffered too much to be able to share fully the Librarian's apparent confidence in their Atn passenger.

The red dwarf grew closer with each successive jump, until finally they emerged into normal space about 30 AUs from the star, out towards the edge of the system. Even this far out, the local environment proved to be infested with the Swarm's countless components, all sucking up the energy necessary for their next mass jump across the Perseus Arm and closer to humanity.

As the Librarian informed her and Bash, there were somewhere in the region of three to four hundred million of the components. Each one was a single node in a distributed network that together made up a single, vast machine intelligence.

And yet, thought Dakota, they still didn't know *why* the Swarms had been set their task of laying traps for intelligent life. And, until they knew, nothing would change; for there would always be Swarms, and other forms of life would always be threatened by them. What little Bash had gleaned from the Wanderer concerning the Swarm was, she felt sure, only one small part of a far larger picture.

'You have no idea how much being here terrifies me,' said Dakota. They were inside a shared datascape, flying through a real-time simulation of the red dwarf system and amidst the Swarm components in their millions. 'The last time I got anywhere near this Swarm, I wound up dead.'

'I don't think it even knows we're here,' said Bash, his mood sombre now that he had seen exactly what they were up against.

Rather than being randomly scattered throughout the system, the greatest number of components were gathered around the star itself. They were arranged in distinct clusters, linked by rivers and channels composed of others of their kind, streaming back and forth.

'Don't be fooled,' she said with a shiver. 'It knows we're here.'

When Dakota first died – before waking in the Demarchy, prior to her escape and finding a new identity – she had gone in search of this very same Swarm. She had made the mistake of bringing one of its components on board, only to discover too late how it had infiltrated the Magi ship she had then been piloting. In the last moments of that life, a copy of her complete mind-state had been transmitted to other Magi ships – one of which had resurrected her.

And now she was back to confront the same Swarm a second time. She had, she realized, come full circle.

'I wonder sometimes how many of me there are,' she said quietly.

She felt rather than saw Bash's frown. 'What?'

'Other versions of me,' she said. 'Other Dakotas.'

'I don't follow.'

'Remember what I told you: the Magi ships all have copies of my mind stored deep in their memory banks. There could be other Dakotas wandering around right now, and I'd never know.'

'I'll admit,' said Bash, 'I'd feel pretty strange if there were other versions of me out there, somewhere. But why on earth would it ever make more than *one* of you? Hell, having to deal with just the one seems bad enough.'

She swiped him with a ghostly virtual limb, and then remembered the Librarian discussing how it had simulated ways of dealing with the Swarm. She found herself wondering if a simulated Dakota had taken part in any of them, and if that other her had known . . .

Dakota? Bash? They both heard the Librarian calling to them, as if from far away. *It's time.*

They watched the Atn as it tumbled away from the Magi ship. They were far enough away from the red dwarf and the components swarming around it that the star wasn't much more than a particularly bright point of light amidst countless others. But a cluster of some tens of thousands of components was busily dismantling a small rocky planetoid for its raw materials, and the Atn aimed itself towards them, soon disappearing out of range.

'Now what?' asked Bash.

'Now we wait,' said the Librarian, 'for the infection to take root.'

Dakota woke several hours later and knew immediately that something had changed. She sat up on her bed and locked into the ship's senses, seeing the way the streams and clusters of components surrounding the star had become fragmented and twisted out of shape. Space around the star was now filled with sparkles and blooms of light.

'Do you see it?' asked Bash, rushing into her cabin unannounced, with an excited grin on his face.

'I see *something*,' she said, pulling herself to her feet, 'but I don't know what it is.'

'The damn thing's at war with itself,' he exclaimed, almost beside himself. 'The components that haven't been compromised by the Atn are attacking the ones that have. That's what all the light is – they're shooting at *each other*.'

She closed her eyes and accessed the ship's real-time simulation of the surrounding stellar environment. The ship had colour-coded those components that had been infected with a viral copy of the Atn's mind-state. They showed up red, while the unaffected components were indicated by tiny points of fluorescent white light. Something about those flowing and shifting patterns of colour made her think of blood cells.

They watched in fascination as, over the next several hours, more than half of the Swarm was subverted and taken over by their Atn passenger. Each subverted component became a new recruit to its enemy's cause, quickly destroying or infecting its neighbours; brilliant beams of fusion energy flashed through the stellar night, destroying components in their thousands on either side. Space around the star soon filled with glowing clouds of superheated debris, as the battle slowly approached its conclusion.

When Dakota finally emerged from her datascape, many more

hours later, she went to find Bash in his quarters. He emerged from his own datascape looking weary but happy.

'I can hardly believe what I'm seeing out there,' said Dakota, taking a seat beside him on his bed.

'We are pleased to say that matters are progressing even more satisfactorily than expected,' said the Librarian, making her jump. She turned to see it had appeared as if from nowhere at the far end of the room.

Bash stared at the entity, momentarily speechless, then shook his head. 'You know,' he groused, 'one day I'd like to see you actually walk through the door instead of just materializing out of thin air like that. Gives me the damn creeps.'

'This is really how the Wanderer destroyed a Swarm?' asked Dakota. 'By altering one of its own components?'

The Librarian nodded. 'Not so difficult, perhaps, since the Wanderer and the Swarm are so similar in many ways. A case of parallel technological evolution, each finding the same optimal solution to a particular set of problems. The Atn were clearly the perfect delivery system for the exploit discovered by the Wanderer. Another few hours, and only ashes and wreckage will remain.'

'So why didn't the Wanderer just grab one of that earlier Swarm's nova drives back when it had the chance?' asked Bash.

'Current observations show each Swarm component destroys its drive before becoming fully compromised. Presumably that earlier Swarm did the same when the Wanderer attacked it.'

'So if not for that,' said Dakota, chilled at the thought, 'the Wanderer might have got what it wanted long ago.'

'It doesn't matter,' said Bash, his expression jubilant. 'We can go home now.'

She shared his joy, despite a bone-deep tiredness. The threat of the Swarm had been hanging over her for so long she barely knew how to adjust to its absence. With it destroyed, she could go home to a people who might never know how close they had come to extinction.

But home to what? she couldn't help wondering, even as Bash reached out to pull her into a rib-crushing hug.

EPILOGUE

One year later

The air was much warmer here on the floor of the chasm, a full kilometre beneath Jarô's surface. Dakota took off her heavy long-coat and glanced upwards, hoping to catch a glimpse of the sky, but saw only a narrow strip of azure streaked with red and obscured by whirling vortexes of dust from the desert far above their heads.

Her gaze dropped lower, following the dark framework of a funicular railway that reached all the way from the upper rim of the chasm to its floor. She and Bash had travelled aboard one of those cars, accompanied by such a cacophony of juddering gears and creaking metalwork that she had wondered if perhaps the whole thing might not simply fall apart around them before it sent them plummeting to the ground.

The air pressure this far beneath the surface was sufficiently high to obviate the need for protective gear, or for even a breather mask to reduce the risk of anoxia, since the atmosphere was otherwise entirely breathable. A town called Amuza Urbo nestled on the chasm floor, its buildings abutting or even climbing the steep walls, like ivy composed of steel and carbon. There was an organic fluidity to the architecture, too, that made this comparison more than apt; for many of the buildings, she had learned, were the product of advanced gene tech, being the distant and highly modified descendants of earth-bound trees and coral reefs.

The streets were packed with people dressed in brightly coloured finery, dancing to music that echoed off the lofty cliffs surrounding them. There were vendors everywhere, selling street food that smelled exotic and enticing to Dakota.

'Trust us to arrive in carnival season,' she said, reaching up to wipe the sweat from her brow. She still felt too warm, even in the soft and light fabrics she had dressed herself in before coming down from orbit. Her intention had been to look nondescript, but that ordinariness instead caused them both to stand out amongst the garish crowds.

She suddenly caught sight of a cluster of women equipped with huge multicoloured wings, which were clearly actual physical appendages rather than costumes. Some of them were dancing around with a man she at first thought was dressed in a bird costume, before realizing that his beak and feathers were real.

Primal and strident, the rhythm of the music beat all around them, setting up a sympathetic vibration in her blood. As she inhaled a lungful of sweet smoke that tickled the roof of her mouth, she glanced at Bash and he grinned back as if the last ten years had never happened.

'Hard to resist, isn't it?'

She nodded: it *was* hard to resist. She could smell raw *sans de sezi* in the air, and through the crowd caught a glimpse of a man – bright-eyed and ecstatic – leaning against a wall as he laughed uproariously, his hands and mouth vividly stained orange from the narcotic spore.

'Come on,' urged Bash, grabbing her by the arm and pulling her into a tight knot of thrashing bodies gathered around a band performing with thunderingly loud amplification. A number of the heaving, gyrating bodies around them wore so little clothing they might as well have gone naked for all the difference it made.

His broad, dark face split in a grin, Bash started to move in time with the beat, taking hold of her hand and whirling her around. She laughed, and just let the music take her, dancing for all she was worth as he spun her around and around.

Then he lost his grip on her and she was immediately swallowed up by the warm, glistening bodies that pressed in all around.

Another reveller caught hold of her outstretched hand, pulling her close to him as they moved together, his eyes shining as his hips moved against her. For the first time in what felt like a very, very long time, she felt a flush of desire, for the warmth of another body pressed tightly against her own.

But then she remembered why they had come here.

She flashed her newfound dancing partner a regretful smile, then pushed her way through the crowd until she found Bash again, drawing him out of the crush of bodies into a less crowded side-street.

'What do I keep telling you?' said Bash, panting from his exertions. 'You need to loosen up, Dakota. Cut yourself some slack.'

'We're here for a reason,' she said firmly. 'Remember?'

He cast a rueful glance towards the carnival throng. Thousands of lanterns had just been released, drifting up towards the mouth of the chasm on rising currents of warm air.

'I remember,' he replied. 'I just hoped I might be able to change your mind about your . . . plans.'

She sighed. 'We already talked about that.'

'I know, but . . .' He looked as if he was about to continue, but instead let out a dramatic sigh. He made a slicing gesture with the side of his hand which suggested *lead on*. They made their way down a street that was both empty and dark.

Amuza Urbo was a purposely low-tech settlement, one of dozens scattered all across Jarô that deliberately made do without data-nets. Jarô itself was a world that people came to because they were running away from something, or because they wanted to reinvent themselves, or often both – the same purpose Kjæregrønnested had once fulfilled for Dakota when she had first become Megan Jacinth. And reinvention was something she had gained some expertise in.

She had hoped that by pretending she was someone else – by taking on the name of a dead girl – she could escape her past self. But now she understood more than ever that she was, and always had been, Dakota Merrick.

They came eventually to an apartment building that looked as if it had half melted. Its walls sagged artfully, the corners twisting where they met the ground.

'And we're sure this is the right address?' asked Dakota.

'As sure as I can be,' Bash murmured, as he came up beside her. 'That's assuming the private detective I paid to locate Stiles knew what he was doing.'

She gave him a weary shrug. 'Only one way to find out.'

They entered the foyer, then made their way up a flight of stairs to an apartment situated on the top floor. Dakota rapped on the door and waited. They heard footsteps and, after a moment, Martha Stiles opened the door. Her eyes widened when she recognized them, one hand clutching her chest as if she was having trouble breathing.

Dakota glanced past her and into the apartment beyond. It looked small and tidy and colourfully decorated. Several bright and glittering 'Tears of Saint Jarô' charms hung from the hallway ceiling.

'Mind if we come in?' asked Dakota, stepping over the threshold before the woman could even form a reply.

They waited in the lounge as Stiles fetched Evie for them. Whenever she had thought about this moment, or what it would feel like, Dakota had imagined feelings of happiness – or of joy tinged with sorrow. Instead, she felt like a weary traveller at the end of a long journey, wanting nothing more than to conclude her business here and be on her way.

She could see how nervous Stiles was as she led the tiny girl through into the room where she and Bash waited. Stiles took a seat on a couch, and Evie blinked wide grey eyes at them before burying her face against Stiles's knee in a sudden fit of shyness. Her hair was thin and pale, and curled around her ears.

Dakota could see how deeply attached Stiles had become to

Gabrielle's daughter. She could see that she feared they had come to take Evie away.

'I've read some official reports about that attack on the outpost,' said Dakota. 'You and Evie here were the only survivors – am I right?'

'It wasn't easy,' said Stiles, helping Evie to climb up onto the couch beside her, where she babbled to herself in little-girl words. 'I was stuck there for more than ten days before a rescue team finally turned up. I told them Evie belonged to one of the staff, and that was enough for them.' Her eyes drifted towards Bash, and she shook her head. 'The last time I saw you, you were a vegetable, completely unresponsive. And now here you are.' Her eyes narrowed. 'It *is* you, isn't it?' She leaned forward slightly and peered intently into his face. 'I haven't made a mistake?'

'You haven't,' Bash smiled wryly. 'I could tell you how I recovered, but you wouldn't believe me – not in a million years.'

They waited in silence as Stiles took time to gather her thoughts further.

'The funny thing is, I hated your guts for a long time,' she said at last, her tone matter-of-fact. Bash and Dakota exchanged a surreptitious glance as she continued. 'I held you directly responsible for bringing those dreadful people down upon us. They murdered everyone I knew there, and I had to stand and watch them all die. And then . . .' Stiles paused and drew a heavy breath. 'But every time I ran things through my head, trying to find a different way of doing things, a way that wouldn't have ended up with so many innocent people dying, I realized I couldn't have done things any differently. I could never have forced you back out after we found you, or abandoned you in the middle of nowhere, not with one of you pregnant and the other operating like a walking corpse. No matter what, I was always going to do things just as I wound up doing them. And that means that what happened was always going to happen.'

Dakota leaned towards her. 'Martha—'

'It took a long time,' Stiles interrupted her, 'but one day I was able to think clearly, and I saw I was wrong to hold you responsible. You were victims just as much as we were. What Gabrielle told me made that clear, however outrageous her story seemed.' She cast a bitter look at Dakota. 'But I can't tell you how much I regret not just letting you take that damn truck the first time you asked for it.'

Choosing her next words carefully, Dakota asked, 'What brought you here, to Jarô? Do you come from here originally?'

She shook her head. 'No, somewhere a lot less colourful. But I had a powerful need to get as far from Redstone as I physically could, and you can't get much further than here.'

Evie pulled herself onto Stiles's lap, making cooing noises. 'Maybe I should have mentioned this first, Martha,' said Dakota, 'but I'm not here to take Evie away. I just wanted the chance to see her before I head off.'

She didn't need to look at Bash to detect his expression. His disapproval was entirely palpable.

Stiles visibly relaxed. 'Then, can you tell me what happened to her?' she asked, looking between the pair of them. 'Gabrielle, I mean. After those people kidnapped her, I thought maybe . . .' Her voice trailed off.

'She died,' said Dakota. 'I'm sorry.'

Stiles's face crumpled a little, and she bowed her head. 'God damn it,' she breathed. 'And those men? The ones who took her?'

'Dead, too,' said Dakota. 'They got what they deserved.'

Stiles nodded tightly. 'Good. I'm glad to hear that.'

Dakota noticed Evie staring at her. She waggled her fingers at the little girl, who smiled uncertainly, glancing up at Stiles for reassurance.

'May I?' asked Dakota.

Stiles rose from her seat, carrying Evie and carefully placing her beside Dakota. Dakota brushed a strand of hair from Evie's face, thinking: *This is the nearest I'll ever get to having a daughter of my own.* And since she and Gabrielle had identical DNA, in a sense Evie *was* her daughter – or the daughter she might have had, if ever she had lived a normal life.

Bash got up from his chair and came to sit on Evie's other side, giving her a hand-sized star prism. She took it, smiling hesitantly.

'Here.' Bash reached down and took hold of it again. 'You have to shake it, like this.'

It started to glow, and Evie gave a tiny cry of delight.

<Dakota?> sent Bash. <I know you're going to find this hard to believe, but this little girl is reading me.>

<I think I can feel it too,> Dakota replied, staring at the child in astonishment. Somehow, incredible as it seemed, Evie was probing the edges of the machine-part of her consciousness – something that should be impossible for anyone lacking implants. <But look at her. There's no way in hell Evie could have machine-head circuitry in her skull, could she?>

She glanced at Stiles, who clearly sensed something was up.

<No,> sent Bash, after stroking the top of Evie's head, which was entirely free of the bumps and crenellations that usually indicated the presence of implants. <This is something else entirely. Look . . . the Ship of the Covenant tweaked the DNA of the original Speaker-Elect, right? And all of you are her clones?>

<What are you thinking?>

<That maybe the Ship of the Covenant did a lot more than just tweak your DNA. Maybe it did something else that would make any children you produced different as well.>

You're not really human, are you? she thought with a chill, staring down at Evie with new eyes. *Part of you is, but the rest is all Magi.*

Evie clearly wasn't a machine-head, but neither was she a normal human girl. She was something new; something Dakota didn't even think there was a word for.

But she was still flesh and blood. She was still Gabrielle's daughter.

Dakota had a fleeting mental image of brightly coloured, fuzzy shapes that moved and twisted in new and enticing ways. A kaleidoscope of feelings and sensations accompanied this image, and she sensed fear and excitement and wonder and curiosity all mixed together. Most importantly, it was coming from Evie.

'Here,' she said, lifting Evie up and handing her back to a puzzled-looking Stiles.

The older woman cleared her throat, after she had settled Evie back on to the couch beside her. 'If you don't mind my asking, just what are your plans?'

'Speaking for myself,' said Dakota, 'I'm only visiting here briefly. Then I'm moving on.'

Stiles nodded with a sigh. 'I've grown . . . rather attached to Evie,' she said quietly. 'But I guess that's obvious.'

Dakota remembered the story about Stiles's dead teenaged daughter. 'I've already said I'm not going to take her away from you, Martha. As a matter of fact, I can't think of anyone better suited to take care of her.'

Stiles nodded, looking slightly stunned. 'Just how long are you going away for?'

'I'm not sure.' Dakota forced a brittle smile. 'Which is one reason why it was important to me to have this opportunity of seeing Evie.' *In case I never get another chance.*

Stiles suddenly looked weary and old beyond her years. 'Then at least promise me that no one else will come and try to threaten or hurt either of us. I've had quite enough of that kind of thing for one lifetime.'

'That's not going to happen,' Bash reassured her. 'But, just in case, I'm personally sticking around here for a while.'

Stiles peered at him. 'You're not going together?'

'I've decided to stay here on Jarô,' he explained. 'I've missed out on a lot of living over these past ten years, so I want to settle in one place and get to know it. And, besides,' he nodded towards Evie, 'I could help out, if you ever wanted me to.'

Dakota watched Stiles sizing him up before nodding hesitantly.

She stood up. 'We should probably be going now. We're staying at a place in the centre of town for the next couple of days.' Dakota recited the address. 'If you need us, you'll find us there.'

'Before you go,' said Stiles, 'I want to know more about just *why* my friends died. What Gabrielle told me wasn't enough for me really to understand all of it. It's been . . . hard to find any real closure, not really comprehending the details.'

'Whenever you want to know them, Miss Stiles,' said Bash, 'you and I are going to go find somewhere we can sit down over a couple of drinks. Because it's the kind of story that takes a long time to tell.'

Having said their goodbyes, they headed down the stairs and out into the night, without looking back.

After walking a few blocks, Dakota pressed her back against a doorway and clasped her hands over her face. Bash knew enough not to say or do anything, beyond resting a comforting hand on her shoulder.

'It doesn't have to be this way, you know,' he said quietly, once she was ready to start moving again. By now they were almost at their hotel. 'I know you've told me to shut the hell up often enough, but let me say it just one last time: You could stay here and make a new life for yourself.'

Even this late at night, there were still a few revellers left, as they trudged together through the alcohol-sodden debris. 'No, Bash,' she said quietly. 'I told you why I can't do that.'

'Dak—'

'Not now,' she said firmly.

Bash once again showed his good judgement by saying nothing more.

Even living in real time for the duration of their journey back to the worlds of the Accord, Dakota had found plenty of opportunity to think.

The Makers were still out there, still carrying on their aeons-spanning project to reshape the universe from within the core of not only the Milky Way but other galaxies as well. The question still remained: *why* had they undertaken this extraordinary project?

Why you? Bash had asked, during one of their numerous arguments. *Why does it have to be you, and not someone else?*

Why not *me?* she had countered. *There's no one else who knows what I know. That means I have to go.*

You told me yourself there were other yous out there, he had retorted. *Other Dakotas.*

But those other Dakotas hadn't experienced all that she had over the last ten years, and that made all the difference. She saw things more clearly now, and no longer blamed herself for things in her past that she should never have blamed herself for in the first place. She understood things that those other Dakotas never could.

Martha Stiles wasn't the only one desperate for a sense of closure. Dakota needed it too, and so it had to be her and no one else. She would travel to the core of the galaxy, and there she would attempt to discover the ultimate purpose of the Makers – and, if possible, find a way to destroy them that didn't mean genocide for the rest of the galaxy.

And if she failed, perhaps one of those other Dakotas would finally get her turn.

They arrived at the hotel, a slim, sideways-leaning shard of dark glass lit by glow-lamps. Bash took a step towards the entrance, then turned to see her still standing in the middle of the street.

'What, you're leaving *now*?' he asked, with a pained look on his face.

'I can't stay here any longer,' she said.

Bash let out a groan.

'Don't,' she said. 'Don't tell me to stay. Please just let me turn around and go.'

She fought to control her emotions. It would be so easy just to stay, never to leave, to watch Evie grow tall and slender and womanly.

And that was precisely why she had to leave as soon as possible, before her determination had a chance to waver.

He stepped over to her and pulled her into a hug that felt likely to crush the breath out of her.

'I'll miss you,' he said, into her shoulder, his voice already muffled with emotion. 'I'll miss you so very much, Megan – or Dakota or whatever damn fool name you're using this week.'

She let him hold her like that for a minute, before carefully extracting herself.

'Take care her of her for me,' she said. 'For both of us. Always watch over her.'

He sniffed, his eyes glistening. 'You'll be back?'

'If it's at all humanly possible,' she said, 'I will.'

She hoped, more than anything, that this was true.

She turned around then and walked away. Heading across the nearby square, she kept walking until she reached the foot of the funicular railway, some of whose vertical cars were the size of small houses. She climbed aboard one and stood facing the wall of the chasm itself as it rose into the night. She was now thinking of the Magi ship waiting, hidden, in Jarô's outer system – waiting to take her to the core of the galaxy . . . and all that might await her there.

TIME LINE

2,000,000 years PHA (Pre-Human Era)

The earliest starfaring Magi cultures form within the Large Magellanic Cloud (LMC).

|

162,000–160,000 years PHA

Maker caches, containing faster-than-light nova drive technology, are discovered in the LMC.

The star drive triggers a rapid expansion of the Magi cultures until they dominate the Cloud.

|

160,000 years PHA

Multiple Nova Wars break out in the LMC, almost entirely destroying the Magi culture.

|

A fleet of Magi superluminal craft departs a devastated LMC for the Milky Way, intent on hunting down and destroying both the Maker caches and the Swarms responsible for seeding them throughout the universe.

|

A few millennia after its arrival in the Milky Way, the Magi fleet is almost entirely wiped out by the Shoal Hegemony. The Shoal subsequently becomes the dominant power throughout a large part of the Milky Way, maintaining a monopoly over nova drive technology stolen from the Magi.

SHOAL TRILOGY

2542 AD (*Stealing Light*)

A human expedition to the Nova Arctis system, piloted by Dakota Merrick, discovers a derelict Magi ship with a functioning faster-than-light drive.

|

2542–2543 AD (*Nova War*)

Dakota and Lucas, along with a Magi ship, are captured by a Bandati Hive. Subsequent events trigger a Nova War between the Shoal and their ancient enemies, the Emissaries.

|

2544 AD (*Empire of Light*)

Following the Shoal Hegemony's retreat from the Perseus Arm, Dakota Merrick locates a Maker Swarm at the same time that the first human-built ships equipped with nova drives emerge from within the Consortium. A later expedition piloted by a resurrected Dakota succeeds in finding a way to bring the Nova War to an end.

EVENTS FOLLOWING *EMPIRE OF LIGHT* AND PRECEDING *MARAUDER*

2545–2570 AD

The Consortium, the legislative body acting as a government for human worlds, is dissolved in the wake of the Shoal's departure and replaced by the pan-species 'Accord of Worlds'. Further human expeditions meanwhile trigger a rapid expansion throughout the Perseus Arm, a period subsequently known as the 'Great Diaspora'.

|

2645 AD

The Three Star Alliance, an independent nation comprising three neighbouring star systems, Alyeska, Kjæregrønnested and Al-Jahar, announces its formation.

|

2647 AD

The Three Star Alliance formally secedes from the Accord.

|

2748–2751 AD

The Accord begins an embargo and a long war of attrition against the Three Star Alliance, in order to gain control over nova drives recovered from a Shoal coreship adrift in interstellar space.

|

2752 AD

The first expedition to the Wanderer, under the command of Gregor Tarrant, sets out from Kjæregrønnested, seat of government of the former Three Star Alliance.

Acknowledgements

These days, if you didn't know better, you'd think there were only two people involved in publishing a book: the author, and whoever hits the button marked PRINT. Most people are at least peripherally aware that there's an editor, and a cover artist, and maybe even a copy-editor or editorial assistant or two. However, the explosive growth of the ebook market has led some to believe, erroneously, that anyone standing between the author and that button are somehow excess to requirements.

I wondered if the reason might be that you don't get to see the names of all the people involved in a book's production the way you do in a movie's end credits. Why not, I thought, do the same in a book? Maybe then people might understand better there's more to this job – sometimes a lot more – than just some guy typing on a laptop. I present to you here a list of some key players involved in getting this book into your hands, and making it a stronger piece of work than it would have been otherwise.

Structural editing – Bella Pagan
Line editing – Peter Lavery
Editorial services management – Eloise Wood
Editorial assistance – Louise Buckley
Copy-editing – Jessica Cuthbert-Smith
Proofreading – Kim Bishop
In-house design – Neil Lang
Illustration – Steve Stone
Marketing – Rob Cox
Publicity – Sophie Portas
Agent – Dorothy Lumley